Lynn Shepherd studied English at Oxford, before working in the City and then in PR. She's been a freelance copywriter for over ten years, and has also published an academic work on the 'Father of the English novel', Samuel Richardson. She lives near Oxford with her husband and two cats.

Also by Lynn Shepherd

Murder at Mansfield Park

Tom-All-Alone's

Lynn Shepherd

corsair

Constable & Robinson Ltd
55-56 Russell Square
London
WC1B 4HP
www.constablerobinson.com

First published in the UK by Corsair,
an imprint of Constable & Robinson, 2012

A copy of the British Library Cataloguing in Publication
Data is available from the British Library

ISBN 978-1-78033-166-9

Printed and bound in the UK

1 3 5 7 9 10 8 6 4 2

For Stephen

Prologue

L ondon. Michaelmas term lately begun, and the Lord
Chancellor sitting in Lincoln's Inn Hall. Implacable
November weather. As much mud in the streets as in a
Flanders field, and almost as little hope, at least for some. It is
the greatest city in the world – quite possibly the greatest ever
known – but on this dark early winter day in 1850 you might
be forgiven for thinking you've been transported, on a sudden,
to a circle of hell even the devil has given up for lost. If a single
man can ever be said to stand for a city, then it is this city, in
this year, and the name of that man is Charles Dickens. But if
that name conjures up colour and carol singers and jolly old
gentlemen, then think again. These streets are no cause for
comedy, and know no tones but grim and grey. More than two
million souls, and as many as a third of them sunk in a
permanent and repellent destitution that will turn your
stomach long before it touches your heart. Night and day
London moves and sweats and bawls, as riddled with life as a
corpse with maggots.

From where we stand, the air is so deadened with a greasy
yellow fog that you can barely see three paces ahead, and risk
stumbling in the street over milk-cans, broken bottles, and
what look at first like rat-ridden heaps of rags, until they stare
back at you with gin-hollowed eyes, and hold out their

1

blackened hands for hard cash. The shops are lit two hours before their time, but the gas gutters, and the windows are sallow and unappealing, the merchandise filmed with the same sticky brindling of soot that will coat your clothes and line your lungs by the time we're done.

But enough. This is not what you came here for. Muffle your face, if you can, against the stink of human and animal filth, and try not to look too closely at what it is that's caking your boots, and sucking at your tread. And keep your pocket-book close as we go – this part of town is as silent with thieves as it is strident with drunks. We have a way to go yet and the day is darkening. We must find him soon, or risk losing him altogether.

Chapter One

The Young Man

The young man at the desk puts down his pen and sits back in his chair. The fog has been thickening all afternoon, and whatever sun might once have shone is now sinking fast. The window before him is as blank as if it has been papered over. For all he can see outside, the room might give on the flat expanses of the Essex marshes, or command the ancient forests of the Kentish heights. Or it might – as indeed it is – be on the first floor of a London lodging-house, in a narrow street not far from the British Museum. That fact is significant in itself, as we shall see, and it is not necessary to be a detective (as this young man is) to make a number of other useful deductions about the character of the person who inhabits this space. He is a single man, this Charles Maddox, since the bed is narrow, the room small, and neither is very clean. He is careless of his appearance, to judge by the waistcoat hanging on the wardrobe door and the tangle of shirts spilling from the chest, but there are other things he does care about, for a large black cat has appropriated the best and warmest chair, which looks to have been placed next the fire for precisely that purpose. He is a sentimental young man then, but more than anything else he is a curious one. For by his possessions shall ye know him, and this room is a mirror of Charles Maddox's mind. He has little interest in languages, so has never come across the word

Wunderkammer, but he has created one nevertheless – a small but perfect 'cabinet of wonders'. Every level place carries its prize – mantelpiece, bookcase, desk, even the wash-stand. An ostrich egg, and a piece of pale grey stone, slightly granular to the touch, printed with the whorl of a perfect ammonite; the blank face of an African mask, bearded with woven fibre, and next to it something black and shrivelled and eyeless that looks disconcertingly like a human head; a wooden box of old coins, and a blue jar filled with shells and pieces of coral; a case of stuffed birds feathered in primary colours that cannot be native to these drab shores, and a scimitar blade with a worn and battered handle that clearly once boasted jewels. There are maps, and prints, and charts of the voyages of the great explorers. And one whole wall is lined with bookshelves, many not quite straight, so that the volumes lean against the slope like dinghies in a wind. We are beginning to form a picture of this young man, but before you smile indulgently at the hopeless clutter, and dismiss him as a mere dilettante, remember that this is the age of the gifted amateur. Remember too, that in 1850 it is still possible – just – for an intelligent man to span the sciences and still attain a respectable proficiency in them all. If, of course, he has money enough, and time. If, in short, he is a gentleman. It is the right question to ask about Charles Maddox, but it does not come with an easy answer.

Nor, it appears, does the task he is presently embarked upon. There is nothing scientific about this, it seems. He stirs, then sighs. London is full of noises, but today even the barrel-organ on the corner of the street is stifled and indistinct, as if being played underwater. It's hardly the afternoon for such an unpromising task, but it can be postponed no longer. He picks up his pen with renewed determination, and begins again. So engrossed is he – so concerned to find words that will keep

4

hope in check but keep it, nonetheless, alive – that he does not hear the knock at the door the first time it comes. Nor the second. It is only when a handful of grit patters against the glass that Charles pushes back his chair and goes to the window. He can barely make out the features of the man standing on the steps, but he does not need to know the name, to know the uniform. He pulls up the sash.

'What is it?' he calls, frowning. What business has Bow Street here?

The man steps back and looks up, and Charles finds he recognizes him after all.

'Batten – is that you? What do you want?'

'Message for you, Mr Maddox. From Inspector Field.'

'Wait there – I'm coming down.'

The message, when he gets it, is no more than two scrawled lines, but such brevity is only to be expected from such a man, and in such circumstances.

'The inspector thought you'd like to see for y'self, sir,' says Batten, stamping his feet against the cold, his breath coming in gusts and merging into the fog. 'Before we do the necessary. Seeing as you're taking an interest in the Chadwick case.'

'Tell Inspector Field that I am indebted to him. I will be there directly.'

'You know where it is? I'd take you m'self, only I'm on my way home and it's the opposite way.'

'Don't worry – I'll find it.'

Charles gives the man a shilling for his trouble, and returns to his room for his coat and muffler. The former is over the back of the chair, the latter – it turns out – under the cat. There is the customary tussle, which ends in its customary way, and when Charles leaves the house ten minutes later, the muffler remains behind. There is probably nothing for it but to buy another one; when he can afford it. He turns his collar up against the chill, and disappears from sight into the coaly fog.

There's no lamp at the corner of the street, just the little charcoal-furnace of the chestnut-seller, which throws a red glow up at her face, and on to the drawn features of four dirty little children clustered around her skirts. Not for the first time, the woman has a swollen black bruise around one eye. As he steps off the kerb, Charles only just avoids being trampled under an omnibus heaving with people that veers huge out of the dense brown haze into the path of an unlit brewer's dray. He springs back just in time, but not fast enough to avoid a spatter of wet dung from hip to knee. It's not an auspicious start, and he hurls a few well-honed insults at both 'bus driver and crossing-sweeper before dodging through the traffic to the other side and heading south down an almost deserted Tottenham Court Road. No street-sellers tonight, and the only shop still open is Hine the butcher, who runs no risk of thieving raids in the lurid glare of his dozen jets of gas. A couple of old tramps are warming their faces against the glass, but paying customers are sparse. The afternoon seems suspended between day and dark, and the circles of milky light cast by the gas-lamps dispel the gloom no more than a few feet around. A gaggle of raggedy link-boys follow him hopefully for a while, tugging at his coat-tails and offering him their torches: 'Light you home for sixpence!' 'Darn't listen to 'im – I'll do it for a joey – whatcha say, mister? Can't say fairer than that.' Charles eventually shakes them off – literally, in one case – and smiles to himself when one lad calls after him asking if he can see in the dark, ''cause yer going to need ta'. Even in daylight, the city changes character every dozen yards, and a fog like this plays tricks with the senses, blanking out familiar landmarks and shrinking distances to no further than the eye can see.

6

Having patrolled these streets for the best part of a year, Charles should know them, if anyone does, but there is something else at work here – an ability he has to render the map in his head to the ground under his feet, which explains the pace of his stride, and the assurance of his step. A modern neurologist would say he had unusually well-developed spatial cognition combined with almost photographic memory function. Charles has more than a passing interest in the new advances in daguerreotyping, so he might well understand the meaning of those last words even if not the science behind them, but he would most certainly smile at the pretension. As far as he's concerned, he's been doing this since he was a little boy, and thinks of it – in so far as he thinks of it at all – as little more than a lucky and very useful knack.

Once past St Giles Circus, the line of shops peters out and the road narrows. A few minutes later Charles stops under a street-lamp before turning, rather less confidently this time, down a dingy side lane. It's unlit, with alleys branching off left and right. He stands for a moment, allowing his eyes to adjust to the dark, and wonders if he should have hired one of those boys after all. He rates his chances well enough against a lone footpad, but for a year or more this part of London has been notorious for a spate of garrotting attacks, and the men who use these miserable backwaters for cover, ply that trade in threes and fours. No one but a fool or a foreigner would venture willingly into such a maze of dilapidated houses, seeming blind and yet teeming behind, as Charles well knows, with a desperate human detritus that has no choice but to call this vile place home. Even the fog seems more malevolent here, funnelling down from the main thoroughfare, and eddying ghostily into archways and casements. Charles takes a deep breath and starts off again, his ears suddenly attentive to the whispers and creakings of the crumbling tenements on either side. Half a dozen times in as many months the ground round here has been shaken by a sudden crash as one of these structures has subsided, throwing a tower of dust into the dirty London sky. The last was barely three weeks before, and when the scavengers moved in to rake the wreckage, they found more than two dozen bodies – men, women and children – huddled together for warmth half-naked, in a room less than fifteen feet square.

The further Charles goes, the thicker the fog becomes, and once or twice he thinks he sees darker shapes and shadows loom and then retreat before him – if they are men they do not show themselves, leaving his agitated imagination oppressed by phantasms. But only too horribly real is the sound of the fever cart, creaking its own slow way through the narrow alleys somewhere nearby, the cries of warning smothered in the dead air. He's more relieved than he'll admit to turn a bend in the alley and see the entrance to a low covered way, with a solitary lamp looming at the farther end. He ducks his head and starts along the tunnel, though not without at least one anxious glance behind; if ever there was a place precisely adapted for thieves to waylay the unwary, then this is surely it. The walls are running with moisture that drips into pools on the floor and slides in runnels down the back of his neck, and he wishes, not for the first time, that he'd been firmer with the cat. He quickens his step, but the further he goes, the more he becomes aware of an all-too-familiar sickly reek. When he comes out into the open, it's to an iron railing and a choked and ruined burial ground, crowded in on all sides by half-derelict buildings, the gravestones all but level with the first-floor windows, where here and there a dim light still shows through the cracked and patched-up panes. The gate is standing open, and there are bull-dog lanterns on the far left side, close by what looks like the twisted stump of a stunted yew tree.

The police.

He can't make out how many there are, but they're expecting him, and one calls across in a voice he recognizes. It's Sam Wheeler – Cockney chipper and as quick as ginger. They worked together for six months out of St Giles Station House. It was Wheeler who'd taught him the ways of the London underworld, and Wheeler who'd been at his side the night Field first took him to Rats' Castle and the rookeries.

'Hey, Chas!' he cries. 'We're over 'ere. Mind where you're walkin' though, or you'll find your body being committed to the ground rather sooner than you bargained for.'

Charles looks around. Humidity hangs like contagion in the atmosphere, staining the mouldering bricks and catching at the back of his throat. He knows all about the risk of infection in a place like this, and finds himself wishing to God he'd never come – never taken a case that has been doomed from the start and can only end in failure. But then he reminds himself that it isn't just a case, it's *the* case – the only one he has, and the only one he's ever likely to have, if he gets himself a reputation for letting people down. He starts to pick his way slowly towards Wheeler, but the spongy earth sinks and sighs unnervingly under his weight. He swallows his scruples and steps on to one of the mossy half-buried stones, but his foot slips from under him on the slimy surface and he loses his balance and lurches forward, landing heavily on his side. He swears under his breath, but as he shifts his weight to get back up, his fingers push down through the mud into something else – something cold and viscid and putrid that comes away in his hand. He jerks his arm away and gets quickly to his feet, feeling the delayed prickle of cold adrenalin as he breathes through his

9

mouth and feels in his pocket for a handkerchief, willing himself not to retch like a woman. He glances across at Wheeler, wondering if he saw, but thankfully the constable's attention is engaged elsewhere.

'Look at that rat!' Sam cries, pointing. 'Did you see it? What a monster! Almost as big as a dog! Ho – there he goes – there – straight under that stone!'

Charles wipes his hands hurriedly and throws the handkerchief from him in disgust. No amount of laundering will persuade him to use that thing again. Then he steadies himself and sets off again, and as he comes closer to the light, he can see that the ground about the tree stump has been disturbed. He edges closer and squats down, telling himself to forget the stench and the squalor and concentrate on looking carefully and thinking clearly. That's what he's good at: using his eyes and applying his mind – just as he was taught by his great-uncle Maddox, the celebrated thief-taker. His parents had named him Charles in Maddox's honour, though not without some misgivings: Maddox might have made a lot of money out of his chosen profession, but it was not one well regarded by the middle classes. Not then, when Maddox was practising, in the early years of the century, and certainly not now. But then again, the Victorian bourgeoisie can rely on a properly constituted police force, which is a luxury their grandparents never had. Thief-taking may never have been a particularly respectable occupation, but it was an essential one, nevertheless, and all too often the only bulwark between order and anarchy. 'Charles Maddox' he is then, the second of that name, but his parents could hardly have expected he would want to emulate his predecessor in a far more significant way, and take up the same base calling. When he turned seventeen, Charles reluctantly agreed to follow his father into medicine in a last forlorn attempt to salvage their relationship, but he lasted less than a year before giving it up and beginning the world again where his heart really lay – with the Detective.

The second officer comes up now and stands behind him, watchful but silent. Charles thinks he's seen him before, but can't remember his name. Clough, is it, or Cuss? Something like that, anyway. His face is as sharp as a hatchet and his skin as dry as an autumn leaf.

'So what do you make of it?' the man says eventually, in the same level tone he might use to buy a brisket or order a beer. Is it indifference – or just an appropriate and commendable detachment? Charles can't be sure.

'Can you tell me who found it?' he asks.

'Couple of lads, playing where they shouldn't. I doubt they'll be back here in a hurry.'

'And it was like this?'

'Nothing's been moved. Not yet.'

Charles bends down and looks more closely, straining his eyes in the low light. Without a word, the man brings the bull-dog lower, and Charles feels its warmth on his skin. It's clear to him now what must have happened. Judging by the exposed knots of red yew root, the last week's rain has washed at least an inch of mud from the surface of the soil. And what it's revealed is the tiny body of a newborn baby, still wrapped in a dirty blue woollen blanket, a scrap of white cotton tangled about the neck. He may never have completed his medical training, but Charles knows enough to make a pretty shrewd guess how long these bones have been here. In this waterlogged London clay, probably three weeks; certainly no more than four. The eyes are long gone, but wisps of pale hair are still pasted to the skull, and the flesh is largely intact, though almost black with putrefaction and scored with the marks of teeth and claws. Indeed, the rats seem to have done an unusually efficient job with this one. One hand is completely gone below the wrist, but the fingers of the other are curled as if to a mother's touch. When Charles lifts the edge of the sodden blanket, the gaping belly is swarming with larvae. But that isn't the worst of it. Underneath the body he can already see the buried blue of another coverlet, and the broken ribcage of another small child. He glances up at the officer. 'Do you want to, or shall I?'

'Be my guest. It's not a job I particularly relish.'

Charles takes a pair of gloves from his pocket, and the officer hands him a small trowel. Five minutes' careful digging reveals three bodies buried under the first, one next to the other, exactly aligned. Indeed, they look for all the world like infants in a cradle. Sleeping soundly side by side, carefully swaddled against the night air. Charles sits back on his heels. 'So what do we think? Are we assuming it's a woman?'

The other man considers. 'Most likely, in my experience.'

'And the same one each time?'

'Hard to tell for sure. Could be two of them. The body on the top's a lot more recent, but the other three are like peas in a pod. Probably all went in together.'

Charles is silent a moment, then shakes his head. 'I disagree. The earth here's been turned over more than just once or twice. And surely even in this light you can see the difference in the bones.'

Not just the bones, in fact, but the flesh. One baby's face is smoothed almost doll-like – unnerving the first time, but Charles has seen many times what grave wax can do. The other two underneath are withering one after the other into parched cages of separating bones, their mummified flesh dried in tight leathery tendons, the closed lids stretched paper-thin.

Charles glances up. 'Whoever this woman was, she seems to have been trying to give them a decent burial – or the nearest she could manage. This last one looks like it even had a handkerchief or something put over its face – as if she couldn't bear to look at it. And yet she kept coming back – kept reopening the same grave.'

He stares at the open pit, struggling for a word to help make sense of it, and comes up only with 'tenderness'. It jars horribly with the evidence of his own senses – not just the sight of decomposing flesh, but the reek of decay eating into his skin and clothes – but the idea has caught his mind, and it will not go away.

The other man is dismissive; he's clearly had enough of this wild goose chase. 'Come on, it's no big mystery. She'd have needed time, even for a shallow grave, and this is the only part of the cemetery where you're not much overlooked. It's just common sense. Nothing more sinister than that.'

Charles nods; the man has a point – he should have thought of that himself. 'All the same, think about what that actually *meant*. Imagine digging over the same piece of earth time and time again, knowing full well what you were going to find. What kind of woman could do that? It goes against every idea we have of the sanctity of motherhood.'

The man laughs. 'Sanctity of motherhood, my arse. I thought they told me you'd been in the police? Most of the women round here have already got too many mouths to feed. Baby farms cost money; a pillow over the face is free gratis, and you know as well as I do that unless they're either very careless, or very unlucky, there's virtually no chance of getting caught. I've lost count of the number of dead babies I've seen fished out of the Thames, or found rotting in the street, but I can number the women we've prosecuted for infanticide on the fingers of one hand. The courts have better things to do with their time. As have we.'

He turns and waves at Wheeler, beckoning him over.

'Come on,' he calls. 'There's nothing for us here. Just another routine child-killing.'

Charles sticks the trowel into the ground and stands up, his eyes glinting. 'So if dumping them in the river is so easy, why go to all the trouble of bringing them here? Not to mention the risk. It's because this place is consecrated ground – that's the only explanation that makes any sense. And that alone means this is a very long way from being *just another routine child-killing.*'

There's a snort, and Charles looks round to see Wheeler staring down into the gaping grave, a half-eaten apple in his hand.

'Jesus,' he says, taking another bite, 'if this is your definition of consecrated, give me hellfire any day. Looks like the last one they put in over yonder had to be stamped on to get 'im in. The coffin's rearin' up out of the ground like the Last Trump's already blastin'. Though at least 'e did *have* a coffin. Unlike these poor little buggers. Any use to you, Chas?'

Charles sees the other man's cool and quizzical eye; he's clearly been wondering all this time what right Charles has to be there, but has decided to say nothing. Charles shakes his head. 'I doubt it. The last anyone heard of the child I'm looking for was sixteen years ago, when it was taken to an orphanage at three months old. These bodies haven't been in the ground anything like that long.'

'You ain't got a lot to go on, if you don't mind me sayin' so,' says Wheeler, his mouth full. 'What's the chance of findin' one solitary kid in a town this size – dead or alive? You might pass it in the street this very evenin' and never know.'

Charles shrugs. 'I have a picture of the mother, and my client hopes the child may take after her.'

'Your client,' says the other man softly, 'must have money to spare – or a very poor understanding of the likelihood of success.'

The tone is purposefully neutral, but the implication is clear. Charles turns and looks the man squarely in the face. 'My *client* refuses to give up hope,' he replies coldly, 'even though I have explained very clearly that our chances are small. I am conducting as detailed an investigation as is possible after all this time, and doing so in the proper professional manner. I resent any suggestion, *Constable*, that it could possibly be otherwise.'

He sees Wheeler's eyes widen and realizes his mistake at once.

'Last I looked,' says the other man, 'my rank was *sergeant*. And if I were you, *Mr* Maddox, I would keep a civil tongue in your head and that temper of yours under control. It's already cost you more than you could well afford. Or so I hear.'

Charles feels the heat rush across his face under the man's steady gaze. The bastard knows. Of course – they *all* know. Charles has never learned the trick of coping with injustice – not as a small child, punished for something he hadn't done, and not now, as a man of twenty-five, unjustly dismissed from a job he loved. The official charge was insubordination, but he knew, and his superiors at Scotland Yard knew, that his real crime was daring to challenge the deductions of a higher-ranking officer – and challenge them as not just scientifically unfounded, but rationally unsound. Looking back, it might have been wiser to make his views known privately – or keep them entirely to himself – but a man's life had been in the balance, and he'd felt then as he does still, that he had no choice. It was no consolation, months later, to find that new evidence had come to light; by that time an innocent man had already been taken to a place of lawful execution, and hanged by the neck until he was dead.

The eyes of the two men are still upon him. He turns, as pointedly as he dares, to Wheeler. 'Tell Inspector Field that I will continue to be grateful for any information he might come across that could have a bearing on my case. I will detain you gentlemen no longer.'

He is out of sight in five yards, and out of earshot soon after, but all the same he keeps his anger in check until he is back at the Circus, then vents the full force of his fury on a stack of wooden crates outside the Horse-Shoe, sending glasses and bottles spinning and smashing across the cobbles, and spewing rank beer on the already filthy ground. He stands there breathing heavily for a few moments, then straightens his collar and pushes open the inn door.

Chapter Two

In Mr Tulkinghorn's Chambers

It's late when Charles wakes, his head wooden with hangover, and the sulphur of fog still in his mouth. The curtains hang open as he'd left them, and a line of sunlight glances across the farther wall. He sits up slowly, as if careful to keep his brain from tilting, and then pushes his hands through his hair and kicks back the twisted sheets. He opens the door and calls to the landlady to send out for half a pint of coffee from the shop next door, and then goes to the wash-stand and pours a jug of cold water over his head and neck, eyed all the while by the cat, who is understandably disdainful of Charles' dismal efforts, having attended rather more thoroughly to his own ablutions some two hours before. As he's towelling his face dry, Charles catches sight of his letter, still unfinished, on his desk. If things had turned out differently last night he might have had something worthwhile to say – a reason to rip up his mealy-mouthed draft and begin again, but as always this case leads only to dead ends. And dead children.

The landlady knocks with the coffee a few minutes later, and as he's fumbling in his pocket for what's left of his money, he sees for the first time that there's a white edge of paper jutting out from under the trodden rope-matting which is all the room can boast of by way of carpet. Someone has slid something under his door. He looks down at it for a moment. He has no memory of seeing it when he got home the night before – not much memory of getting back at all, if truth be told – but he knows it wasn't there when he left. Strange. He's on the point of calling Mrs Stacey back up, but recalls that Tuesday evening is her Harmonic Meeting, and the maid had probably taken the opportunity to sidle out the back and meet that greasy pot-boy from the Three Tuns. He bends down and slides the piece of paper from under the mat. It's a very superior kind of paper, he sees that at once. Fine-textured, heavy, and ostentatiously sealed with thick red wax. The paper of a very superior kind of man. The kind of man who does not expect to be refused, and does not care to be kept waiting.

Lincoln's Inn Fields
Tuesday, midnight

Sir,
I would be grateful if you could present yourself at my chambers, at eleven o'clock tomorrow morning. There is a small matter of business I wish to discuss with you.

Your obedient servant,
Edward Tulkinghorn
Attorney-at-Law

Charles knows the name. Who, in his line of work, does not? A hard, gruelling and arid man; widely feared and rarely worsted. Such words apply to Mr Tulkinghorn, as they apply to many other eminent London lawyers, but Tulkinghorn of the Fields is, all the same, a man apart. There is hardly a noble family in England that does not have its name inscribed on one of the locked iron boxes that line his room. He speaks only when he can charge to do so, and offers no opinion that has not been paid for, and handsomely. Little is known of him beyond his accomplishments in Chancery, and how he spends that portion of his time that has not been purchased is his private secret. There, he acts for himself alone, and he is never more careful than with his own confidences. To be consulted on a matter of business by Edward Tulkinghorn is an event of some moment, even for the great; to be – perhaps – employed by him, a professional distinction so distant that Charles can scarce allow himself to contemplate it. He has, in any case, very little time to do so. The appointment is less than an hour away.

He washes again – quickly, but more carefully this time – and retrieves a shirt from the closet. It's been worn, but not too often, and it's the best he has. He smoothes his unruly hair as well as he can, and retrieves his comb from where it is currently doing service as a bookmark in the second volume of Erasmus Darwin's *Zoönomia* (Charles has recently chanced upon a new work by the great man's grandson, but considers him, on this showing at least, to be far inferior to his illustrious forebear).

A quarter of an hour later he leaves the house. The difference in the day is dazzling, and the events of the night before begin to seem nightmarish and unreal, a hallucination of the poisonous air. It is hardly possible to believe that such a hell-hole exists, on such a bright, cold morning. Charles retraces last night's journey as far as the Circus, though progress through the crowds is rather slower than it had been through the fog. Little boys tug at his coat-tails offering walnuts and apples, housewives pick over fruit and vegetables, and tiny children risk trampling to sift up the cigar-ends swilling in the gutter with the rest of the refuse and excrement. The local whores are out in force already, and Red Suke winks lewdly at Charles as he goes past. And it's hardly surprising – it's not just his clear blue gaze and thick bronze curls, though they undoubtedly have their effect – there's something about the way he walks, a swagger that is not quite a swagger, that draws the eye and catches the attention, and has got him into trouble more than once. And even though you will never get him to acknowledge it, even to himself, that trouble is not always or exclusively of the female variety. Suke is clearly in a cheerful mood, having downed her usual three morning quarterns of gin and peppermint before presenting herself for paying custom.

'Where's you off to in such a rush, Charlie? Got y'self a sweetheart, have yer?'

When he turns and grins at her, she hoots with laughter and replumps her ample décolletage in his direction.

'You can al'as fall back on me, Charlie boy. Though falling for'ards might be more to the purpose.'

The air is raucous with hawkers' cries, and heaving with the hot smell of open-air cooking. For someone who's had nothing to eat since lunchtime the previous day, the aroma of sizzling fish is too much to bear. Charles decides he will indulge himself, just this once, even if it means no eggs for breakfast tomorrow. Though on this showing, it may not surprise you to learn that he goes without his eggs more often than he has them. The decision made, he shells out a penny for a toasted bloater wrapped in bread and eats it greedily in three bites, licking the salt from his lips and wiping the butter from his chin with the back of his sleeve, having forgotten until it's too late that he no longer owns a handkerchief. As one would expect, none of the usual pickpockets are yet abroad – thieves are alone in loving the fog, and weather like this is no environment for profitable dipping. A couple of the Fenhope lads are making faces at themselves in the boot-maker's window, but the next moment they're gone, disappeared into the huddle of women gathered round a stallholder's table. At least we must assume it is a table, since no square inch of the surface is actually visible under the jumble of teapots, crockery, artificial flowers, plaster of Paris night-shades, clothes-horses, tea-caddies, and tins of rat poison. It looks like some absurdly over-elaborate version of the memory game – as if at any moment the proprietor might whisk across one of the much-darned sheets drooping over his head and challenge his customers to name every rag and cast-off. Then again, you might well counter that this dishevelled display bears more than a passing resemblance to our own young man's muddle of assorted curios. But if you were to say such a thing to Charles, he would merely look at you blankly: he collects scientific specimens; these people trade in trash.

A scatter of crows cackle into the sky above his head as he crosses into Holborn and heads towards the City. The crowd thins a little but the traffic is as heavy as ever. Wagons and hackney-coaches rumble past him, and he's relieved, in the end, to turn into the relative tranquillity of Lincoln's Inn Fields. Mr Tulkinghorn has not specified a number, trusting, perhaps, that a man like Charles should either know it, or be able to find it without undue exertion. If it is any sort of a test, then Charles passes it easily and presents himself at the impressive and oddly Egyptian-looking facade at precisely five minutes before eleven. The door is unlatched before he has raised his hand to knock and swings open to reveal a middle-aged clerk, a little out at elbows, who is showing out a bald, timid-looking man with a shining head and a clump of black hair sticking out at the back. Having completed this task, the clerk turns to Charles, who does not, apparently, need to give his name.

'Mr Tulkinghorn is expecting you. Follow me, please.'

They pass the high pew where Charles' guide normally sits, and proceed at an appropriately ponderous pace up the imposing staircase to the first floor, where Mr Tulkinghorn is sitting in state behind a large writing-table, at the far end of a room painted the colour of blood. The blinds are drawn and the green lamp is lit; the bright day clearly has no business here. Mr Tulkinghorn seems not to have noticed Charles' presence, though the creak of the floorboards must have given him away the moment he entered. The air is close with the must of old paper, but Charles is uncomfortably aware that there is also a distinct under-tang of fried fish, which can only be his own personal contribution. All the same, it is at least another slow minute before Mr Tulkinghorn lowers the paper he has been reading and removes his spectacles. Charles makes sure to keep his eyes fixed upon him, all the while making his own private map of the precise configuration of the room. To the left, a cabinet of parchment scrolls and leather-bound law books, the lettering all but dissolved into the spines; to the right, the shadowy portraits of eminent and anonymous men, ranged one by one between the long windows; and on the wall behind Tulkinghorn, a rack of iron boxes in niches that resemble nothing so much as a *columbarium*, a last repository for cases long dead, and a hiding place for secrets still very much alive. The surfaces are dusty, like Charles' own; but clear, unlike his own. There are no papers visible, aside, of course, from the one Tulkinghorn has been reading. 'Has been' being the phrase, since the lawyer has now placed that paper carefully on his desk and raised his eyes to meet his visitor.

'You have been recommended to me.'

It's not the opening Charles expected, but it is, all the same, a promising one. He waits; Tulkinghorn waits. There's a chair on Charles' side of the desk, but he's not invited to use it.

Tulkinghorn picks up a piece of broken sealing-wax and weighs it in his hand. 'It is a – somewhat delicate matter.'

'Most of my work is.'

Tulkinghorn raises an eyebrow. 'You mean the Chadwick case? That, if you don't mind me saying so, is a waste of your time. I would say a waste of your talents, but I am not sure, as yet, how far those talents extend. You will never find that child, as more seasoned police officers than you have already discovered. If the earth has not swallowed it, this city has. Even if it lives, it will be as depraved and degenerate as the rest of its class. You could not find it, even if you searched every thieves' den and rookery lair in London.'

Charles has his own views on that score – and reasons of his own that we may yet discover, for his dogged persistence in continuing with the case – but he elects not to share them. And if it surprises him to find Tulkinghorn so well informed, he is not going to pay his interlocutor the compliment of showing it.

'You said there was a recommendation?'

'Ah yes. It was Inspector Bucket. Of the Detective. I believe you know him?'

It's like a blow to the gut. *Bucket*? There are, undoubtedly, people who might have mentioned Charles' name in Tulkinghorn's hearing, but the list is not long and Bucket, surely, is at the furthest and most remote end of it. What on earth can possibly have induced him to do anything to advance Charles' interests? Indeed, Charles would have laid a good deal of money he does not possess on the inspector doing everything in his power in the opposite direction. It was Bucket who'd had him dismissed from the police – Bucket whose judgement he'd questioned with such disastrous consequences. His mind is racing, and he is all too aware that Tulkinghorn is watching him with extreme though concealed attention. Does Bucket, perhaps, feel guilty? Even the famously infallible inspector must have accepted by now that he made a terrible mistake in the

Silas Boone case. Perhaps he feels, now, that if he'd listened to Charles, the man might never have hanged. So is this his way of making reparation? Boone is beyond even Bucket's long reach now, but Charles is alive and has to earn his bread somehow.

'I am aware, of course,' continues Tulkinghorn, 'of your family antecedents. Inspector Bucket was, I believe, something of a protégé of your great-uncle in his youth?'

Charles nods. 'He worked for him for a time, before joining the Detective, and I dare say he owes much of his subsequent success to my uncle's methods. As, indeed' – this with the slightest bridling that the lawyer does not fail to register – 'do I. Mr Maddox has been my teacher and mentor since I was a boy.'

'Indeed so. And now you are a young man. A young man, moreover – or so I have been informed – of intellect and discretion. The matter I wish to discuss with you requires both qualities, but it is the latter that is my paramount concern.'

'I understand.'

Tulkinghorn eyes him. 'Possibly you do. But I shall repeat the point nonetheless. Discretion in this case is all in all. My client in this affair is a man with an unimpeachable reputation. A man trusted with the confidential business of the highest in the land.'

For one wild moment Charles thinks the lawyer is referring to himself, but Tulkinghorn has not finished.

'You will have heard, I think, of Sir Julius Cremorne?'

As Tulkinghorn is to the law, so Cremorne is to high finance. The latest in a long family line to head one of the City's oldest and most astute merchant banks; a prime enabler of imperial trade, and lender of first resort to the country's largest corporations. Even – it's rumoured – an adviser to the Queen. Yes, Charles has heard of Sir Julius Cremorne, but he cannot begin to imagine what such a man could possibly want with him. His bafflement must be legible in his face, because

24

Tulkinghorn gives the ghost of a smile. It is not an expression that finds an easy home on his impassive features.

'The case is not, of itself, a taxing one. The need for discretion arises purely from Sir Julius' rank and repute. In all other respects it is utterly trivial. But it must, nonetheless, be resolved, and with dispatch. I am afraid, Mr Maddox, that there will always be those who seek to besmirch eminent men for their own nefarious purposes. I have seen it happen many times before, and the more spotless the family credit, the more zealous such villains seem to be to compromise it.'

'I see,' says Charles, who does not, quite. 'Perhaps you could—?'

'Of course. You will want details. It is in the nature of your profession.'

A noise. So low as to be almost inaudible – little more than the slightest creak of the ancient boards, but Charles is suddenly alert. Is it possible that there is someone else in the room? He'd noticed the elaborate oriental screen when he came in, and thought in passing that it sat rather oddly with the austerity of the rest, but he had not suspected its role might be more than decorative.

'Sir Julius,' continues Mr Tulkinghorn, looking at Charles from under his bent grey brows, 'has been receiving letters. Very unpleasant letters.'

'Letters of a threatening nature?'

Tulkinghorn considers. 'Nothing specific. Merely the expression of a vague but undeniably malevolent intent.'

Charles frowns. 'But as you said yourself, it cannot be the first time that Sir Julius has been harassed in a similar way. Why should this particular example concern him so much?'

Tulkinghorn places the tips of his fingers together. 'Sir Julius has always gone to extraordinary lengths to protect his wife and daughters from the less seemly consequences of his public position, and in this endeavour he has, until very recently, been entirely successful. Unfortunately, the eldest Miss Cremorne is about to be married, and the house has, as a result, been thronged at all hours of the day by dressmakers, provisioners, flower-sellers, and I know not what. In short, there has been an unwarrantable breach on the part of one of the footmen, such that one of these infamous letters was given directly to Lady Cremorne's own hand.'

'There have been how many, so far?'

'Three. The earliest some five months ago; the most recent, only last week.'

'May I see it?'

There is, perhaps, a slight hesitation on the lawyer's part at this request, but he takes out a ring of keys from his waistcoat-pocket and unlocks the desk drawer. The letter has been placed on plain brown paper, under a small oblong paperweight carved of some highly polished black substance. From where Charles is standing it looks, improbable as it sounds, like two slender fingers, one slightly longer than the other, the fingernails carefully incised. He's still staring at it when Tulkinghorn leans forward and hands him the paper. One sheet only, soft with frequent handling, with marks here and there in a dark and dirty brown. The handwriting is not educated, that much is both obvious and expected, but there is strength in it, and considerable resolution.

I naw what yow did
I will make yow pay

Charles looks up, 'Was there no cover?'

'I believe it was mislaid.'

'But it was posted, not delivered by hand?'

Tulkinghorn nods.

'And the others? May I see them?'

'Possibly. If they have not been disposed of. I will enquire.'

'And Sir Julius has no idea what this latest letter refers to?'

Tulkinghorn spreads his hands. 'Like the others – anything and nothing. You know what the people who commit these affronts to decency are like. And you can also imagine, I am sure, the effect of such a missive on a lady's mind. The matter must be settled with all possible speed: there must be no recurrence.'

'So what do you want me to do?'

'Discover the culprit and tell me his name.'

'As simple as that. Even though, on the face of it, this letter could have been written by any one of a thousand men.'

Tulkinghorn inclines his head. 'Even so. It is a complex puzzle, I grant you; if it were *not* so I should not have required assistance to resolve it, and I should not have hired *you*.'

He has him there; Charles is intelligent enough to know he is being flattered, but human enough to pride himself on that intelligence, and crave the credit for it.

Tulkinghorn gets to his feet, as Charles folds the paper and puts it in his breast-pocket. 'I will expect you to keep me fully informed. If you have expenses, you should apply to Knox. He, likewise, will require you to render a comprehensive account.'

The clerk shows Charles back down the stairs and out on to the square. He has been in the house less than twenty minutes. He walks slowly to the corner and waits to let a carriage go past, then stoops for a moment to refasten his boot. So it is that he does not see that same equipage come to a halt at Tulkinghorn's door, or the man who emerges from it. He is a little below middle size, this man, pale-faced, and about five-and-forty. His beard is shaven on his chin, but grows a fine rich brown on his cheeks and his upper lip, though his most distinguishing feature is concealed at present by a black leather glove: he bears an unsightly red scar on the back of his hand, the result of an unfortunate wound received some years since while travelling on the Continent. He stops a moment on the top step and looks about him, but by the time Charles straightens up he has disappeared inside, and the groom is closing the carriage door. The panel bears a rather striking black swan on its coat of arms, which Charles glances at idly before turning and walking away. Heraldry was rather a hobby of his, as a boy, and somewhere on his crowded shelves there is still a tattered old scrapbook of the armorial bearings of the English peerage. But these arms, arresting though they are, he does not recognize.

The man, meanwhile, is ascending the stairs of Tulkinghorn's house much as Charles had done. But he, unlike Charles, finds his host waiting to greet him at the door of the room. Tulkinghorn bows solemnly and leads the way to a smaller ante-chamber on the far side. They cross the floor under the opulent if rather faded ceiling, which seems to depict some sort of allegorical figure, reclining among flowers, clouds, and chubby pink-cheeked cherubs, and pointing with a plump arm which – from where we're standing, at least – seems oddly foreshortened. Tulkinghorn's new visitor admires the ceiling, having seen it many times. He considers it rather fine, of its type; Charles thought it obscene.

There are three other gentlemen already seated at the round table in the ante-room, two of them smoking, and a third man with a finely trimmed beard, who has just emerged from the recess behind that extremely useful oriental screen.

'So?' It is the oldest of the men, upright and self-possessed, with fine white hair and an equally fine white shirt-frill, perfectly starched. 'Is he our man, or not?'

Mr Tulkinghorn takes his place at the table. 'I think, Sir Amyas, that young Mr Maddox is ideal for our purposes. Bright, but not dangerously so, and very much in need of gainful employ. He has sufficient astuteness to do what we ask, and judgement enough not to probe any further.'

There is a silence. The last gentleman to arrive shifts in his seat, clearly not yet convinced. 'I am sure I need not remind you why it is absolutely imperative that my own particular part in this business should remain a matter of the utmost secrecy. You *say* this young man is unlikely to discover the truth, but what if he should—'

Mr Tulkinghorn holds up a hand. 'He will not. Indeed he cannot. As far as he is concerned, he is investigating a distressing but ultimately inconsequential incident, involving only Sir Julius Cremorne. It is impossible he should discover the full extent of the affair. He knows enough to locate the culprit, nothing more.'

'That's all very well,' says the bearded man quickly, looking round the table, and shifting rather stiffly on his old-fashioned mahogany-and-horsehair chair. 'None of *you* face the m-meddling of a vulgar and impertinent upstart—'

'Hardly that, surely,' murmurs Tulkinghorn.

'– none of *you* run anything like the risk you expect *me* to assume. We've all had those damnable letters, but I'm the only one menaced with exposure by this plan. I told you before, Tulkinghorn, and I'll tell you again – I d-don't like this. I don't like it at all. And as for that latest abomination—'

'My dear Sir Julius, we have, as you say, discussed this already, and at some length. In the first place, your letters are among the most recent, and we may hope that their trail has not, therefore, gone completely cold. In the second place, it will be far easier to convince our young man that, for a gentleman in your position, such letters are little more than an occupational commonplace. No one, after all, has any great love for bankers.'

Sir Julius sits back in his chair, his face very red. 'To speak frankly, I fail to see why we need this *Maddox* at all. That other f-fellow has always given perfect satisfaction in the past.'

'The circumstances have changed, Sir Julius, as well you know. What is it that good Mrs Glasse says in her housekeeping compendium? "First catch your hare." Mr Maddox has the skills we require to complete that particular task, but you have my assurance that I will – as always – make my own arrangements thereafter. And if he proves foolish enough to delve deeper into the affair than the task demands, I will make it my business to ensure that he does not live to profit by it.'

'You m-mean—'

The lawyer gives a small grim smile. 'It would not be the first time such a problem has occurred, Sir Julius, and I hope the other gentlemen will do me the justice of acknowledging that whenever such a circumstance has arisen, I have never once scrupled to take whatever steps were necessary to eliminate it. If young Maddox insists on putting himself into the like category, I shall not hesitate to have him dealt with in the like manner, and with the like expediency.'

There is an unsettled silence, broken only by the puttering of the coal fire and the breathing of cigars. The man with the scarred hand glances at Cremorne, but he is half-turned away from the rest and will not meet his eye. He looks to the lawyer.

'And the lady? What of her?'

Mr Tulkinghorn sits back in his chair. 'I have, as promised, concluded my enquiries. It appears that the lady in question is indeed in possession of certain facts that, put together, could allow her to discover our secret.'

There is a gasp at this, but once again. Tulkinghorn holds up his hand.

'The word I used was "could". I did not say "will". I very much doubt that my Lady Dedlock has any idea of the significance of what she knows, or how to connect what must appear to her to be little more than a random collection of meaningless scraps.'

'All the same—'

'All the same, I am not proposing that we sit idly by. Trusting to luck is, in general, a notoriously unreliable defence, but it seems in this case it has been singularly favourable. It has come to my knowledge – I need not trouble you how – that my Lady has a secret of her own. A dire and shameful secret that threatens to bring stain and ignominy on the proudest of lineages. I have suspected it a long time – fully known it only a little while. And now my Lady knows that I know it.'

'And you intend to expose her?'

Tulkinghorn shakes his head. 'Not yet. Perhaps not at all. Once disgraced she would have nothing to lose, and time on her hands to ponder those facts which at present are the very last and least of her concerns. No, gentlemen, better by far that she remains where she is, dragging out her present life at my pleasure, from day to day, from hour to hour, wondering when the blow will fall, and when the dark and lonely path she chose so long ago will at last find its end.'

Sir Julius looks at him narrowly; his agitation has somewhat subsided, and with it his slight but perceptible stammer. 'I should not like to have you for an enemy, Tulkinghorn. You show neither pity, nor compunction, nor hesitation. I congratulate you.'

Tulkinghorn bows, the faintest possible colour in his grey cheeks. 'I am obliged to you, sir. Indeed, the circumstances could hardly be more propitious. I caution, as always, against the slightest complacency on our part, but I am perfectly easy in my own mind. I do not think my Lady will be troubling us again.'

Chapter Three

Hester's Narrative

I have a great deal of difficulty in beginning to write my portion of these pages, for I know I am not clever. I always knew that. Even when I was a very little girl I knew, and I would confess it to my doll when we were alone together, and ask her to be kind and patient with me. And she would sit there in her little chair, with her bright smile, and bright pink cheeks, and I would sit by her and chatter on, telling her all my childish secrets, and knowing she would understand and never blame me. I would run up to my room as soon as I came home from school, and tell her all that I had done, and all that I had said, in that great expanse of hours since I had left her there that morning. Though I rarely had much to tell of what I had said, because I never said very much at all. I was always a very diffident child, very shy, and fearful of putting myself forward, though perhaps I had, in consequence, a rather observant way about me – not a clever way, or a quick way, no indeed! – but a quiet way of noticing things, and events, and people, especially when they are people that I love. Though it is possible that I flatter myself even in that.

The first person I loved so tenderly as this was my mother. My earliest memory is of our tiny up-and-down cottage with a trellis of honeysuckle around the door, and a pretty little garden where cherry trees would blossom in spring, and snowdrops nestle among the snow in the winter of the year. Though when I think of this little house now, it is always summer, the sky blue and the view of the meadows hazy in the heat, and a sweet warm breeze. I would sit in the sunshine on the tiny veranda, playing with my dear old Dolly, while my mother sat in her own chair at the little tea-table, with its white cloth and its delicate china pot, all wreathed with jasmine and roses.

My mother was, I think, the prettiest lady I ever saw, with her beautiful golden curls and the loveliest eyes in her gentle tender face. People have told me since that I resemble her, and sometimes I catch a glimpse of myself in the glass and think I see my mother's face. But even if I am not so pretty as she was, I remember that the gentlemen who visited us in our little house were always quick to praise my looks. When I was still a very little girl, one of these gentleman – tall and severe to my lowly eye – bent down and touched my shoulder, saying, 'Do you know how pretty you are, child?', smiling all the while at my mother, where she sat at her needlework before the fire, and the little bird sang in its cage above her head.

I had a very happy childhood altogether, surrounded by my mother's love, and the companionship of the girls at the local school. I was the smallest there by a good deal, and they all made such a pet of me, kissing and cosseting me, and calling me their little marmoset. My mother shook her head at these frivolities, saying she was afraid I would be spoiled by so much attention. I think this was why she discouraged me from inviting my friends home; at least I think that must be the explanation, for I cannot remember any parties at the cottage in those days. Or not, at least, for my own friends; aside from the gentlemen who visited my mother, our lives were very retired and tranquil. As I grew older, my mother was careful to instruct me in my duties and obligations, telling me to be always diligent, submissive, and obedient. "Do good to those around you, child," she said one day, as I stood at her bedside, "and you will always win their love. That is all that matters. Nothing else. You must always remember that." The tears come to my eyes when I think of her shining face as she said this, her skin so pale and her eyes so bright! It is my weakness, I know, but I cannot help it. But there! I have composed myself again now, and can go on with my story.

It seems to me now that I had very little time with my mother, after this. I remember strange women in the house I had never seen before, and the sound of cries that seemed to go on through a whole night and the following day. The women looked at each other when they thought I could not see, and one of them took something away wrapped in a coverlet that I never saw again. It was that day, I think, that one of the women clasped me by the hand and led me upstairs to my bedroom under the eaves, bidding me to be as quiet as a little mouse, and give my mother no further cause for distress. I was terrified to think that anything I had done could have brought about such turmoil and wretchedness, and lay awake the whole night pondering all my petty and unconfessed misdemeanours, which now lay as heavy on my soul as mortal sins.

I do not remember how long this went on – ages and ages it seemed to me then. Days of whispering and bewilderment, and the women casting such stern looks upon me that I knew all this misery was indeed my own fault, and I deserved no better.

'Where is Mother?' I asked at last in my childish way. 'Why does she not let me see her?'

'Your mother is in a Better Place,' said one of the women, pronouncing the words in so serious and awful a tone that I was quite overwhelmed. I could not understand why my mother should have gone on a journey and left me behind, or how anywhere could be better or happier than our own little home that she loved so much. The woman was one of our neighbours and not, I think, unkind, and seeing my eyes fill with tears she drew me on her knee and explained as best she could that my mother had gone before me to Heaven, and if I was good, and dutiful, and said my prayers every day, and went to church every Sunday, I might hope to meet her in the Hereafter. I did not know if this was the Better Place she had spoken of; but I did comprehend – albeit dimly – that I was not to see my mother again, not for many and many a year, and that all that waste of empty time must be filled with good deeds, and good works, and self-sacrifice. I wept alone in my little bed that night, and for many a night after that, gripping my Dolly tight in my arms and wondering what was to become of me. It was a long time indeed before I was able to quiet my sobs by recalling what Mrs Millard had said, and telling myself firmly that this was no way to be going on. 'Hester,' I would say to myself, 'this will not do! Duty and diligence are to be your lot, and it is through duty and diligence that you will see your mother again.'

They put me in a black frock and sent me for some days to lodge with our neighbour and her husband, a big, close-lipped religious man who looked grimly upon me, and quoted verses from the Bible as if they applied chiefly and particularly to me. '*You shall not bow yourself down to them, nor serve them,*' he would intone in his booming voice. '*For I the LORD your God am a jealous God, visiting the iniquity of the fathers upon the sons to the third and fourth generation.*'

My mother had read from the Gospels many times, telling me stories about our Saviour, and talking to me always of God's love for his children, so I hardly knew what to make of the dour and vengeful Jehovah Mr Millard talked of. All I did know was that I was very sinful, and very wicked, and very much in the way.

One dark and rainy afternoon I came home from school with my books and satchel, hoping, if possible, to slip upstairs before Mr Millard saw me, but his wife had clearly been looking out for my return, and came towards me as soon as I closed the door behind me. She took me by the hand and led me into the best parlour – a room I was never allowed to enter without permission, or by myself – and presented me to a gentleman of a very distinguished appearance, dressed in black and drinking tea, whom I had never, to my knowledge, seen before.

'This,' said Mrs Millard in a confidential tone, 'is the child. This is Hester, sir.'

The gentleman sat forward in his chair and beckoned to me. 'Come here,' he said. Let me look at you.'

Then he asked me if I would be so kind as to take off my bonnet, and when I had done so, he said, 'Ah!' and afterwards, 'I see. Yes. Quite.'

And then he leant back in his chair again, and picked up his tea-cup, and Mrs Millard said, 'That will be all, Hester. Go and play now, there's a good girl.'

So I made him the curtsy my mother taught me, and left the room.

I think it was a few weeks later, and the winter nearly gone, when the gentleman in black reappeared. I was sent for by Mrs Millard, and found him in the same place in the parlour.

'I have news for you, Hester,' he said. 'Your Guardian has arranged for you to be placed at an excellent establishment, where you may finish your education, and find a secure home that will offer you every appropriate comfort and amenity.'

I knew not what to say. I had never heard I had a Guardian, and only the vaguest idea what the word might mean.

The man was watching me closely, and seemed concerned to give me what reassurance was within his power.

'You need not fear, Hester. Mr Jarvis is a kind man, and you will want for nothing, of that I am sure.'

I could not speak, not then, because my heart was overflowing with gratitude for this unknown Guardian and his kindness to me, and I think the gentleman sensed some of this, because he reached over and patted me gently on the shoulder and said,

'Run along now, child. I have business to talk with good Mrs Millard.'

And so it was that exactly a week later I left the only place that I had ever known, and travelled by stagecoach for London. Mr Millard showed no discernible emotion at my departure aside, perhaps, from relief, but Mrs Millard had a softer heart and wept many sad tears. I do believe she had become quite fond of me, in the short time we had had together. When she gave me one last kiss, and adjured me to tread always in the paths of righteousness, I felt so remorseful and despondent that I threw my arms around her and wept myself, saying it was all my fault, and that Mother would never have left me if I had been good.

'No, Hester!' she returned with a sad smile. 'It is just your unhappy lot, my dear. And whatever Mr Millard says on the matter, I believe in my heart that our Heavenly Father does not visit the sins of the fathers upon the children, and will not hold you culpable for the circumstances of your birth, but only for the rectitude of your own conduct.'

I wondered a little at these words, but the coach was already at the gate, so I had no time to ask her what she meant. She turned then and went into the house, and I never saw her again. I had no friend left now in the world, and no protector, except, perhaps, for my new and as yet unknown Guardian.

I looked back at the house until I could see it no more, and then wiped my eyes and cast my gaze instead at the landscape unrolling before me. It was a very beautiful day, with the new buds on the trees, and the fields pricked with the first green shoots of the year. After a very long and rattling journey, during most of which I was quite alone, the coach finally came to a halt and a lady opened the coach door and said, 'I am Miss Darby. You must be Hester.'

'Yes, ma'am.'

'Come then. Mr Jarvis is waiting for us.'

My boxes were put into a small green pony carriage by a maid in a starched white apron and cap, dressed altogether rather more formally, to my eyes, than the servants I was used to seeing in our country village. But that was only to be expected.

'We have been looking forward to your arrival, Hester,' said Miss Darby, 'and I am sure you will find the Solitary House a congenial home.'

'The Solitary House, ma'am?'

She smiled. 'It has acquired that name over the years, though I believe it was once known as The Peaks or Three Peaks, or some such. It has, as you will find, a rather secluded situation for a house so close to London and hence, I suppose, the name. Those of us who have lived there a long time hardly think it strange any more.'

Presently we drew up to a little lodge, and waited for the keeper to open the gate, before trotting up a long avenue of trees to a broad sweep before a large porch. It was a tall redbrick house with yellow-framed casements, and squares of blue and green glass in the windowpanes. On one side a bay had been thrown out one floor up, creating a view over what seemed to me to be a large and very pretty lawn, bordered with flowers, with beyond it an orchard and a vegetable garden. I heard a bell ring as the trap stopped, and I found my heart beating very fast as Miss Darby got down and helped me to descend. The door opened, and a man appeared. It was not the same person I had seen at Mrs Millard's but another gentleman. He had a broad smile and a full beard, and came down the steps briskly and took me by the hand.

'Welcome to the Solitary House, Hester. I think you will be very happy here.'

I felt the colour flood my face as I tried, without much success, to say some words of thanks, but Mr Jarvis seemed determined not to notice anything was amiss, and drew my hand through his arm as if it was the most natural thing there could be.

'Come,' he said. 'Let me show you your new home!'

From that moment I felt quite at my ease with him, and knew in my heart how blessed I was to have found someone I could trust so completely, and in whom I could confide so unreservedly.

He showed me to my little room, and truly I felt myself at that moment the luckiest girl in the world. It was a bright, homely room, with a well-tended fire in the hearth, and a high metal-framed bed with smooth white pillows. The window looked down upon the flower-garden, and across the heath to the far-away steeples and towers of London, almost ethereal that day under a light silvery cloud. I turned to Mr Jarvis with tears in my eyes, wondering how all this could be, and almost overcome, saying 'Oh, thank you, thank you!' again and again. But he merely placed his arm about my waist, and made me sit down on the little chair by the fire and take some of the tea that had been thoughtfully placed there in preparation for my arrival.

'My dear Hester,' he said kindly, a few moments later, 'how you are a-tremble! Your cup quite clatters against the saucer.'

How could I not be moved? Sitting there with him, seeing him smile upon me, and feeling, for the first time since my mother died, that I was valued and cherished, and had a place in the world.

I put my arms about his neck and kissed him, and he gently patted me on the head and handed me a handkerchief scented with lavender. 'There! There!' he said. 'There is no cause for tears. This is your home now, and you will find no one here but those who wish you well.' At least, that is my memory of what he said. 'Wish', I am sure it was.

He got up presently and stirred the fire, then sat back once again in the easy-chair. I had by then folded my hands upon my lap and quite recovered myself, and Mr Jarvis started to talk to me as naturally and easily as if we were acquaintances of long date. The look on his face at that moment was the very image of his innate and generous goodness – I saw that expression for the first time in that moment, but for many years now I have seen it every day, and when I close my eyes it is there still.

'Indeed, Hester,' he began, 'I am in hopes that you will play a full part in our little community. I have been told you are a young lady of sense and usefulness; indeed it is obvious to anyone who has been but a quarter of an hour in your society. Some of your fellow boarders are occasionally a little dejected and melancholic – such a thing is quite common and normal, especially when they first come to us – but I feel sure that in such circumstances they could make a friend of you, and benefit immeasurably from being confided to your care.'

I hardly knew what to say. 'I hope you have not formed too high an opinion of my abilities,' I began. 'I am very young and I am afraid I am not clever either. I will do my best, but I am very concerned lest you should expect too much of me and then be disappointed.'

He waved his hand at this as if all my fears were quite groundless. 'I think it very likely that you may prove the good little woman of The Solitary House, my dear,' he smiled. 'Remember the little old woman of the nursery rhyme?

Little old woman, and whither so high?
To sweep the cobwebs out of the sky

'The Solitary House has its own little clusters of cobwebs, Hester, like all such houses. But you will sweep every one out of the sky for us in the course of your time here. I am quite confident of that.'

And that was how I came to be called Old Woman, and Little Old Woman, and Cobweb, and Mrs Shipton, and Mother Hubbard, and Dame Durden, and so many other things of a similar kind that I began almost to think myself the stooped and wizened creature my names seemed to imply.

I soon adapted so fully to the daily routine of The Solitary House that I could hardly remember any other life, and my years at the cottage with my dear mama seemed like a far-off golden dream. It was a happy and ordered existence we led, and nothing disturbed the calm serenity of our days. There was a place for everything, and a time for everything, whether reading, or baking, or laundry, or tending to the garden. I have had several different companions during the years I have lived here, but at that time we were four boarders, including myself. There was Amy, and there was Caroline, and there was Augusta. Such pretty names they all had, or so I thought. Amy was small and slight with huge grey eyes and a timid look, and a tendency to hear noises and take fright at the slightest untoward sound or gesture. I do believe the dear little thing took to me at first sight, and by the end of the week she was following me round like a tiny devoted dog, and creeping into my bed at night, whispering that she had heard the ghost on the walk again, or there were cries in the night, or phantoms scratching in the roof above her bed. Caroline I found almost forbidding, or at least at first. I was introduced to her by Miss Darby the day after my arrival, in the big room downstairs, where she sat at a writing-table looking dissatisfied and sullen, her fingers covered with ink, her hair untidy, and her satin slippers scuffed.

I saw her looking at my own dress, plain and serviceable as it was. 'You think a lot of yourself, I dare say,' she said bitterly. But I could see there were tears in her eyes, for all her angry words, so I took a seat by her and tried my best to look her friend.

'Come, come, Miss Caroline,' I said, 'a little care, a little tidiness – a pin here and a stitch there, and I could make you as fresh and lovely as a spring day. Lovelier far than I could ever be.'

I put my hand in hers, but she pulled it away saying she was tired. Miss Darby shook her head and touched Caroline's forehead, observing that it was hot, and she would have one of the maids fetch a restorative that would help to calm her. Miss Darby then said a few more quiet words to Caroline and she presently put down her pen, and straightened her dress as well as she could.

'There,' said Miss Darby brightly, 'that's much better, Caroline. You're almost presentable for once. Why don't you take Hester upstairs and show her your room?' adding in an undertone to me that the chamber was as much in need of attention as its owner. I did what I could to bring a little order, and saw at once that this was a great relief to its occupant, who stood wringing her hands in the centre of the carpet, not knowing, it seemed, whether to fling her arms about me, or berate me for my meddling. I had not long finished my tucking and tidying when there was a soft tap at the door and it opened to reveal Augusta, hand in hand with little Amy. The latter slipped to my side and whispered that Augusta had just had one of her fits, but Miss Darby had been on hand, and all was well now. I went to Augusta and gave her a kiss, and she smiled timidly at me, though her cheeks were deeply flushed and her eyes still a little wild. Poor girl! I saw her suffer many of these seizures in the months that followed and I am sad to say that they got worse, if anything, over that time. It was not long before I recognized the tell-tale signs. A strange expression would pass across her face, and then she would suddenly stiffen in the most alarming manner, and fall to the ground, no matter where she was; her limbs would thrash about, her mouth would froth, and she would become so rigid and tense that the slightest touch seemed to hurt her. When the fits were particularly bad, her eyes would roll round so that naught but the whites were visible, which was especially terrifying to dear little Amy, who thought it signified that poor Augusta's soul had been seized by a evil spirit, so I would always take care, if I was nearby, to take Amy apart and sit with her, telling her a fairy story, until Miss Darby had made all peaceable once more.

I spent the next quiet, happy months at The Solitary House, surrounded by my friends, protected by my Guardian, and contriving to make myself as useful as I was cheerful. Then one August morning, Mr Jarvis called me to see him. The garden was in its full summer glory, the air fragrant, and the birds singing. When I opened the door of Mr Jarvis' room, I saw at once that he was not alone. The two of them were standing by the fire talking, and they turned towards me when they heard my approach. Oh, she was so beautiful! Such lovely golden hair, and such a pure and innocent face! I thought at once of my mother, and of the likeness of her I still kept close to my heart, and I was – for a moment – a little sad. I think that this lovely girl divined this somehow, for she came to meet me with a smile and kissed me, with nothing in her eyes but affection and acceptance. Oh, the joy and relief I felt at that moment!

'This, Hester,' said Mr Jarvis, 'is Clara. And this, Clara, is the Little Old Lady I told you of before. If The Solitary House is a happy house, it is because Dame Durden makes it so.'

He said this out of his love for me, nothing more, and knowing that I almost fear to write it down, in case it should seem like vanity, but it is unlikely, after all, that anyone will ever read these pages but me.

Clara took my hands in hers and led me to the window-seat, and she had such a enchanting way with her that we spent the whole of the rest of the morning sitting there with the sunlight upon her beautiful hair, talking and laughing together. I saw Mr Jarvis look his approval, and knew at once that he had designed we should be friends, and that I should do what I could to make the dear girl comfortable and content with us. In the days and weeks that followed we became inseparable, and Mr Jarvis was so good as to allow us to move to adjoining rooms on the ground floor, opening on to the garden, where I would walk before breakfast with my darling. I called her so even then, and it is so natural to me now that I cannot think of her in any other way! She would take my hand in hers, and tell me I was a dear creature, and her best friend, and we would both look up to where Mr Jarvis stood watching us at the big bay window.

I remember repeating to my Guardian some such charming words of hers, as we sat together one evening – not for my own vainglory – oh no! – but because – well, just because.

'What a weight off my mind it is that she should love me!' I said. 'It is so reassuring to know that a beautiful girl like Clara wishes me for her friend! It is such an encouragement to me!'

'And why should you need anyone else's encouragement?' he said, taking my chin gently in his hand. 'Clara is by no means the only beautiful girl here. Nor even the most beloved.'

I, very much abashed, hardly knew where to look, and when at last I had the courage to glance up, I saw him looking at me with that careful fatherly look of his that I had come to know so well. I took his hand and kissed it, and held it in mine.

In a little while he smiled, and drew one of my pale flaxen curls through his hand.

'So let us hear no more, Hester, about your looks.'

Chapter Four

A New Lodger

'My journeys into Africa were exclusively devoted to science, and
to the study of nature, but I could not help bestowing some
attention to the advantages that might be derived from the
civilization of that most fertile portion of the globe. I shall therefore
touch here and there upon the practical, as well as upon the
scientific, results of my expedition. I may premise that I had
prepared myself for the task I have undertaken by studying natural
science under some of the most distinguished professors in several
universities, and that from my earliest youth the observation of the
phenomena of nature had excited in me the liveliest interest.'

The room is full tonight, and the number of portly and be-
bearded gentlemen crowding the rows of seats is making up
for the rather inadequate fire at the far end. Cigar smoke is
hanging heavily overhead, and it's obvious that the portly
gentlemen are sweating gently under their starch and barber's
cologne. The speaker on the dais at the front is small and lean,
with heavy whiskers, thinning hair, and a little beard sharpened
to a perfect point. He looks rather like the Prince Consort, and
speaks with a very similar accent, though someone better versed
in these things than I am would tell you that he is, in fact, Austrian.
A former Consul-General, no less, and his presence here,
therefore, is something of a coup for this as yet rather minor

47

geographical society, which has only fairly recently acquired another adjective before its name, and has yet to take possession of the large and distinctive redbrick premises it will later occupy on Kensington Gore. Baron von Müller has a map pinned to an easel and a small table to his left, which holds a number of interesting items, some instantly identifiable, others rather less so. We have just been listening to his opening preamble, and it's a fair sample of his rather self-important, amplifying style. No doubt it comes with the territory, in every sense of the word.

His subject tonight is 'A Scientific Journey through Africa', and he is clearly going to take his time about it. Some twenty minutes later he is still 'proceeding slowly across the immense steppes', though there is no hint of impatience from most of his audience. But if the august members are increasingly intrigued by the identity and purpose of the tray of props, they are about to be enlightened. One by one, the Baron proceeds to hold up these prize samples of what the African continent offers to 'the commercial, industrial, and intellectual people of Europe'. They are, to wit, and in order: a piece of gum Arabic (smooth, slightly clouded, amber-coloured, the size and texture of a bar of soap), a large ivory tooth (known – the Baron tells us – as a *masheket,* due to the fissure running through it, which he carefully points out), a jar of tamarind (small brown peanut-shaped pods), a sliver of ebony (cut thinly from unpolished trunk, with a light outer skin and a dark inner core), a handful of pressed senna leaves (dried now and faded), and – finally – two large ostrich feathers. The latter, at least, needs no accompanying explanation; there is not a gentleman in the audience whose wife does not possess a fan or head-dress embellished with plumes just like these. But the table has not yielded up all its treasures yet, though it is some minutes more before we find out what the final item is doing there.

The Baron resumes: 'At Melpess, in the vicinity of Lobehd, where I had spent some time for the purpose of collecting objects of natural history, I made in April 1848 the acquaintance of a man, from whom I wanted to buy several animals, who for the first time put me on the trace of the unicorn, or *anasa*, hitherto considered a fabulous animal. The man had often seen the animal living in the Chala and dead among the tribes. It is the size of a small donkey, has a thick body and thin bones, coarse hair, and tail like a boar. It has a long horn on its forehead, and lets it hang when alone, but erects it immediately on seeing an enemy, when it becomes stiff and hard.'

The Baron smoothes his moustache and looks up and down the rows of faces turned towards him. 'Moreover,' he continues, and then pauses, prolonging his moment. 'Moreover, I was able, at no inconsiderable expense, to obtain an example, and return with it from the darkest heart of Africa. Gentlemen, I present to you now the only authenticated example of a unicorn horn ever to be brought to these shores!' He lifts the final item in his hands with a theatrical flourish, and stands there, awaiting the wonderment. He's given this performance before, and this is always by far the most rewarding moment.

The horn in question is perhaps three feet long, not entirely straight, but almost so. Dark, highly burnished, and twisted in a thick spiral towards the base. There is no question that it does indeed look uncannily like the representations of unicorn horns that everyone present has known since boyhood, not least on the royal coat of arms. The room is silent for a moment, and then the murmuring starts. Quiet at first, but then louder, with here and there a word discernible.

'Good Lord.'

'Quite extraordinary.'

'Never seen the like.'

49

The noise continues for some moments more. And then – improbably – there is the sound of laughter. Loud, incredulous, and outrageous laughter. As you would expect, this is rather a rare occurrence for such a learned institution, and the members start moving cumbrously in their chairs to see what's going on. It's coming, they find, from a seat at the back; it's coming, as we can now see, from none other than Charles Maddox. The officer of the society who has been chairing the proceedings rises to his feet.

'Order, please! His Excellency deserves the courtesy of a considered hearing.'

It makes no difference; the noise is rising to a din. He picks up his gavel – normally an object of far more ornament than use – and strikes it against the wooden block.

'Would the gentleman in the back row care to explain himself?'

Charles smiles. 'Gladly,' he says, and gets to his feet. 'I have read a number of papers on the subject,' he begins, 'and they have only served to confirm my belief that there is not, and never has been, any such species as the unicorn. The very idea of such a creature is, quite frankly, an insult to the intelligence of this society—'

The Baron had returned to his seat, but he is on his feet again in an instant, his face red. '*You*, sir, I take it, have never even set foot on the African continent.'

'I have not. And therefore I can offer no actual *proof* – scientific or otherwise – that this creature does not, in fact, exist.'

'There you are – what did I say! The man is an ignorant fool—'

'But what I *can* do is prove beyond all doubt that the horn you are holding is *not* what you claim it to be. That it is, in short, a fake, and that if there is indeed a fool among us, it is far more likely to be *you* than *me*. Though in your defence, you are not the first to be taken in by cunning and opportunistic natives, and I dare say you won't be the last.'

Uproar now. The room is in chaos. The chairman raps his gavel again, and motions Charles to the front.

'You had better be able to make good your claims, sir, or be prepared to make a full and unreserved apology to our esteemed guest.'

Charles looks unperturbed by either the words or the portentous tones in which they have been uttered. He makes his way briskly up the centre aisle to the mutterings and – in some cases – the downright disapproval of several of the audience. He does not, after all, look the part of a serious scientific mind, being every bit as untidy as when we saw him last and a good twenty years too young to have any sort of legitimate opinion. He leaps the steps to the dais two at a time and takes the horn from the Baron's hands. He turns it, weighing it lightly, and running his fingers from tip to root. Silence descends. You could, in fact, hear a pin drop.

A moment later, he looks up at the chairman and grins (something else these walls rarely get to see). 'As I thought. This horn was taken from an adult bull of the *Taurotragus oryx*, or Common Eland. An antelope common in precisely those parts of Africa that the Baron has been describing to us in such exhaustive detail.'

He tosses the horn back to the Baron. 'It is, I grant you, a fine and unusually large example, and will make an admirable addition to the wall of your ancestral *Schloss*. Appropriately labelled, of course. I am sure that a man who has "studied natural science under some of the most distinguished professors in several universities" would not wish to leave his visitors in any doubt as to what this *actually* is.'

51

The Baron is only halfway through his prepared paper, but Charles does not stay to hear it – he has better things to do with his time. How long it takes for the rest of the room to return to anything like its previous attentiveness, he neither knows nor cares.

Outside on Regent Street the night is clear but frosty, and though he is not far from home, the sight of a green Bayswater heading his way tempts him, for once, to take the omnibus. It's very full – no surprise at this time of night – and Charles struggles to find a seat between a little testy man with a powdered head, and a sturdy brown-faced woman in a grey cloth cloak who's gripping an umbrella with a wooden crook and has a market-basket full of greens wedged between her knees. The 'bus grinds its slow way past brilliantly lit shops and strolling crowds, and Charles eventually swings down the step at the bottom of Tottenham Court Road.

It is, perhaps, some five minutes later that he first gets the sense that someone is following him. It's happened many times before, especially on fast-darkening evenings like this, but it's no less alarming for that. He stops, and turns as if nonchalantly, but sees no one. A minute later he steps quickly down his own small side street and slips into the shadow of a doorway. And now he knows he's not imagining it: he can hear heavy boots, and even heavier breathing. One man only; that at least is something. He waits, his heart pounding, but when he springs out, grasps his pursuer by the throat and throws him against the wall, he starts back in disbelief.

'Abel Stornaway – what in God's name do you think you're doing? I could have killed you!'

The old man is leaning against the wall, spluttering. 'Mr Charles, sir,' he gasps, his Scotch tongue tempered by the best part of fifty London years. 'I never meant to startle ye. Yer

52

landlady wouldna let me wait in yer room, so I was keepin' an eye out—'

'Let me guess – from the snug of the White Horse?'

Stornaway smiles weakly. 'A wee nip ne'er goes amiss on a night like this. And then when I saw ye go past I couldna keep up with ye. The legs bain't what they once were, and that's a fact.'

Charles looks at him. He is – what – seventy-five now? Even eighty? He has a pitiable old scarf round his neck and a much-worn and often-mended pair of gloves, but neither will be much good in these freezing temperatures. Whatever it is that's dragged him from his comfortable fireside, it must be important.

'Look,' he says, 'let me make amends for Mrs Stacey's lack of hospitality. She is a kind woman at heart, but her infatuation with Gothic novels has her seeing ghosts and vampyres under every bed, especially after dark. Come back to my room and I'll have her get us some hot coffee. And then you can tell me what this is all about.'

Stornaway is soon installed in front of Charles' small fire, with a mug gripped in both hands and the powerful aroma of coffee filling the room. The cat wakes, stretches languorously on the bed then turns himself slowly upside-down, inviting adulation. Stornaway takes his time to get to the point, but Charles is in no hurry and sips his own coffee patiently, stroking the cat and contemplating his companion. Stornaway bears all the marks of his brutal career: twisted fingers gnarled with scar tissue; a nose that's been broken more than once, and the thin white mark of a knife wound running from his brow to the corner of his mouth. He was lucky not to lose the eye; Charles' father even let drop, some years before, that another such encounter left him with a fractured skull and a metal plate holding his head together.

'It's the guv'nor, Mr Charles,' he says eventually, his face troubled.

Stornaway is not a man given to delicacy of feeling, or finding problems where none exist, and Charles is troubled in his turn, not least because it's been rather longer than he cares to admit since he last saw his great-uncle. Maddox spent the summer on a long-postponed tour of northern Italy, but he must have returned to his house near the river at least six weeks ago, and Charles has still not found the time to visit. Given the relationship they have – or had; given what Charles said of him only yesterday (and every word of that was true), this lapse might strike you as rather odd. It might strike you, too, that there must be a reason for it that Charles seems rather reluctant to admit. What this might be we may yet discover, but it is, in itself, instructive: he may be a meticulous observer of the habits and behavioural patterns of other creatures, human or otherwise, but he is singularly blind to his own. Abel, meanwhile, has said nothing, but Charles is in no hurry. Best the man comes to it in his own way.

'He's not his'sen, Mr Charles. Not at all. Not since we got back.'

'Is he unwell?'

Stornaway looks perplexed. 'That's just it. I dinna rightly know. One day he's as right as rain, the next he dinna seem to know who I am. One day he just sits there in his chair, starin' into space mumblin' to his'sen; the next he's as sharp as a razor, setting everything to rights from the state o' my collar to the state o' the nation.'

Charles puts down his mug. 'I suppose he is very old now.' He's trying to be reassuring, but he's not as confident as he sounds. Maddox has an incisive mind, yes; but he was never a belligerent man.

Stornaway, meanwhile, is nodding. 'Aye, that's what's I thought me'sen. Mrs McLeod, who comes in twice a week to do for us, her husband is in the same declinin' way. More a little chiel than an old man she says. If that's all it were, I could manage. But these last few days, things have changed.'

He is, all unconsciously, rubbing his left arm and Charles leans forward and pushes the sleeve gently back. Stornaway does not resist and that, more than anything else, tells Charles that something is seriously wrong. There's a livid bruise from elbow to wrist and darker marks where fingernails have dug into the flesh.

'Did he do this to you?'

Charles has never seen tears in Stornaway's eyes before, but he sees them now.

'He dinna mean it. I was just trying to help him get his'sen dressed – you know how partic'lar he is about such things. Everythin' has to be just so – coat, shirt, stock, wesscit.' He shakes his head. 'He accused me of attackin' him. Tryin' to rob him. Told me to get oot and nae come back.'

Looking at his companion now, Charles is prepared to bet that harder words than this were thrown at him and the memory of those words is far more distressing than any pain he feels from the wounds to his arm.

'Was that the only time it happened?'

Stornaway shakes his head. 'Nay. It happened again this mornin'. Only this time it were Mrs McLeod as bore the brunt. She's an old lady her'sen, Mr Charles, and canna be expected to suffer ill-treatment. That's when I realized som'at had to be done. And I thought a ye.'

Charles nods slowly, then drains his mug and puts it on the table.

'You did the right thing. I'm glad you came.'

Stornaway is in no state for more nocturnal wandering, so Charles picks up a hackney cab at the stand in Tottenham

Court Road, and hands over – without any compunction whatsoever – one of the new-minted shillings Knox advanced him only yesterday. It's a very short hop by four wheels and the two of them are soon set down outside a tall and elegant house in one of the smart Georgian streets on the south side of the Strand. It is – and always was – an excellent location for a man in Maddox's line of work. Not fifty yards from the river in one direction, and a brisk walk from Bow Street in the other.

There are lights burning in the first-floor windows, as there are all along the facade. By comparison with the hectic jumbled streets further north, the architecture here seems to exude its own atmosphere: you can hear the roar of the traffic on the Strand, but it is curiously remote. Here, all is harmony, order and proportion. Or so it appears outside; inside, as Charles soon finds out, it's a very different story. The moment Stornaway opens the door, they hear the sound of voices. A man's raised in rage, the words shrill and incoherent; a woman's, pleading and anxious; and a third that carries on steadily all the while: the unmistakable emollience of a professional at work. Charles sees a flicker of apprehension on Stornaway's face and hurries ahead of him up the stairs. He knows and loves this house but he's never seen the drawing-room in this state. There are papers and books flung in all directions, a windowpane broken, a chair overturned, and a plate and dish-cover upended on the floor. An elderly woman is on her knees, trying – rather ineffectually – to stop a large serving of veal and gravy seeping into the Turkey carpet. The man at the centre of all the sound and fury is his great-uncle, but Charles barely recognizes him. When he last saw Maddox, he still retained all the fine presence of his middle age – the same energy, the same acuity, and the same resonant voice he used to such trenchant effect with patron and perpetrator alike. The scar above his eye had softened a little with time, but in every other respect he was still, in essence, the Maddox of Charles' childhood. The man before him now is a meagre shadow of that former self, his face sunken and his back bowed, and his old red silk dressing-gown is gaping open over a white night-shirt that – Charles sees with horror – is soiled, and still wet. His hair is well-cut but grown out ragged, and his whiskers need trimming. There's a long rope of spittle hanging from one side of his mouth. Knowing who and what this man once was, it is a pitiful sight, and the worst of it is that Maddox himself seems more aware of it than any of them. He calls out to Charles as the corpulent doctor struggles to trammel his flailing arms and get him back into a chair.

'I've told this fat scoundrel he can take that filthy stuff back where he found it – they're trying to poison me, you know, him and that crabbed old witch – eh? Eh? You hear me?' Maddox strains towards the woman on the floor and aims a kick in her direction. He's too far away to harm her but the woman cowers in terror all the same. 'Ha! Lost your tongue now, have you? You can't pull the wool over *my* eyes, you shrivelled old hag!'

'Come, come, sir,' says the doctor, the beads of perspiration standing out on his brow. 'Just a few drops of this medicine and I guarantee you'll feel better in a trice. Ah! You there, whoever you are,' he says, catching sight of Charles in the doorway, 'give me a hand here, would you, the old fellow is quite raving.'

Charles is quick to oblige, but not quite in the way the doctor expected. He seizes the man forcibly by the shoulders and pulls him away, then encircles his great-uncle in his arms and sets him gently on the sofa, feeling, for the first time, just how gaunt and thin he's become. The old man's anger vanishes like a summer storm. He's suddenly as meek as a kitten, staring up at his great-nephew nervously, his shoulders huddled as if it's only now that he feels the icy draught slicing through the room. Charles kneels before him, smoothes back his rough grey hair, and pulls his dressing-gown closer about him. It isn't much better, but it is something. He stands up and turns to the doctor.

'Thank you, Mr—'

'Boswell. Lawrence Boswell, of Devereux Court, the Strand. Mrs McLeod was—'

'Well-meaning, but ill-advised. We will have no more need of your services tonight.' He turns to Stornaway, who has appeared now in the doorway. 'Abel, do you still keep the keys to Mr Maddox's strong-box?'

Stornaway nods.

'In that case,' says Charles, returning to the doctor, 'if you call tomorrow with your bill, I shall see that it is paid without delay.'

But the doctor is not so easily dismissed. He has been asked for an opinion and he intends to give it.

'Are you a physician, then, sir?'

'No. I have some knowledge in that field, but—'

'But not qualified? Not a practitioner?'

'No, sir. I am not.'

'May I then venture to suggest that this old man—'

'Mr Maddox,' says Charles softly. 'His *name* is *Mr Maddox*.'

'That Mr Maddox is clearly in need of more considered medical attendance than you can possibly give him. This infirmity of his requires such constant care and surveillance as only a—'

'No,' says Charles. 'Out of the question.'

'I could recommend a most reputable establishment.'

Charles moves a little closer to him, his voice even lower now. 'Did you not hear me? *I said, no.*'

There is something in the young man's blue stare that gives the doctor pause. And it is not merely the ferocity of his determination.

'Is there,' he begins, more hesitantly – the young man is still standing very close – 'any history of, shall we say, similarly distressing disturbances of mind in Mr Maddox's near relations?'

'Absolutely not.' The response is as quick as a reflex. If there is something – a half-memory, half-suppressed – then Charles gives no sign. He turns again to Stornaway. 'Abel, would you mind seeing Mr Boswell out, please? And Mrs McLeod, perhaps I could speak to you for a moment?'

The old lady has been standing by the window, twisting the dish-cloth in her hands, but now she grips the arm of one of the elbow-chairs and sits down heavily, glancing fearfully every now and then at Maddox, who has started to whimper to himself. Charles may be angry with her for meddling, but he cannot deny that she should never have been expected to handle his uncle alone. A few moments later Stornaway reappears, rather out of breath.

'I'm so sorry, Mrs McLeod. I had nae idea. He'd seemed biddable enough when I left.'

Mrs McLeod shakes her head fretfully. 'He took against the veal. Heaven only knows why, he always liked it well enough before. I had it sent in special from that chophouse he's so partial to. It's a crying shame he never married,' she continues, 'then he'd a'had someone to care for him in his old age. Or mebbe a son or daughter of his own.'

Charles is not so sure; he remembers Maddox saying on more than one occasion that most of the people he knew would have done far better to leave marriage alone, and yet when his other long-serving assistant had married – rather late in life – he bought the couple a little cottage with a plot of garden, and sent George Fraser off to a happy if rather dull retirement in Walworth. He was always nothing if not generous to those he cared for. And it's remembering that which decides Charles now.

He goes over and sits down next to her. 'Mrs McLeod,' he says kindly, 'I'm sincerely grateful for everything you've done for my great-uncle, and very much aware that I should have been here more often myself, these last weeks. But that, at least, is going to change. That officious doctor was right about one thing: Mr Maddox needs constant care, and I cannot possibly ask you to undertake such a heavy task – I gather from Stornaway that you have troubles enough of your own.'

A nod here, and the glisten of a tear.

'So, this is what I propose. Tomorrow morning I will give notice at my lodgings and have my belongings sent here. There's a perfectly adequate suite of rooms upstairs which will do very well for me, with a little soap and water.'

'Oh, I can do that for you, Mr Charles,' she says quickly.

He smiles. 'That would be very kind, but I would be even more grateful if you could help me find a valet for Mr Maddox, and a maid-of-all-work to cook and clean. There's plenty of room in the servants' quarters downstairs, and that way there will always be someone at hand if Mr Maddox should feel unwell.'

He is, he knows, descending to as much euphemism as the wretched doctor did, but he cannot really see any alternative.

'I've never had a servant, so I haven't the faintest idea how to go about hiring one, but I'm sure you'll know exactly what to look for. And I would be extremely appreciative, needless to say,' he adds hurriedly, hoping she understands what he means.

Mrs McLeod seems to be regaining her composure; her hands finally stop their nervous fluttering and she folds the dish-cloth and lays it neatly in her lap.

'I'd be happy to do anything as will help put things to rights, Mr Charles.'

One problem solved, then, but Charles now has another, though it's at least a full minute before he notices it. It's only when he glances across at Stornaway, fidgeting by the door, that he realizes that what has come as a relief to Mrs McLeod has had quite the opposite effect on the old man. Of *course* – he lives in one of those very rooms downstairs that Charles has just been casually disposing of. Charles quickly gets to his feet and moves towards him. 'I do hope you'll stay too, Abel,' he says, putting his hand on Stornaway's arm. 'It may take my uncle a while to get used to so many new faces, and having you here will be a great comfort. And not only to him. To me, as well.'

The old man smiles, showing the gap in his front teeth that he's had for all the years that Charles has known him. 'Whatever ye say, Mr Charles, whatever ye say.'

A little less than two miles away, as the London crows fly, in an immense but dreary house, in a dull but elegant street, a great lady is bored to death. My Lady Dedlock may partake of the finest entertainment London affords, by night or by day, but finds not the least diversion in any of it. This boredom of hers is a chronic condition, and has been much magnified this evening by a correspondence that will insist on obtruding on her notice. She sits by the fire in her boudoir, glancing wearily at the letter in her hand. Having acquired a great quantity of relations on the occasion of her marriage, and mostly of the poor variety, she has, it must be admitted, very little consideration to spare for those belonging to her acquaintance, and finds it incomprehensible that she should even be applied to on such an ineffably tedious subject.

61

There is a knock at the door. The footman. Mr Tulkinghorn is downstairs, my Lady. Mr Tulkinghorn, would, if it please my Lady, be grateful for a few minutes' conversation. Will my Lady receive him, if the time is convenient? It would appear that it is not, for she heaves a silent sigh, and for a moment it seems that the request will be refused. But it is not. She will see him.

She gives this acquiescence in her usual haughty and careless manner, but when the door closes, there is an expression on her face that is unaccountable in one so high, so admired, and holding so unassailable a position at the centre of the fashionable world. But so it is. And so it is, also, that when the insignificant little man in the old-fashioned black waistcoat is ushered into the room a few moments later and stands before her, her lips are white and her voice, for a moment, falters. For a moment only, but this man has a practised eye in such matters. He sees, moreover, that the letter she was reading – whose handwriting is, perhaps, familiar to him – lies now on her dressing-table, discarded and forgotten. These are, in themselves, but the smallest of signs and tokens, but Mr Tulkinghorn can reckon their value, and to the last farthing.

Chapter Five

Signs and Tokens

Moving Charles' paraphernalia of personal effects proves to be a rather larger job than can be accomplished in a single morning. Thunder the cat likewise takes a good deal of persuading to leave his comfortable and accustomed billet and suffer the ignominy of being carried in a wicker basket halfway across town, banging every stride against his master's knee. But by early evening a stack of boxes and trunks has finally been hauled up the stairs in Buckingham Street to the large bare resounding room at the top of the house, which Mrs McLeod has spent much of the day cleaning. And when she hasn't been scrubbing and washing she's been at the nearby hiring-office, picking out two candidates for Charles to inspect. The lad, Billy, seems both sensible and sturdy, with an open good-natured face and a ready grin. The girl could hardly be more different. She is small, almost too fragile for the heavy chores she will have to do daily, up and down four flights of stairs. But she is capable and accustomed to hard work – or so the manager of the hiring-office insists.

'I know that's what they always claim,' says Mrs McLeod, conciliatory, 'but I took one look at her hands, and I could see she's a good worker. You don't get calluses like that from arranging the flowers, you can take that from me. She does have one drawback though – but maybe you won't see it as such. She don't speak. They couldn't tell me if she can't, or just won't, but I suppose the end result is much the same.'

There's something else I have not yet mentioned, and nor, for that matter, has Mrs McLeod. In her defence, the point is so obvious that Charles can see it for himself. I do not have her excuse and you, of course, can only see what I allow you to see. So here it is: the girl is beautiful, and she is black.

'What do you think, Mr Charles?' says Mrs McLeod, an anxious note creeping into her voice at his prolonged silence. 'There weren't many to choose from, I have to say, but she has good references and at least she won't be gossiping with tradesmen all day long.'

Charles is still looking at the girl, demure and self-contained in her apron and white cap, her eyes down, her hands motionless. As motionless, in fact, as all those drawings in his books and maps upstairs, but those crude sketches could never have prepared him for the delicacy of these features, the gleam of this perfect skin. So if he stares now it's because he's struggling to reconcile what he thought he knew with what he can actually see. It's not the first time such a thing has happened, of course – he's a scientist, after all – but in the past, the specimens have invariably been either invertebrate, or inanimate.

'They weren't sure of her real name,' says Mrs McLeod, breaking into his thoughts. 'Something long and fiddlesome in her own language, they thought. But she will answer to Molly.'

'Molly it is then,' he says, making an effort. 'Thank you, Mrs McLeod. I'm sure they will both do very nicely.'

And so they do. So much so, in fact, that before two days are out, it's hardly possible to remember living any other way. The drawing-room is put to rights, the broken window mended, the newcomers installed. Thunder takes the longest to adjust of all of them, but once he's learned to avoid the loud and erratic old human on the first floor, he soon becomes reconciled to his new home, especially after he's had his way with the rats in the basement, and discovered a route out of Charles' eyrie on to the leads, where he can king it over the feral felines and prowl the chimney tops by starlight. Up at the top of the house the boxes and trunks start, slowly, to be unpacked and placed on the attic shelves, but when a sheaf of Chadwick documents slips from the atlas where Charles has stashed them and spill all over the floor, the thought occurs to him that it might be useful to have somewhere more professional to keep his working papers. Followed swiftly by the recollection that there is a small but serviceable room down on the ground floor where Maddox used to receive his clients, and where Charles might now receive his. If his ego is flattered by the idea of following so literally in his great-uncle's footsteps, he has the good grace to acknowledge it. And it's not as if Maddox will need it again; in the last two days he's been by turns rambling and raging, but the man Charles once knew has not returned.

Tucking the papers back in the box for the time being, he makes his way downstairs and pushes open the office door. It clearly hasn't been used for some time. There's a smell of damp, and a spider's web sagging from the (rather dirty) windowpane. As for furniture, there's a hard spindle-backed chair, a small walnut desk, and a wall of shelves. Nothing more. The upper levels are stacked with boxes, most coated with grey dust; the lower ones are largely empty, though the marks on the wood suggest they once contained the books now ranged in the drawing-room above. But it's what remains that attracts Charles' eye: a line of leather-bound memorandum books. His uncle's case files.

He is, suddenly, a small boy again. Standing at the entrance of this same room, summer sunlight glancing through the half-closed shutters. No damp in the air then, but the delicious aroma of baking drifting up from a kitchen that boasted not only a cook but two kitchen maids and a scullion: in those days it was Maddox's business to know and be known, and some of the most eminent men in the land would eat regularly at his table, and count themselves privileged in the invitation. Charles remembers being surprised at finding this door open, and pausing at the threshold, tentative and fearful, knowing he shouldn't be there. Then catching sight of the book open on the table and creeping forwards to look at it. Struggling at first with the handwriting, but making out a word here and there, and so engrossed in doing so he never heard his uncle's tread.

'And what, exactly, do you think you're doing, young man?'

Maddox's face – when Charles summoned the courage to look up at it – was unsmiling but not unkind.

'Prying into my papers, I'll wager, or so it would seem.'

Charles can remember, even now, the hot flush of shame, and the lurch of his stomach as Maddox laid a heavy hand on his shoulder.

'Do you not recall what I told you?'

A nod, then another, quicker.

'And what was that?'

'That all that passes between a detective and his client is confi— confi—'

'Confidential,' said Maddox, with emphasis. 'Quite so. And what does confidential mean?'

'Secret.'

'Exactly so. Secret, and not to be shared with anyone, however small, and however inquisitive.'

Maddox had sat down on the chair then, and lifted Charles on his knee, the wood creaking beneath their weight. 'One day,' he said, touching him lightly on the brow, and smoothing

66

his hair, 'one day, young Charles, when you are older, and the people in these files dead and gone, I will let you read about these crimes, and show you how I resolved them. But not today. Today I am too occupied, and you are still too young. So run along now, and have Cook give you a glass of milk. But ask politely, mind.'

Charles moves now towards the shelf and works back along the spines, wondering if he can find that same book, and read the pages he read that day, such a long time ago. He pulls out the volume for 1834 and is struck for a moment by the coincidence: it was this same year that Chadwick's grand-child went missing from the Convent of the Faithful Virgin orphanage. Not that he expects to find anything so commonplace here. Here it is all forgery, and coining, and housebreaking, and theft. Profitable investigations, as the neatly noted fee receipts demonstrate, but rather lacklustre, from a purely professional point of view. He closes the book and pulls another at random from the shelf: 1811. Now this, it seems was quite another story. He spends half an hour enthralled by an extraordinary murder case at a Northamptonshire mansion, only to turn the page at the end and find himself confronted by what will prove to be one of the most infamous crimes of the nineteenth century: the Ratcliffe Highway murders. Charles already knows the bones of this story – the savage and apparently inexplicable murder of Timothy Marr and his family in their East End draper's shop, followed twelve days later by a second equally brutal killing spree, which left the landlord of the nearby King's Arms with his throat cut, and his wife and maidservant likewise. Charles – like most of his contemporaries – has always thought the man arrested for these murders was in all likelihood the one who committed them, even if he killed himself in jail before he could be tried. But as he winds deeper and deeper into

Maddox's notes, he finds inconsistency after inconsistency in the evidence, and failure after failure in the official police investigation – inconsistencies and failures that are amply and fascinatingly described, by the way, in a more modern account of exactly the same events by one of our most revered crime novelists (though the Baroness of Holland Park does not come to quite the same conclusions as the master thief-taker of Buckingham Street once did). By the time Charles is a dozen pages into Maddox's notes, he's already questioning whether the same lone killer can possibly have committed all these crimes, and is starting to wonder how on earth his uncle got drawn in—

'The Home Secretary asked for my help.'

He looks up, just as he looked up all those years ago, only the man in the doorway now is bent and grey and leaning heavily on a stick. Though Billy's good offices are clearly in evidence, for his hair is brushed, and his dressing-gown newly washed.

'That was indeed what you were thinking, was it not?' says Maddox, coming slowly into the room. 'How I came to be involved in the Ratcliffe Highway case?'

Charles starts forward and helps Maddox to the chair. 'Are you sure you should be on your feet, Uncle?'

Maddox waves his hand dismissively. 'Don't fuss, boy. You're as bad as that damn Stornaway – man's turned into an old mother hen. Show me the book.'

Charles slides the volume towards him, and the old man looks at it for a moment, turns back a few pages, reads a paragraph here and there, then returns to where Charles left off.

'So what have you concluded thus far?'

Charles scarcely knows what to say, caught between his bewilderment at this utter and unlooked-for change in his uncle's demeanour, and a dizzying sense of being still that same little nine-year-old boy, frantic to gain his great-uncle's good opinion but never quite measuring up to the task.

'Well, I—' He hesitates. 'From what I've read, I think it likely that the second murders were the work of other hands.'

'The latter plural was, I take it, intentional?'

'There were two men seen running from the inn soon after the attack.'

'Indeed. Go on.'

Maddox's tone is cool, non-committal; Charles can't tell whether he agrees with him or not. He swallows, and plunges on.

'I think the first murder was a robbery that went wrong, probably committed by someone with a grudge against Marr. That's the only way I can account for the degree of violence involved. I also think this man must have been involved in some way with the Marrs' servant girl – she was rather too conveniently out of the way when it happened, and seems to have behaved rather suspiciously thereafter.'

Maddox nods. 'And the second murders?'

'Made to look like the Marr killings, and in that respect almost entirely successful. But this crime was far more methodical in its execution, and seems to have been driven by something quite other than passion or revenge.'

'Or robbery,' says Maddox. 'The only item missing was the landlord's watch, which would have been next to impossible to sell, since it bore an engraving of a man's name. Bravo, my lad, you've made noteworthy progress since I saw you last. Indeed you seem to be applying my principles with no small success. After all, there is no problem, however intractable, that cannot be resolved by the steady application of—'

'Logic and observation,' finishes Charles with a smile. 'I can still remember the very first time you told me that. I was six years old, and you were visiting us in Berkshire. I'd found a broken window in the stable-block, and came rushing back in to tell you we'd had a burglary in our midst.'

Maddox, too, is smiling now. 'But having conducted a thorough inspection of the scene, we were able to determine that the glass had fallen *out*side the building, not *in*, and the breakage was therefore far more likely to be down to a stable-boy's carelessness than a determined assault on your father's property.'

He sits back in the chair. 'I recall we undertook a number of similar "investigations" that Christmas – the Strange Death of the Vagabond in the Ditch being one of them. Though I seem to remember we concluded he had merely had the misfortune to become intoxicated and fall asleep on the high road on an unexpectedly cold night. Did I not set you to write me an account of that?'

Charles grins. 'Indeed you did. I have it even now. It took me a whole week – I was so desperate to impress you.'

'As you did. As you do still.'

Charles flushes, just as he did when his uncle caught him in his office all those years ago, but now it is from pleasure, not guilt. They sit in silence for a moment, feeling the old relationship returning, the old closeness reinstating.

'So was I right?' says Charles at length. 'About the Ratcliffe Highway murders?'

Maddox sighs. 'As correct as my own conclusions at the time, and just as likely to be disregarded. If you had finished reading my account, you would have found that I was unable to persuade the authorities to pursue my theory of the case, and after the hapless Williams was found dead in his cell, they were only too eager to draw a line under the whole unfortunate episode.'

'But you don't believe he was the killer.'

'Certainly not at the King's Arms, because he had a perfectly robust alibi. And when I examined his remains in the prison mortuary, the corpse bore all the signs of a violent struggle. I suspect it was not suicide, as the turnkey claimed, but murder. Indeed, by that point I was firmly of the opinion that a large part of the evidence against Williams had been fabricated, and I had my own suspicions as to who might have done so. But given who those men were, and the public standing they enjoyed, I could not hope to convince Bow Street without concrete proof. Which I never found.'

Charles turns to the end of the case and finds a single final word. One he has never seen in these pages before: 'Unresolved'.

'They buried him like a felon on the public highway,' says Maddox quietly. 'With a stake through his heart.' He looks away, his face troubled now. 'It was my only other failure. That – and Elizabeth.'

Charles starts. He has not said her name since he left his father's house for the last time six years before; has not heard it said since he was last in this house a twelvemonth before. Hearing it now, so unexpectedly, he feels the iron close again about his heart. This is what he has been evading, all that time; this is what he feared, coming here again. And yes, there was some tiny, hidden, shameful part of his mind that saw his uncle's madness as a relief. A guarantee that they would not – *could* not – ever speak of her again. Only Maddox is not mad. Not any more.

Charles takes a deep breath. 'You did everything you could. You weren't there when it happened, and by the time you arrived it was too late to—'

'That is no adequate excuse. If anyone could have found her, *I* should have been the one to do it. Taken like that, in the middle of the day, barely yards from where her mother was standing—'

Charles says nothing, knowing, just as Maddox does, that his mother never forgave herself for that moment's distraction, those few minutes when her infant daughter was out of her sight.

Maddox strikes his hand against the arm of the chair. 'I should have *found* her – what use are skills like mine if I cannot use them to spare my own family from a lifetime of regret and self-reproach?'

Charles shakes his head, but the memory, so long stifled, will be suppressed no more. And as if in revenge for such long denial, the pictures in his head are more vivid now than the day it happened – the sounds more intense. He sees the soft curves of his sister's face, and the tiny golden curls escaping – as they always did – from under the edge of her straw bonnet. Sees himself being told to watch her by his mother. Hears the taunts of the street-boys because he was holding her hand. Feels himself letting that hand go, and turning away to play, his back to her all the while despite her tears. Hears then, and now, and ever after, his mother's agonized cry. It was *his* fault. It had always been his fault. Not just what happened that day, but what it led to. It was all his doing. And he has never had the courage to confess it.

'Is that why you did it?' His uncle's voice breaks into his thoughts, and Charles looks up – not flushed now, but white in the face. Maddox wasn't even there that day – surely he cannot possibly suspect—

Maddox is watching him thoughtfully. 'Is that why you took the Chadwick case? Because you hope to find not only a lost grand-child, but a lost sister too?'

Charles turns away and walks to the window. On the other side of the street two children are playing with a ball, and a little grey dog is racing around them, barking and wagging its tail.

72

'I took the case because I need the money. That's all.'

Maddox turns, rather laboriously, to look at him. 'I suspect, my dear Charles, that you are not being completely honest in that response. Not least to yourself. You know what I have always said—'

'That a detective must never allow his own feelings to become engaged by an investigation, for they will only impede it. I know, I know, but I have never been as consummate a professional as you always were.'

It may be that Maddox himself has not always followed his own dictates as strictly as this might suggest, but of this the old thief-taker gives no sign.

'Take care, Charles,' he says eventually. 'I fear you will find neither child now, after all these years—'

'You're not the first to say that.'

'But you run a very grave risk of losing your *self*.'

The old man watches as the young man by the window stiffens, and then drops his head. Maddox has, in fact, long suspected what really happened the day Elizabeth Maddox disappeared, and is saddened that the boy has never felt able to confide in him. But he knows better than to probe. His great-nephew resembles him in far more than merely name and intelligence; neither is adept at intimacy, and both are very well-practised in the evasion of emotion. It may even be – though Maddox has never considered this – that the protégé has patterned himself on the mentor in this, as in so much else. And with the past Maddox knows he has, and the secrets Maddox knows he keeps, is it any wonder Charles finds it easier to keep people at a distance – to investigate them as suspects, or study them as species, or even buy their bodies by the finite hour. Anything to avoid an equality of exchange.

All this while Charles is still at the window, but Maddox can see now how rigidly he's gripping the window-frame, and he thinks again of the image that has come to him so many times in the presence of this young man – an image of a bright sheet of smooth paper, folded and folded and folded again until it is nothing more than a hard tight knot, closed into a fist.

A moment later Charles has turned to face him again. Their eyes meet, but the old man barely has the time to register the look on the younger's face before Charles turns quickly away and leaves the room. He can hear Maddox calling after him, but it's only when he is halfway up to the attic that he hears the thud from below, and when he looks back down over the banisters, he sees the old man sprawled on the lower landing, his stick flung from his grasp. And then pandemonium breaks loose. Molly with bandages, Billy with brandy, and – last, but worst – Abel Stornaway, who deciphers what has happened in a moment.

'What was he doing on the stairs all by his'sen?' he says, as he lifts his master's head. There's a graze to Maddox's cheek, and a wildness in his look now, that makes the eloquence of the last hour seem like a distant dream. 'He bain't as steady as he was, Mr Charles – he needs watchin' all the time.'

Charles has nothing to offer by way of excuse, and there's an accusation in Abel's eyes that he cannot counter. Between the four of them they eventually manage to get the old man to his feet, but by the time they get him back to the drawing-room he's already starting to mutter and struggle.

'Should we send for the doctor?' asks Charles meekly, as Stornaway settles Maddox into his chair.

Stornaway tucks a rug over the old man's knees and shakes his head. 'The cut is not sae bad. And that doctor would only scare him the more. Leave him be, Mr Charles, just leave him be.'

Sunday morning, and all the bells in London are ringing. Some near, some distant, this from Christchurch, Endell Street, that from St Paul's, Covent Garden; all marking a different moment for the passing of the hour. Charles is still asleep, despite the noise, one arm thrown back, his legs tangled up in his sheets much as we saw him once before, only this time someone else is managing his laundry, and the sheets are clean. There may have been a tap, there may even have been the sound of the door opening. Something of the sort there must have been, because when he opens his eyes he sees Molly standing at the end of his bed with a letter in her hand. He sits up with a start and feels, for a moment, absurdly embarrassed, as if she had caught him atop a whore. The girl sets the letter down on the table by the bed and leaves the room, her bare feet almost silent on the wooden boards. She does not smile; she merely delivers the message and is gone. Charles rubs his eyes with the heel of his hand, aware, for the first time, of the smell of hot rolls and bacon that has drifted in through the open door. Letter first, then wash and breakfast.

Lincoln's Inn Fields
Sunday morning, eight o'clock

Mr Maddox,
If it does not interfere unduly with your devotions, I should like to see you this morning at your earliest convenience. I have the two letters that you requested at our last meeting.

Your obedient servant,
Edward Tulkinghorn
Attorney-at-Law

Charles looks at the note, and then sits back, his face thoughtful. The domestic demands of the last two days have not left him any time to set about the practical task of tracking Tulkinghorn's culprit, but his mind has been hard at work all the same. Only what it's finding for him so far are not answers, but more questions.

Charles has, on the face of it, no obvious reason to be so sceptical about such an unexpected and well-paid commission, but sceptical he is, and even more so now. He's always had an excellent instinct for a lie, and his time in the Detective has done nothing to dull it. And what that instinct is telling him now is that a man like Tulkinghorn would never deign to deal personally with such a mundane affair, even for a client as consequential as Cremorne. The fact that he *is* so doing – and that even such a trivial matter as the delivery of supposedly insignificant letters cannot be delegated – is as eloquent, to Charles' mind, as Tulkinghorn is taciturn. Charles, of course, did not see what we saw, and cannot know what we know, but he's certain all the same that there's something the old lawyer is not telling him. But what that is, and how deep it goes, even we cannot yet fully imagine.

Lincoln's Inn Fields looks particularly beautiful this morning, the trees frosty against a brilliant blue sky, and somewhere among the branches, a blackbird singing. Charles presents himself as before, and as before he is shown upstairs, though progress is somewhat impeded by a little group of people in the hallway, gathered around a wizened and vociferous old man in a chair and a black skull-cap, attended by a lean female with a thin and wasted face. An angry altercation breaking out at just that moment, Charles leaves Knox to clear the house of such undesirable riff-raff and makes his own way upstairs. He arrives, as a result, rather sooner than his host seems to have anticipated, since Mr Tulkinghorn is not at his desk – is, in fact, still in a little ante-room Charles did not notice on his first visit, and from which come voices and the smell of fine tobacco. Charles catches sight – so briefly it is no more than an impression – of three men sitting round a table, and a fourth, older, grey-haired, standing upright with his back to the door. A moment later Tulkinghorn appears, closes the door firmly behind him, and moves, rather quickly for him, back to his wonted position of state behind the desk.

'Good morning, Mr Maddox.'

'Mr Tulkinghorn.'

As before, the lawyer takes the ring of keys from his waistcoat-pocket and unlocks the desk drawer. As before, the papers are placed on a plain brown sleeve. Two sheets. Tulkinghorn hands them to Charles.

'This arrived six weeks ago, the other some three months before that. As you will see, our anonymous correspondent seems to be lacking in either imagination or vocabulary. Or, indeed, both. It does not seem to me that they add a great deal to the evidence already at your disposal, but here they are.'

There is, indeed, a dogged persistence in the content of the letters:

I naw what yow did
Yow cannot hide from me

Yow sins will find ee out
I will make yow pay

'You were going to ask about the envelopes?'

'I have put enquiries in hand. I am not hopeful, but if they can be found, I will have them sent to you.'

Tulkinghorn is about to close the drawer again when he notices that Charles is eyeing the strange black paperweight.

'Such curios interest you?' he says, as if casually, picking it up and holding it towards Charles in the palm of his small dry hand.

Charles reaches out and takes the object. 'It's Egyptian, I think? Obsidian?'

The old man raises an eyebrow. 'Indeed. It came from a mummy discovered by Giovanni Belzoni in the Valley of the Kings. Some high-ranking official, buried with his master. I saw the body unwrapped before my very eyes. Some of my noble clients have a taste for the macabre, and such evenings are, I believe, becoming rather fashionable. This amulet was found among the linens. I was taken with it, and my client was good enough to present it to me. A small token of recognition for many years of loyal service. Of course, there are some who condemn such acts as sacrilegious – even accursed – but that, I am sure you will agree, is mere ignorance and uncouth superstition.'

If he did but know it, this hard, dark artefact is a rather interesting metaphor for its equally impenetrable owner. Tulkinghorn may not understand exactly what role it played, but if such things interest you, you can see these selfsame fingers in the British Museum, which is where – by a circuitous route that need not concern us – this object now finds itself. And as the label on the case will tell you, these long thin fingers were a tool of the embalmer, designed to hold the incisions closed after the organs were removed, so keeping malign forces at bay, and the body intact for all eternity. Whatever his view of the possibility of an afterlife (and if he has one, he keeps it as private as his opinions on every other matter of note), this is a role Mr Tulkinghorn would have appreciated, and one in which he is, in his own field, unsurpassed.

When he gets to his feet a moment later, Charles is intrigued but not unduly surprised to observe that Tulkinghorn has no intention of discussing the letters with him any further; he seems, indeed, solely concerned to show him off the premises with all dispatch. But when they reach the door of the chamber, he appears to change his mind, and turns to Charles with what passes, with him, for a smile.

'Perhaps it would interest you to see my little collection? The top of the house is let off now in sets of chambers, but I still keep the lower floors, where the coolness of the temperature and the dryness of the atmosphere are ideally suited for my purpose.'

It could hardly be more contrary to what Charles was expecting, but nonetheless he accepts with alacrity. Tulkinghorn leads him down towards the ground floor, but stops on the half-landing by a door that is so cleverly concealed by the veins and swirls of faked marbled paintwork you could pass it by nine times out of ten and never even notice. He lights a candle and the two of them make their way down a spiral stone staircase to the echoing regions below the deserted mansion. The stairs are dark, and the candle throws the lawyer's enormous, quivering shadow against the curve of the wall. But strange though it seems, the air brightens as they descend, and when they reach the foot of the staircase, Charles sees why. He's in a small hexagonal chamber that opens into another, much larger room, lit from above by a huge conical dome of yellow glass with a stone rose in its centre. They must be at least two floors below ground, but the room ahead of him is double-height, with a catacomb of corridors opening away from him in all directions. The architecture is astounding, but even that retreats into insignificance compared with what it holds. It is like some *augmentum ad absurdum* of Charles' own former lodgings – objects stud every surface, every wall, every shelf, as well as every passage and alcove within view. It is, quite simply, the largest and most extraordinary collection of classical statuary Charles has ever seen. Not even his beloved British Museum can rival this. Stone, marble, terracotta, alabaster – every texture, every colour from pearly ivory to a rich polished black. Funerary urns and a statue of Apollo, horn-eared gods and a snake-haired Medusa, busts of ancient emperors and fragments of vase, heads in profile, heads in relief, tiny broken details mounted on plaques, and perfectly intact slabs of huge architectural frieze. Tulkinghorn eyes his visitor with a quiet but obvious satisfaction.

'Most of the best Greek and Roman sculpture is in here,' he says, as if casually, 'but I think Egypt is your own preference?'

Charles has no preference of the kind, but he has no objection to seeing what else his host is prepared to show him. Tulkinghon leads him towards the dome, and he sees now that this space is not a room at all, but a gallery round another, lower chamber that opens now beneath him, half-plunged in darkness, and dominated by a huge stone trough, throned on pillars and deeply carved with symbols and runes. No – not runes, thinks Charles, leaning over the balustrade as his eyes adjust to the light. Not runes but *hieroglyphs*, and it's not a trough but a sarcophagus – an enormous, perfectly preserved Egyptian sarcophagus. He starts and turns to Tulkinghorn, remembering suddenly where he has seen this before.

'But this is—'

'The sarcophagus of Pharaoh Seti I. Indeed.'

'But you said—'

'That I was given the amulet. That is quite true, but we are speaking of two distinct occasions. The sarcophagus had to be paid for.'

'May I go down?'

'Of course. You will find the stairs in the corner over there.'

Charles heads round the gallery to the far side, but when he gets there he finds himself unexpectedly confounded. He knows this is where the stairs are supposed to be (and he is, as we know, rather better than most at finding his way), but when he turns the final corner by a niche containing a life-size statue of Pan, he finds himself face to face with – himself: a life-size reflection of himself. The glass is slightly convex, and the mirror so cleverly sited and angled that it makes the room seem at least twice its real size. It also serves, very effectively, as a blind alley, an optical illusion that can only be designed to lead the inexperienced visitor astray. What sort of man could possibly—? Charles turns and looks backs to the other side of the gallery. Tulkinghorn is still standing there. Standing and watching. A curious expression on his face – his customary sardonic superiority, yes, but something else as well, which in another man might suggest a barely suppressed excitement. The combination is unsettling, and Charles is struck suddenly by the conviction that more than half of the lawyer's pleasure in this exquisite collection lies in the power it affords him to withhold that pleasure from everyone else. Even – or perhaps especially – those he ostensibly brings to see it. He has not merely constructed this astonishing gallery, and at unimaginable expense, but contrived every stratagem at his disposal to deceive the eye: light, shadow, looking-glass, *trompe l'oeil*. Indeed, as Charles now realizes, this space that seems designed for display has actually been created for another purpose altogether. An enfilade of architectural subterfuges that bestows with one hand what it conceals with the other. There are, unquestionably, incomparable treasures here, but not so many as the eye believes it can see – some are mere illusions, others tantalizing glimpses forever out of reach. Charles looks slowly about him, re-adjusting his mental map, and attempting to penetrate beyond the dazzle of remarkable objects to the bones of the building that must lie behind. Tulkinghorn is the Daedalus of this labyrinth, and no one understands its secrets better than the man who made it. He feels, surely and uncomfortably, that his host is toying with him, much as Thunder does with the mice behind the skirting-boards, when the weather is wet and there is nothing better to do. It takes a few minutes, but he eventually realizes that the catacomb effect is nothing but a spectacular sleight of hand: four of the six narrow passageways that appear to lead off the gallery are only mirrored alcoves. There is only one way in, which means there can be only one way down.

'I congratulate you,' says Tulkinghorn, when Charles emerges eventually beneath him. 'Many visitors never negotiate that particular little puzzle. Even the more astute take rather longer than you did. You will find a lit candle in the small niche on the right-hand side. If you hold it carefully inside the sarcophagus, you will be able to appreciate fully the translucent quality of the stone. There are also, as you will see, some signs remaining of blue inlay, but sadly the alabaster has not aged well.'

His tone is almost cordial, as if Charles has passed some obscure initiation.

'It is extraordinary, Mr Tulkinghorn. The whole collection. Quite extraordinary.'

The lawyer inclines his head. 'I am gratified you think so. But I am afraid I will have to draw your exploration of it to a rather abrupt conclusion. I have a luncheon engagement with a baronet, and I cannot keep him waiting.'

Charles arrives home just in time to be too late for his own lunch, but Molly scrapes together the remains of the boiled beef and greens, and he elects to take his plate into his great-uncle's room and sit with him while he eats. The slight graze to Maddox's cheek has all but healed and – to Charles' relief – he seems to retain no memory at all of how he came by it. Though if Abel has anything to say on the matter, it's doubtful Maddox will ever move much beyond these four walls again. He is quiet today, but Charles has not the experience yet to know the difference between the quiet of composure, and the quiet of catatonia. His eye-glass and his watch are ready to his hand, though he has not yet picked up either of them; but perhaps he just needs something to stimulate his curiosity.

Charles finishes his meat and puts the plate on the floor beside him, then takes the Cremorne letters from the inside of his jacket.

'Do you have a moment, Uncle Maddox?'

The old man eyes him, rather warily.

'I have just acquired a new case, that I would like to consult you about.'

It may be the magic word 'case', or perhaps it's something in Charles' tone, but Maddox is suddenly alert.

'What's that? Speak up, boy, I can't hear what you're saying through all that mumble.'

'I have a new case, Uncle. A problematic one. I wanted to ask your help.'

'Go on, then, get on with it. I dare say you've got all the facts in the wrong order, just like you used to in the old days. Always went at a problem like a bull at a gate. All over the place. Hopeless.'

It might strike you that this runs rather counter to Maddox's last expressed views on the self-same subject, and it may not be a coincidence that the old man's tone is rather shrill. Charles edges forward in his seat, trying not to mind.

'The client has been receiving letters—'

'Letters? What sort of letters?'

'Offensive letters. Anonymous letters. My task is to find out who sent them. That alone will be difficult enough, given how little I have to go on, but I'm convinced there's more to it than what I've been—'

Maddox doesn't appear to be listening. 'Is that them there?'

Charles hands them over. The old man's hands are trembling slightly, but his mind suddenly seems completely steady. He picks up his eye-glass and looks first at one letter, and then another, turning them over carefully several times. But then, to Charles' horror, he takes one and flattens it against his face, breathing heavily. Charles tries to seize it, but Maddox will not let it go, and the two of them struggle, the flimsy sheet crumpling and tearing between their fists.

'Uncle – please—'

'What do you think you're doing? Let go of me, you fool!'

'But—'

Billy has heard the fracas from the adjoining room and appears at the door, his bright round face frowning and concerned. 'Everything all right, Mr Charles? Only—'

'Everything's fine, Billy,' says Charles quickly, embarrassed to be found in this ridiculous position, playing tug-of-war with an elderly man over a piece of wretched paper. 'There's no need to worry yourself. Go down to the kitchen, would you, and ask Molly for some tea.'

'Right you are, Mr Charles. I'll be back in a jiffy.'

When Charles turns back to Maddox, the old man's face is very red and his chest is heaving.

'I'll thank you, Charles, to show me an appropriate degree of respect. My age, if nothing else, surely commands that much.'

It is as if a switch has been flicked – an analogy which is at least thirty years away, by the way, though the snap of a magic lantern will do almost as well. Maddox is looking at Charles now with as clear a gaze as his nephew can ever remember.

'I'm sorry,' he stumbles. 'I did not intend—'

Maddox's eyes narrow. 'No, I dare say you did not. Now, to business. These letters of yours. You have, I presume, drawn the first and most obvious conclusion?'

It's Charles' turn to redden now. 'Yes – that is, no—'

Maddox smiles, his eyes twinkling. 'Well, that is no more than I expected. Have you forgotten all I taught you already? Logic and observation, my boy, logic and observation.'

He smoothes the torn paper against his leg and hands it to Charles. There is no trace of a tremor now.

'Examine this – carefully, mind – and tell me what you find.'

Charles takes the paper and stares at it.

'Well,' he says slowly, after a few minutes. 'The writing is not educated—'

'Indeed.'

'—and is in a man's hand.'

'Indubitably.'

'He has some cause for grievance against Sir Julius, which he clearly feels very deeply, but does not specify. Is that significant?'

'Perhaps. Perhaps not. Go on.'

Charles looks up. 'That's all. I can infer nothing more.'

Maddox smiles broadly. 'Come, come, my lad. Surely you can deduce a little more than that? Do you not remember what I used to tell you when you were a boy? A letter is far more than a sequence of words written on a page – it is a *physical object*, and in that respect is frequently far more eloquent than its creator intended.'

Charles looks again at the letter in his hand. 'The paper is poor, that much I can see, but that doesn't get us very far. And as for anything else—'

'Smell it.'

Charles gapes. '*What?*'

His great-uncle is clearly enjoying himself. 'Go on – smell it. It will not bite you.'

Charles brings the letter slowly to his face. It's faint at first, but as the paper brushes his nose, he pulls his head away, coughing.

'My God, whatever that is, it's absolutely disgusting.'

'Quite so. Absolutely nauseating, and absolutely un-mistakable. An exceedingly unpalatable combination of cattle fat, rotting meat, and dog excrement.'

Maddox sits back in his chair, and joins his fingertips together. 'Is it not obvious? Your culprit, my dear Charles, is a *tanner.*'

Charles' eyes widen. This man is remarkable, completely and utterly remarkable. Who else but Maddox would have even thought to put the letter to such a test? And who else but he would know how to interpret what he found?

'Moreover,' Maddox continues, 'the text itself is not quite so devoid of interest as you seem to believe. You stated – quite correctly – that the author of this missive is uneducatcd. But he is not – perhaps – as illiterate as you might assume. This word here,' he points a gnarled finger, '*naw,* and here *yow*—'

'I took them as mere spelling errors.'

Maddox shakes his head. 'I am sure you did. Because that is exactly what they would have been had you yourself written them – indeed, had almost any Englishman written them. But there is one region of this kingdom where this orthography is quite common. I had occasion, some years ago, to be employed by Sir Jonathan Evershed, at his estate at Launceston. The infant child of one of his tenant farmers had been found murdered in her cradle. The perpetrator – inconceivable as it

86

sounds – proved to be the family's young maidservant, a girl of no more than fourteen years. She claimed to have been incited to the deed by a gentleman in black, who came to her bed in the dead of night. She was caught in the very act of attempting to strangle another child.' His voice falters for a moment. 'I endeavoured to persuade the magistrate that this was *prima facie* evidence of a diseased mind and that the girl was, in consequence, quite unaware of the nature, character, and consequences of the act she was committing. But I failed.'

He stops and seems to be gazing back into his own mind, seeing again, as Charles cannot, the crowd of silent bystanders gathered about the gibbet, and the thin body swinging slowly, slowly, under a leaden April sky. A moment later he shakes his head, and resumes. 'A most deplorable case, but the point I wished to make was that in the course of that inquiry I had occasion to interrogate a number of local villagers and labourers from the surrounding district. Your suspect, my dear Charles, is *Cornish.*'

Charles sits back in his chair, dumbfounded.

'I am very sorry, Uncle. When you put the paper to your face just now, I thought, well, I thought—'

'You thought I was going mad. Deranged. Like that poor dead girl, seeing people who do not exist, hearing voices that are not there.'

A shadow crosses his face, and all his old self-assurance shrinks to fear. He reaches forward and grips hold of Charles' wrist. 'There are days now, Charles, when I cannot see beyond the dark – when I cannot trust my own body – when I can barely untangle my own *thoughts*. Do you know what that is like – for a man like *me*? Listen to me, Charles,' he whispers, his grip even tighter. 'These people watch me night and day, but *you* are the one I trust. Which is why I want you to promise me something.'

87

'If I can—'

'Promise me you will not let them take me away. Promise me *I will not lose my mind.*'

The old man's eyes are locked on his own. Charles opens his mouth to reply, then—

'Here we are, Mr Maddox,' says Billy cheerily, bumping down a tray of tea on the table beside them. 'Hot and strong, just the way you like it.'

The old man slumps slowly back in his chair, his head against his pillows, his mouth open. The moment has passed; the light in his eyes has gone out.

Chapter Six

A Wintry Day and Night

When Charles opens his eyes the following morning, he can tell at once that the weather has changed. He already loves this room – the way river reflections play across the ceiling on sunny days, flickering chains of light into bright geometric shapes. But not today. This morning the room is filled with that off-white over-white glow that means only one thing: snow. He dislodges a heavy and very sleepy cat from the counterpane and goes to the window to look out over the roof-tops. The flakes are coming down in huge clumps, slow and steady, and the skylight overhead is gradually layering with translucent grey. There's a perfect inch of snow on the parapet, and on the ledge, a track of large, fastidious pad-prints to show where Thunder beat a tactical retreat sometime during the night.

The house is suddenly very cold, and Charles gets dressed quickly among his heaps of boxes; he really must find time to arrange his collection properly, now he finally has the space to do it. He slides a hand, half-automatically, down the side of one of the cases to reassure himself his pistol-case is still where he left it. And if you're surprised to find he owns such a thing, it is not, after all, so very unusual that he should: just like any other young man brought up in the country in the first half of the nineteenth century, he learned to handle a rifle hunting rabbits as a boy, and thinks no more of owning a gun than of taking laudanum when he has a tooth-ache, though both would brand him a dangerous delinquent now. He is, by the way, rather good at shooting, and keeps his hand in at a little rundown gallery he knows near Leicester Square. He is also – as you have just seen – assiduous to ensure that the pistol is always safely stowed. But for all his precautions, and all his care, this gun of his may still prove to be his undoing.

The only person up and about downstairs is Molly, who's on her knees raking out the hearth in the drawing-room. He stops on the stairs a moment, then takes a step or two into the room.
    'It's cold today.'
    She tilts her head slightly towards him, as if to show she's heard, but does not look up; there is no break in the slow, methodical movement of her large rough hands across the sooty tiles. He wonders if she's seen snow before; wonders, in fact, how long she's been in England, and whether the unforgiving sunlight of her native land – wherever that is – might not now be stranger to her than the dank grey London streets. He eats what he can find in the kitchen (bread and butter only, since the bacon is still frying), and then trudges through the thickening snow to the Strand, a flurry of white flakes settling on his eyelashes and his hair and his coat (though this time, at least, he has retrieved his muffler).
    There's an even longer queue than usual for the omnibus, and Charles can barely feel his feet by the time it arrives. He has to change twice more before he's finally heading south towards the river, the gritty, partly frozen snow churning under the wheels like gravel and the horses slithering on the icy stones. It's not the best day for such a journey, but now he has both a genuine lead and a point to prove, and not just to his client, but to himself: the next time he and Tulkinghorn meet,

he wants it to be at his request, not the lawyer's. And given that knowledge is power – especially when it comes to a man like Tulkinghorn – if there is indeed something about this case the old man is concealing, Charles wants to find out what that is, so he can decide for himself what information to give, and what to keep. All of which makes perfect sense, of course, but since as far as we know he's had no new information, how is it that he's suddenly so sure of where he should be going? And where – for that matter – *is* he going? That question, at least, is easy enough to answer. Maddox told him he's looking for a tanner, and that being the case, even a half-competent London detective would know where to start: Bermondsey. This densely packed district barely one mile across holds more tanners, curriers, fellmongers, parchment-makers, wool-staplers, leather-dressers, and glue-makers than the rest of the country put together. Dyeing they do here too, though dying has been more prevalent of late – over six thousand were killed by cholera in the last year, so overcrowded is this strip of land hard by the Thames, and so hard the subsistence for those who live here. As the 'bus hauls slowly over London Bridge, the footways on both sides are thronged with people, some workers, some tradesmen, and some poor stitchers from south of the river, carrying huge canvas bags made for the wealthy wool-merchants on the other side. The snow is too thick to see far in either direction, but Charles can make out the dark wharves and wherries of Shad Thames, and further away still, the dim outline of Jacob's Island, with its warehouses, docks, bridges, and alleys, bristling with the masts of ships. Less lethal now than once it was, but still an infamous slum, the houses clustered thick and the rooms cramped and stinking, overhanging water that clogs with refuse, and sewage that empties hourly into open ditches.

It will not surprise you to find that this part of London is not much frequented by the idly inquisitive (though Charles Dickens himself will make almost exactly this journey in a few months' time). Nor is it an area that Charles knows well, so when he swings down from the 'bus at Tooley Street, he asks the driver what he suggests.

'Start with the Skin Depository, guv. Up ahead off Bermondsey Street. On yer right.'

The quadrangle of buildings proves surprisingly elegant for such a down and dirty trade, but there's no disguising what's really being bought and sold here. Men with stained hands and soiled aprons press close against him, and laden carts push at him through the throng, leaving a trail of dark, viscous slime matted with hanks of animal hair. Inside the Depository there are stacks of hides and wet skins piled in bays on every side of the courtyard, horns still dangling from slices of skull, and while the buyers do their rounds in their black coats and tall hats, picking over the merchandise and questioning its quality, a horde of bedraggled little boys follows them from carcase to carcase, stripping them of any flesh still edible, however rotten it smells. Charles suddenly feels rather ill. The air is sickly with blood, and the snow is treading red into the mud under his feet. He's wearing the wrong boots for this. He takes as deep a breath as the evil air will allow, and heads for one of the more respectable-looking fellmongers. A slight little man with a thin, nasal whine. He's courteous enough to start with, but lapses into indifference when it becomes clear Charles has not come with money to spend. He claims to know nothing of the tanneries, and even less of the men who work there. In any case, there are scores of them – hundreds even. But if Charles is intent on such a hopeless quest, he should probably start by enquiring in Long Lane. There must be a good twenty establishments there.

*

And so it proves. Charles has never really thought much about leather production before, and even though Maddox's words should have prepared him for something of what he's about to find, the reality still comes as a shock. If the smell was rank in the market, it's ten times worse here. The first tannery he finds has a narrow entrance under two overhead gangways, and when he reaches the inner yard he finds a group of men stripping a cartload of new hides of their last scraps of bone before loading them into one of a score of lime pits. Another heavier man has a wet hide slung over a wooden frame, and is deftly stripping the hair and spongy white fat with a two-handled blade. In the corner, a coil of steam rises slowly from a bating tank of pale, cloudy water; there are brown sticky clods floating on the surface, and believe me, it's only too horribly obvious what they are. Looking at the man at work on the carcase, Charles no longer questions how the letter sent to Sir Julius Cremorne gained its distinctive smell – it must be next to impossible to rid their hands of the stink; though what strange thread it is that connects two men from such disparate strata of London society is even more obscure to him now than it was before. He makes his way carefully across the yard towards the man; the snow has all but stopped but the whole area is an inch deep in slop and grease, and most of the workers are splashed to the knees.

'Could I talk to you for a moment?'

The man looks up, then back at his work. 'I'm busy. What are you – police, or what?'

Charles shakes his head. 'No, not police. But I am looking for someone.'

The man looks up again, for longer this time, but says nothing.

'I'm trying to find a man who does a job like yours.'

'Thinking of openin' a tanner's, are you? Nah, I didn't think so somehow. Look, I don't know who you are or what you're after, but I'm not about to get some other poor bugger into trouble. 'Cause trouble's all that can be comin' from a face like yours.'

Charles wants to deny it but knows he can't. Lying is the one tool of his trade he's never really mastered. He tries another tack. 'Sounds to me like you come from round here.'

The man eyes him guardedly. 'What's that to you?'

'I assume most of the men who work here are Bermondsey boys?'

The man puts the knife down and looks Charles full in the face. He's a big man, and thickly built, with a shaven head and a dark indistinct tattoo on the side of his neck. '*Bermondsey boys?*' he echoes, his voice barely able to contain his contempt. 'What are you, some kind of bloody nancy? Looking for a bit of local rough and ready?' This last is accompanied by a particularly lewd gesture, and before Charles can react, he's reached out a hand dripping with fat and taken him by the chin like a girl, to the coarse amusement of the rest of the yard. 'Well we might just be able to help you there, what do you think, lads?'

Something flickers red in Charles' brain, and though he's barely half the man's weight, he seizes his thick wrist and tries to force his fingers away. 'Get your stinking hands off me.'

The man comes closer and brings his face within a kiss of Charles'. 'Oh really?' he says softly. 'So you don't like the way I smell? Well in that case, why don't you take your pretty face and your fancy voice, and *hook it*. We don't take to the likes of you round 'ere, and we look after our own. Am I makin' myself clear?'

The man puts both hands on Charles' chest and pushes him roughly away. He stumbles, landing flat on his back in the muck, and only just misses drowning himself in the bating trough. The viscous white filth is clinging to his face, and he wipes it away in furious disgust. He gets to his feet and retreats across the yard with as much dignity as he can manage. One or two of them grab at his backside as he leaves, and when he reaches the gate, the yard behind him, the air is raucous with laughter and strident whistling.

He made a complete mess of it, he knows that. Well-spoken stranger asking leading questions; small wonder the man was wary. He should have known better. At the building next door he adopts different tactics, and opts to speak to the manager, not the men, but it doesn't get him much further. The man is harassed and only half-listens, but he claims he doesn't know of anyone from Cornwall working in the area. And nor, indeed, does anyone else Charles asks. One owner thinks he recalls a man who might have been from those parts, but it was months ago and he can't remember his name; another can only think of a young lad who had 'a strange accent – thick as soup – we could hardly make out what he was saying half the time', and a third refuses to speak to him at all, all the while eyeing Charles' filthy trousers with obvious suspicion. By the time he reaches the end of the street, he's beginning to wonder if he's wasting his time. He considers for a moment asking in the Fellmongers' Arms, but a glance through the window at the group of silent men smoking together in the gloomy taproom convinces him otherwise. He's not sure he would even want to drink in there. And in any case, it's getting late. He's had enough.

The journey back is very uncomfortable. It's not that he's wet through from shirt to feet (though he is), or even that once the Bermondsey smell abates somewhat he finds he's ravenously hungry (though he's that too), it's the looks of those around him that make him shift in his seat and look determinedly out of the window. The 'buses are more and more crowded the closer he gets to home, but even though the last one up the Strand is packed full, the only person willing to take the seat next to Charles is the smallest son of a large and alarming lady with spectacles and a prominent nose sitting opposite, who flaps her handkerchief in front of her face and says, 'Oh, dear me, this is most trying, most trying!' very loudly indeed, to no one in particular, for a whole slow half a mile. The child looks absolutely ferocious with discontent, and glowers at Charles' reeking trousers as if he can never forgive the injury being done to his olfactory nerves. By the time Charles gets to Buckingham Street he wants to tear his clothes off and dump them in the nearest ditch, and as soon as he reaches the house he rushes down the back-stairs to the kitchen, looking for Molly and hot water.

Both of which he finds.

She's standing before the kitchen grate, stripped to the waist, a bowl before her and a wash-cloth in her right hand. He's never seen her without her starched white cap, and her hair is cut so close to her head that he can see the exquisite curve of her skull, the delicate hollow at the nape of her neck. He's seen naked girls many times, but never one so unadorned. Her breasts are as flat as a boy's, the nipples erect and tender in the cold air. The dark skin, the white cloth, the cool milky light from the kitchen window; it is as perfect, and as motionless, as a Vermeer. How long he stares at her, he could not have said; it's only when she lifts her face to his, and meets his eyes for the first time in that house, that he shifts his gaze and turns away, his cheeks burning.

'I – I wanted some hot water. To wash.'

She drops her eyes and nods, then pulls her chemise up about her shoulders.

He turns, and leaves the room.

Halfway up the stairs he hears a noise behind him, and sees Stornaway emerge on to the landing beneath.

'Mr Charles!' he calls. 'Someone here to see ye.'

'I need to change my clothes before I see anyone. Who is it – can they wait?'

'A Mr Chadwick, it is.'

Charles stops. 'I see. Please give him my apologies, and say I will be down without delay.'

He's been dreading this interview; dreading it, and putting it off. But now he has to think of something to say, and quick. He peels off his revolting clothes and kicks them into a pile by the bed, then upends the cat from his next-cleanest shirt, there being no time to unearth a new one from the (still half-unpacked) trunk. He keeps his back purposefully to the door, so that when the girl comes with the water he does not see her. Ten minutes later he is almost fit for decent company; five minutes more and he is downstairs.

Mr Chadwick has appropriated the only chair in the office, though Charles can hardly begrudge it to him. He's a frail old gentleman, neat and well-dressed, with a little grey head and a bearing that would have been stately but for a trembling in one of his hands and a certain rigidity in his limbs that makes it difficult for him to sit comfortably in his seat, and reduces him to moving in quick small shuffling steps.

When Charles opens the door, his visitor is rather ostentatiously consulting his pocket-watch.

'Mr Chadwick, I am glad to see you. I hope you are well.'

The old man puts up his watch and looks at Charles over his gold eye-glasses. 'I should be a great deal better if I had not

97

chased around town half the morning looking for *you*. Could you not have informed me that you had removed here? A mere two lines would have sufficed, but instead of that, I not only had to waste both time and money being carried to your former lodgings, but then endure the indignity of being forced to enquire for your landlady at a common – and, I may say, most *insalubrious* – public-house.'

Monday, thinks Charles. Mrs Stacey's Linen Box committee day.

'I am very sorry you were inconvenienced, sir.'

He wants to suggest going for a second chair, but feels that in his client's eyes he has not yet earned the right to sit down.

'Well, sir? What have you to say for yourself?'

'I apologize for my oversight, sir. My great-uncle was taken ill, and I had no alternative but to—'

The old man waves his hand impatiently. 'Not that, not that. The *investigation*. Have you, or have you not, made any progress in discovering my grand-child?'

'I have, as you know, interviewed the beadle in charge of the workhouse where your daughter died—'

'Where they *told* me she died. There were no records, you know, no grave.'

Charles looks rueful. 'I doubt there are many workhouse inmates who are accorded the dignity of an individual resting-place. As for the lack of proper records, it was, was it not, some time later that you first enquired?'

Chadwick starts to rub his left thumb and forefinger together; it is a tic he has, which usually indicates he is becoming anxious.

'You know very well, Mr Maddox, that my wife and myself had been estranged from our daughter for some months before her death, and you know very well the reason why—'

'You discovered she was with child.'

The old man is now somewhat flushed about the face; the trembling in his hand is noticeably worse.

'I never could comprehend how such a calamity could have come upon us. Not seventeen years of age, brought up piously in a devout home, watched over day and night, schooled in the strictest observance of her religion, and ever mindful of her duty to a God who is both watchful and avenging—'

'But merciful too, surely?'

Chadwick looks at him sharply. 'That is not for us to say, and certainly no business of *yours*. I may tell you, Mr Maddox, that even in the face of such a terrible blow, I took no hasty step. I searched my conscience, I consulted members of our families, I spoke to my brother-in-law, and I sought spiritual advice from our minister, a most exemplary man, held in the highest esteem, and a most ardent speaker whose sermons draw attendance from many miles around. And there was not a dissenting opinion among them: it was our duty, as Christians, to cast her out.' His voice falters slightly. 'They all agreed, I tell you. Cast her out.'

'But you changed your mind,' says Charles quietly.

'My wife became ill. She had argued, from the first, for leniency.'

There is a silence. The old man is breathing rather heavily.

'Constance made me promise, on her death-bed, that I would do everything in my power to find our daughter and the child, and forgive her. I have taken that as a sacred trust. This is why I persist in this unhappy pursuit. Even after all these years. Even against my own better judgement, and the express advice of my family, who consider the venture doomed to failure.'

Charles clears his throat. 'As I said, I have interviewed the workhouse beadle, Mr Henderson, and he has confirmed that there are no useful records remaining from that period. However, after a good deal of prompting, and a certain amount of financial inducement, he did finally remember that a Miss Jellicoe, who was then on the staff, might still be living. He promised to obtain her address for me, but I have not, as yet, heard from him. She would be very old now, but she may remember something.'

Chadwick nods; the trembling in his hand has not abated.

'I have also,' continues Charles, 'seen the superintendent of the orphanage. They, like the workhouse, seem to have either mislaid the relevant papers or never kept them in the first place. However, the superintendent did recall his predecessor telling him of an outbreak of smallpox, which he believes was probably around the time in question. I am afraid we must prepare ourselves for the possibility that your grand-child fell victim to that terrible disease, when still barely a few months old.'

Chadwick nods again, more stiffly this time. 'Anything else?'

'I have talked to some of my former colleagues in the Detective. They have promised to inform me if they come upon anything that might assist us. I will, of course, maintain regular contact with them on this matter on your behalf.'

'See that you do,' says Chadwick. His moment of weakness has passed, and his voice has regained some of its former irritability. 'And see that you keep me informed of your progress. And rather more frequently than you have hitherto, if you please. Good day to you.'

The visit has, on the whole, gone as well as Charles could have hoped, but he still feels shamefaced enough to sit down and write a second time to Henderson, to enquire whether he has yet succeeded in discovering an address for Eleanor Jellicoe.

That done, and a late lunch eaten, he allows himself the indulgence of an hour or two at the British Museum. He needs to decide what to do next in the Cremorne case, and he has, as yet, no clear idea. But he thinks best when he walks, and it's a good step to Bloomsbury, even though the weather has closed in again, and the snow is starting to fall. Outside in the street, a thin track of muddy wet paving has emerged between the frozen heaps of blackened slush, and every now and then a slab of compacted snow slips with a dull thud from the summit of one of the neighbouring roofs. Charles has left the house and is heading carefully towards the Strand when he hears his own name. It's Tulkinghorn's clerk, coming slowly towards him through the swirling flakes. There's a carriage waiting at the top of the street.

'A package for you, Mr Maddox. Those envelopes you were wanting.'

Charles thanks him and opens the packet. There are three of them. All post-marked from the Charing Cross sorting office, but all collected at different receiving-houses – receiving-houses, moreover, that are at least a mile distant from one another. He sighs. He'd been hoping they would turn out to have been posted in the same place. That would have narrowed the task down to a manageable margin. But it had always been a bit of a long shot: even the most dunder-headed criminal would have known to take that elementary precaution. He tucks them inside his coat and sets off again, more quickly this time. He thinks best when he's walking.

The carriage pulls slowly away, and overtakes Charles a few yards further on, though he barely registers its passing, so thick is the air with the darkness of the day and the density of the snow. And so it is that he walks the length of the Strand without being in the least aware that his footsteps are being followed, and all his movements as closely watched as if he, too, were a prize specimen – one no less worthy of scrupulous surveillance, but far more vulnerable to an observing but unobserved eye. As Charles will, in due course, discover.

Chapter Seven

Hester's Narrative

I don't know how it is I seem to be always writing about myself. I mean all the time to write as little as possible about myself, and am most vexed to find how much I seem to be taken up with the little doings of my own life, but there it is.

My darling Clara and I were so happy together, and so busy in all our daily employments that the months seemed to fly by. There was rarely a night when little Amy did not contrive to steal into my bed, and rarely a morning when I did not wake to find a flower on my pillow or a ribbon, or some other little token of love. Everyone was so kind to me, and showed me such unstinting affection, that I thanked God every night that I had found such a home, and such friends.

And all the more so, since there were times – a very few – when I was not as well as I would have liked, and was forced to keep to my room for some days together. At such times I would lie in my bed and hear how quiet the house was, and know that it was kept so out of consideration for me, and I would shed tears then, that were as precious to me, in their way, as the most delightful happiness could ever have been.

As summer came round again, I began to see Mr Jarvis walking in the garden with a little old lady in a worn squeezed bonnet, who would sally about with him with great stateliness, carrying a threadbare velvet reticule. After I had seen the lady several times at the same time of day, I contrived one morning that Clara and I should take our own exercise at that same hour. We strolled out into the garden, and it was not long before we came upon the old lady examining the roses, as Mr Jarvis was giving some instruction to the gardener on the other side of the lawn.

'Oh!' said she, as soon as she saw us. 'The wards of The Solitary House! I have heard so much about you! I am most honoured to make your acquaintance. It is not often that youth and hope and beauty find themselves in such a place as this.'

'Quite mad!' whispered Clara to me, with one of her playful looks, keeping her voice low so the old lady would not hear her.

'You are quite right, young lady,' she replied, much to Clara's surprise and embarrassment. 'Quite mad! I was not always so, though,' she continued, with a bright smile. 'I had youth and hope myself once, and, I believe, a little beauty. Not a beauty as bright and gilded as yours, but beauty all the same. But none of that matters any more now.'

Clara had by now lost all her pretty confidence and become a little frightened, shrinking close to my side, so I endeavoured to humour the poor old lady and said that we were very pleased to be introduced to her.

'I am most honoured, I'm sure!' she said with a bow. 'I see so little company these days. My friends are very kind, but my room is small, and my poor birds are rather confined. Not at all what I was once used to. I cannot but admit that it is rather mortifying.'

'You keep birds?' I asked, noticing that Mr Jarvis had now become aware of our presence.

'Oh yes! Larks, linnets and goldfinches. I like to keep them about me, as I find the days rather wearisome, and sleep does not always come as readily as I would wish. It is such an affliction, is it not?'

I noticed that even when she asked a question, she never waited for a reply, but chattered on as though no one else was there, and I began to wonder whether it were not the result of many years of retirement and seclusion, with no one but herself for companionship.

'Ah!' she said suddenly. 'Here is your good benefactor, come to check me in my ramblings!'

It was, indeed, Mr Jarvis, who came up just then. 'So, Miss Flint, I see you have met our Dame Durden and her lovely friend?'

'I have indeed, sir,' she said simperingly, with her head on one side. 'An honour! An honour indeed!'

'Miss Flint enjoys sitting here on fine days,' he said to us with a smile. 'It is extremely conducive to her health, and I am happy to make the garden available to her.'

'Oh yes,' said the old lady, with a wistful look. 'I come here every fine day, when I am well enough. It is so lovely in the summer-time when the birds are singing. I cannot allow my own birds to sing much – they disturb my neighbours, and that would never do, would it?'

'No indeed,' said Mr Jarvis, taking the old lady kindly by the arm. 'And now I fear you are tiring. We must not over-tax your strength.'

The old lady gave a profound curtsy, and the two of them walked slowly away; we could hear her prattling to him the whole way down the garden.

'Mad, quite mad!' said Clara laughingly, who had regained her composure. 'I wonder Mr Jarvis lets her come here.'

We made another turn about the lawn and came upon Miss Darby, walking with Amy and Augusta. I have to say Augusta looked much the better for a little air. Her hair had nearly grown back, and there was the rosy flush of health on her cheeks. Amy came dashing up to me straight away. It was hard to believe so much time had passed, so similar was she to the little childish creature I met on my very first day at the House.

'Hester! Hester!' she cried. 'Can you guess what has happened? No indeed, I think you never can – who could ever have expected such a thing!'

She was by now jumping about in such excitement and tugging so at my hand, that I had to look to Miss Darby for illumination.

'Miss Amy is merely pleased at the prospect of a new companion,' she said, attempting to quiet her.

'I see,' I replied, turning back to Amy. 'And what is the new young lady's name?'

'But that is the thing!' cried Amy. 'It is not a young lady at all. It is a young *gentleman.*'

I cannot say I was sorry it was a young gentleman. A young woman had joined us at The Solitary House some few weeks before, and I know that Mr Jarvis was concerned that she had not settled as well as she might have done. She was always quiet and obedient with Miss Darby and the maids, this Anne, never giving any trouble, and never anything but sweet-faced and docile. Quite their little pet, I suppose I should say. I was not envious of her – how could I be! – but she seemed to me to be a withdrawn, resentful, bitter person, and I think Mr Jarvis shared my view, though we never spoke of it. That sounds very harsh and judgemental on my part, and I am sorry for it, for I know I was not fit to judge, and moreover had neither the right nor the wisdom to do so, even if he did. But my memory may not serve me well, or it may just be my own fancy. Everyone else made quite a fuss of her, as I think I said.

To return to my story, when we went downstairs to luncheon that memorable day, we found a young man sitting beside Mr Jarvis. His name was Roderick, though he said his friends always called him Rick, and he begged that we would all do the same. He was nineteen years old, and he was an orphan. This fact alone made him particularly interesting to Clara, who was, as I think I may have said, an orphan herself. Young as she was when her mama died, whenever she talked of her, tears would come into her eyes, and she spoke of her father as everything that was honourable, upright, and virtuous. Rick really was the most handsome young man, with a blithe open face and the readiest laugh; indeed, I heard him laugh very often, not just during the course of that first meal together, but throughout our acquaintance. He found cause for merriment in everything from the quality of the beef (not very good, it must be admitted) to the rather dour features of the portraits on the walls, which he proceeded to christen by new and very improbable names – one stern-faced lady with a prominent chin was at once dubbed Miss Wisk, while a group of several heavy-looking gentlemen in waistcoats and thick whiskers were known from that day onwards as Boodle, Doodle, and Foodle. Everything gave him cause for mirth, everything seemed to catch his attention – most especially Clara. All the young ladies were very taken with him and eager to engage him in conversation, not least my own little Amy, but I saw from the first that it was Clara who drew his gaze. And how could it be otherwise? No young man could be unmoved by her beauty, and add to that her lively spirits and pretty ways, and it was no surprise to me to see him addressing himself to her more than to any other person present, even Mr Jarvis. Within an hour, Rick had confided to her that he meant to be a great lawyer one day, and had boxes full of books and documents waiting to be unpacked upstairs.

'It is a fine and admirable profession,' said Mr Jarvis, in a serious tone, 'but it requires a great deal of study and hard work, and conscientious application.'

'Quite so,' said Miss Darby. 'Most conscientious.'

'Oh, you need not worry about that,' said Rick in a careless manner, his eyes on Clara. 'I shall give it my best shot. I always do.'

I am sure I believed him at the time, but in the weeks that followed, I began to wonder how he was finding the time to devote to his chosen profession, since he seemed to walk with us every morning and sit with us every afternoon. He was forever admiring Clara's skill with a needle, or contriving an excuse to ask her to sing. I saw it, and I know that Mr Jarvis saw it too. One evening, when I was making tea with Miss Darby, and Clara was sitting at the piano with Rick at her side, I observed Mr Jarvis come to the door and stop a moment, watching the two young people, and at that moment Rick bent to speak a word softly to Clara and she raised her head to smile up at him. It was such a happy picture, and all at once it seemed to me that it might presage an even happier future.

I remember that Mr Jarvis' look was more than usually thoughtful as he stood there, and that he exchanged a glance with Miss Darby, who rose a moment later and took a cup of tea to Clara, before taking a new seat by the piano next to her. I remember, too, that Mr Jarvis' eyes met my own, and though he said nothing, it seemed to me that I could read his thought, and that he shared my precious hope, and he too looked forward to a day when Clara and Rick might be even dearer to one another than they were already.

Buoyed by the conviction, I saw no reason to fear for my darling pet, though I could not but notice that I was never thereafter allowed to be their only chaperone, and either

Miss Darby or one of the other maids would always sit with us when Rick was present. I did what I could, however, to prevent Amy from absorbing too much of his time. I am sure it was nothing more than her usual girlish vivacity, but she was always asking him to tell her stories, or carry her pig-a-back, or play at Wild Beasts under the piano. My careful remonstrances, gentle as they were, seemed to have but little effect, and I began to wonder whether my influence with her – such as it was – had not started to wane. Certain it is that the little trinkets and nosegays that had appeared on my pillow almost every morning now appeared no more. I was not disappointed at this – I had never, after all, thought myself in the least bit deserving – but I confess I was rather relieved when Miss Darby began to step in to check Amy's more excessive exuberances. It was evident by then that Clara was becoming a little irritated with her, and I think I may even have heard her raise her voice to her on one occasion, though in that I may be mistaken. Not that Clara need have worried, for Rick had eyes only for her.

It was very soon clear to me that they were both of them head over heels in love. Not that I could say anything, of course, or even divulge that I knew what was happening. But I was always ready to divert Miss Darby and allow them a few moments of private conversation, so that sometimes I wondered whether I was not becoming quite devious. Needless to say, I would never have done so had I not believed that Rick was as noble and praiseworthy a creature as there possibly could be, despite a certain restlessness that occasionally caused me a little unease. The tenderness and patience he showed to the importunate Amy was touching to observe, and in Clara's presence he became the most attentive of young men. As for Clara, I had never seen her look so beautiful. She blossomed before my very eyes, and took on new womanly ways, and little innocent feminine wiles that must have been utterly enthralling to her charmed admirer. He loved her dearly, and I do not think she loved him any the less.

I scrupled to tell Clara that I had discovered her secret – indeed, it was so obvious to me that I could scarce see how either of them could hope to hide it. And one morning before breakfast, when I had finished helping Caroline with her dressing, I found Clara waiting impatiently for me in my room.

'Hester, Hester!' she cried, closing the door behind me and standing for a moment with her back pressed against it. 'I thought you would never return!'

'What is it, my pet?' I asked, going to her. 'Have you been unwell again?' For indeed, her eyes were unnaturally bright, and the hair on her forehead was damp against her skin.

'Oh Hester!' she cried. 'I have a secret to tell you! I have been wanting to tell it for so long – so very long! Please forgive me!'

And what secret might that be, my beautiful darling girl?

'What is it, Clara? Shall I try to guess?'

'Oh you could never guess! How could you guess such a thing?'

She stopped and looked at me, and had I not known better, I might have thought she was afraid. I put my arms about her, and she buried her head against my breast.

'It's about—' she began in a whisper. 'It's about—'

It was so touching to have her clinging to me in that way, hiding her face, and to know that her tears were the tears of joyful love, that I was not above teasing her a little – a very little.

'Let me guess, my own pretty one,' I said soothingly. 'Could it, perhaps, be about a certain gentleman?'

I heard her give a little gasp.

'Now, I wonder who it can be?' said I gaily, pretending to consider.

I felt her stiffen in my arms, and burst into sobs. 'Oh Hester, he says – he says he loves me dearly. That no one will ever treasure me as he does, or love me more.'

'And did you think you could conceal such a thing from your own Hester?' said I with a smile. 'Why, I have known all about it for many weeks now!'

Clara held up her flushed face, the tears still staining her cheeks, 'Yet you never said anything,' she said wonderingly.

'It was your secret, my pet,' said I. 'And I knew you would tell me in your own good time.'

'But now I have – you don't think it wrong of me, do you?'

How could I have said so, looking at her lovely anxious face? I shook my head. 'Of course not,' I replied encouragingly. 'How could he not love an angel as beautiful as you, and being an angel, how could you not return that love?'

'But that's not quite the worst of it!' cried Clara, holding me even tighter and hiding her face once more upon my breast.

'Why, you never mean to say that you—' I began with a smile.

'Yes, yes!' she sobbed. 'Even that – even that! And now you know it all. You know everything!'

I told her, laughing, and to her utter consternation, that I had known that, too! And then we sat together for a while over the dying fire, and after a little while Clara was quiet, and soon it was as if nothing at all had ever happened.

Chapter Eight

A Morning Adventure

The accuracy is exceptional. The fragility of the shimmering stained-glass wings, the sharp serrations on the articulated legs, and the density of the improbably long and heavy body. In reality, this creature is barely an inch long, but at this magnification there's something faintly horrifying about the size of those eyes, and the monstrous efficiency of that hooked proboscis. And if you're wondering where we are, this is the third room of the Northern Zoological Gallery of the British Museum; we are by the table marked *Hymenoptera*, and we – like Charles – are looking at a display devoted to bees. It's only one of eight similar cases in this overcrowded room – in fact, there's barely an inch of floor or wall space in either direction that doesn't have its neatly arranged array of eggs, shells and mounted insects, or its furred or feathered exhibit staring beadily down from a glass case. The sheer variety of death on display here is rather overwhelming – even a little sickening – but as this room confines itself only to the banal and British, it lacks the glamour of the more exotic Mammalia room with its lions, tigers and bears, or the child-catching appeal of the stuffed giraffes in the central saloon. Combine that with the wintriness of the weather, and you'll understand why there are only half a dozen other people here. One of them is a stocky man with a balding head and thick grizzled eyebrows who's

making detailed notes in a black pocket-book on the subject –
it would appear – of honeycombs, though the cells in his
drawing look rather more circular than hexagonal, so it seems
he is not a very accurate draughtsman. Far less so, certainly,
than the man who made the drawing Charles is still admiring.
Charles has never had the patience to produce work as detailed
as this, but he can recognize a proper scientific precision when
he sees it.

'Apiology interests you? Or are you, perhaps, an api-
culturist?'

The voice behind him is a soft Lowland Scottish, the man's
pale face stippled with sandy freckles.

Charles turns to him and smiles. 'I doubt you could produce
any honey worth the eating within five miles of here. But the
study of insects in general, yes, that does interest me. And these
illustrations are particularly fine.'

The man's flush of pleasure betrays him.

'They're your own?'

He bows, and extends his hand. 'James Duncan, at your
service.'

Charles frowns. 'James Duncan? Not the James Duncan of
The Naturalist's Library, surely?'

'The same. I am gratified to find that you know it.'

'I am a great admirer of the series,' says Charles, shaking his
hand. 'And the entomological volumes, in particular, are
excellent of their type. I was especially interested in your
description of the formation of swarms – one can only have the
highest respect for such a prolonged and painstaking effort of
observation.'

Duncan bows. 'I drew heavily – as you no doubt know – on
the work of Monsieur Huber—'

'Of course—'

113

'—but all the same, I do not think I am being unduly immodest if I say I was able to add a number of useful deductions of my own. Indeed, since that volume was published, I have pursued my study of bees rather further, and am considering a new work on the same fascinating subject.'

They have started to walk back down the gallery, and as they pass the man with the pocket-book, Charles notices that he is eyeing the two of them with distinct interest.

'You may remember,' continues Duncan as they walk, 'that I asserted that a honey bee can fly up to two miles in quest of food. Indeed, there have been well-authenticated instances in which they have been known to have covered double that distance, but these are relatively rare. The subject of my more recent interest, however, is the fact that they often appear to make the deliberate decision *not* to forage in the area immediately surrounding the hive, despite the fact that the source of provender therein may be plentiful, and the effort required to harvest it proportionately less.'

Charles looks across at him. 'That is curious. How do you explain it?'

'I suppose one must conclude that it is a act of self-defence. That they are attempting – in a purely instinctive manner, of course – to prevent predators or parasites locating their nest. Interesting, is it not?'

It's not merely interesting, thinks Charles, his hand going automatically to the folded envelopes in his coat pocket; it might very well be the breakthrough he's been looking for.

He's tempted to accept Duncan's offer of a glass of beer and more debate about bees – under normal circumstances there's very little else he'd rather do – but he has an idea in his head now, and he needs to find somewhere quiet to test it out. He gives Duncan his card and the two of them part on the most affable terms on the museum steps. When he gets back to Buckingham Street, most of the windows are already dark, though there are sounds from the kitchen that show Molly still has tasks to do before she sleeps. He stops for a moment outside his great-uncle's room and is relieved to hear him sleeping soundly – if rather noisily. The old man has been troubled by bad dreams, and on more than one occasion since Charles moved in, the whole house has been roused by shouting in the early hours. Charles does not care about being woken up – he has a talent for sleeping that rivals his cat's – but his uncle has already suffered one fall which Charles knows he should have prevented, and for that reason if none other, Billy now has a truckle-bed in the drawing-room every night.

Once up in the attic, Charles lights the lamp, and drags his copy of Cruchley's New Plan of London on to the makeshift table. He gets the envelopes out of his pocket, and starts to mark the locations of the receiving-houses on the map in red ink. The last one done, he steps back and contemplates his handiwork. The crosses form a perfect arc around the northern rim of the East Westminster postal district. Had he not met Duncan, he might never have thought of it – or seen it as merely an arbitrary and meaningless scatter. But not now. Now he has a new way to interpret what he sees; now he can find a pattern in this apparent randomness. The man he's seeking may well be no more conscious of what he's doing than the bees Duncan is studying, but Charles is prepared to bet his motive is exactly the same. Like them, his first priority is self-protection; like them, he's prepared to travel much further than he needs, to conceal his quarters from anyone who might want to track him down. Charles leans forward again, and looks more closely at the details of the streets. Armed with his new insight, the answer seems obvious. The heart of the arc marked

115

on the map is no more than a mile from this very room. One of the most infamous, intricate, illicit districts in this dirty, dangerous town. That maze of streets, courts, lanes, and narrow alleys, already immortalized – if that's the word – in Dickens' *Sketches by Boz*. A place teeming with people, and thick with crime, and Charles' destination as soon as it gets light.

Seven Dials.

And as we wait for the slow dark hours to pass, we might do no worse than stand, as Dickens himself once stood, in the irregular square at the crossing point of the seven narrow passages that give this place its name. Dickens talked of arriving 'Belzoni-like, at the entrance', and if you're thinking that you've heard that name before and recently, then you're right. It was this same Giovanni Belzoni who brought back the sarcophagus that holds pride of place in Mr Tulkinghorn's labyrinthine collection. It was this same Belzoni, moreover, who was the first to find the entrance to the inner chamber of the second pyramid of Giza, and the first to penetrate inside. Hence, I suppose, Dickens' choice of analogy. It is certainly true that Egypt can hold no darker ways, no more obscure secrets, and no more forbidding, claustrophobic tunnels than those that confront us here. In the brightest daylight it's hard to see far, the air is so dense with grit and coal smoke, and even a 'regular Londoner' would hesitate to come here by night, as we have. So let us explore a little, while we wait for Charles.

We could do with him now, though – if only for his near-perfect sense of direction. It's doubtful any cartographer has ever ventured anywhere near these tightly interlocking streets. The traveller who trusts to John Rocque's serene and civilized version of the city – some hundred years older than the map on Charles' desk – will come in full expectation of a symmetry of orderly boulevards in a seven-point star, as formal and considered as a London Versailles. What he will find instead is squalid and rat-infested passageways that open suddenly and erratically into uneven rutted courts, where barefoot children wallow with the dogs and play at tip-cat and battledore among the rags and paper gathering in drifts on the pavement. In these shops, third-hand counts as spanking new and most of the articles are so made-do and mended that it's hard to make out what they might once have been. The public-houses and gin-shops are only now, well past midnight, closing their doors and evicting their staggering and roaring clientele into the cold, where their shabby womenfolk are sitting on the steps, their shoulders slumped, waiting – as they have these four hours – for their men to emerge.

Some of these tall, high-ceilinged houses still cling to a fast-crumbling memory of grandeur, but if their dimensions impress, their interiors will dismay: this district is populated not by the house, but by the room – even by the closet. Whole families inhabit six feet square – one in the front shop, one in the back kitchen; two sharing three rooms upstairs. Most of the men are labourers, most of the women prostitutes, even, it is whispered, that so-called 'lady' trying to keep up a genteel appearance in the attic storey. Cages are stacked in every alley awaiting the morning trade, for – unlikely as it sounds – half the bird-fanciers and animal-dealers in London have made this quarter home. There are huddles of bony fearful rabbits, and birds of every conceivable kind – fowls, doves, fancy pigeons, owls, hawks, parrots, love-birds. An irony that last, if rather an obvious one, since there is little love lost between all these people cramped in so little space. Even at this hour, brutal quarrels are breaking out between those above and those below, and the sound of stamping on paper-thin floors is contending with the drunken bawling of the Irishman two doors down, who beats carpets by day and keeps his hand in by night on his wife and children.

As dawn approaches, the darkness finally starts to thin, and all of a sudden the light seems to gather and surge. The sky is grey now, not black, and there are the first signs of life that isn't four-legged or verminous. Coster-mongers and street-sellers are some of the first, but it is not too long before the dilapidated shops begin to open their shutters, and scrawny children appear on the doorsteps, chewing husks of stale bread.

By the time Charles arrives, close on nine, the matrons of the manor are in full voice, and as full dress as their wardrobes allow, or their profession expects. A little local difficulty has been simmering nicely for a good quarter of an hour and, fuelled now by gin, is about to take a turn for the physical. The urchin children are gradually abandoning their shuttlecocks and settling down for far finer entertainment – and free, too.

'Go on, Kat!' hollers one of the women standing by. 'Don't take no nonsense from such as 'er – the dirty tramp! Tear 'er eyes out!'

'You're a one to talk,' cries another. 'I know where you was last night – question is, does yer 'usband?'

'Does he even care, more like!' shouts a third from the safety of a doorway, and for a moment or two there's the risk of a sideshow skirmish to the main event. Kat, however, is not to be distracted; she has a score to settle.

'Come on then – out with it!' she hisses. 'You was up to it again wiv my Johnny last night, weren't yer? Don't you start lying to me neither, 'cause I can sniff out when yer lying soon as look at yer!'

'Go to it, Kat,' yells one of the lads from the door of the gin-shop. 'She ain't even 'alf your size – no contest!'

The other woman is now looking rather flushed about the face. 'Bah,' she spits, 'who'd a'blamed him if he was – I mean, who'd look twice at you, you stinking alley cat! Yer name suits yer and no mistake!'

'Who are you calling an alley cat?' screeches the other, rushing at her rival and seizing her by her thin dress. 'You – you *hussy*!'

The two fall finally to blows to the whistles and cheers of the crowd, and the barking of a number of lean and hungry dogs, who set to in a gutter brawl of their own.

Charles has been standing watching all this time, hoping he won't have to intervene, but old habits die hard, and even though he no longer has the hat, stock and belt, he still has the mind of a policeman. Though as he's about to find out, that can be a troublesome quality without a uniform to back it up.

'Come on, girls,' he shouts, darting between them and endeavouring to push them apart. 'That's enough of that.'

It's too much to hope that someone else might weigh in and help him – they're enjoying it far too much – and in the next minute or two he gets as many kicks and scratches as either of the women. But he finally manages to get the sturdy Kat off-balance and push her firmly against the nearest wall. It's only when he hears the whoops and cat-calls that he realizes he has each hand on an extremely large and half-uncovered breast. He steps back at once, pulling away as fast as a scald, feeling the hot blood flood all over his face. Worse still, Kat is not at all offended, indeed seems to have taken quite a shine to him, and is now leaning against his chest and leering in his face in a lop-sided, half-slurred way.

'Get home with you, and sober up,' he says curtly. 'And think yourself lucky I didn't call the constable.'

There's a sting under his eye that argues for a deeper cut than the ones on his hands, but there's not much he can do about that at the moment: he has no intention of going anywhere near the water in the drinking fountains here. The crowd is starting to disperse, now the show is over, and a few moments later a shuttlecock shoots so close by his face that he feels it skim his cheek. He wheels round, but the children are too quick for him and all he sees are dirty heels disappearing down a side street. He's starting to feel irrationally thwarted; this is not how this morning was supposed to be going. He had a clear logical plan, and now everything's muddled and confused. He stands for a moment contemplating the seven public-houses that ring this square. Two of the hard-faced women in the crowd are about to disappear into the Clock House, and he hesitates a moment before following them in.

Once he finally attracts his attention, this first landlord is not unduly taciturn, but what Charles hasn't allowed for is the sheer quantity of drinking-dens in this district, and the extraordinary lack of curiosity their owners seem to share about even their most regular customers. If the man he's looking for really is a tanner, and lodges anywhere near here, surely someone must know who he is, but four hours and four times that many inns later, Charles is nowhere nearer a name. But perhaps his luck is about to change.

He's left the last till last, because he knows from experience that it's the best this place can boast, and therefore – to his mind – rather out of reach for a common workman. Right on the margins of the Dials and everything the Dials is not: bright, gleaming, gaudy, and pricey. One of the largest and handsomest gin-shops in the West End of town, glittering with mirrors and plate glass and brazen with gilt. As Dickens himself found when he visited the same establishment, every window shouts its advertising slogan – *The Out and Out, The No Mistake, The Good for Mixing, The real Knock-me-down* – and every wall holds its

'Genuine Endorsement' for an obscure sub-species of gin we've now long since forgotten, including some – like Cream, Honey, and Butter – which seem to be trying to sell themselves on the basis that they might just be good for you. One or two even claim to be 'medicated', though how, and with what, they do not say. When Charles gets to the door, he can hear the drone of voices even before he pushes it open. It's lunchtime now, and trade is brisk. The inside is – if anything – even more dazzling than the outside, with a long gleaming counter, a spacious saloon (crowded nonetheless), and lines of green casks behind brass rails labelled with names like Old Tom and Samson. On display behind the bar is an array of glossy spirits bottles, and two well-upholstered young women for whom the term 'buxom wench' would have to be invented, if it didn't already exist. They look remarkably similar, these two, right down to the red and black striped bodices and artfully arranged beauty spots, and they're clearly as adept at dispensing drinks as they are at repartee, as the raucous laughter of the group of young men leaning on the bar proves.

'Put another nice warm rum in there, would yer, Lily,' says one with a wink, 'and if you want to put yer nice warm hands somewhere else in the meantime, then I'm sure I could come up wiv a few helpful suggestions.'

'That's enough of your filth, Harry Murray – if Mr Dudley hears talk like that he'll 'ave you out on your ear'ole soon as look at yer.'

She sounds annoyed, but she's blushing all the same.

'Aw – you wouldn't tell on me, would yer, Lily?' he smirks. 'Not when I'm so good to yer.'

He reaches out to pinch her cheek, but she's too agile for that (or perhaps she just knows this routine all too well already) and ducks away in plenty of time, to the vast amusement of the rest of the lads. They're by far the gayest and best-dressed posse in the place, for despite the gorgeousness of the surroundings, most of the clientele are decidedly down-at-heel. There are three washerwomen on a bench by the door, a group of bricklayers (to judge by the dust) clustered at the far end of the bar, and two old men who've drunk themselves maudlin, leaning against one another and managing thereby to stay reasonably upright, at least for the moment. There's a pinched-faced woman in a worn great-coat spattered with fish-scales, waiting quietly for one of the full-blown barmaids to fill her little flask, and two or three wan-looking children who can barely reach up high enough to put their bottles on the bar. One of the hawkers Charles saw in the street an hour ago is now touting his boiled trotters to the assembled drinkers, though it seems most of them would rather spend their penn'orth on something rather stronger. Charles scans the dingy crowd and finally locates the landlord, who has a fire of his own in a cosy snug, where he can keep an eye on his girls without getting caught in the draught from the door, which swings open every few seconds, leaving most of the room as cold as the street outside.

Charles orders as small a dram of rum as he can get away with. He's already had rather more than he should, but no self-respecting landlord is going to waste his time on a man with no drink in his hand. The fellow here looks affable enough, with his puckered red face and mustard whiskers, and tight round belly. Charles edges through a gang of loud labourers who seem undecided whether to clap each other on the back, or clatter a fist into each other's faces. They've clearly been at this some time, and show no sign of coming down on one side or the other for a good while yet, though a gambling man would probably bet on their level of aggression rising in reasonable proportion to the amount of drink they put away.

'Mr Dudley?' says Charles, with a silent acknowledgement to his unwitting informant behind the bar.

The landlord looks up and takes his pipe out of his mouth. 'Who's asking?'

He's not particularly hostile, just curious.

'I was wondering if I could ask you a couple of questions. If you have time.'

This may well strike you as rather abrupt, given everything I just said about the way Charles has been going about his business so far this morning, but remember that this is a very superior establishment, and he's pretty sure he's not going to discover very much useful here. Frankly, he just wants to get it over with.

Dudley looks him up and down.

'I've seen you before, haven't I? A while back. I've a good memory for faces.'

Charles flushes, caught off guard. It's such a long time since he patrolled the streets – either here or anywhere else – that he thought he was safe from embarrassing recognitions. This was never really his patch, after all, and no one else he's spoken to this morning showed any sign of knowing who he was. Out of the uniform he's just another punter; in it, just another rozzer.

'Well—' he begins.

'That's right,' interrupts Dudley. 'You were with that other fellow – Wheeler, is it? Little feller – carrot-top. I remember now – he used to come in 'ere a lot at one time. Saw you in the street with him once, nibbing a couple of dippers. That was you, weren't it?'

No point in dissimulation now. Charles – like those pickpockets – has been well and truly collared.

'I'm not in the police any more. I'm working on my own.'

The man looks sceptical. 'I've heard *that* one before. So what do you want with me – or my shop for that matter?'

'Nothing,' says Charles quickly. 'At least nothing I'm aware of. I'm looking for someone who may lodge nearby. Someone who could well drink in here.'

Dudley snorts. 'You've got your work cut out – hundreds come through these doors.'

'I know, but you might know this one. I think he works in Bermondsey. In the tanneries.'

The man's face does not change, but he drops his eyes and looks away. Charles knows what that means.

'You know who I'm talking about, don't you? Who is it?'

He spoke too eagerly, and Dudley draws back. 'I'm not sure as I should say any more. Not to you. You haven't even said what this is about.'

Charles shrugs, faux-nonchalant. 'Suit yourself. Though there could have been something in it. For you, that is.'

Dudley looks at him narrowly. 'Money, you mean?'

'Could be. If you lead me to the right man.'

'How much?'

Charles does a quick mental calculation. He needs to offer enough to loosen the man's tongue, without making him suspect how important the information really is.

'A thicker?'

Dudley's eyes widen. A sovereign is no poor return for a few minutes' idle chat. Idle chat, moreover, that's very unlikely to have any disagreeable personal repercussions.

'Well,' he begins slowly, 'I'm not saying as he's definitely your man – I only saw him a few times – but there was a tanner in 'ere a few weeks ago. Got bawling drunk and had to be hauled out by the pot-boy.'

'Has he been in since?'

'Once. Twice maybe.'

'Do you know his name?'

Dudley shakes his head. 'Can't help you there.'

'And that's it?' snaps Charles. 'That's all you have?'

'Like I said, I only saw him a few times—'

Charles makes to get up – 'If you think I'm parting with good money for that—' – but Dudley holds him back. 'Not so fast,' he says. 'I may not be able to tell you *who* he is, but I'm pretty sure I know *where* he is.'

'You mean—'

Dudley smiles knowingly. 'Absolutely. The pot-boy didn't just haul him out. He hauled him *home.*'

Chapter Nine

Bell Yard

The pot-boy in question seems sharp enough – an active, curious sort of a lad whose wits have been filed so fine by life's knocks and scrapes as to earn him the general nickname 'Razors' – but when he leads him to what turns out to be a dark and boarded-up house in St Clement's Lane, Charles' first thought is to turn on the boy and ask him what he's playing at. The ramshackle building flutters with bills for penny-theatres, law-writers, and dancing-schools, and all the windows are broken. No one lives here, and clearly no one has, for a good long time.

Razors is already turning to leave when Charles seizes him by the ear and jerks him back. 'I thought you said you brought the man here?'

'Oi – that hurts! And it's God's 'onest truth. I took 'im right 'ere. That's where 'e lived.'

'Don't mess with me, lad – look at the place.'

'Ain't my problem, mister. This is where 'e lived and this is where I brought 'im. It weren't boarded up then. He lived up there – up the back stairs. Took me 'alf an 'our to drag 'im up there, and no tip neither.'

He's now looking rather pointedly at Charles, who gives him tuppence and shoves him on his way. He gets no reply when he knocks on the doors either side, but there's a small butcher's shop two doors down, with the gas already lit and a crowd of women with knotted hair and torn shawls standing in front of it, contemplating the slabs and hunks of rancid greenish meat. There are no cuts here Charles recognizes; all that can be said for it is that it's meat, and it's just this side of edible; even then it's more than most of the women can afford.

He pushes his way to the front of the crowd and manages a word or two with the harassed proprietor. The house, he finds, was closed down weeks before, when the floorboards in the ground floor caved in on an open sewer choked with corpses. It turned out the landlord had excavated his basement and started a lucrative side-trade in bargain burials, with standard no-frills interments for less than half the price of the official graveyard up the road at St Clement Dane's. With two slaughter-houses nearby no one had even noticed the smell. Something that might also explain, Charles realizes suddenly, why a tanner might choose to lodge in a place like this. A quarrel now breaks out in the queue of women outside, but before Charles loses the butcher's attention altogether, he manages to elicit the one fact that has been eluding him all this time. The one fact – small though it seems – that will make all the difference.

A name.

A name that even Charles recognizes as unmistakably Cornish. William Boscawen, late of this parish. Lodging now at Bell Yard, Holborn.

It's an area, as it happens, that Charles knows well. Part of that warren of courts and lanes behind Lincoln's Inn, and hard by the far more palatial residences of Lincoln's Inn Fields that number among them Mr Tulkinghorn's tall and blank-faced house. Another fact that cannot – surely? – be irrelevant. Bell Yard, by contrast, is narrow and dingy, and the lad he corners by the entrance points him towards Cook's rag and bottle shop at the far end of the court. First impressions are not encouraging. The windows are all but pasted over with old law notices and Offers to Buy, and the other side of the glass is stacked to obstruction with oddments of iron and brass, and shelves of dirty used bottles of every conceivable shape, purpose, and colour. Inside the shop there are tables of chipped plates, tin pans and old rusty kettles, and the broken remnants of a horse's harness hanging on a hook, as well as sack after sack of assorted unsavoury rags, human hair, and ancient laceless boots and shoes, none of which seem to be in pairs. A sudden movement at the back of the unlit shop betrays the presence of what Charles can only deduce is the said Cook, eponymous owner of this unprepossessing emporium of unconsidered trifles. A squat, hairy man with spectacles and a moth-devoured cloth cap, his eyes wary and his brows low.

'You there!' he says, coming towards him, a guttering candle in his bony hand. 'Have you anything to sell?' He looks Charles up and down, then: 'Or perhaps you're interested in the room I have to let? It's a fine room, even if I do say so myself.' He squints at Charles slyly. 'You can live up there as private as you like. I'll ask no questions. Even if you should want to bring "company" home. Know what I mean?'

He winks obscenely at Charles, who returns his gaze with a controlled composure.

'I've come to see one of your tenants – Mr Boscawen. Is he in?'

The man screws up his eyes. 'Not him. Never here at this time of day.'

'May I wait inside? I've come a long way.' A lie, of course, in the literal sense, but not perhaps in the metaphorical.

The man ponders him for a moment, and then steps aside to let him pass.

128

'You can wait if you want. You may even find something to interest you in my shop,' he continues, as Charles stands looking about him, 'though most of it is mouldering in cobwebs, and the rest rotting in the damp.'

There's certainly a smell of something in this close, dusty little room, but it isn't rot. Or damp, for that matter. The air reeks so strongly of cheap gin that Charles starts to feel a little light-headed.

'You a friend of his?' asks the man warily.

'An acquaintance.'

Charles' tone is steady, but the old man's penetration is unnervingly sharp.

'What do you want with him then?'

'That's between me and Mr Boscawen.'

The old man sniffs and lowers himself carefully into a rickety chair. 'Never heard no one talk like that who weren't police. Or one of them accursed lawyers I see about here.'

'Then you'll be relieved to hear I'm neither.'

The cook nods slowly. 'If you're going to hang about, there's nowhere to sit. I don't go in for entertaining.'

'Perhaps I could wait upstairs?'

'Perhaps you could.'

'Would you mind?'

'It's not for me to mind. You *say* you're a friend of his, and I'm in no position to know if that's true, or if there's something else you're after.'

It's too dark in this gloomy room to see whether Charles flushes at this, but I can tell you he does. He turns away to hide his awkwardness, and sees for the first time that there's a narrow staircase in the corner of the room. He doesn't wait for further permission but makes his way quickly through the assorted lumber and up the uneven stairs. The first room he comes to is

129

obviously the one available to let. A cramped empty room with one or two scraps of old furniture the landlord has clearly extracted from his more presentable stock. The door to the attic at the top of the house is closed, but even on the landing Charles can tell that the air up here is bad; a cloying mix of soot, sweat, and the scummy fatty smell he remembers only too well from his jaunt to Bermondsey. The room itself turns out to be large – much larger than the one downstairs – but there is little in it apart from the remains of a coke fire in the grate and a low bed covered with rough ticking. Much more interesting to Charles, though, is the desk in the corner, with its pile of twisted paper and stumps of pencil. Boscawen is no man of letters, if this illegible and barely literate scrawl is anything to go by. But there is no mistake: Charles has seen this writing before. The letters posted to Sir Julius Cremorne were sent by this man.

There's a creak on the stairs, and Charles stuffs the scrap quickly into his pocket before turning to face the beady eye and watchful face of the owner of the shop.

Only it's not him. The man filling the doorway is thick-set, dark-faced, bearded. His hands black with grime, his trousers worse. And he has some sort of cudgel in his right hand.

'Who are yow, and what dusta think yow doing?'

Charles takes a step back without even realizing he's doing it. 'I – I was interested in the vacant room. I must have made a mistake.'

The man moves towards him, and Charles can now see the landlord standing blinking in his shadow, a furtive smile twisting his face.

A moment later Boscawen has seized Charles by the collar and lifted him almost off his feet. He's about to protest when the man's heavy fist hits him dead centre and he drops heavily to the floor, completely winded. He rolls over, trying to get back up again, but Boscawen has him by the hair and hauls him to his feet. His face this time. Jaw, cheek, temple, nose. Slumped again. Retching. Something hot running into his eye. By this time things are getting a little blurred round the edges, and there's a sharp pain in his right side that wasn't there before. Up again, and he braces himself, but this time nothing comes. The man brings his face close to Charles', and he can feel the heat and stench of his breath.

'If I find ee anist here agen, or hear yow've been arsting any more questions arter me, sure'nough I will give ee such a basting as will gut the bettermost of ee. Are'ee hearing me?'

Charles wants to answer back – wants even more to spit straight in the man's face – but his lips are so swollen he cannot form the words. Boscawen's fingers tighten on his neck, and he nods. The next thing he knows, Boscawen is dragging him to the door and throwing him hard down the first flight of stairs. Then the door slams above him, and he lies there for a moment, gazing up at the landlord, who is silently watching him, his eyes narrowed and a curious, almost exalted expression on his face.

By the time Charles drags himself the short distance to Lincoln's Inn Fields, the night is falling, and with it a sharp icy sleet. Anyone with any sense would have found a cab and gone home, but we already know that there's a certain stubbornness about Charles that does not always serve him well. More than one passer-by eyes him nervously in the street, and he's lucky not to encounter a constable, since he would quite probably have taken one look at his bludgeoned face and taken him in for further questioning.

Knox peers at him warily from behind the door, and it's some moments before Charles can persuade him to open it and let him in.

'Mr Tulkinghorn is dining, sir. Was he expecting you?'

'No, he wasn't, but I'm here now and I want to see him.'

Knox shakes his head. 'I'm not at all sure you're in any fit state to—'

The fury festering in Charles' mind heaves suddenly up and boils over. He seizes the pinched little clerk by the arm, and pushes him roughly to one side, then strides up the stairs to Tulkinghorn's room and throws open the door. His client is sitting quietly in his usual place, a plate and knife and fork placed neatly before him. To one side there is a glass and a bottle of port more than fifty years old, drawn from what remains of a bin that was laid down long ago in the cellars that lie deep beneath the house. He has eaten his bit of fish, brought in as usual from the coffee-house nearby, and is now sitting in twilight, sipping his wine. The sound of the door swinging open brings him to himself with a start. The sight of Charles, grey with dust, where he is not reddened with his own quickly darkening blood, is something of a shock and – frankly – quite unprecedented at this hour, and in this place.

'Mr Maddox. I was not aware we had arranged to meet today.'

'We hadn't.'

'In that case, I assume you must have something both urgent and significant to impart. Something that – evidently – cannot even wait for a bath and a change of clothes.'

Charles walks towards him slowly, taking the paper from his pocket, his eyes never leaving the lawyer's face. He comes to the table and lays the crumpled sheet on it with exaggerated carefulness. It is, perhaps deliberately, just beyond Tulkinghorn's easy reach. The lawyer looks at it, and then at Charles, then makes a gesture towards a second chair. 'Will you join me in some wine? I can have Knox fetch another glass.'

'No. Thank you, but no.'

'It is a very old wine, Mr Maddox. And a splendid one.'

'All the same.'

The lawyer nods, and swirls the amber fluid round and round slowly in his goblet. The room fills with the fragrance of the warm south.

'So what is it you have brought me?' says Tulkinghorn at length. If it's a poker game these two are playing, it is Tulkinghorn who has blinked first.

'I have discovered the man you asked me to find.'

Tulkinghorn sits back in his chair, and brings the glass to his lips.

'I gather from your unsavoury appearance that your quarry was not best pleased to be located.'

'There was an – altercation, yes.'

'What did you tell him?' The question is quick, possibly a little too quick, and they both know it. Tulkinghorn shifts in his chair.

'I told him nothing. He found me in his room, that's all.'

'And what do you know of him?'

'He is a Cornishman by birth, but works now as a tanner in London. In Bermondsey. And as this piece of paper will prove, he is quite definitely the man who wrote those threatening letters to Sir Julius Cremorne.'

'But you have no idea why he did so – no suggestion to offer as to his reasons?'

Charles shrugs. He, too, wishes he had found the answer to that question – but only because he would have so deeply relished the pleasure of withholding it. 'I wasn't in the room long enough to find out. Always assuming there was something there to find, of course. After all, didn't you claim he was in all probability just another motiveless malignant?' He's rather proud of the phrase, which he's heard somewhere before, but it's hard to say all those 'm's without slurring. His mouth keeps filling with blood, and two of his teeth feel loose.

'Indeed I did,' says Tulkinghorn quietly, 'and it seems I am very likely to be proved right. Who is this man, and where does he live?'

'His name is William Boscawen. He lodges above a rag and bottle shop at the bottom of Bell Yard. You might walk it from here in less than a quarter of an hour. Take it in as part of one of your customary evening perambulations.'

The lawyer betrays nothing beyond the slightest, almost imperceptible, widening of the eyes. He is not used to other people knowing his private movements. He takes out his handkerchief and starts to clean his spectacles, then – in no apparent hurry – opens his drawer, unlocks a small strong-box and takes out a purse of money. He does not open it or count the contents, but tosses it lightly across the table. This also, perhaps deliberately, lands just beyond Charles' reach. The two of them look at each other silently for a moment, then Charles leans across and picks up the purse. He's halfway to the door when Tulkinghorn calls him back.

'And the letters, Mr Maddox?'

Charles spins round. 'I'm sorry?'

'Could you return the letters I gave you? And the envelopes, of course. I assume you have them with you.'

Indeed he does, but something about the look in the lawyer's eyes prompts a prevarication.

'No. I'm sorry. I don't have them here.'

'In that case I will send Knox for them in the morning. Ask him to come up, would you, as you leave?'

Charles nods.

'And Mr Maddox—'

'Yes, Mr Tulkinghorn?'

'I'm told the chophouse on the corner does very good steak. You might request one if you are passing that way.'

'I'm not hungry.'

'Not to eat, Mr Maddox. For your eye.'

After the door closes, Tulkinghorn sits silently, once more sipping his wine. He is to all appearances more imperturbable and impenetrable than ever. At length he opens his desk drawer again, extracts a sheet of paper and starts to write. Knox appears a few moments later, and stands at the door, awaiting his instructions.

Tulkinghorn looks up and places his pen on his desk. 'I will have a letter to take in half an hour. For Curzon Street. We have a name.'

Chapter Ten

A Discovery

The great bell of St Paul's strikes midnight, and one by one the towers and spires of the city go through their hourly catechism of answer and reply, making the night air hum and jangle, so that at last, when all is still, the silence that descends is electric with after-echo. The fog came on again just before dusk, but it is clear now, and from where we are, we can look down upon the clustered roofs of Bell Yard, and the ramshackle huddle of its dilapidated buildings. But even as we watch, a sudden shadow darkens the moon, a skein of cloud carried on currents so high and distant they have no power to stir the dark slow flakes that are settling soundlessly on these slates and window-ledges and chimney-stacks. For some reason the atmosphere seems denser than usual, the falling soot blacker and more sulphurous. Come closer, come with me down into the rag and bottle shop, and your breath will thicken with every pace, until we penetrate the heart of this unnerving ticking silence and push open the door at the top of the stairs. The desk is as we left it, the grate still empty, and the papers scattered as before. But this time, on the bed, there is a man. His head is thrown back at an odd angle so that you cannot see his face, but there, on the coarse and yellowing coverlet, there is a dark and spreading stain.

*

When the dawn starts to seep through the half-shuttered windows of Charles' room the following morning, he turns over drowsily to shut out the light and wakes with a hammer jolt of pain. The ache in his right side has sharpened to a howl, and his face feels twice its usual size. He puts out a hand tentatively and feels along his jaw. He was worried last night that it was broken, but it seems not. That's something, at least. He hauls himself up and over to the wash-stand, thankful that it has no mirror to reproach him; he doesn't even want to imagine what he looks like. The water is cold and stings, but somehow that helps, and he's got to the point of slowly pulling on his clothes when there's a commotion on the stairs and the door flies open without a knock. It's Stornaway, bent half-double, heaving for breath, his face red.

'Mr Charles!' he gasps before he's even in the room. 'Something's gone off. Ye have to come.'

Charles feels his way back to the bed and sits down heavily; he can barely see out of one eye. It's only now that Stornaway gets a proper look at him.

'The good Lord save us – whatever have ye done to ye'sen?'

Charles takes a deep breath. 'I got into a – disagreement. That man I've been looking for took quite unreasonable umbrage at discovering me snooping through his things, and decided to make his displeasure known in concrete form. At least that's what it felt like.'

Stornaway is not deceived by the lightness of his tone. 'Ye ought to get a doctor to look at that face.'

Charles shakes his head – once only, when he finds how much it hurts. 'No need. I've had worse.'

Stornaway smiles. 'Aye, so have I, but it dinna make 'em smart any the less. Let me at least send up Molly with some hot water and bandages.'

'I don't need coddling. I need a drink.'

'I'm not sure as that's such a good idea.'

'And what were you saying just then? When you came in?'

Stornaway hesitates, 'Well—'

'Come on, man – you don't drag that old body of yours up three flights of stairs on a mere whim. You must have thought it was important.'

Stornaway suddenly looks a little abashed. 'The other night when ye were talking to the guv'nor, I heard ye say – that is, I weren't eavesdropping, but I couldna help but overhear—'

'For heaven's sake get on with it, man!' snaps Charles. 'You may take it as read that if I was concerned about privacy I'd have locked the damn door.'

'Ye said ye were looking for a tanner.'

Charles snorts and opens his arms. 'And as you can see, I have found him!'

But Stornaway isn't laughing. 'I heard it from the post-boy this mornin'. There's been a fire. In Bell Yard—'

Charles is out of the room before he has even finished his sentence.

When he gets to the rag and bottle shop, there's little left to see, but from what there is, Charles deduces at once that the fire started in the corner of the shop, then ran up the walls with sickening speed and into the shrivelled hovels on either side. There are at least twelve dead. So far. Among them a family of six caught in their sleep in the attic next door, and an old woman who seems to have been sheltering in the lee of the shop door. In the centre of the blackened rubble there's another body slumped in its chair, the skull mouth gaping, and shreds of cloth soldered into the cracked bone. The air is still fluttering with the scorched remains of old withered paper as Charles picks his way carefully through the smouldering embers towards the constable standing on the farther side. 'Good morning, Ainsworth. Any idea what happened?'

'Not difficult to guess, Mr Maddox. Look at this place – 'ard to think of better tinder. And I gather from the neighbours that the proprietor was in the 'abit of taking liquor. Was – to put not too fine a point on it – a notorious drunkard. Easy to see a candle overturned by a drunken 'and, sir. We've both seen that enough times. Even easier to see this lot going up like a Roman candle. Must 'ave been like bloody Guy Fawkes 'ere last night.'

'Where's the lodger? The one upstairs – is there any sign of him?'

Ainsworth gestures towards the back of the shop. 'See there – that pile of wood and timber? Part of the roof fell in. Compacted two whole storeys together like a stack a' playing cards. If your man was upstairs, he wouldn't have stood a chance.'

Charles starts in the same direction but Ainsworth holds him back. 'I wouldn't go no nearer, Mr Maddox, sir. Too dangerous by 'alf. The rest of that roof could come down at any minute. And it looks like you've 'ad one too many close shaves already.'

Charles shoots the man a glance but ignores his protests. It takes a few minutes to clamber across the deathtrap floor, but it's worth it, when he gets there. Under the rubble of singed joists and boards he can see a foot. A man's foot. Blistered red by the fire but essentially intact. As is the body, when he hauls the planks off it. He crouches down and looks more closely. The back is broken, but that could be the result of the fall; no way of telling either way. But not even the fiercest fire, in Charles' experience, ever left its victims with their throats cut. And not just cut – scored so deep that the head is all but severed from the shoulders. He sits back on his heels. There's only one conclusion he can draw: Boscawen was dead long before the fire started.

Charles stands up and moves back towards the source of the fire. There's no mistake here either – the tang is unmistakable. Sharp, woody, slightly resinous. Camphene. Notoriously – even dangerously – combustible, but still used to light lamps by half the householders in London. Half the householders, yes, but not, as Charles well knows, by this one. This fire was no accident; it was arson.

Back at Buckingham Street, he sits for a while with his great-uncle. The room is quiet and Maddox is sleeping in his chair, his breath coming in soft erratic lifts and grunts. Somewhere in the house, Billy is whistling. Charles reaches for the notebook in his pocket and his fingers brush the package of Cremorne letters. Apparently Knox called at the house in his absence, and will call again later. Tulkinghorn is clearly concerned to retrieve his client's property, though why there should be such urgency, especially now that—

But that, of course, is the crux of the matter. Not only why Tulkinghorn should have involved himself in such an apparently banal business in the first place, but why a man like Boscawen had to be eliminated in so brutal and permanent a manner. For there is, to Charles' mind, no possibility of coincidence in this affair. Within hours of Boscawen's name becoming known in Lincoln's Inn Fields, the man was dead.

Maddox stirs and comes slowly to, blinking.

'Charles!' he says after a few moments, 'you have returned, I see.' He stops and screws up his eyes, peering at his great-nephew. 'I hope the deplorable condition of your physiognomy is not mirrored in the state of your investigation?'

Charles smiles; it's obviously one of his uncle's good days. 'Quite the opposite. The investigation has closed and you were right. On both counts, in fact. He was a tanner, and he was a Cornishman.'

'Ha!' says the old man, snapping his fingers. 'Exactly so! So did you find out the truth of it? Such behaviour, from such a class of man, can hardly be a random act of gratuitous malice.'

'I'm sure you're right, Uncle, but I am unlikely to get to the bottom of it now.'

'Ah, I gather your suspect was not forthcoming.'

Charles' tone is sardonic. 'Certainly not when I last saw him, but even less so now. He's dead.'

Maddox raises his eyebrows, trimmed now, regularly, by the ever-diligent Billy. 'Now that puts quite another complexion on the affair. You are not, I take it, about to inform me the demise was accidental?'

Charles shakes his head, and gives his great-uncle a short resumé of the last day's events. The old man sits listening quietly, nodding occasionally, and now and then asking a question: timing, physical evidence, sequence of events. At length he sits back in his chair. 'You did not tell me that it was Tulkinghorn who had commissioned you. Had you done so, I would have advised you in the strongest terms not to accept the case. I have had dealings with Tulkinghorn of the Fields myself, though it was some years ago, and we were on opposite sides of the matter in question. He was a formidable opponent, even then, and utterly merciless in the defence of even the most insignificant interests of his clients.'

'But you were successful – you prevailed?'

Maddox laughs drily. 'We came, shall we say, to an accommodation acceptable to all parties. I think each man knew he had met his match, and neither was willing to pursue a confrontation that would assuredly have been the ruin of one of us, if not both. He has since paid me the ultimate compliment of one practitioner to another, and avoided me. As I have him. But you should know that even in so-called compromise he was utterly implacable. I am not, therefore, as surprised as some might be that this pillar of the law employed you to find a man solely for the purpose of having him killed. Nor is this the only time I have seen our profession made use of in such a fashion. Indeed, I can remember half a dozen similar incidents in my own career. In my case, however, I do not think I can recall a single instance where the culprit in question did not amply deserve his fate – indeed most of them would have received precisely the same adjudication at the hands of the law, could an adequate case ever have been brought. But you know next to nothing about this Boscawen, and there is, as far as we know, no such accusation to be made against *him*.'

Charles leans forward and puts his head in his hands. His jaw aches with a deadened throb, and he cannot rid himself of the uneasy conviction that he has been royally duped. After everything he sacrificed in the name of principle in the Boone case, despite the suspicions he's had from the first that there was something darker driving Tulkinghorn's demands, he's still allowed himself be lured straight into the trap the lawyer laid before him. He looks up and sees Maddox watching him.

'I was just thinking about another case. The one that got me dismissed from the Detective.'

Maddox's eyes narrow. 'I believe I warned you at the time that you had nothing to gain from setting yourself in conflict with Bucket. I know the man, if any does, and he does not take kindly to opposition from any quarter, and even less from his subordinates.'

'But I was right – you *know* I was right – Boone wore a heavy ring on his right hand – if he really had strangled that man, there would have been the marks to prove it—'

Maddox raises one hand. 'I agree, I agree. But that changes nothing. All the other evidence pointed the other way, even if most of it was at best circumstantial, and at worst trumped up. Boone was doomed long before he took the dock. As were you, the moment you submitted that report to Superintendent Mason. It was a noble sacrifice, but a futile one. Do not do the same thing now.'

The two of them sit silently for a moment, then Maddox leans across and puts his dry and freckled hand on his nephew's shoulder.

'Something tells me that once again my advice is not going to be taken,' he says softly, though there is no resentment in his voice.

Charles looks up. 'I'm sorry, Uncle, but I can't just leave it at that. Tulkinghorn has lied to me from the start. There was never anything gratuitous or random about those letters. I couldn't work out what was behind it before, but I know now – this Boscawen clearly had something on Sir Julius Cremorne – something so dangerous that they had to kill him for it.'

There's a brief knock and Billy appears in the doorway. 'Sorry to disturb you, Mr Charles, but that man Knox is here again. To collect a package, he says. Seems to think you'll know what he means.'

'Tell him I'm not here.'

'But I already—'

'I don't care. Tell him I'm not here.'

Billy's cheeks are rather pink, but he makes no further protest and backs out of the room, closing the door behind him.

Charles turns back to find his uncle's eyes upon him, and despite his injured and swollen face, there is a lift to Charles' chin that Maddox knows only too well.

'As far as I'm concerned, this case is only half over. I have Tulkinghorn's money, and I intend to spend it finding out exactly what it is he doesn't want me to know.'

Tulkinghorn himself is at this moment letting himself into his large and silent house. He's been on his travels again, having numerous clients with estates in the country, and other business of his own, that calls him often from town. All the same, it is undeniably strange, this way he has of moving from place to place. He seems always to arrive before he is expected, and yet his carriage is heavy, and his horses slow. And when he returns to London, as he has just done now, it is never by day, and rarely from the direction one might naturally have assumed.

From where we stand, invisible in the silent square, we can see that his tight dry features seem rather more animated than usual this evening. He no more believes in 'happiness' as a concept than he believes the moon to be constituted of under-ripe cheese, and if – contrary to all expectation – he has once or twice experienced a momentary sensation that could conceivably merit such a word, he no doubt deemed it an unpardonable lapse. But all the same there is an unaccustomed urgency in his gait tonight – an unusual energy in his manner as he takes a candle from the clerk's desk in the hall and walks noiselessly up to his hidden door, and then down into his private labyrinth, where there are artefacts seen only by him, and secrets known only to him, and spaces that no one but himself has ever penetrated.

Chapter Eleven

Covering a Multitude of Sins

*I*t *may be that you are the only one left who can resolve this mystery.*

Charles sits back in his seat, and puts his pen on the desk. It's rather a good conclusion, even if he says so himself. And it also happens to be absolutely true: if Eleanor Jellicoe will not help him, he can see no other way forward in the Chadwick case. Hence the letter to which this is the postscript is a careful mixture of the polite, the professional, and the pleading, which has taken him a good two hours to write. But now it is done, and now it can go, and he can turn his whole attention to Cremorne. This is meat much more to his taste and he has the whole day mapped out clearly in his mind. And mapped is indeed the word, for there are parts of this great city that will yield secrets about great men, if the right questions are asked, and of the right people. Charles' first destination, then, is Lombard Street, the very soul and centre of that part of London where the city acquires a capital letter, a Corporation, and a police force all its own. Discount-houses, stock-jobbers, ship-brokers, marine and insurance companies, share-speculators, share-scammers: Lombard Street and its branching tributaries are bankers to the world. And there, only yards from the Bank of England, sits Cremorne de Vere (Estd 1675), one of the oldest and most commanding of a clutch of old and commanding family banks gathered about the only such institution entitled to both a capital letter and the definite article. Cremorne de Vere is a graceful stone building somewhat reminiscent of the Royal Academy, erected by an ancestor of Sir Julius' with a penchant for all things Venetian. It is there still, looking rather like an elderly queen dowager these days, a little bumped and tarnished round the edges, and crowded now by presumptuous *arrivistes* in polished metal and plate glass. But some things do not change, even in a hundred and sixty years, and one of those would seem to be the need to post two supercilious flunkeys at either side of the entrance, as if the imposing porch were not intimidating enough. Charles, as we know, is not a man to be easily intimidated, but all the same he has absolutely no intention of bowling straight up to the front door. He's much more interested in what he might discover round the back. He's read his Donne, and even if he hadn't, his profession has taught him often enough that he who seeks the truth 'about must and about must go'. So about he is now duly going – to the nearest dining-house in fact, it being nigh on noon. After all, Lombard Street does not trade merely in money: gossip here is as valuable as gold.

Charles accordingly betakes himself to the nearest suitable establishment, a Victorian version of fast food known by the wonderfully descriptive name of a 'slap-bang' – you slap down the money, and they bang down the food. The shop-front has a fine display of artificially whitened cauliflowers and artificially plumped-up pork, but it's not really the food he's come for. The glass inside is steamed-up and the sturdy waitress is as plump and pink as the pork in the window. She shows him to a table in a private booth and is somewhat surprised to find he prefers a seat on a bench already occupied by a cluster of young clerks, but as Charles has already noticed, three pint pots of half-and-half are making these young men usefully voluble. He orders a beef cutlet, unfolds his copy of *The Times,* and settles down to listen, though that's harder than it sounds with the shouting from the kitchen, the bustling of servers in and out, and the crash of cutlery and tin plates being slammed down on the tables. The clerks have made short work of their plates of mutton and French beans, and one of them proposes another.

'Thank you, William,' says a second, whose clothes seem to have seen better days than he has: they, at least, must once have been *à la mode.* 'I really don't know but what I will take another. And I would not object to a morsel of that cabbage neither.'

'A man needs his nourishment, Tony. Specially a man embarking on a new professional connection, as you might call it. Last term you was most certainly on the wrong side of the post. Things looked very bleak then, and now look at you. Quite the man about town.'

'I will not deny it, William. I was on the wrong side of the post. If any man had told me this time a twelvemonth that I should be as hard up as I found myself then, I should have – well, I should not have credited it.'

'Fallen on your feet now, though, Tony my lad. Most definitely fallen on your feet. I have the pleasure of drinking your good health and good fortune.'

They raise their pint pots and drain them, and call for another.

'I never doubted that something would turn up,' continues the aforementioned Tony in complacent tones, 'and hey presto, so it did. I see a very smiling prospect before me, so I do.'

'I always knew you'd do well there, Tony. Didn't I say as much? After all,' says William with a wink to the others, 'the

147

l-l-lord and m-m-master is not a man easily impressed, or so I h-h-hear.'

This seems to amuse them all immensely, and Tony looks a trifle abashed. 'Well, we didn't actually *meet,* not in actual *person.* You can't expect a man like him to concern himself with everyday matters like that.'

William winks again as Tony continues: 'I will admit it's not quite the elevated position as I've been accustomed to, but you have to start where you can and work your way up. And I know for a fact there were at least a dozen other applicants. A bank like Cremorne can take its pick.'

Charles glances across at this, but none of them is paying him the slightest attention.

'It's certainly a fine institution,' says one of the others, a tiny wizened little creature with a short neck in a tall collar.

'None better, Chick, none better. One of the City's finest and no mistake.' Tony squares his shoulders as he says this, as if his new employer's cachet is already bolstering his own. 'You should think of making such a move yourself, William. Better prospects in banking than the law, these days.'

'If only I had the energy I once possessed, Tony!' says William with a theatrical sigh. 'But there are chords in the human mind—'

'All the same,' interrupts Chick, who seems to have heard this particular maudlin strain from his friend before and to be anxious to avoid it, 'I did hear a whisper there was a little difficulty at Cremorne a while back. Something about clients losing money and creditors threatening to sue.'

Tony waves his hand with what might, perhaps, be a rather exaggerated nonchalance. 'Oh there's nothing in that, Chick. Take my word for it. Nothing at all.'

'Really?' replies Chick, his simian eyes narrowing. 'I'm

sure I heard as how some of the nobs at Cremorne de Vere had put clients into investments they knew were going to fail, while wagering the other way with their own cash. I heard as how certain notable customers have had their pockets well and truly picked, and had to be paid off handsomely to keep quiet about it. "Irregularities", that's what I heard.'

Tony has by now gone rather red about the ears. 'Now, William,' he says with somewhat forced joviality, 'what do you say about pastry?'

'Marrow puddings,' he replies instantly. 'What about you, Chick?'

'Aye, aye!' says Chick, eyeing Tony with a knowing look. 'Thank you, William, I would not say no to a marrow pudding.'

'Three marrow puddings and three small rums, Poll!' calls William.

The waitress duly returns with another stack of plates and flat tin dish-covers and clatters them down, and the clerks fall to it again. Charles meanwhile takes the opportunity to pay quietly for his meat and potatoes, and leave.

The air outside is cold and damp after the heated atmosphere indoors. Charles pulls his collar closer round his neck and turns towards the West End. His next port of call is in that direction, and a walk will warm him up. He has plenty of time to kill, after all; Haymarket doesn't wake up until well gone dark.

In fact it's near eleven when he finally gets there, and the evening's business is in full swing. The pavements are full of women strolling and men observing, and the eating-houses, cafés, bars and assembly rooms that line the thoroughfare are packed with buyers and sellers who have already reached an arrangement for the evening amenable to all concerned. It's a pretty fair bet that every female Charles passes is a prostitute, since no respectable woman would run the gauntlet of this street at this time of night, but you would never guess it from their clothes. The harlots here ape the society lady in every frill, flounce, and well-curled feather. Charles has had all afternoon to form a plan and has decided to start, geographically as economically, at the top, and work his way down. This means Great Windmill Street and the Argyll Rooms, an enterprise newly opened by a particularly wily proprietor who's turned money made in wine into a crimson and gold palace of forbidden pleasure. He's a shrewd man, Robert Bignell, and his Rooms offer an irresistible combination of drink, dancing, illicit gambling and sex. All the vices the Victorian gentleman deplores so vehemently in public, and indulges in so greedily in private. And at the Argyll Rooms, vice does at least come at a very reasonable price, and there's no risk of encountering the wrong sort of whore. Even the architecture observes the most meticulous social distinctions, with the lower orders downstairs, and the aristocracy elevated to the balcony above. Charles pays his shilling and stands for a moment in the lofty hall, contemplating the motley collection of City clerks, small tradesmen and jobbing tarts parading it on the dance floor, and the satined courtesans and their clients lounging on the velvet benches above, drinking iced champagne and casting languid looks down on the spectacle below. The music is so loud it's hard to do anything other than watch – or drink – and for a while he does just that, noting here and there a face he knows, if only from the newspapers. He's trying to spot a likely candidate among the hard-pressed staff, and his patience finally pays off. He drains his glass and makes his way slowly around the hall to the bar, where he takes a stool at the quieter right-hand end.

His quarry is small and wiry, with a thin little moustache and something of a strut in his way of cocking a tray, and sweeping a napkin. The next time he comes within earshot, Charles hails him and orders a drink, but the man never looks him in the eye. All things considered, that's not so very surprising. When he returns ten minutes later to collect the glass and offer a refill, Charles puts out a hand and touches him on the arm. The man flushes; he's misunderstood the gesture. But it can hardly be the first time it's happened. He looks for a moment at the hand resting on his arm, and then – finally – raises his eyes to Charles' face.

'Hello, Jacky,' says Charles. 'Fancy meeting you here.'

The flush deepens, and the man looks quickly back down the bar to where the slick and self-important maître d' is supervising what is clearly a new and not very experienced recruit.

'Don't worry. He won't hear anything from me. Not yet, anyway. Is there somewhere we can go? Just to talk, you understand. Nothing "else".'

Jacky leans forward. 'I've a break in ten minutes,' he hisses. 'Round the back. By the kitchen door.'

Charles nods. 'But I'll be keeping an eye on you. If I find you've given me the slip, I'll feel honour-bound to have that little chat with your governor after all. Do we understand each other?'

The man glares at him for a moment, then nods. There's a tiny spasm under his left eye that wasn't there before.

He keeps Charles waiting, for all that. Half an hour later he's on the point of going back in and hauling Jacky out in front of the lot of them when the kitchen door opens and the man sidles out, looking more edgy than ever. He stops in the

151

doorway and takes a small screw of paper from his jacket, then stuffs a penn'orth of tobacco into his cheek and starts to chew.

'They don't let us have pipes in there. Not while we're working. And I can't stay long. They'll have my arse if I'm not back in five minutes.'

'Let's get it over with, then.'

Charles gets out a folded piece of newsprint and pushes it under the man's nose. It's a page from the *Illustrated London News*, and it took him most of the afternoon to find it. The quality of the illustration is not as good as he'd hoped, but it's a likeness nonetheless. A likeness of Sir Julius Cremorne.

'Recognize him?'

Jacky shifts his tobacco to the other cheek and carries on chewing. 'If that's who I think it is, he's a regular. Twice – sometimes three times a week. Drinks a lot of brandy, gambles a lot of money. Ideal client for a place like this.'

'Who does he come with?'

'Couple of other stuffed shirts. Same crowd mostly. Sometimes there's a stiff old geezer with grey hair, but usually it's another younger cove with a bad mark on the back of his hand. Looked to me like a knife done it – he usually keeps his gloves on, but I saw it once when I was on privy duty.'

You and I have seen this man before, but Charles, of course, has not, which means he cannot possibly realize the significance of this otherwise trivial observation.

'What about the girls?'

The man looks at him but says nothing.

'Don't be coy with me, Jacky. I know as well as you do why men like him come to a *place like this*.'

Jacky's shaking his head. 'Yeah, he likes the tarts. Has his own type, like most of 'em. Blonde's his favourite, but most of all he likes variety, him and the other one both. And they like to *share*, know what I mean?'

Charles' face is grim. 'Anything else?'

Jacky eyes him narrowly. 'There was another geezer he came with once – now he's a different kettle of fish altogether. I seen him before. He don't come for the girls, that one, he comes for the *boys*. Guardsmen if he can get them, specially the young ones, but he ain't that fussy. I should know.'

He moves closer, all his previous jumpiness gone. 'You know too, don't you? I mean, you might look all innocent and like butter wouldn't melt,' he whispers, 'but you and I know better. *Don't we?*'

And then the kitchen door opens, and there's the sound of an angry voice calling his name, and Jacky is gone.

Back out on Haymarket, the lights are even brighter, the music even louder, and the crowds even thicker. Charles has just stepped aside to allow a blue silk train the space to pass when he feels a small cold hand slide into his, and another close tightly around his balls. 'Fancy a frig, mister?'

He knows the voice; has known it, in fact, these five years and more. The girl standing behind him is tiny and her impish features heavily made-up, but there's life and real affection in the bright green eyes. She's arrayed in an expensive and extremely fashionable combination of ruby satin and white lace that clashes jauntily with her anything but expensive accent. Though as Charles well knows, she can mimic the gentry to perfection when it suits her – in fact this talent of hers has been more than a little useful to him in the past. He may have met her first in the exercise of her profession, but she's been invaluable to him since in the pursuance of his own, both official and unofficial. Informer, undercover agent, decoy, spy: Lizzie has been all of this to him, and more. As well as a true and unfailing friend. But there is one more fact about Lizzie Miller that you need to know, and will not discover from anything these two are about to say: she is the same age, almost to the day, as the sister he has lost. That other Elizabeth who had the same golden hair, and the same bright green eyes; that other Elizabeth he has never, in all this time, ceased to search for.

'I got your message,' the girl says now with a smile, before looking up in his face and sensing his unease. 'Somefing up, Charlie?'

'It's cold out here, Lizzie, do you want a drink?'

She shakes her head. 'The old hag is watching us – see? Over there, pretendin' to look in the shop winda?'

The woman's probably no more than fifty but looks and dresses like an old crone. As drab as Lizzie is gay, with strands of dry grey hair escaping from an old straw bonnet and dirty marks on her patched cotton dress.

'She's checkin' up on me – makin' sure I don't 'ook it in the bloody frock she spent so much money on. She won't be too fond of you neither, so you'd better be quick, whatever it is.'

The girl moves away from the glare of the lamp, and Charles follows her into the comparative shadow of a closed doorway, where he fishes inside his coat and pulls out his sheet of newsprint.

'Have you ever seen this man?'

Lizzie squints at the page. Those green eyes of hers are not just very pretty, but very long-sighted, and the smudgy images all look alike to her. 'Bloody 'ell, Charlie, that could be anyone! Dark coat and a beard – is that the best you can do? Half the blokes in London look like that, and most of them are down 'ere at least once a week. I must 'a shagged a dozen like that in the last two nights alone.'

'He's a banker. Sir Julius Cremorne. You must have heard of him.'

Lizzie snorts. 'If I 'ad a shillin' for everyone as 'as told me they was a lord or a sir or a bloody judge, I wouldn't 'ave to drop me knickers to buy me bread. You'll 'ave to do better than that.'

'He stammers,' says Charles suddenly, the words out before he's even had the conscious thought.

'What's that?' says Lizzie, her voice dropping.

'I think – I'm not sure – but I think there's a good chance he might have a stammer. Why – does it remind you of someone?'

The girl puts out a hand and leans heavily against the wall.

'What is it, Lizzie?' says Charles, grabbing her by the shoulder. 'You know him, don't you?'

She turns and spits into the street, which tells him far more than anything she's yet said: she's hardened to her life, tough as it is, not usually so easily rattled. 'Oh yeah,' she says bitterly, 'I've seen him.'

She looks up and past Charles' shoulder. The older woman is moving through the milling crowds in their direction. She's surprisingly agile for such a stout matron, and she does not look pleased.

'Look,' says Lizzie in a quick whisper, 'come and see me Monday – I'm off to Brighton for the weekend first fing wiv one a' me reg'lars – Bert 'Itchins – remember 'im? – but I'll be back Monday. Come and see me in the afternoon. But meanwhile—'

She's about to say something else, but the old woman is already upon them. 'Are you buying, sir?' she says tartly, breathing gin fumes in his face. 'Because if not, Lizzie has work to do, and I'd thank you not to occupy her.'

Charles and Lizzie exchange a glance. She looks – to his eyes – pale and stricken under the paint, but he'll get no more from her with her iron-eyed minder in tow. Monday seems a very long way away, but it doesn't look like he has much choice. He's going to have to wait.

Chapter Twelve

The Letter and the Answer

The following morning brings a reply from Eleanor Jellicoe, and an invitation to call on her that afternoon at her house in Brixton. It's a grey, drear day of low cloud and fine, almost imperceptible rain. Not a morning that tempts you outside; indeed, the sort of morning that seems made for domestic preoccupations, especially those you've been finding excuses to avoid for weeks. Like unpacking. Though to be fair to Charles, he has made a certain amount of progress since we last took a look round his attic refuge. There are now four shelves of books, more or less neatly arranged, but the rest of his precious collection is still bedded in sawdust in three large crates. He leaves the warm bedclothes to the cat, who bunches them up into a curled nest, and calls to Billy for his breakfast to be brought up on a tray. And then he gets to work. With so much more space at his disposal than in Percy Street, he can have the luxury of a rather more scientific organizational principle, and he spends a happy half-hour deciding which system to employ to group his objects. And so it is that he does not hear the door open – does not hear the girl's feet, bare as ever, whatever the temperature – approach across the wooden boards. Hears nothing, in fact, until the plate and tin mug clatter to the floor and he turns to see her face.

He has never seen a look of such abject terror before; never, indeed, seen the phrase 'horror-struck' as anything other than a ludicrous hyperbole fit only for one of Mrs Stacey's Gothic novels. But there are no other words. Her eyes are dilated black with fear and her mouth is distorted like a cry of pain. He starts towards her, out of pure instinct, but she staggers back from him, her lips moving soundlessly. And now he knows – the *what* anyway, if not the *why*. He is holding the menace in his own hands. One of the centrepieces of his collection, acquired – at a price – from an explorer recently returned from the left bank of the Niger, and about to occupy pride of place under 'Ethnographical' between the shrunken South American head and a Chinese *urh heen* fiddle (which is a rather finer example, in fact, than the one on display at that very moment on the upper floor of the British Museum).

The bearded mask.

He stands there, looking down at the thing lying there in his hands, and realizes with a jolt that this is surely the point. To him it's just a 'thing' – a treasured thing, a beautiful thing, but a thing all the same – a mere artefact, collected for its craftsmanship and prized primarily as an intriguing if uncivilized curiosity. Words like 'demon' and 'magic' and 'soul-eating' may be nothing but quaint pagan concepts for him, but he has only to look at the girl to know that it is not so for her. What little he understands of the purpose and use of such masks comes straight (or crookedly) from the mouths of European missionaries, but even such partial and ill-informed accounts are enough for him to know that she might now believe herself cursed – as a woman and an uninitiate – merely for laying eyes on it, just as surely as he profanes it with the touch of his sacrilegious hands. Charles is the one who feels accursed now – cursed by carelessness – and he plunges the

158

mask back in the sawdust with a hot flush of shame before turning back to the girl.

'It's gone. I'm sorry – I had no idea.'

Molly is still standing on the same spot; the only difference now is that there are huge tears coursing silently down her cheeks, tears she makes no effort to wipe away. Charles is seized with an immense, irrational desire to touch those tears – to put his fingers gently against that face. But he does nothing. Embarrassment? Fear of rejection? Mere clumsiness? Some or all of the above, no doubt. And perhaps – more to his credit – a sudden realization that this girl, too, must have been considered, at least by some, as little more than an intriguing if uncivilized curiosity. Which is enough, all things considered, to stop him doing anything other than stand there, unmoving, until he hears the sound of Billy coming up the stairs, and seizes the excuse to move swiftly to the door and close it behind him, leaving Molly standing exactly where she was, surrounded by the ruins of his uneaten breakfast. As he clatters down the stairs, Charles tells himself he's doing it for her sake – protecting her from Billy's all-too-perceptive eyes – but I suspect that this time he's being disingenuous, and I'm reminded of the old truism that it's the lies you tell yourself that are the worst lies of all. Something Maddox tried to tell him only a few days ago, though without very much success.

Half an hour later, Charles is on a large red omnibus lumbering slowly over Westminster Bridge. The traffic heading into town on the opposite side of the road is almost at a standstill – a line of carriages, carts, wagons, carriages and hackney coaches stretches back to the far end of the bridge and beyond, the carters cracking their whips and swearing. Crowds of clerks and office workers are making their equally hindered way on foot. Dark grey figures on a pale grey day; a palette of neutral tones. As soon as the 'bus turns down the Brixton Road, Charles realizes with something of a start that it must be two years or more since he came this way. He can still remember fields backing on to the rather elegant houses that line this street – marshy scrubby tracts of unloved land, in the main, but green all the same. Now the seep of the suburbs is absorbing these last remnants of countryside, and what once were villages are gluing irrevocably together in lacklustre London leakage. Meadow after meadow pass them by, segmented now into residential building plots. Here and there the outline of a street has been cut, and two or three show-homes stand on the corner sites. They look sharp enough, these little model houses, their paintwork unpeeled and their small squares of rudimentary garden marked out with posts and string, but those who buy them may find the workmanship belies the sprightly exterior. Corners are cut here, as well as built on. Further down the road, the 'bus rumbles past other sites which have clearly not attracted such an encouraging level of interest; here the ground is merely squared into foundations, with large confident notice-boards posted along the fence proclaiming 'This Ground to be Let'. Further still, and we're into dirty shanty settlements, where the dogs fight, the weeds grow rank, and rubbish is dumped daily by contractors unconstrained by such nice concepts as 'Health' and 'Safety'.

Eleanor Jellicoe's house proves to be one of a low unfinished row that peters quickly into a quagmire of red clay and gravelly rubble. The few feet of trench outside her gate suggest that digging did at least start on the drains, but from the smell and the slowly caving walls it appears work has stalled. And yet the thin elderly lady who opens the door to Charles seems remarkably unconcerned by the makeshift state of everything about her. There's a plant in a pot on her windowsill, and her little cottage is as neat as she is; it occurs to him as he looks around him that she must spend her whole life cleaning.

'Mr Maddox?' she says. 'You are prompt, I'll say that for you. After a lifetime of working to a strictly regulated timetable, my hours are now my own, but I still appreciate those who respect the punctuality of their appointments. Will you come in? I have made tea.'

The tray of miniature blue and white cups and saucers is set in a sitting-room barely large enough to hold them both. Everything seems to be constructed slightly less than life-size, and Charles finds himself stooping like Gulliver. He looks about for a chair sturdy enough to hold him, but there is only one other. He perches awkwardly, worried it may not hold his weight.

Miss Jellicoe pours, presents, and takes charge. 'Now. Your letter indicated that you had received my address from Mr Henderson. I gather, therefore, that what you have to ask me concerns my time at the Camberwell workhouse?'

Charles gets out his notebook, hearing the little chair creak alarmingly.

'Though I am not sure whether I will be of any use to you, I'm afraid. My memory is not what it was.'

Charles doesn't believe a word of it; he's prepared to bet the mind behind those enquiring eyes is as sharp as it ever was. He thinks, with a pang, of his great-uncle, not realizing that she has seen the look of sorrow cross his face.

'It is a difficult case, the one you are working on?'

He hesitates, momentarily wrong-footed. 'No – not especially – that is, yes, of course, for those directly concerned. But I am hoping to be able to offer my client some sort of conclusion – an answer to his questions, at least.'

161

Miss Jellicoe folds her hands in her lap, and sits back in her chair, clearly waiting for Charles to begin.

'The incident in question took place some sixteen years ago—'

'In 1834.'

'In 1834, exactly. A young woman was admitted to the workhouse that May in circumstances – well, shall we say, in—'

Miss Jellicoe nods. 'She was with child? I thought as much. I'm afraid that was – and *is* – an all too frequent occurrence. We must have had scores of pregnant girls come through our doors in the course of a year.'

The numbers, if nothing else, are not encouraging, but Charles makes an effort to seize back the initiative. 'This young woman was very young indeed. Not much more than seventeen. Pale hair, very slender. Does that remind you of anyone?'

Miss Jellicoe takes a deep breath. 'I can recall at least a dozen girls that might fit such a description, Mr Maddox. There were, as I said, all too many of them, and a sad proportion were quite as young as that, if not younger.'

'This girl's name was Chadwick. Her father came looking for her some months later, but by then both mother and child were long gone.'

'Oh dear,' says Miss Jellicoe with a sigh. 'Your client wasn't the first father to repent a rash condemnation made in haste, and he won't be the last, I dare say.'

'He was told his daughter had died in child-birth, and the baby removed to an orphanage.'

Miss Jellicoe gets up from her chair and goes to the window, looking out over the half-desolate landscape. There's a group of labourers working at a distance; the noise of their digging just audible in the misty air. A moment later she looks back to Charles, her face troubled.

'There was one young woman – but she did not call herself Chadwick, I'm quite sure of that.'

'She may have gone under another name. I'm sure that's quite possible.'

She returns to her chair and adjusts her shawl. The house is, indeed, extremely cold, and Charles notices for the first time that the room may be clean, but their two chairs and the low table are the only furniture, and there are neither coals nor ashes in the grate. No fire has been lit here for days. He wonders suddenly, looking again at her gaunt face, if he is idly consuming a whole day's ration of provisions.

'This girl,' she continues, affecting not to notice his glance around the room, 'if it was indeed her, stayed only a few weeks with us. She was very poorly both before and after the child was born, and we did not think she would survive. The child was removed as a precaution. A sad case, a very sad case.'

'I'm sorry, I don't think I take your meaning.'

'It was badly deformed. The child, that is. The spine was twisted, and the face strangely drawn on one side. It gave quite a disquieting appearance. I am afraid to say I have rarely seen such a face outside a circus. Or one of those deplorable travelling freak shows.'

She shakes her head, disapproving, and Charles remembers, with a quick rush of self-disgust, his own boyish delight at being taken to one such in St Giles. Even at that age he was, to be fair, far more interested in the wax models and mechanical contraptions, and what he now knows were – at best – pseudo-scientific displays of bottled foetuses and two-headed calves, but he still remembers the wretched look on the face of the trapped and tamed giant in the room at the back – *Before Your Very Eyes, Ladies and Gentlemen – From the Snows of the Himalaya to the Streets of London – Chico, The Tallest Human in the Known World!'*

163

'None of us thought the poor mite would survive,' continues Miss Jellicoe, recalling him to the present. 'And of course there were those who said it was God's will. The outward manifestation of sin and depravity.' She shakes her head.

'What happened to the young woman?'

'She was taken away.'

She sees his face and quickly raises her hand. 'No, no – not in *that* way. A gentleman came and took her with him. Said he was a relation of hers. As far as I remember, she was barely well enough to walk, but he insisted. But did you not say that your client's daughter had died?'

'That's what he was told, but there are no records. No proof.'

Miss Jellicoe looks at her hands in her lap. 'I was rather unwell myself soon after the young woman left. I cannot answer for what records were kept – or not kept.'

'Do you know what happened to the child?'

She shakes her head. 'As I think you know, there was an outbreak of smallpox around that time. Many children died. I fear such a weak and undersized baby would have been only too susceptible to that terrible disease. God forgive me, but in such cases death itself is often far preferable to the probability of an even more dreadful disfigurement. Nonetheless, I am sure it would have received only the best of care in Peckham.'

Charles frowns, and flicks quickly back through his pages of notes.

'I have here that the Convent of the Faithful Virgin Orphanage is in Norwood?'

Miss Jellicoe nods. 'Indeed it is – I know it well, and it is an admirable institution. But the child was not sent there.'

'Are you sure?'

'Quite sure. The baby was sent to Mrs Nicholls. In Peckham.'

'And she was—?'

'A dedicated and Christian woman, with the welfare of the babes in her charge always at heart.'

Her cheeks are now rather pink, and she looks away.

'They put the child in a baby farm,' says Charles softly.

'As I said,' she retorts, 'it was a reputable and highly respected establishment. I heard nothing but good reports of it, the entire time I worked at Camberwell. I can assure you, Mrs Nicholls' was a model of its kind.'

Charles does not press her, but he's not fooled either. The practice of baby-farming is not yet as prevalent as it will become later in the century, and won't become a public scandal for at least another twenty years, but his time in the police force has taught him what can really happen to children in such places. All too often the so-called respectable women advertising so innocuously in the newspapers for 'children to adopt or nurse' were little better than child-murderers, prepared to take an unwanted baby off its mother's hands for an appropriate fee. No questions asked, and never to trouble them again. No surprise, either, that Miss Chadwick's newborn child should end in such a place – the younger and sicklier their charges were, the better the baby-farmers liked it; several pounds for a few weeks' work was a handsome return, and the death of such an infant was so common as to raise not the slightest concern, official or unofficial.

There is a silence. After a moment or two, Miss Jellicoe shifts in her chair, and bends to the table to collect the cups. There is a closed look on her face, and Charles knows he has his cue to leave.

They return to the tiny hallway and he turns to thank her. He expects her reply to be as perfunctory as possible, but she surprises him by asking where he plans to go next.

'Back to town, but my destination is unconnected with the present case. I head for Curzon Street, Mayfair.'

And now it is her turn to look surprised. 'How curious. My last nursing engagement was in that very street. Number forty-six.'

Charles strives, not very successfully, to conceal his astonishment. 'You worked for Sir Julius Cremorne?'

'Strictly speaking, no. He was my employer, of course, but my patient was his wife. Poor lady. That such a thing should have happened.' She sees his uncomprehending face, 'You obviously do not know the story. Lady Cremorne suffered a bad fall some four or five years ago. She was found one morning at the bottom of the stairs. Her back was not broken, but she was lamed in the hip and has been in great pain from that day to this. I never heard her complain, all the time I nursed her, but she will not walk again.'

Charles frowns. 'I find it hard to understand how such an accident could have taken place in such a well-attended house.' He looks at her downcast eyes. 'Were there rumours about it at the time?'

But he has pressed her too much; she looks at him sharply. 'It's neither my place to comment, nor yours to pry.'

The next moment the door has shut behind him and he's standing on the rough unmade road, quite alone.

Chapter Thirteen

Hester's Narrative

I debated very much whether I ought to inform Mr Jarvis about what Clara had told me. She had not enjoined me to secrecy, but neither had she given me leave to talk of the matter to anyone but her. In consequence I was very doubtful whether I had a right to speak of it, and sat up half the night thinking and pondering. At last I came to the conclusion that I might do so, because I knew in my own heart I had only her good in mind, and only her and Rick's joint happiness in view. I hope this may not seem trivial. I was very much in earnest.

Accordingly, when the morrow came, I went to Mr Jarvis after breakfast, and said I had something delightful to tell him. He was in his own room overlooking the garden, as he always was at that time of the day.

'Then you must tell me what it is, little old woman,' said he jovially, putting down his pen.

'Mr Jarvis,' said I, gaining confidence from his smile, 'do you recall that night soon after Rick first came to The Solitary House? When Clara was playing the piano, and Rick was with her, and they looked so fine and well-matched sitting there together?' When our eyes met, I wanted him to remember the moment, and now there was an expression on his face that told me that he did.

'Yes, my dear?' said he, with perhaps just a very little impatience now.

'What I foresaw that night has come to pass,' said I. 'Clara and Rick have fallen in love. She has told me so.'

He sat considering for a minute, and then asked me a question or two, concerning what Clara had said, and how I had replied.

'You are not angry with them, are you, Mr Jarvis?' I asked, at length. 'They are, it is true, very young, and many years must pass before they can think of marrying. But I am convinced their love is true and will stand the test. Even if any dearer tie must be very far off.'

'Very far off,' echoed he, with a suitable gravity. 'Very far off indeed, I fear.'

'I hope I have not done wrong, sir,' I said then, 'in encouraging their attachment?'

'How could our Dame Durden ever do wrong?' said he, laying his hand a little heavily on my head, and looking into my eyes. 'But we must take care she does not overburden herself in the concern she shows for her fellow boarders. For there are others here who deserve her attention, and a Guardian who has first claim on her love.'

We spoke no more on the subject, either then or at any other time. I admit that I did expect him to raise it again, but I am – no doubt! – making too much of my own importance. I do know – or at least I believe – that he spoke to Clara, and I am sure, to Rick too. What I am now about to say has long been a cause of regret to me, and I have blamed myself many times, but I must steel myself to it and be as truthful as I hope I have always been in these pages. I am sure Mr Jarvis spoke to Rick, because I observed with pain that Rick and he were never quite as frank and genial with one another thereafter. Rick was civil – more civil, if anything, than hitherto – but all the same, a coolness arose between them that worsened as the months progressed. I feared from the first that this was all my fault, and that a corresponding coolness might develop between me and my darling, but it was not so. It is true that she became somewhat distracted and listless as the weeks passed, and seemed more often indisposed. Her appetite, likewise, was a little affected and no doubt for this reason, she took ill of a low fever.

I remember everything about that day – the weather, the circumstances, exactly where I was, and what I was doing. I even remember the little paisley shawl I had gone to fetch for Clara from my own room. We had been sitting together working, and I observed that her fingers were blue, even though the fire was lit and burning brightly. I was returning with the shawl and had my hand on the door, when I heard the key turn in the lock on the other side. I was concerned at once, for never, in all our time together, had either of us ever fastened our doors against one another. I called to Clara at once to let me in, and my apprehension was only augmented when I received a reply not from my darling, but from Miss Darby.

'Not now, Hester,' she called. 'There's nothing the matter; I will come to you presently. You will be with Miss Clara soon.'

But it was long, very long before my darling pet and I were to see each other again.

Within a few short hours, Clara had become very ill. Miss Darby moved her to a chamber upstairs, on the other side of the house, and though I begged on my knees to be allowed to nurse her, my Guardian would not even permit me to enter her room, saying I might catch the contagion of her disease.

So I wrote her a letter telling her that I loved her, and Rick loved her, and she had to get well for both our sakes. But despite all this, my poor darling grew worse and worse, and for many days we almost despaired that she would ever recover. How much I reproached myself then for not taking more care of my darling! How much I would have given to have taken her place, and restored her to the sunlight, and the sweet dreams of happy love!

My only comfort was my Guardian's tenderness and affection, which never failed, all that terrible time. Never had he been more protective of me or more assiduous of my comfort; never had I needed his care and kindness more. He would sit with me, and hold my hand, and I would cling to him as he kissed and consoled me. Nor was this the only instance of my Guardian's love, at this time, and I should not let it pass without gratitude and recognition. One evening, while Clara was still very ill, there came a gentle knock at my door. I said, 'Come in!' and there on the threshold was a pretty girl, dressed in a starched white cap and grey dress.

'If you please, Miss Hester,' said the girl, 'I am Carley.'

'And what brings you here so late, Carley?' said I, in some surprise.

'If you please, miss,' she replied, 'I'm to attend you, at your Guardian's request.'

I put my hand to my heart, it beat so fast, so overcome was I by this new instance of his solicitude for me.

'There's no need to cry, miss,' said Carley, helping me to my chair.

'I can't help it, Carley.'

'All will be well now,' she said with a smile, and patting my hand. 'You will soon recover your strength, and before you know it, you will be able to join Miss Clara once again.'

She smoothed my hair, then set about her functions, going about the room putting things to rights, and finally she folded my camisole and took it away.

You will wonder how I occupied my days, all the time that poor Clara was away from me. I had my duties, of course, and all the little tasks I took on to make myself useful about the house; indeed I re-doubled my efforts, in an effort to distract my thoughts and alleviate – in my own small way – the burden Clara's illness placed on the maids. Likewise I would often see Miss Flint in the garden. Soon after Clara fell ill, Mr Jarvis encouraged me to seek her out and talk to her. He knew I had always done my best to humour her poor distracted mind, and I think he hoped that in doing so now I might be brought to think less of my own sorrows, and gain a juster appreciation of all the blessings I still possessed. The first time Miss Flint saw me walking alone, without my pet, she came running towards me, her bonnet and shawl all awry, crying aloud in the utmost distress, 'Oh my dear Miss Hester, what sad news!'

I do not know if she wept more or if I did, but I do know that she soon had to put her hand in her little reticule and search among the paper matches and dry lavender for a pocket-handkerchief, and I had to take out my own. I led her to a little bench, where she sat holding the cloth to her eyes with both hands, shedding tears.

'Be so good as to let me have my cry out, my dear,' she said. 'I am a little rambling today, I fear, but if you will forgive me and not mind my tears, then I will be quite recovered presently.'

So I let Miss Flint cry, and I let myself cry, and it did us both good.

In a little while I composed myself and attempted to lead Miss Flint to talk a little about her own history, and how she came to be with us, which would, I thought, quiet her mind and draw her from sad thoughts. But I was much mistaken. She immediately became quite distressed, and looked about her in the most pitiful way. 'Oh I must not talk of that! Do not press me, my dear!'

I seized her agitated hands and held them fast in my own, doing my best to soothe her, saying I would never have raised the subject had I known the effect it would have. But she became ever more fretful, and I began to wonder whether my darling was not right when she pronounced Miss Flint to be a little mad. It happened to be at that moment that I perceived Miss Darby wheeling Augusta towards us down the gravel path, at which sight poor Miss Flint became quite irrationally distraught, and seizing her little reticule, quite ran away. I worried very much about this for some hours and spoke to Mr Jarvis about it that very evening, but he assured me that the poor thing was often given to such sudden and absurd flights of fancy, and would be quite her old self when next I saw her, and would probably have no recollection of the incident at all. And so, to my immense relief, it proved.

I also, of course, found myself spending rather more time than I usually did with the other girls during my darling's illness. My pretty room had become a source of pain to me; I could not bear to sit there on my own in the evenings, thinking of what Clara and I would have been doing together at that moment if she were there, so when my Guardian was not with me, I would sit in the drawing-room with Caroline and Augusta and the others, with good Miss Darby in attendance. Caroline was not nearly as reserved as she had been when I first came to The Solitary House; indeed Miss Darby told me she had made considerable progress, and could nowadays often be permitted to sew by herself and cut out her own work. Miss Darby was good enough to ascribe much of this encouraging improvement to my own influence, but I am sure that very little of it was due to anything I had done. At first Amy was not supposed to know (and indeed did not know) why Clara was not among us, but as the days lengthened to weeks she was eventually told what the matter was. She was always such a sprightly child, and I suppose it was unreasonable of me to expect such news to dampen her girlish chatter, or quiet her constant skipping about. It is as well that we hardly saw Rick during all that dreadful time – I imagine he was as anxious about Clara as I was – I am sure of that! – but Mr Jarvis told us he had a great deal of study to do and had no time to devote to anything else. Little time, as I said, for conversing with us and I cannot say I am sorry. Not for my own sake – oh no! – but because one might almost have thought Amy saw Clara's illness as an opportunity to ingratiate herself with him. I know there was nothing in it – that it was only her way – but she became rather insistently vivacious; one might almost have said flirtatious, if that were not such an incongruous, not to say unpleasant, idea.

It seemed many sad weeks before they finally told me that all my desperate prayers had been answered, and God had spared my darling. She was still very ill, still very weak, but she would live, and she would – at last – be restored to my side.

Then it was several long slow days more before they finally let my pet come and stand behind the window-curtain and talk to me where I stood in the garden, looking up towards her blinded casement, and loving her beautiful voice even more than when I used to hear it every day, and there was not a minute of the hour when we were not together.

And then at last there was that longed-for afternoon when I was finally allowed to go upstairs and see my dear girl, sitting up in bed for the first time, and propped by soft pillows. She looked well, my Clara, but not, perhaps, as lovely as she once was. There were hollows now beneath her pretty eyes, and a thinness to her pale cheeks. I had hoped that we would return to our old ways and our usual confidential manner, but as her strength slowly returned, I began to notice a change in my darling. I cannot say what it was that first made me think of this, and even now I find it hard to lay my finger on this word, or that gesture, but sure I was all the same, that what Clara had suffered had altered her in some way I could not define. She loved me as much as she ever did, I knew that, but there was a secret sorrow about her now, which she did not speak of. And one day, when I stole to her room and found her sleeping, it seemed to me as I watched her that even her always beautiful face – that face I knew and loved so well – was different now in some strange new way, and not the same as once it was.

Chapter Fourteen

Springing a Mine

Drawing a chair before one of the coffee-room fires to think about him at my leisure, I gradually fell from the consideration of his happiness to tracing prospects in the live-coals, and to thinking, as they broke and changed, of the principal vicissitudes and separations that had marked my life. I had not seen a coal fire, since I had left England three years ago: though many a wood fire had I watched, as it crumbled into hoary ashes, and mingled with the feathery heap upon the hearth, which not inaptly figured to me, in my despondency, my own dead hopes. I could think of the past now, gravely, but not bitterly; and could contemplate the future in a brave spirit. Home, in its best sense, was for me no more. She in whom I might have inspired a dearer love, I had taught to be my sister. She would marry, and would have new claimants on her tenderness; and in doing it, would never know the love for her that had grown up in my heart. It was right that I should pay the forfeit of my headlong passion. What I reaped, I had sown.

'For heaven's sake, let me hear no more of this sentimental claptrap! Can you not find something decent to read in that great stock of books of yours?'

Maddox aims a swipe of his walking-stick at his great-nephew's ankle, which very nearly meets its mark. He is lucid today, if a trifle cantankerous; Charles' idea of reading *David Copperfield* to him started auspiciously enough, but as time has gone by Maddox has become increasingly restless, first muttering occasionally under his breath, and now breaking out in open rebellion.

'Don't you like Dickens, Uncle?' says Charles. 'They were queuing at the bookseller's for this last instalment – I very nearly didn't get one. Everybody wants to know if there's going to be a happy ending.'

Maddox snorts and looks at him with undisguised contempt. 'Life rarely provides what you so tritely term a "happy ending", and certainly not in the mawkish fashion to which this fellow seems so attached.'

'What would you prefer? I think I have a Miss Austen somewhere.'

Maddox sniffs. 'At least that woman could write decent prose, which is more than I can say for this hack of yours.'

Another swing of the stick, which this time succeeds in knocking the pages out of Charles' hands.

'Though even *she* seemed to consider a wedding an ending, rather than a beginning. It is usually quite the opposite way around, in my opinion. And in my experience.'

Charles frowns. 'I didn't think you ever—'

'No, no, of course not,' Maddox snaps. 'I was not talking about *myself* – I was referring to the observations I have made of other people. Marriage is at best a hazard, my boy; at worst, a snare from which there is no relief, and no escaping. So you mind my words, next time you find yourself following a well-cut spencer down the Strand.'

It's doubtful any woman has worn such an out-moded article these last twenty years, but Charles knows what he means. The next moment Maddox is wiping his hand clumsily across his eyes, and banging his cane heavily on the wooden floor.

'Where is that wretched girl? It must be well past noon. What's got into her lately?'

Charles gets to his feet, feeling more than a little responsible; he's been trying not to notice, but Molly has become uncharacteristically unreliable ever since the incident in the attic. 'I'll go and see what's keeping her.'

Down in the kitchen the delay is quickly explained. The air is full of steam and there's a tray overturned on the table, and something leaking from under it that looks suspiciously like Maddox's lunch. Molly is doing her best to clear up the mess, while Billy is standing nervously in the corner of the room, looking red-faced and awkward.

'What's going on here?' says Charles quickly, addressing himself – ridiculously, in the circumstances – to the girl.

She looks up quickly, then resumes her scrubbing. He can see the tension in her pale, rigid knuckles. He turns to Billy. 'What happened? Come on – out with it – I haven't got all day.'

Billy becomes – if that's possible – even redder about the face. 'I was just trying to help – I mean, the tray's heavy up all those stairs—'

He's not a good liar, and even if he were, Molly has stopped scrubbing and is looking straight at him. Her mute recrimination reverberates through the room.

Charles turns to Billy and grabs him by the arm. 'If you touch her again, you'll be out of here quicker than I can kick you, and counting yourself lucky to collect dog-shit for a living. Do you hear me?'

Billy is wincing. 'I hear you, Mr Charles. Look it were only a bit of fun – she probably didn't understand, being one of *them*—'

'I don't care what she is, you will behave properly in this house or get the hell out of it. I won't tell you again.'

177

He throws the lad from him and pushes him out of the door, which means he doesn't see the quick smirk on the boy's face as he disappears back to the scullery. For Billy has just had one of his suspicions well and truly confirmed. As far as he's concerned, it's a truth universally acknowledged that gentlemen only stick up for servants when there's something in it for them, and in this case it's not difficult to guess what that something might be. Despite the pain in his arm, he's grinning slyly to himself as he sidles back to his boot-blacking.

Charles turns to the girl. 'Is there anything else Mr Maddox can have for lunch?'

She nods, her eyes cast down, and steps quickly to the pan smoking on the stove, where she takes a long wooden utensil and fishes a pudding wrapped in muslin from the boiling water. It's so hot she can't handle it at first, but it's eventually unwrapped, plated, and on the tray. Then she collects a knife and fork and moves to the door, glancing once and once only at Charles before disappearing in her turn. Charles is left in the kitchen, feeling rather stupid and extremely hungry. In all probability he's just given away his own meal; he's rather partial to steak pudding and Molly makes a very good one. He's still standing there a moment later when his eye is caught by the rapidly cooling cloth lying discarded by the stove. There's something about the pattern left on the fabric – the pleats radiating from where the pudding was wrapped – that he's sure he's seen before. Seen before, and seen recently; but his power of recall has deserted him for once, and he cannot for the life of him think where it was.

He returns to the drawing-room, and takes his seat by Maddox again. The old man has rather disordered table manners these days, and sometimes forgets which implement to use. Indeed when Charles enters he is hacking at his pudding with his fork, while the knife lies unregarded on the tray. There are dribbles of gravy on his shirt, and a smear across one cheek. Looking at him now, mumbling and staring, it's hard to credit that only a few minutes before this man was sharp, astute, categorical. This happens so often now that Charles is no longer surprised, but all the same he's by turns baffled and horrified by the speed of the change – Maddox's mood can plummet and soar as quickly and as violently as his command of his reason. Most of the time he seems completely unaware of these sudden and vertiginous shifts, but there are occasions, much like the one we saw once before, when his face is haunted – when he grips Charles' hands and stares out at him from eyes that are a long way back, and drowning in the dark. It's as if a rent has been torn in his mind, and corners of his character long dormant – or long controlled – are flooding through in rising and regular tides, one moment overwhelming all that made Maddox the man he was, the next ebbing back to reveal the battered wreckage left by the last swell. Even now, more than a century later, there's no aid or succour for those devastated by this disease but patience and understanding, and a great deal of what Thomas Hardy will call 'watchful loving-kindness'. Charles is doing his best to provide all this, but he lacks a map, to use another obvious if pertinent metaphor. So he sits longer than usual with Maddox, aware that he hasn't been at home much these last few days, and that he has hours to make up in his own conscience, if nothing else.

The meal finally eaten and the tray removed, Charles fishes in his pocket for his notebook and starts pulling together his thoughts about Sir Julius Cremorne. He's done more digging since we last saw him and is diligently pursuing both of the two fronts that have now opened up to him, both the pecuniary and the promiscuous. Like any self-respecting detective – then or now – Charles had his contacts in Fleet Street, which was then very much a physical location and not merely a metonym. And he has been mightily intrigued to find that there is no word – whispered or otherwise – on that crowded chattering thoroughfare about Sir Julius' less than reputable after-dark existence, which suggests that the man may well be prepared to go to considerable lengths to keep it that way. Indeed it showed all the signs of being an extremely productive line of enquiry, but it has already run into the sand; as far as Charles can see, there's only one way that Boscawen could have met Cremorne or his associates – one way that he has any chance of tracing, at any rate – but a tanner would have been very rough trade even for the lowest end of the West End 'sodomitical' clubs, and a series of discreet enquiries has turned up nothing. Of course, Cremorne's companion could simply have picked the man up casually on the street and concluded his business in a darkened alley, but in 1850 homosexuality is still a capital offence, and the risks of such a rash proceeding would surely be higher than any transitory danger-driven satisfaction it might provide. Nor is there any evidence that Cremorne's own tastes extend in that particular direction, which still leaves the letters unexplained. It may be that Ockham's razor applies here as it does in so much else, and the simplest explanation is indeed the right one, but if that's true and it's Cremorne's own whoring that has been behind this all along, Charles is struggling to fit Boscawen into that all-too-commonplace picture. London is at once the most swarming and the most stratified city in the world – class and nationality forge unseen barriers as remorseless as barbed-wire, but as Dickens never ceases to remind us, sin and contagion observe no such boundaries and permeate every order of society up to the proudest of the proud, and the highest of the high. But what deadly link can it be that binds these two men so wide asunder? 'Only connect' is proving a difficult aphorism to follow, and Charles has been forced, however reluctantly, to park the idea for the present, merely for lack of avenues to pursue. Nor is high finance proving much more fruitful. Charles has turned up the names of a number of investors who might have a legitimate complaint against Sir Julius' bank; several of them are prominent men in their own right, but most are wealthy enough to withstand this little local difficulty and none, as far as Charles can see, would have any cause to resort to the services of a man like William Boscawen to resolve the problem. But there is one fact of which he is completely unaware, though I do not see why you should share his ignorance: all four of the men who gathered together in Tulkinghorn's chambers nearly two weeks ago appear somewhere on this swindled list. What Charles *does* know, thanks to his friend at the *Morning Chronicle*, is that at least two of the other names are rumoured to have received substantial payments from Cremorne de Vere – no doubt for silences rendered – and a third is menacing to file a suit in Chancery. But given that institution's reputation for ruinous and soul-crushing delay, Charles suspects the prospect of litigation to be more in the nature of a lever than a real threat.

A few minutes later, Stornaway returns with the newspaper and sits down on the sofa to read it to Maddox. Stornaway is not much bothered by what he reads, and Maddox is – now – not much bothered by what he hears, so the two of them move jerkily from a review in Hyde Park, to a meeting in Manchester, to a thunderous account of a recent shipwreck in the East Indian seas – dreadful sights – death and dying – thunder and lightning – heaps of bodies cast on the shore – young physician steps forward – saves hundreds – clothes dozens – cares for the injured – buries the dead. By the time Stornaway reaches the point where the wretched survivors are falling at their saviour's feet in adoration, Charles has grown rather irritated with the hero of this piece and decides it's time to slip away. The day is wearing on and he has an appointment to keep. In Curzon Street.

It's a fine day and the demi-monde are out in force; those with title, fashion, money, or merely nothing better or more pressing to do are taking advantage of the pale and watery sunshine to stroll in the rather breezy air and gossip in their latest finery. There are, today, quite shockingly delighted rumours of something amiss in a mighty marriage, a whisper that the husband, poor unfortunate man, has been sadly used, and his lady no better than she should be, for all her pride, beauty, and insolence. The promenaders are passing on all sorts of delicious speculations on this subject, snips and scraps of which reach Charles' ears as he skirts the ribbons and flounces set equally aflutter by the steadily increasing wind, which is whipping up the last leaves left on the pavements into sudden eddies and squalls.

Curzon Street looks lively this afternoon – rather livelier than Charles was expecting at this time of day, and it's clear from the bustle of activity outside number 46 that something out of the ordinary is afoot. There are servants rolling out a strip of crimson carpet and attaching flower garlands to the gleaming railings, and two footmen in powdered wigs are erecting a red and white striped awning over the steps. And then Charles remembers – as you probably do – that the eldest Miss Cremorne is about to be married, and to the son of an earl, no less. These are no doubt the preparations for one of the innumerable splendid and excessive society parties deemed necessary to mark such a momentous event. But given all this activity, Charles is somewhat surprised that his new informant has the spare time to devote to idle tale-telling, so when he asks at the tradesman's entrance he's exasperated but not unduly surprised to find that the man is no longer in Sir Julius' employ; that he has, according to the vinegar-faced housekeeper, been banished bag and baggage that very morning and not before time, neither. No wonder the man was so willing to dish the dirt on his erstwhile employer – he must have seen this coming when Charles first ran him down two days ago, and decided that discretion no longer had as much currency as cold hard cash. But that particular equation only works if Charles can find him and conduct the exchange. The housekeeper claims a sour disregard for anything concerning the blackguardly Milloy, but when Charles asks the footmen at work on the awning, one of them tips him off that the Graham Arms, off City Road, might be a good place to start, 'It being Monday, and all. But the show don't start till late. About nine, front row, right-hand end. If you want my advice.'

Charles walks slowly back towards Park Lane and crosses into the park. It's still too early to call on Lizzie, so he walks on until he finds a bench and sits down to contemplate the crowds and collect his thoughts. A nursemaid passes, followed, somewhat sulkily, by her young charge, a toy hoop dangling unregarded at her side. The girl is wearing a large straw hat, tied with a ribbon, with coils of sleek brown hair twisted above each ear. The nursemaid is demure in a simple dark dress, but her charge is resplendent in a wide skirt of fashionable plaid, stiffened with corded petticoats, which are not quite long enough to cover her white lace pantalettes. The dress is expensive, clearly, but not very comfortable, if the little girl's face is anything to go by.

'I don't *want* to go for a walk today,' she says, stamping her miniature kid boot. 'It's cold.'

'I'm sorry, Miss Tina, but Mr Freeman gave strict instructions before he left for the depot. He's concerned for your health.'

'Papa *always* says that.'

The nursemaid sighs; however intractable young Tina may be, it's apparent the servant has more than a morsel of sympathy for her. She bends down and touches the girl's pouting face. 'Shall we go and find some gingerbread? There's a stall at the end of the Row.'

The girl looks sceptical. 'Papa says it's bad for me.'

The maid pinches her cheek affectionately. 'What the eye don't see, the heart won't fret over. It'll be our little secret. What do you say?'

'Yes please!' cries the girl, her small oval face now wreathed in smiles. Charles watches them move – rather more quickly now – towards Rotten Row, the girl skipping from side to side as she swings her nursemaid's hand. He gets out his notebook again and spends some minutes reading – again – the notes he made after he left Eleanor Jellicoe's house. Lady Cremorne's unlucky accident may have been just that – both adjective and noun – but Charles isn't buying any of it. The more he discovers about her husband, the more he dislikes the man – and the more he's convinced that he has a death at his door, and it's one that no awning can cover or garlands disguise. But the question still is *why*. What could a semi-illiterate Cornish tanner like William Boscawen have on a man as powerful – and as protected – as Sir Julius Cremorne?

In the meantime a couple have strolled in his direction. They too seem to have emerged from Curzon Street and they too appear to be in quest of a park bench. The man is upright, hearty and robust, with a lively quick face; the young woman slender and graceful, but with her features concealed by a heavy veil. They are talking together with such ease and intimacy that Charles takes them at first for husband and wife, but as they draw closer he sees that the man is nearer sixty than fifty, while the woman must be less than half that age. She is – indeed – young enough to be his daughter, but there is something that suggests to Charles that she is not. He cannot say what that is – the merest hint of a more than fatherly concern in his manner, or an even subtler assumption of equality in hers? The relationship is ambivalent, it seems, even ambiguous, but it is undoubtedly a happy one. They stop by the next bench, clearly as delighted with the day as they are with each other's company. It is only then that Charles realizes that there is something protruding from under the low hedge no more than a yard from where they are standing.

Charles sees it all as if in slow motion – the man bending to check whether the bench is dry – the young woman gasping and holding her hand to her face – the man turning to her and then following her line of sight – the woman sinking on to the bench – the man torn between his concern for her, and the horror of what's suddenly before him. A moment later Charles has pushed straight past him and is on his knees, doing what he can to put himself between the young woman on the bench and the body of a young girl lying motionless on the damp hard earth. She can't be more than eleven or twelve, and her thick red hair and pale white face are both ground in dirt. She has a thin cotton shirt clinging to her shoulders but very little else, and a pair of shoes that are far too big for her, tied to her feet with string. Charles takes off his coat and is just tucking it round her when he realizes that the young woman has joined him, and is quietly chafing the girl's hands and rubbing her temples. In a few moments the girl begins to stir, and her lips look less bluish, and she eventually opens her eyes and stares, somewhat wildly, at Charles.

'Leave me alone – I ain't done nuffin'!' she cries, pulling away from him.

'Hush, hush,' says the young woman. 'There is no cause for alarm. This young man is just trying to help you.'

'He ain't police?' says the girl in terror, huddling against her.

'No,' says Charles. 'I'm not police.'

The young woman looks up at him. 'Perhaps you might withdraw for a moment, sir? I will endeavour to put her more at her ease. And then we can decide what best to do.'

Charles steps back to the bench, and takes up a position next to the man. They both watch in silence as the young woman rests the girl's head on her shoulder, whispering to her gently all the while as she takes out her own handkerchief to wipe the dirt from her face.

'The lady seems to have a talent for compassion,' says Charles, in undisguised admiration.

The man looks at him quickly, then resumes his careful assiduous gaze. 'I doubt there is a man or woman in London who has more kindness and forethought for those around her than the lady before your eyes. The brightness about her is the brightness of angels.'

'Your daughter, sir?'

'My ward. These ten years and more. And she repays my care twenty-thousandfold, and twenty more to that, every hour in every day!'

Charles falls silent; humbled, perhaps, by the barely suppressed emotion in the man's voice. After some moments the girl seems calmer and the young woman helps her to her feet. She places an arm about the girl's shoulders and brings her slowly towards them.

'Sarah has need of a hot meal, and then somewhere warm to sleep.'

Charles looks at her, and then at her gentleman companion. 'I can fetch something from the stall on Park Lane.'

The young woman inclines her head. 'If you would be so good. And in the meantime we will confer about what is to be done.'

When Charles returns with tea and a hot meat pie, the two of them seem to have reached a decision. As the girl crams pieces of pastry into her mouth without any refinement whatsoever, the young woman explains that she's been living in a lodging-house in St Giles, 'but has had a disagreement with the proprietor. When she was unable to pay for last night's accommodation in advance he refused her a bed, which is quite deplorable, especially on such a cold night. Anything might have become of her.'

To Charles' mind, 'anything' already has, and often. He glances at Sarah, who stares back at him, her eyes wary. An unspoken communication passes between them, and he knows that the version of events she's given the young woman is very far from the truth of it. Perhaps she's trying to protect her protector from the brutal reality of the rookery padding-kens; perhaps she has a shrewd eye for a soft touch; either way, the girl suddenly looks far more the whore she probably is than the unlucky innocent the genteel pair clearly believe her to be.

'Where is it?' he says. 'The lodging-house?'

The girl's eyes narrow. 'Church Lane. McCarthy's.'

Charles nods. 'I know it.'

And he does. Last time he saw the place it was high summer and the largest of the small rooms had fourteen coarse beds, the grey linen rife with vermin and the occupants not much better. Even with every window and door open the stench was unbearable, and when he put his hand to the blackened wall he'd found it crusted with cockroaches. There was nothing but a bucket for sanitation, and no possibility of privacy for any personal function, be it menstrual, matrimonial, or excremental. In some rooms whole families were sleeping in the same bed, even in the middle of the day; in others, two or three girls as young as Sarah had no choice but to share with men much older, and from there to actual prostitution was the smallest of tiny steps.

The young woman turns to Sarah. 'We will accompany you. I am sure if we were to speak to the proprietor—'

The girl's eyes widen and Charles quickly interposes, 'There's no need to trouble yourself, miss. I will see the young lady home. I am sure you have more important things to do with your day.'

The young woman seems to stiffen slightly. He cannot see her face through the veil, but her beautiful voice expresses gentle reproach. 'There can be nothing more important than Christian charity to our fellow beings, Mr—'

'Maddox. Charles Maddox.'

'You undertake to accompany her safely to Church Lane?'

Charles bows. 'I will consider it a sacred duty,' he answers, wondering, even as he says the words, what it is about this young woman that leads him to behave – and talk – so uncharacteristically.

She turns to the girl. 'If you are again in difficulty, please apply to the Asylum for the Houseless Poor in Cripplegate. It is only open on freezing nights, but it is a respectable place, and if you give my name to the superintendent, he will ensure you are treated well.'

She presses a card into the girl's grasp, but from the way Sarah squints at it, it's clear to Charles, at least, that she cannot read. It's high time to go.

Feeling more than a little foolish, he offers his arm to Sarah and bows to the couple. The man shakes the girl's hand in farewell; more, it seems, as a discreet means of passing her a coin than for reasons of politeness. As he and Sarah walk back towards Park Lane, Charles sees the young woman standing watching them for some minutes, before her companion touches her gently on the arm and they turn away.

'Gawd, did you ever see the like?' says Sarah gaily, biting the sovereign then rubbing it against her bare thigh. 'Fell on me feet there, eh?'

Charles frowns; it's not so very different from what he himself is thinking, but putting it into such coarse words seems something akin to a profanity.

'She was very kind to you,' he says tersely.

''Course she was. Makes no difference to 'er.'

'Do you want to go back to McCarthy's? Or to that other place she mentioned?'

'Cripplegate – Christ no! 'Ave you seen the place? Tried it out when I first came to Lunnon. Terrible bloody dump. But I ain't goin' back to McCarthy's neither. Some 'orrible old tooler wanted some for free, and then kicked off when I told 'im he could pay up or 'ook it. And then I was just settin' meself up for the night on that bench when some bastard nicked me coat. Christ it was cold.'

Charles looks sideways at her, but his sympathy stalls when he realizes the young woman's handkerchief is tucked into the neck of the girl's shirt. And, more to the point, there's a small grubby hand digging round in the pocket of the coat he has – perhaps unwisely – left wrapped around her. He hauls her round to face him and drags the coat, none too gently, from her shoulders and puts it back on.

Sarah laughs. 'Don't worry, mister – I ain't robbed yer! And I didn't rob 'er, neither,' she adds quickly, seeing his face. 'She *gave* this to me, cross me 'eart.' She holds out the handkerchief

189

in one hand and sets it fluttering in the breeze. 'Nice bit a'cloth though – I know a few fogle-hunters'd give me a good few bob for this.'

Charles tries to snatch it from her but she's too quick – suspiciously quick, in fact, and he catches hold of her wrist with one hand, and checks through his pockets again with the other. Only then does he let her go, and they continue, rather less comfortably, on their way.

'You don't 'ave to come wiv me,' says the girl sulkily. 'I'm all right on me own.'

'I said I would, so I will. Where do you want to go?'

Sarah shrugs. 'I'll find somewheres. Always 'ave before.'

Charles sighs, 'I think I know somewhere you can stay for a day or so. If' – this with a glance at her shoes – 'you're capable of walking a mile or so.'

For a few shillings he can probably persuade Lizzie to put her up, and for a few shillings more ask her to keep an eye out for the girl for a while. Sarah's chosen a dangerous profession; she may well need someone decent to turn to.

Sarah enjoys their walk far more than Charles does. He stops her at the first second-hand clothes stall they come to on Oxford Street and makes her invest part of her new wealth in a decent if rather threadbare military coat. It takes what he considers an unconscionable time to root through all the jumble, but Sarah eventually picks out a dark green merino shawl, badly stained on one side but fringed with bright emerald silk. Thus decked out she becomes animated, almost coquettish, and he's forced to acknowledge that she has an eye for colour if nothing else. The green makes richer the red in her hair and the swing of the man's coat flatters her slender tomboyish figure. For a moment – just a moment – he feels a distinct and absurd stirring of desire, which he stifles ruthlessly by reminding himself that this girl can't be more than a few years older than the little Park Lane princess he saw earlier, as suffocated by her stiff plaid as she clearly was by parental anxiety. He quickens his pace and forces Sarah to run to keep up; the sooner this enforced excursion is done with, the better.

When they eventually reach the house near Golden Square there's no sign of life, but that's no great surprise at this time of day. He tells Sarah to wait at the front, and goes down the narrow alley at the side to the shabby one-up-one-down cottages at the back, thrown up some years ago on what was once a leafy garden. Lizzie lives at number 5, but there's no answer from her door. The only ground-floor window is covered with a thick curtain, no doubt to keep in the heat from the meagre fire. Charles knows where she keeps the spare key, and decides that his own need to have done with Sarah is more pressing than Lizzie's for a few more minutes' sleep. When the door creaks open, his eyes are momentarily blinded by the contrast between the bright sunshine outdoors and the darkness inside. He knows this room well – he's slept here more than once himself – but as his senses adjust, something about it strikes a strange note. It's a small squalid space, no more than ten or twelve feet square, sparsely furnished and damp for nine months of the year. But behind the bed, on the left-hand wall, the unplastered brick seems to him oddly dark – in fact not just dark but thick with something that – he sees now – is dripping its slow way on to the floor and congealing in pools on the bare boards.

Blood.

Appalling, inconceivable quantities of it. Charles stands there, almost stupefied. The room is like a slaughterhouse, and it's only much later that he will realize exactly what it is that's strewn about his feet in such raw glutinous slabs. For the moment, all he can see is what's on the bed. *What*, not *who*, for identity – personality – self – have been brutally obliterated. It's Lizzie, but he only knows that because he knows the little rose tattoo still visible on her right shoulder. She's turned towards him but does not face him – cannot face him because someone has taken a knife to her skin and hewn her pretty features away, leaving only a sodden coagulating mass of flesh. The policeman in Charles computes – almost automatically – that this must have been some time after the killer hacked her throat through with such ferocity that he can see her spinal bones; the man in him has the tiniest moment of relief that she was spared that, at least. Though whether she was still alive when her breasts were sliced off and her torso ripped open from neck to thigh is far less clear. Coils of gut and offal are dragged across the tangled bedding, and her legs gape open in a gruesome parody of birth, or sex. Charles is hit suddenly by a memory – an image of himself on that bed – of Lizzie in not so very different a pose – and he staggers, reaches for the wall to stop himself sinking and spews acid vomit all over the floor.

A moment later he hears a sound in the court outside and Sarah's voice calling to him. He forces himself out of the room into the open air and shuts the door.

'Find a constable,' he gasps hoarsely, wiping his face with the back of his hand, then – louder – '*quickly!*'

As soon as she's gone, Charles drops slowly to the ground and sits there, his back to the door, his mind and heart in tumult. It's only when he hears the sound of feet coming back down the passage-way – five minutes later? ten? – that he opens his eyes and looks up. Sarah stands there, looking down at him, and beside her – amazingly – is the round red face of Sam Wheeler, who seems as astonished to see Charles as Charles is relieved to see him. He tries to get up, only to see a cloud of prickling stars and slide back down. He feels Sam's hand on his shoulder. 'Take it easy, old mate. Looks like you've had a shock.'

'It's in there,' says Charles weakly. '*She's* in there.'

He doesn't see Sam's concerned look back at him, as he pauses on the threshold before pushing open the door. The next thing he remembers is Sam crouched down next to him, talking softly in his ear.

'The doctor's on his way and I've sent one of my lads for reinforcements. But before they get here, I need you to tell me what happened. We need to get this straight. Just between you and me – you follow? So I know what to say.'

Charles is starting to stammer something incoherent when he realizes there's a strange tone to Sam's voice. He looks up at him. 'Christ, Sam, you don't think I had anything to do with this?'

Sam should look shamefaced, but doesn't. 'Well you found 'er, didn't you? Remember what Inspector Field always says – he who 'appens on it 'appen done it. And I mean – look at you.'

Charles glances down and realizes, for the first time, that there's blood on his hands, which means there's probably some on his face too. It must have come from the door, or the wall, because he can't remember touching anything else. He looks up to Sam. 'I've been here half an hour – no more. Ask the girl, she'll tell you. And you know as well as I do that this must have happened hours ago – probably some time last night. Get your lads to start questioning the neighbours.'

Sam doesn't seem to be listening. 'But you knew 'er, didn't you – that woman in there – it's that Lizzie Miller, ain't it? Hard to tell under all that blood, but I thought she was lodgin' round 'ere last I 'eard.'

'Yes it's her, and yes I knew her. I was bringing that girl here to see if she could cadge a bed for a few days. That's all.'

'So 'ow come you 'ad a key? That's what the girl said.'

'I didn't *have* the key, I just knew where she kept the spare. I've only been here once or twice – three times at the most.'

'So when did you last see her – Lizzie?'

Charles hesitates, aware that the truth sits a little awkwardly with what he's just said, but that lying is probably worse. 'A few days ago. And no,' he continues quickly, seeing Sam's face, 'it wasn't here, and it wasn't for that. I met her in Haymarket. She had some information for me.'

Sam frowns. 'What sort of information?'

'I can't say. It's to do with a case.'

'Come on, Chas! You wouldn't take that for an answer if you was in my shoes! Here you are, up to your elbows in blood and gore and nothin' but a twelve-year-old whore to back you up. I need more than that – you know I do.'

'Jesus, Sam – do you seriously think that if I'd been responsible for that – that – *butchery* – in there, I'd have walked away with just a few piffling splashes on my damn hands? The man who did that must have been absolutely saturated with blood by the time he'd finished with her.'

Sam is shaking his head. 'There's no proof you didn't kill 'er hours ago. You could have burned what you were wearin' by now and come back 'ere all washed and brushed with a witness in tow, just to throw us off the scent.'

They stare at each other and there's a moment when Sam wonders if his old colleague is about to hit him, but then Charles shakes his head and sighs 'In that case, you'd better get your bracelets out and take me in. But in the meantime you can send a constable to Buckingham Street, where Abel Stornaway will happily confirm I was nowhere near this place last night.'

Sam opens his mouth to say something, but we'll never know what it was, because they're interrupted at that moment by the arrival of the doctor – a very respectable old gentleman with grey hair and spectacles, carrying a large black bag. He is surprisingly composed in the face of the savagery inside, and betrays nothing more than a certain pallor about the jowls when he re-emerges to inform them – somewhat superfluously – that all life is extinct.

'The victim has been dead a good few hours, I should say. Difficult to tell exactly which of the blows killed her, but I suspect it was the incision to the carotid artery.' He wipes his hands on a large white handkerchief. 'As I'm sure you are aware, there are remnants of viscera all over the room. Someone will have to gather them up and ensure they accompany the corpse to the mortuary. I will forward my own report to Inspector Field in due course. Good morning to you.'

As soon as he's gone, Charles gets to his feet, brushes down his coat and holds out his wrists. Whereupon Sarah starts shouting, 'Leave 'im alone – he didn't do it – 'e was wiv me!'

It takes two constables to constrain her, and she's only finally persuaded to calm down when Charles warns her she risks joining him in the cells if she doesn't. Another half-hour later and we find her in a back room of the Bow Street station-house, giving a statement to one of Sam's fellow constables and, by the look of her, rather enjoying the attention. Charles, by contrast, is neither in an interview room nor the cells but sitting, thanks to Sam, in an arm-chair by the fire in the front office. All the same, he hasn't yet been allowed to dispense with the cuffs, and in any other circumstances that fact alone would have seen him pacing and raging like an infuriated animal. But he has no energy left for exasperation. To all appearances he is – unusually for him – doing absolutely nothing, beyond gazing idly at the yellowing police notices pinned to the walls.

£100 Reward – **Wanted** for **Murder**
Dead Body Found
Missing Child

He stares at the words, reads them again, consciously and deliberately, but however hard he tries – however earnestly he tells himself Lizzie was in all likelihood long dead before she was disfigured – he cannot take his mind's eye from that room – cannot change the hacked flesh on the bed for the Lizzie he knew – the Lizzie he cared about as much as he's ever cared about anyone, and who needed someone in her life to do that, for all her hard-boiled confidence and self-sufficiency. All the while two police officers are calmly filling in forms at the front desk (though they do eye him surreptitiously every now and again), and other than the occasional muffled thumps and shouts from the cells below, the station is as quiet as he has ever known it.

Wheeler is not back until nearly five, whereupon he slumps into the chair opposite Charles' and runs a hand through his wiry red hair.

'Bloody 'ell, Chas, I ain't never seen nothin' like that before, and I 'ope I never do again. She weren't just disembowelled, you know – 'alf 'er insides were missin' and the rest was all over the floor, includin' the fish and potatoes she'd 'ad for dinner. Quite put me off me lunch, that did. What in God's name 'ad the poor bitch done to deserve that?'

'Did you talk to Abel?'

Wheeler nods. 'Confirmed you was at home all night. As did that boy of yours. Billy, was it? Seems 'e had cause to look in on you in the early hours, though 'e was pretty vague as to why.'

Charles nods, his face grim; he has his own theories as to what – or who – Billy was expecting to find.

'Did you question Lizzie's neighbours?'

Wheeler nods again, and pulls his ring of keys from his pocket to release Charles' cuffs.

'No one saw 'er between eight and eleven last night, but one person thought they spotted 'er in the pub after that. She was obviously 'avin' a good night – she kept half the courtyard awake when she got back 'ome, singin'.' He shakes his head. 'Poor little cow. Never 'ad much to sing about at the best of times.'

'So when was the last time anyone saw her alive?'

'Chap called Bert 'Itchins saw 'er on Oxford Street around two. She tried to cadge money off 'im, but 'e told 'er she'd cleaned 'im out after three days in Brighton, so she homed in on another mark. Luckily for us they stopped for a bit of a fondle under a gas-lamp and 'Itchins got a good look at 'im. Youngish bloke with a pale face, hat pulled down over his eyes, and a long dark coat. Quite well-spoken but no toff, 'Itchins says.'

Charles rubs his wrists where the cuffs have scratched his skin.

'There was one weird thing, though,' continues Wheeler, rubbing the back of his neck. 'When we looked through the room we found the fire was so 'ot last night the spout of the kettle had 'alf melted off. Some of 'er clothes 'ad been burnt too. Does that make any sense to you? Do you remember it being particularly 'ot in there?'

Charles shakes his head, all the while wondering how he could have missed that – the door was locked, the curtains drawn – after what had gone on in that room, surely a wave of stinking heat should have assailed him the moment he opened the door, but he can't remember that at all – can remember nothing but what he *saw*, as if his body could only deal with so much, and all his other senses had shut down.

197

'Your case don't involve a bloke in a long dark coat, by any wondrous chance?' asks Wheeler, looking at him sideways, his face thoughtful.

Charles forces himself to concentrate. 'No,' he says eventually. 'I'm sorry, Sam. The man I'm investigating is much older and most definitely a toff. But if I come across anything, I'll let you know. Can I go now?'

Wheeler sighs. 'On your way. And try to stay out of trouble this time.'

Charles nods, but when he's half-way to the door, Sam calls after him, 'You know what the bosses are like round 'ere – they don't like coincidences.'

Charles stops and looks back at him. Coincidence? It hadn't even occurred to him that Lizzie's death might be anything but a coincidence.

But what if he's wrong?

Chapter Fifteen

A Struggle

The Graham Arms has ceilings as low as the company it keeps. Even at a time when pubs make little effort to be appealing, this one seems extraordinarily unconcerned to offer the potential customer anything other than the sport he's come for: drinking is most definitely second-best to spectacle here. Charles eyes the blackened spirits tubs with distaste and opts for the beer, which proves to be only marginally more palatable. It's nearly nine now and the parlour is filling up; so much so that the proprietor is moving people along the bar and calling regularly to 'Place your orders, gentlemen, before the entertainment begins.' Charles looks about the room, compiling his mental inventory, just as he always does. There's an old white bull-dog with swollen pink eyes sleeping on one of the chairs before the fire, and on the opposite side, a wiry brown terrier with a patch over one eye and a tendency to growl whenever anyone but its owner gets too close. Above the bar there's a cluster of leashes hanging on hooks, with pride of place going to a silver collar, which a notice proclaims will be awarded to the winner of a major rat-match in a few days' time. Rather more disconcertingly, the parlour walls are hung with stuffed champions in cases, labelled with lists of their most infamous kills. A number of aficionados are inspecting these specimens with some interest, and Charles' first thought is that it's like some gross lampoon of the Mammalia Saloon, but another minute's reflection suggests that perhaps it's is not so very different, after all. Two of the spectators are talking at the bar just along from Charles, one obviously a regular, with a bright red and green 'King's-man' neckerchief knotted about his throat, the other a stout balding gentleman in black, with a double chin and a perspiring forehead. The sort of man you cannot imagine at twenty – or with a full head of hair. The only thing he seems to be drinking is lemonade, and he's making lengthy and detailed annotations in a large black notebook. Charles thinks – suddenly – that he's seen him before. And in fact he has – at the *Morning Chronicle*. Mayhew, that's his name. Henry Mayhew.

'Now that *there* is a dog,' says the man with the neckerchief, pointing to a stuffed grey terrier posed with a large black rat in its mouth. 'It was as good as any in England, though it's so small. I've seen 'er kill a dozen rats almost as big as 'erself, though they killed 'er at last.'

'So how was that?' asks the bald gentleman eagerly, pencil at the ready.

The man sucks his teeth. 'Sewer-rats like that are dreadful for giving dogs canker in the mouth, and she wore 'erself out with continually killing 'em, though we always rinsed 'er mouth out well with peppermint and water while she were at work. When rats bite they're poisonous, and an ulcer is formed, which we 'ave to lance; that's what killed 'er.'

Charles loses interest and turns away. The room is now filling up, and it's as fine a cross-section of lowish London life as you could hope to encounter – costermongers, soldiers, tradesmen, servants – as well as here and there a couple of foreign gentlemen looking, it must be said, a little apprehensive, and no doubt wondering what they've let themselves in for. The four-legged company is almost as diverse – and as numerous. Some dogs are twitching on laps, some stand with their back legs quivering and tails bent between their legs, and others (the more aggressive, these) are tied for precaution's sake to the legs of chairs, growling through gritted teeth. The favourites among them are being examined for form as minutely as racehorses, their limbs palpated and their teeth examined, and on the far side of the room there's a man boasting loudly that his dog once killed 'five hundred rats in five minutes and a half – I kid you not'.

Charles has been watching all this while for Milloy, and is surprised to find the small commotion at the street door is down to his arrival. He's as far now from the liveried little man of Curzon Street as it's possible to get, draped in a great-coat with a fur collar, with a cane in one hand and a pair of white gloves in the other. His hair – what there is of it – is smooth upon his head, and wiped down every other minute with a large silk handkerchief. From the quality of his reception he is clearly not merely a regular, but extremely well-respected in this neck of London. Waiters snap to it and a glass of milk punch appears on a tray at his elbow before he's three paces into the room.

'Now, Jem, when is this match coming off?' he asks impatiently and despite the quick assurance that they're at that very moment getting ready, Milloy starts threatening to leave at once if he's kept waiting much longer. This seems a mite unreasonable, but it produces a flurry behind the bar and another milk punch, so perhaps it has the desired effect. Milloy proceeds to process around the room, looking at each animal in its turn, and exchanging a word here and there with the owners, who spread their dogs' legs and bare their teeth so he can see them at most advantage. The gilt clock over the bar then strikes nine and the proprietor calls for order, announcing

201

that the pit above is open for business. Everyone rises at once, and the crowd parts to allow Milloy to be first up the stairs. Wondering distractedly how a footman has established himself in such an exalted position – and how much money it must take to sustain it – Charles takes his place in the line of punters streaming up the wooden staircase. The line pauses at the top and Charles retrieves a shilling from his pocket and places it in the proprietor's clanking canvas bag.

The room that opens in front of him has a small circular arena in the centre, built from planks of whitewashed board, and brightly lit by an array of gas lamps. There are chairs ranged round it in rows, and a recess on one side that's clearly reserved for special guests; it's no surprise, therefore, to see Milloy taking his seat there. The audience rush for the front row, and those who don't make it clamber on the tables at the back to get a better view. The air is filled with speckles of sawdust, and the whining of the dogs straining on their owner's laps. The proprietor brings out a rusty cage seething with huge black rats, and the noise rises to an unbearable cacophony of howling and barking. Milloy is in the arena at once to inspect the game, and one of the dog-fanciers takes the opportunity to try to sell him a spotted terrier he claims is a 'very pretty performer, you mark my words'. Milloy calls for a dozen rats, and makes to drag them out of the cage himself, despite a stern warning from the proprietor.

'One of my lads was bitten bad by one of these blighters only yesterday and took so bad we had to send him home. Doctor said bits of its teeth was embedded in the boy's thumb. Had to pull the bits out with pliers – you should have heard him scream. Never knew he had such lungs on him.'

Milloy laughs, but he takes a rather nervous step backward all the same. By now the rats are swarming across the floor –

one makes to run up Milloy's leg and he shakes it free to the loud laughter of the crowd. The spotted terrier is growing more and more frenzied, and Milloy climbs out of the arena and gives the signal for the dog to be loosed. The rats run in all directions, and the spectators start banging the sides of the pit in unison, shouting, 'Kill! Kill! Kill!'

Some rats fight back, tearing the dog's muzzle with their teeth, others scramble frantically for chinks of escape in the smooth white boards, but all end eventually with their backs broken or their heads wrenched off. The dead are swept unceremoniously into a heap in the corner and another fifty loosed in their place, which the man next to Charles says are all sewer and water-ditch rats, and certainly stink like it. They cluster and cringe and run blindly about as the impatient audience awaits the next dog. People start cat-calling and banging on the tables until the proprietor's young son appears with a bull-terrier that's already frothing at the mouth with excitement, and straining so far forward that its studded collar is almost choking it. The proprietor calls for a stop-watch and the dog is finally dropped into the pit.

'Rat-killing's *his* game and no mistake! Where'd you get him?' shouts one of the men in the front row.

The landlord grins. 'I'd back him to kill against anybody's dog at eight and a half or nine.'

The watch is stopped after four more raucous minutes and the boy catches up the writhing dog, its eyes bulging and its tongue bloody. The proprietor calls for more drink, and as the waiter takes the orders, Charles takes the opportunity to slip down to the front and reaches across to touch Milloy on the arm.

'Milloy? Remember me?'

The milk punch seems to be having an effect. Milloy looks at him a mite blearily for a moment and then slaps him on the back.

203

'Maddox, isn't it? Good to see you, my friend! Are you here for the ratting?'

'No. I'm here for you. To finish our conversation.'

'Pity. Sport of gents, this, my lad. And you can win a pretty penny at it too. Take my word for it.'

Charles can well believe it; no doubt it explains both Milloy's flamboyant appearance and the impression he gives of not being unduly concerned to be no longer in paid work. It might also account for the handful of money he now takes from his pocket, in preparation for the next bout.

'It won't take long,' says Charles quickly, seeing the proprietor making his way across with another cage of rats. 'I just wanted to ask if you've remembered anything more about those anonymous letters sent to Sir Julius Cremorne?'

Milloy is already counting out coins. 'Can't remember what I said – remind me.'

'That there were three of them. That they came through the post. And that the writing was rough.'

All of this information has, of course, been in Charles' possession since that very first encounter with Tulkinghorn in Lincoln's Inn Fields; what he's after now is something else – something he *doesn't* already know.

Milloy finally looks up. 'Ah – now I recall. Though I am sure my memory would serve me better if—'

He smiles broadly and glances, ostentatiously if rather unnecessarily, at the stack of coins in his palm. Charles doesn't need to be nudged twice. He holds a sovereign over Milloy's hand, then pauses and looks him in the eye before letting it drop. 'This had better be good.'

'Oh it is – it is. I have no doubt of your complete satisfaction.'

Milloy catches the eye of one of the men in the front row and puts ten shillings – well over half his weekly wage in Curzon

Street – on the next dog. Then he turns back to Charles and starts to speak. His voice is low, quick, and suddenly not at all slurred.

'There is one salient fact that seems to be eluding you. The last one wasn't a letter. It was a *package*.'

Charles stares at him, then puts a hand into his coat pocket and pulls out the envelopes Tulkinghorn gave him. *That's* what the cloth on the kitchen table had reminded him of. He can't remember ever registering it consciously, but in the glare of the gas lamps overhead he can see the same pattern on one of the envelopes – a network of creases so faint that someone must have used a hot iron to flatten it out. But it's still there, and now he knows what it means. There was something inside that envelope – something neither the lawyer nor his client wants him to know about. Something, therefore, of desperate significance.

He looks up at Milloy. 'Do you know what it was?'

Milloy shakes his head. The next round is about to begin and he has to raise his voice to make himself heard. 'All I can tell you is that Sir Julius went as white as death when he opened it. Gave orders there and then that any more like it were to be put into his hands, and his alone. The butler told me afterwards it looked for all the world like he'd seen a ghost.'

Out on the street the fog is starting to come down, but even that's a relief after the reeking atmosphere inside. As the mist gathers, the buildings are starting to soften into looming abstractions, mere blocks of shadow without facet or feature. Charles stands for a moment, breathing in the night, then starts down towards the City Road. The street is almost empty of people, with here and there only a sleeping drunk, or a loud one. So there is no one to see the slight figure in the long dark coat emerge from a doorway behind Charles and slip an arm about his neck. No one to catch the glimmer of a blade in the yellowish light. No one to see Charles stagger to his knees, and fall forward, gasping, into the mud. And no one, I can assure you, anywhere near close enough to see the man stoop down over the body at his feet, and bring his face close and low against his victim's ear.

'Whatever you're playing at, it's over. Do you hear me?'

Charles feels his wrist grasped, and winces as his arm is wrenched behind his back.

'This is by way of a warning. Next time, I won't be so subtle.'

The blade is warm against the skin, the cut white cold, like an electric shock.

And then the heat.

The darkness.

Chapter Sixteen

Sharpshooters

When the clear cold sunshine slides between the shutters of the attic at Buckingham Street the next morning, the first thing it finds is a pile of jack-towels discarded on the floor. White towels they must have been, but they're stained now with blotches of a rusty deadened red. Slowly, slowly, the sun inches obliquely through the silent room – the corner of a table, a chair, the beautiful coil of a sleeping black cat – until it finally edges across the bed, and touches the two bodies lying there. They are together, there is no doubt about that, but they lie now slightly apart, their naked limbs barely meeting. One is a man. His face and body show the signs of recent violence – old bruises ripened to a greenish yellow, weals and grazes all but mended – but there is also a new bandage bound tightly about his hand, and a smudge of deep scarlet where new blood is still seeping through. The other is a woman, her black skin luminous against white sheets bleached almost dazzling by the strengthening sun.

I suspect you've been expecting this. I suspect, in fact, that you've been expecting it for a good deal longer than at least one of the two people involved. But the fact that it *has* now happened is only half of the story. You will want to know how, and you will want to know why – or at the very least, why now.

So we will back-track, just for a moment. Charles clearly did not bleed out his life in the mud of the City Road as you might have feared. But by the time he came to, his assailant was long gone and he was staring, somewhat dazedly, into the face of one of the early-morning coffee-vendors so common in that part of town. The man was shaking him vigorously by the shoulder, worried – clearly – that he had a corpse on his hands. His barrow was pulled up against the kerb behind him, smoke rising gently from the charcoal burner, and even with his hand pulsing like underground thunder, Charles was almost overwhelmed by the glorious smell of freshly made coffee. The man helped him roll over and lever himself up, and it was only then – with the man's staring eyes round with fear – that he realized, finally, what had happened. The little finger of his right hand was gone. Severed below the knuckle with one slicing incision. Strange what the mind does with such explosive irrevocable information – all Charles could think was how expert this cut must have been – how sharp the knife – not who did this, or what the consequences might be. You don't die of such a wound as that, even in Victorian London, but there was a lot of blood on the pavement and more still throbbing from the wound. Was it the medical or the police training that kicked in next? Or merely the adrenalin? Who knows. Whichever it was, Charles managed somehow to staunch the worst of it with the coffee-seller's handkerchief, and then stagger with him to the nearest cab-stand, where the man was clearly mighty glad to see the back of him. Nor was the cab driver particularly pleased at the prospect of a haemorrhage all over his hansom, and Charles had to pay well over the odds for the fare – 'You're goin' to get blood all over me seats, mate. That'll take hours to get off. Three shillin's to the Strand – take it or leave it.'

It was near five when he got back to Buckingham Street, and Molly had clearly just got up – she hadn't yet put on either her apron or the ungainly cap that covered her hair. He had no idea what he looked like and loomed at her out of the night like a dead man, his coat drenched and the blood still running down his arm where he was holding it clutched to his chest. He'd seen terror on her face once before, but for some reason he didn't have the energy to analyse, he did not see it now. His mutilated hand looked far worse in the glare of the lamp, but the girl did not flinch. The wound was bathed and cleaned, brandy poured, bandages brought, and hot water carried up to his room so he could wash. Only he could not wash, because he couldn't use his right hand. So the girl came back and stood behind him as he sat in the tub and the water around him ran red and redder still. As the brandy kicked in and the pain dulled, he shut his eyes and tried to close his senses down to only the smooth rhythmic rasp of the cloth against his skin. He willed it to be neutral – willed it to be nothing more than an impersonal physical sensation entirely distinct from the girl – but every now and again he felt the quick edge of a fingernail, or the lightest skim of the fabric of her sleeve, and as his body started to respond, he sensed the pressure shift to his shoulder, his neck, his chest, and knew that her face was only inches from his own. And then, without warning, the movement stopped and when he opened his eyes he saw there were tears in hers. What could he do but what he'd once dreamed of doing, and touch that cheek. The girl, in her turn, pushed her face hard against his hand like a cat, and as the two moved slowly together, a rush of energy ripped through Charles' body and all pain was forgotten in a surge of desire.

And now it is morning. The air is still; motes of dust catch in the sun. Thunder is dreaming of rabbits, and his small whimpers and twitches are the only noise in the otherwise silent room. Until a bell rings somewhere downstairs and the girl starts awake, aghast at the light, and what that tells her about the time. There are half a dozen tasks already neglected, and she slips quickly and silently from the bed, gathers up her clothes, and leaves without a sound. Charles stirs and turns over, aware, somewhere deep in his sleep, of a shift, and an absence. When the door opens ten minutes later, the breakfast tray is borne by Billy, who puts it down, none too quietly, on one of the packing cases and starts to move about the room, muttering self-righteously about the mess. He picks up the towels and starts to fold them for laundry, but comes to an abrupt halt when he sees the stains. He looks across at Charles, and sees that the hand lying on the pillow is swathed in bandage and the shirt lying half in and half out of the hip-bath is rinsed with red. His eyes widen and he hovers for a moment in almost pantomimic hesitation, before turning and all but running out of the door. By the time Abel Stornaway has scaled the stairs, Charles is sitting up and pouring coffee with his left hand, and spilling at least half of it on the floor as a result.

'Good heavens, Mr Charles!' wheezes Stornaway, his hand still on the door-handle. 'Should I send Billy for the doctor?'

Charles smiles weakly. 'Another brandy would be more to the purpose, I suspect, Abel. But no – there's no call to trouble the doctor at present; he would only tell me to do what I've already done. Would you please ask Molly' – this with a slight flush – 'if she would come up in half an hour and bind the wound again, and in the meantime I will need Billy to help me get dressed.'

'Ye're never going out in that state.'

Charles leans over and lifts his pistol-case from the box where it has been all this time, then looks up at Stornaway.

'It would appear,' he says drily, 'that I've been in a far more vulnerable state than this for the best part of a week, had I but

210

known it. But I am ignorant no longer. Tulkinghorn has made a serious mistake in showing his hand so crudely. If I didn't know Cremorne had something dire to hide before, I do now.'

He flicks open the case with his left hand and looks at the gun. 'Abel, am I right in thinking you know your way round one of these?'

'Of course, Mr Charles,' says Stornaway, somewhat taken aback. 'I had a pair of Nocks me'sel until only a year or so back. And your great-uncle swore by his Manton flintlocks. Finest gun-maker in England, that's what he allus used to say.'

'Excellent. This one hasn't been fired for a while, so I need you to clean it and have it ready for me by the time I'm dressed. I've let myself get out of practice – quite possibly dangerously so.'

Dressing, eating, bandaging, all take far longer than he has patience for, and somewhere in the midst of it all he has a strange flash of almost gratitude towards his attacker that he did nothing worse – nothing that might have condemned him to such maddening slowness for ever, and not just for the time it will take this wound to heal. But the feeling is fleeting; he knows this was only ever meant as a warning, and that if he encounters the man again there will be no question, and no vacillation: it will be death, or nothing. By midday he's finally making his way through the crowded back-streets and alleyways between the Haymarket and Leicester Square to a long whitewashed passage which leads in turn to a large low brick building with a rather battered sign over the door that says GEORGE'S SHOOTING GALLERY, &c. Inside he finds half a dozen gentlemen at the targets, each stripped to his shirt, and all being assisted with weapons, powder, shot, and the occasional refreshment, by a strange little man with a large head, and a face smeared with gunpowder, dressed in a green-baize apron and cap. He spots Charles straight away and comes limping towards him – well, not exactly towards him, for he has an odd way of shuffling round the room with one shoulder against the wall and heading off at a tangent to where he really wants to go.

'Nice to see you, Mr Maddox, sir,' he says. 'The guv'nor ain't here at the moment, but I expect him shortly.'

'Can I pay for fifty shots?'

'By all means, Mr Maddox. The stall at the end is free at the present – that's your preference, as I recall?'

'It is indeed, Phil, thank you.'

The little man helps him off with his coat, noticing – but knowing better than to remark – that his client's right hand is tightly bandaged, but also that someone has so contrived it that it appears he should still be able to hold a gun. And indeed he can, as five minutes' shooting proves. Firing the pistol is not an issue, though aiming it accurately quickly proves to be. Charles becomes increasingly red-faced and irritable as shot after shot goes wide, and the slick gentlemen in the stands next to his slip him condescending glances. He could out-shoot the lot of them – yesterday. It's as he feared – he's resisting admitting it, but the injury is not as insignificant as he insists, and his usual sure aim has quite deserted him. Not to mention the fact that he's still in severe pain and took a shot of brandy to numb it, neither of which are helping matters. Fifteen minutes later he wipes away the sweat beading on his brow and goes over to the rough oblong table near the door, where Phil is now busying himself preparing coffee, no doubt in anticipation of his master's return. Charles throws himself into a chair and casts the gun on to the table in front of him. Phil says nothing and concentrates instead on boiling the water, and stirring the coffee grounds. The need for conversation is obviated, in any case, by the arrival

212

of the gallery owner, a fine hearty-looking man of fifty or so, with a barrel chest and a slow and deliberate tread. He looks every inch the old soldier, from his weather-beaten face to his upright army bearing, and though he is clean-shaven now (every morning, by Phil), at moments of anxiety or reflection you will see him smooth his upper lip with his hand, as if his military moustaches were still there. He takes a seat beside them, nodding to Charles and making no more remark than his assistant on the bandage – now touched with blood – about his hand. He takes out his pipe and lights it with slow solemnity, then Phil pours coffee for the three of them and his master sits back with his mug and sets his pipe between his teeth. He takes his time, but eventually he leans forward with his elbow on his knee and stretches his neck a little. 'How's the aim?'

Charles shakes his head. 'Hopeless. I didn't make the mark once.'

Phil seems to be avoiding his master's eyes, and the latter fans his cloud of smoke away in order that he may see Charles more clearly. 'In my experience,' he says at last, folding his arms upon his chest, 'a good aim is a matter of mind, eye, and hand, marching in step, the one with the other. Now it seems to me, Mr Maddox, sir, that your mind is what it ever was; your eye, the same.'

'But not my hand,' says Charles grimly, holding it out before him and feeling the change of position in a throb of pain. A thin runnel of red has leached from beneath the bandage and stained his cuff.

The trooper nods, his face serious. 'What accident have you met with, sir? What's amiss?'

'I no longer have all five fingers on my right hand. I thought it would make no difference to my grip. But alas, it seems I was mistaken.'

213

The trooper nods, then takes his pipe from his lips for a moment and knocks the ashes out against his boot.

'It's a question of balance, I should say,' he says finally. 'Balance and weight. You have been accustomed to hold the pistol in a certain way. Now you must make an adjustment. A compensation. D'you follow?'

Charles shrugs. 'I've been trying to do so, but my shots still go wide.'

The trooper swallows the rest of his coffee, then puts his mug down and gets lumberingly to his feet.

'If we give our full minds to it, sir, we may come upon an answer.'

The two of them return to Charles' stand and start again. For a good while they seem to be making little progress – shots fly as wide as they had before – but then the trooper hits on the idea of holding the gun with both hands.

''Tis not how the gentlemen do it, sir,' he says. 'But needs must. Needs must.'

It feels odd at first, and Charles does indeed receive scornful glances from those at the other stands who have not yet abandoned the gallery for luncheon at their club, but there's no doubt of its efficacy. The second hand gives him precisely the measure of control and counterweight he needs, and he has just made his first mark when the two of them are distracted by footsteps in the passage and a commotion at the door.

The trooper casts an eye in that direction, evidently concerned, but Phil has forestalled him. Charles cannot see who it is and can only – for a moment at least – register Phil's low tones, and Phil's grimy hand on the door. No one is more surprised than he is when it becomes obvious from the noise that the intruder is a woman. She is young and, to judge by her accent, French.

'You know who I am,' she says in a shrill and angry voice. 'You take my money many times – it is money as good as any man's – I demand to enter dis place!'

'I'm sorry, madymosselle, but orders is orders. The commander says I am to refuse you entry. And round 'ere, what the commander says goes.'

She has by now so far encroached on Phil that Charles can see her profile against the wall. She is a black-haired woman, with large wary eyes, and a drawn and hungry look, and flesh so thin and taut that the bones of her face seem to press against the skin. It's clearly not the first time the Frenchwoman has been there – or made trouble when she has; the trooper frowns, and folds back his sleeves, then makes his stately measured way to the door.

'You will not gain entry here, mistress.'

The woman laughs out loud in rather an affected manner, and stands her ground.

'I will not, eh?'

'No,' he says heavily, 'you will not. Even if I have to carry you out. Make no mistake, I don't want to do it. I would rather treat a lady such as yourself with the respect she is due. But if I must, I will. You may be sure of that.'

She looks the trooper up and down, knowing that even her ferocious determination is no match for a man of his training.

'I will not forget zis,' she says scornfully between clenched teeth. 'You have not use me well. You have been mean and shabby – as mean and shabby as that miserable lawyer in Lincoln's Inn Fields. You will be sorry to cross one such as I!'

She turns on her heel, and with what she clearly imagines to be an aristocratically contemptuous flick of her cloak, she is gone.

The trooper shakes his head and returns to Charles.

'My apologies, Mr Maddox, sir.'

215

'It's no inconvenience to me. But I admit to some surprise at seeing a lady here.'

'She's no lady, sir,' says the trooper, 'though I might have called her one, out of courtesy. I have all sorts, here. Mostly they come for skill, like you, but some just for idleness. There are even ladies of title and fashion who come here merely to amuse themselves between morning calls and the milliner's. I keep a case of pocket pistols in the drawer there, expressly for the purpose. But when you own a place such as this, you have to be on your guard. I have a long nose for such as she – such as come with revenge in their hearts and dreams of score-settling and I know not what. She is one of those, sir, if I am not very much mistaken, and a dab she is at hitting the mark. I don't know much of women, Mr Maddox, but she's an erratic, that one, that much I do know. I don't want her on my conscience.'

This is quite considerably the longest speech Charles has ever had from the trooper's mouth, and he can see from the creases on the broad brown forehead that the Frenchwoman, whoever she is, has been troubling him for some time.

'I'm sure she means nothing by it. It's no doubt just her way – they are an impassioned and capricious race. I don't think you need worry unduly.'

It sounds trite, even to his own ears, but it seems to go some way to reassure the trooper. Though, as we shall see, he will be far better advised to take no notice whatsoever of Charles' advice, and remain fully and vigilantly on his guard.

When Charles returns to Buckingham Street the house is silent. Billy has been dispatched on afternoon errands and Abel is nowhere about. He hesitates for a moment, wondering what best to do, then goes quietly down the back stairs towards the kitchen. He hasn't seen Molly on her own since – since *then* – and feels he has to cross that line – establish how the two of them are to go on. But when he reaches the half-closed door he's stopped in his tracks by the most ordinary and at the same time the most astounding thing in the world. The sound of a girl's voice. Molly is singing. But there are no words, only a low cadenced humming to a melody unlike any Charles has ever heard before – indeed unlike any conventional European notion of what a 'melody' actually is. But whatever it is, the sound seems to reach inside his head and ring to a deeper rhythm than four-four time. He stands listening, wondering if she's done this before and it's just that he has never heard her. He knew the girl could not speak and thought – wrongly it seems – that she was incapable of any sound. Something else he has assumed, and must now re-assess. But this small check – insignificant as you may think it is – is still enough to make him reconsider, and then retreat silently back the way he came.

Up in his great-uncle's room he finds both master and attendant sleeping peacefully over the subsiding fire. Charles pokes the smouldering coals and retrieves the newspaper from the floor at Stornaway's feet. Then he pours himself more brandy-and-water and sits down on the sofa. It's a long time since he's sat doing nothing, but yesterday is catching up with him. We would call it post-traumatic stress and wonder how he could possibly cope with such a serious injury without analgesics, but all such concepts are equally alien to Charles. He sits back and closes his eyes for a moment, lulled by the alcohol, the warmth, and the soft pattering of the fire. When he opens them again, the room is in darkness.

'I let you sleep. You looked to be rather in need of it.'

Charles starts. It takes him a moment to recognize the voice, though he has known it all his life. Stornaway has gone and

Maddox is watching him quietly from the other side of the hearth. The long dark shadows cast by the low firelight give his face an austere, almost classical air.

'Are you intending to tell me what has happened to you, or am I required to guess?'

Charles struggles to sit up, forgetting – but not for long – that he can't put any weight on his right hand.

'I was – waylaid. By Tulkinghorn's hired henchman.'

'You are sure of that?'

'As sure as I can be. He'd been sent to warn me off, and took a little personal memento with him to make sure I took the point.'

He holds up his hand.

Maddox raises an eyebrow. 'A rather brutal tactic, but without doubt an effective one. There is no infection?'

Charles shakes his head. 'The girl is a very efficient nurse. The wound is clean, and I know what to look for.'

Maddox nods, reflectively. 'I, too, lost many things in the course of my career. My faith in my fellow men, my freedom on occasion – albeit temporarily – and once, and once only, something more important than either of those things. But I never suffered a loss quite so tangible as yours. Your sangfroid, if I may say so, is admirable.' And he is, indeed, looking at Charles with an expression in his eyes his nephew cannot remember seeing before.

Charles shrugs, though his new-found self-possession is clearly not quite all Maddox believes it to be, for there are hot tears prickling his eyes now. He's spent so much of his life managing for himself and expecting nothing from those around him – so long without a mother, in the coolness cast by a distinguished but distant father – that kindness always comes to him as a shock, and it's kindness that has undone him now, not pain, however intense, or self-pity, however justified.

'At least I know now that I'm not wasting my time,' he says eventually, and then explains, as concisely as he can, what he discovered at the Graham Arms.

'But you have no clue as yet as to what this package contained?' says Maddox thoughtfully, when he has finished.

'No,' says Charles, 'but whatever it was, it terrified Cremorne enough to get Tulkinghorn involved – and Boscawen killed. This, my dear uncle, is no ordinary case of petty blackmail. There's something base and corrupt at the bottom of it all – something Cremorne absolutely cannot afford to come to light. That's why I know it's no coincidence I was attacked as soon as I left the rat-killing. I'll bet this thug has been following me for days and knew exactly what Milloy was going to tell me.'

'No doubt.'

They are silent for a moment; the only sound the prim ticking of the ornate French clock on the mantelpiece.

'There's something else—' begins Charles tentatively. He's been wondering whether to mention this – in fact, ever since he saw the butchery done to Lizzie's ravaged body he's wanted to talk to Maddox, get advice from Maddox, elicit from Maddox some part of the unparalleled insight he has into man's inhumanity to man. But in the two days since the murder, the Maddox he needs has been all but gone. But now, at last, the great Regency thief-taker has returned, and the flailing madman who took his place is stilled.

'What is it, my boy?'

'Do you remember the police coming here yesterday?'

Maddox frowns. 'No – or at least—'

He stops, and the old terror creeps back into his face – the terror of knowing how much he no longer knows, of how black the blank spaces are becoming – and Charles realizes his mistake.

'No matter, Uncle,' he says quickly. 'It was just—'

'But I *should* know – if there are officers of the law in this house – *my* house – then *I* should be the one to—'

Maddox's voice is catching that slightly hectic edge that Charles knows he must at all costs avoid. Not just for his uncle's sake, but his own.

'Really – it is no matter, Uncle, I doubt they even crossed the threshold. They were merely enquiring as to my whereabouts the previous evening.'

Maddox looks sceptical. 'And why should they wish to know that?'

'Because I discovered a body yesterday. A girl I know – a whore – was murdered.'

'There is nothing so very extraordinary about that, I fear.'

'The point is not that she was killed, but *when* she was killed, and how.'

'Go on.' Maddox's voice is clear again and his gaze steady; his mind has teetered but swung back from the shadow.

'I saw her a few days before. The only reason I found the body at all was because I'd arranged to meet her there. She was going to tell me something – something about Sir Julius Cremorne. I don't know what, but I'm guessing it had something to do with what I found out at the Argyll Rooms. Because despite Cremorne's public reputation for high principles and a happy family life, he's been regularly debauching a whole host of young women.'

'That, I am afraid to say, is not so very unusual either. At least among those of Sir Julius' class. But I admit it is hardly something a man in his position would want bruited abroad.'

'But this girl wasn't just killed. She was *slaughtered*. With the same skill, and no doubt the same knife, that opened William Boscawen's throat, and was subsequently used on me.'

220

The details are soon given: first Boscawen, then Lizzie. The scene in Agnes Court plays again, reel by reel, through Charles' head. For some reason he finds himself recalling more than he remembers seeing at the time, but it's not so much the horror of it now as the utter banality. The clothes folded neatly on the chair. The boots placed by the fireside. Maddox is all silent calculating attention as he talks, his eyes half-closed, nodding now and then. When Charles has finished, Maddox does not respond straight away but takes a deep breath and stares into the fire. After a few moments – just when Charles fears he may have lost him once again – he starts to speak.

'Did you find your finger?'

The question is so ludicrous – so darkly black-comical – that Charles doesn't know how to react. Is this his uncle's infamous wit, or is it just another example of his inability, so frequent now, to tell the acceptable from the offensive?

'Well, I—' he stammers.

'It is a perfectly serious question, Charles. Did you find your finger?'

Charles gapes at him. 'I can hardly say I looked for it.'

'But it was nowhere obvious – nowhere about you when you came to your senses?'

'No – but the rats may well have had it by then. You know what it's like on the City Road.'

'All the same,' says Maddox. 'And you are sure that some of this unfortunate girl's internal organs were missing?'

'Most of them were lying in pieces about the room, but I was told later at the police-station that the heart was definitely absent.'

'And the breasts were also removed?'

'Both of them. One was lying by her feet, along with what appeared to be her liver. Though there was so much disembowelled flesh I cannot really be sure.'

221

Maddox nods. 'You perceive the pattern?'

A pause, then, 'No, Uncle, I cannot say that I do.'

Maddox sits back. 'Men such as this – men attracted to the point of compulsion by violence so extreme it violates every natural instinct or moral constraint – they are very rare, but they do, in my limited experience, exhibit very similar characteristics, both as a sub-species and as individuals. By the latter I mean that each murderer will have his own habits, and his own preferences, whether it be weapon, setting, victim, or some other little ritual or attribute which may elude the eye of even the most experienced of detectives. As to the former, I have encountered more than one instance – like the present one, indeed – where the perpetrator has felt himself compelled to take something from the victim, not so much a *memento mori* as a *memento delectare* – a way of reviving the illicit excitement generated by the crime long after the actual deed has passed. You will recall, I am sure, our conversation about the Ratcliffe Highway killings, and the watch that was taken from the body of the landlord of the King's Arms – an obvious instance of an otherwise meaningless piece of pilfering that can only be explained by the murderer's need to retain a material keepsake. But I am sure that you, as a scientist, are at least as well-qualified as I could be to venture an opinion on this subject.'

Charles, perhaps unsurprisingly, is in no state to offer an opinion on anything of the kind – if Maddox is right, even the pieces of the puzzle he thought resolved will need to be put back together in a new configuration. He's been assuming all along that Tulkinghorn hired some Cockney bludger to do his dirty work, but is it possible that Cremorne committed these crimes *himself?* He could have found out from Tulkinghorn where Boscawen was lodging, and he could just as easily have followed Lizzie home and slipped into the courtyard unseen in the small hours. And he could – equally easily – have followed Charles to the Graham Arms. But was that really the voice he'd heard when he was lying face-down in the dirt? It didn't sound like a man of Cremorne's age – or one of his rank for that matter – and Charles is sure there was no stammer. But his recollection is fragmentary at best, and the voice never much more than a whisper.

Maddox, meanwhile, has settled more comfortably in his chair. 'Perhaps I might join you in a brandy, Charles?'

'Of course, Uncle,' says Charles, getting quickly to his feet. He pours the brandies and when he hands Maddox the glass his grasp is firm.

'I agree,' Maddox resumes, 'that it is a reasonable hypothesis to presume, until contradictory facts intervene, that these killings were each the work of the same perpetrator. Our next task, therefore, is to ascertain what these crimes tell us about the man who committed them. There is one fact, of course, that obtrudes immediately on our notice.'

He looks at Charles, who takes a sip of brandy in an endeavour to buy time. Maddox smiles, and continues, placing his fingertips carefully together.

'Perhaps "fact" is too strong, since the available evidence is not extensive enough for a robust deduction, but I posit that the individual with whom we are dealing is a swift, skilled and ruthless killer. Of *men*. He is, by contrast, a slow, cruel and utterly depraved murderer of *women*. A man who takes his time to inflict the utmost pain and degradation on his female victims, and who clearly derives an intense and degenerate gratification from so doing. That, to me, suggests a man who has – to say the least – an unhealthy relationship with the fairer sex. A relationship founded on the desire to dominate, and humiliate. Further investigation of Sir Julius' habits and history might, therefore, be instructive, especially as—'

He stops, and frowns, then waves a hand quickly back and forth in front of his face, as if swatting a fly. But it is winter, and there are no flies. Charles sits forward and puts a hand on his arm. 'Uncle? Is everything all right?'

'I was about to say something, but it is eluding me.' He raises his hand again and covers his face, as if the light is dazzling him. 'What was that? Who's there – I know there's someone – show yourself – damn you – *show yourself*—'

He reaches blindly for his cane and makes to seize it, but Charles forestalls him, then moves quickly to the bell and rings for Stornaway. By the time he arrives, Charles can barely keep Maddox in his chair. The old man is kicking and biting and bawling profanities so disgusting Charles can hardly believe he ever knew such words, far less used them. He's almost embarrassed to have Stornaway hear all this, but apparently with no reason: he's either heard it all before, or can dissociate it entirely from the man he has served and revered for over half a century. It's a lesson, of a kind, and despite being in no fit state to fend off the vehemence of his uncle's blows, Charles does what he can to help, and they finally manage to bring Maddox back to some sort of calm. Stornaway silently motions Charles away and kneels down in front of his old master.

'There now – is that better for ye? Would ye like me to bring ye anythin'? Some water perhaps?'

Maddox eyes him with a leering look, then nods and slips his gaze away. Stornaway looks up at Charles. 'I've noticed he's allus worse as the day draws on. But I think we'll be a'right now, Mr Charles, if ye have other things to do.'

It's the gentlest, most courteous dismissal you could ever devise, but it's a dismissal all the same. Charles nods and is turning to go when Stornaway calls to him.

'Mr Charles, ye've dropped some'at here.'

'I don't think so, Abel.'

Stornaway bends down behind Maddox's chair and hands Charles a slip of twisted paper. It's in his uncle's handwriting. Not, alas, the confident flowing hand of his maturity, but the weak looping scrawl that's a sad gauge of Maddox's deteriorating grasp – both of his pen and of his mind. This scrap certainly seems to have been written from a clouded place: as far as Charles can see it's nothing more than a string of random numbers and letters.

'Do you know what this means, Abel, if it means anything?'

Stornaway takes the paper and looks at it, then nods. 'Aye, it does. It's a reference to one of the newspapers in those boxes downstairs. He devised a system a' his own for organisin' 'em. He'd have me file anythin' as might prove to be useful. And many's a time it was.' He sighs. 'There's a pile down there I never got round to doin'. Don't suppose I ever shall now.'

'Can you find it for me – this newspaper?'

'I'll do me best, Mr Charles, but it looks to me that there's some'at missin' here. There should be seven figures, not six. But I'll go see if Billy's back and can sit with the boss, and then I can get to it rightaway.'

Narrowing the reference down to one of the boxes in the office proves to be fairly straightforward; working out what, in all the solid stack of newsprint it contains, Maddox wanted Charles to see is quite another. Stornaway can give him no further guidance, beyond saying that the papers have not been logged in chronological order, but according to the nature of the crime as Maddox defined it. Charles is left with the prospect of a dreary evening that may, in the end, lead him nowhere. Nonetheless he has the fire lit in the room, and asks Billy to bring up a decanter of wine and his dinner, when it's ready. Then he brings down a more comfortable chair from the drawing-room and settles himself by the oil-lamp to read. As he makes his way through the box, page by page, he finds he is confronting the painful reality of his uncle's slow and painful descent into the dark. The sheets are covered with annotations in black ink, but as with his uncle's handwriting, so with his subject matter: there is a terrible distance between the confident magisterial comments that mark the older newspapers, and the impenetrable scratchings on the more recent ones. In consequence it takes longer than it should to decipher exactly what crimes this box records, but when he does, Charles' heart starts to beat a little faster and he grips the page he's holding until the elderly paper crackles in his hands.

The crime referred to hereunder is archetypical of that committed by the 'sequential killer', by which I mean it exhibits a gratuitous brutality, allied with an extreme, not to say excessive, ceremoniousness in the way the corpse has been performed upon, plundered, and positioned.
NB: This man will kill again, and has very likely killed before: investigate the possibility of earlier instances.

The date at the head of the page is August 1817 – far too early to have any bearing to the Cremorne case, but it's the theory, the *thinking*, that has Charles turning up the lamp and emptying the box on to the floor. He's sure now that this is what his uncle was trying to tell him – that a crime so elaborate as the murder of Lizzie Miller cannot possibly be a single unique act. That it must, in fact, have been preceded by other similar outrages – killings that display some of the same characteristics, if not the same degree of premeditated cruelty. Now he knows what he's looking for, everything suddenly accelerates. Within minutes he has the pile of print in two groups – those too old to be relevant, and those recent enough to be plausible. He rearranges the latter heap chronologically and works backwards in time – six months first, then ten, a year. And then he finds it. No more than a paragraph, at the bottom of a column entitled 'Accidents, Inquests, &c'. The story in question clearly sits under the third of the three categories, though a mere '&c' hardly seems strong enough to contain it:

Frightful Murder near St Giles

A dreadful murder took place last Monday week, in the vicinity of Church Street, St Giles. The mutilated body of Mrs Abigail Cass was discovered shortly after midnight by a Police-constable of the St Giles sub-division. We are assured that the unfortunate lady was of unblemished character, and appears to have been the victim of a spontaneous and frenzied attack by an assailant armed with a knife. It is not known what led to this awful crime, and every effort is being made to bring the killer to justice.

Were it not for Maddox's notes, Charles might never have noticed it – there's nothing, after all, so very unusual about this report, which resembles a dozen others appearing in the London press every day. Though there is perhaps a coded message here you would not habitually find – the writer is clearly signalling that this was no common streetwalker, and words like 'mutilated' are rare, even for the more sensational papers. It's irritating not to have the name of the officer who found the body, but that's an omission that can soon be remedied. But what was a respectable woman doing in that part of town in the first place, and what link can there possibly be between her and a whore like Lizzie? And what can either of them have to do with the strange persecution practised by William Boscawen, and the violent death meted out to him by way of retribution?

Chapter Seventeen

The Track

Charles fights up to consciousness, beating the dream back, forcing himself awake. It was the same dream, the same nightmare he'd had ever since he was a child. It was never monsters or ghouls that terrorized him – he'd never had that sort of imagination – this dream's terror lies entirely in its mundanity. Just his small self, his five-year-old self, following his mother through the garden of the house where he was born. He could tell he was just a little boy because the plants and flowers were taller than he was. There were huge furry bumblebees and bright butterflies as big as his small fat hands. It was always the same, always identical. The sky as blue as cornflowers, the huge white clouds billowing like yeast, and up ahead of him, his mother, walking gaily, and holding his baby sister nestled in her arms. He could see her pretty print dress and the red hair coiling in ringlets down her back and lifting lightly in the warm breeze. And he wanted so much to walk with her – to have her turn and see him – take him by the hand – but however hard he tried to catch her up, she was always just too far away – however loudly he cried out, she never acknowledged he was there, never took her eyes from her tiny sleeping daughter. He knew she could hear him, but she wouldn't turn round, he called to her again and again but she never looked back, never turned her head—

He sits up, sweating despite the cold. It's still dark outside and the fire died hours ago. At his side Molly stirs, and whimpers, then falls silent once more. Charles slips from the bed softly, so as not to wake her, and goes to the window. The sky is clear and the moon full and bright, ringed with a thin greenish edge like the peel on a fruit. Ice is already starting to cloud the glass. He breathes on it and rubs it with the sleeve of his nightshirt. Anything – *anything* – to dispel the image of his mother's face. Not the face he'd longed to see in his dream, the beautiful face of the mother of his infancy, but the face he last saw more than six years ago. The face he has tried ever since to forget.

His wound is throbbing and he loosens the dressing, concerned still about infection. He goes to the washstand and slowly unwinds the lengths of cloth, clumsy and left-handed, before sinking his arm into the basin. The shock of the cold water against his skin is raw, but then soothing, and the pain ebbs gradually down. He's still sitting there at five, when Molly wakes and helps him change the bandage before going downstairs to stoke the kitchen fire and clear the hearths. Charles is just about to leave an hour later when a note is delivered from Mr Chadwick. It's in reply to Charles' own letter of a few days before, enquiring whether his client can think of anyone who might have taken his daughter from the workhouse. The response is concise, and characteristically curt.

As I have explained to you on at least three previous occasions, I have no information whatsoever as to the identity of the father of my daughter's child. I can only surmise that this was the gentleman responsible for her removal, though he has forgone any right he might once have had to such an appellation through his own corrupt and vicious conduct.

I shall expect a report of your progress within the week.

F.H.C.

'I've told you already, I don't know, and even if I did, I couldn't tell you.'

We are now at the desk of the police-station in Bow Street, in front of a hefty constable Charles doesn't know, and who clearly doesn't know who he is either.

'Look, sir,' he says with a practised theatrical sigh, 'you *say* you know Inspector Field, and that may very well be so, but he's not *my* inspector, and *my* inspector would take a pretty dim view of me divulging anything in our files without the proper authority. So until you can show me such authority, then I'm afraid the answer is going to remain the same: no.'

Charles stands there, drumming his fingers on the desk, but he's beaten and he knows it. The constable now makes a great show of ignoring him and carrying on with what he's doing, and summons a pink-faced young man from the back of the office to collect a stack of paperwork. Charles turns away, only to find himself face to face with the sergeant he met at the graveyard. It seems weeks ago, but it's actually barely two.

'Maddox, isn't it?' says the man. 'What can we be doing for you?' He's eyeing Charles' bandaged hand with some interest, but he conforms exactly to our previous experience of him by pointedly refusing to ask.

'He was enquiring about the Cass case, sir,' interjects the constable. 'You remember – about a year ago. That woman we found up at Church Street – had been cut up good and proper.'

The sergeant nods. 'I remember,' he says slowly. 'You seem to take rather an unhealthy interest in that part of town, Mr Maddox, if you don't mind me saying so. What's got you poking around in that old case?'

'I was wondering which of your officers was first on the scene.'

'And why should that concern you?'

Charles wonders for a moment if what he's about to do is all that well advised, but decides he has little real alternative. He takes a deep breath. 'I believe the man who killed Abigail Cass may have struck again. But I cannot be certain of that until I know more about the first attack.'

'Struck again, you say?' This with a frown. 'And where was this, precisely?'

'Near Golden Square, on Sunday night. Woman by the name of Lizzie Miller.'

'Can't say it rings any bells. Whore, was she? Must be, in that neighbourhood. Street robberies like that – ten a penny.'

'But this one wasn't a street robbery. She was killed in her own room. I think she knew the man who killed her, and I think Abigail Cass may have known him too.'

The sergeant manages a thin smile. 'Correct me if I'm wrong, but it seems to me that these two crimes have very little in common. What makes you think there's a connection?'

'The newspaper report of the Cass death mentioned a "frenzied attack". It sounded unduly brutal for what you appear to be dismissing as a petty alleyway assault.'

If he was hoping that would draw the sergeant out, then he's misjudged his man; he's far too wily for that.

'This other girl – Lizzie Miller – was practically eviscerated. Breasts cut off, heart cut out, face removed. Does any of that sound like Abigail Cass? I can't believe you wouldn't remember something like that, if it happened on your patch.'

Is it Charles' imagination, or was there just the merest flicker – the merest trace of a flicker – in the sergeant's eyes? But it's not enough – not on its own.

'Can you look at the file for me? Or better still, let me look at it? It would only take a minute.'

The sergeant is no longer meeting his eye, 'That's not possible, I'm afraid, as the constable here has no doubt already informed you. Police files are confidential – you should know that better than anyone. Was that all?'

Outside, the sky is clear and bright and the street is heaving with traffic, both on foot and on wheel; Covent Garden is creating its usual gridlock. There are greengrocers' vans, costermongers' carts, and row upon row of donkey-barrows backed up all the way down Bow Street to the Strand, while their owners wait their turn to unload. The men are catching a last coffee from nearby stalls, and groups of women in rough shawls are sitting on the kerbs, smoking pipes. The smell of cheap tobacco is layered with the earthy aroma of fresh-dug vegetables, and the stronger wafts of scent from wagons laden with oranges. Some of the costermongers' carts are bright with new brass, but most are drawn by cowed and miserable animals, the barrows patched together with pieces of sacking and bits of old rope. On both sides of the road the pavements are stacked with sacks of produce – cauliflowers, carrots, swede, turnips – and shreds of cabbage are being trodden slippery underfoot in the mud. Women have baskets of apples balanced on their heads, and some of the men are managing whole stacks of them, so that from a distance a squadron of wicker giants seem to be lurching and swaying up the street. Charles' eye is caught suddenly by the sight of a girl in a thin print frock weaving her way through the crowd, a basket of violets over her arm and auburn curls under her velveteen bonnet. He's sure it's Sarah – how many girls have hair that shade? – but when she turns in his direction he realizes his mistake at once. This girl must be at least fifteen and the hair, now he sees it against her face, is far too garish to be natural. He looks away, anxious not to catch her eye and have her misinterpret his interest, and finds himself feeling a vague sense of disappointment. Which is, of course, ridiculous. He has no interest in Sarah – no desire whatsoever to see her again. He's so absorbed in reminding himself of this fact that he starts like a gazelle when someone touches him on the arm.

'Mr Maddox, is it?'

It's the thin little constable who was loitering at the back of the police office. He looks painfully young, his skin blotched with pimples. His collar is at least one size too tight and is chafing his neck, much as his presence there appears to be chafing his conscience. He looks round furtively before speaking again. 'Percy Walsh, sir. Constable Percy Walsh. Look, I probably shouldn't be talking to you. The sergeant would have me strung up.'

'Is it about Abigail Cass?'

The lad's eyes are flicking from Charles to the crowd to the door, and back again. 'You were asking which officer found the body? Well, it were me. I can tell you what you want to know.'

Charles tries to disguise his sudden rise of excitement. 'Can you spare me ten minutes? It won't take long.'

Walsh nods. 'Wait for me by St Paul's, in the piazza – I'll be with you as soon as I can.'

In the piazza business is already brisk and the air is thick with costers' cries: 'Three a penny, two shillins the lot'; 'Best quality leeks, just look at the shine on these beauties'; 'Fine apples, mister – 'apenny each – you won't get no gawfs 'ere.'

Some of the market lads are washing themselves at the pump and others are gathered round the birdcatcher's pitch, poking fingers in the cages and whistling at the merchandise.

Charles buys a coffee from a stall under the colonnade, and after a moment's reflection buys another for Walsh. It seems the least he can do, and he even goes as far as to buy a piece of seedcake from an old woman with a face as brown as a walnut. He eventually spots the young constable weaving his way through the crowd, and smiles to himself at the combination of aversion and abuse his starched uniform provokes. Walsh narrowly escapes being pelted with overripe fruit, and when he makes it to Charles' side he suggests they go into the churchyard, where they will be out of sight – and out of shot.

'So,' says Charles, once they've found a bench, 'you were the one who found Abigail Cass.'

The constable takes a gulp of coffee, and nods. 'It weren't my usual patrol – I were covering for another lad who'd got his leg broke following a thief through Rats' Castle. Fell into one of them traps they lay for us and ended up half-drowned in a vat of sewage.'

'So what happened – what did you see?'

The lad's face veers from red to pale. 'I ain't never seen nothing like it, I can tell you. First up, I thought it was something off a Smithfield cart – some sort of animal carcase with all the guts spilling over the road. But straight away I knew I was wrong – there's no butcher as would take his wagon up that route. And the closer I got, I could see it was a woman, despite the wreck he'd made of her. There was blood everywhere.'

'*He?* Who? Did you see him?'

Walsh shakes his head. 'Not me. All I saw was what he'd done.'

'Go on.'

Walsh takes another noisy swallow of coffee. 'I tell you one thing, I ain't never seen the inside of a human body like that before. He'd cut her wide open and thrown her innards across her face. What there was left of 'em. Doctor told me afterwards that half her organs were gone, and we never did find 'em. He also said the man must 'ave known what he was doing, because

235

it'd have taken him at least an hour to take a body apart like that.'

'What was missing, exactly, do you know?'

Walsh fishes in his pocket and gets out a small black leather notebook. 'Uterus and its appendages, upper portion of the vagina, posterior two thirds of the bladder. But that weren't what killed her. She'd had her throat cut. Ear to ear.'

He mimics the action, left to right. Charles notes it and wonders if it was deliberate.

'And what pose was the body in?'

Walsh frowns and looks again at his notes. 'I'm not sure I follow?'

'On her back, on her face – what? Did it look as if he'd arranged the body in a certain way?'

'Oh, I see,' he says, his face brightening. 'Well now you come to mention it, it did look a bit odd. A bit *artificial,* if you take my meaning. She was on her back, like you said, but her knees were up, almost as if—'

He blushes suddenly; he is, after all, very young.

Charles saves him further embarrassment. 'As if she was having sexual relations?'

'Exactly, sir. That was what struck me. That and the blood. Like I said.'

Charles nods grimly. The constable's experience is a mirror image of his own.

'Were there no reports of people hearing her cry out?'

The constable shakes his head. He starts on the seedcake with what is – in the circumstances – commendable enthusiasm.

'No one heard nothing,' he says, his mouth full of cake. 'But the doctor thought she'd been gagged, which might account for it – her tongue was twice its normal size. Seems he probably killed her quick, then took 'is time with the rest of it.'

236

'So no witnesses at all,' says Charles with a sigh.

'I didn't say that. Though I'm not sure "witness" quite covers it neither.' He starts coughing, and specks of cake splutter down his uniform.

Charles can barely contain his impatience; he seizes the lad by the shoulders and pounds his back. He's so thin Charles can feel his shoulder-blades, even through the thick layers of cloth.

'When I arrived at the scene,' Walsh says eventually, his voice still strained, 'first thing I saw was this young lad running away down the alley. Shabby little urchin he was. Anyway, it was pretty dark down there, but as far as I could see this lad'd been bending over the body – we found out after there were at least two rings missing on her left hand. Anyways, I tried to catch 'im but he was too quick for me, and I thought I'd seen the last of 'im, but as luck would have it I came upon 'im again a few days later, when I was on me way home. Turns out he's a crossing-sweeper on one of those streets off Holborn. Newton Street, if I remember rightly. I saw a man talking to the sweep from a distance, and naturally I thought the boy might be importuning the gentleman, so I approached 'em both, and that was when I recognized it was the same lad I'd seen in the alleyway.'

'And what did he tell you – the boy?'

'Not much. Claimed he "never saw nothink" and "never done nothink" and he was going to "hook it, just like 'e was told to".'

'What do you mean – "like he was told to"?'

'That's what I wondered. Sounded to me like someone had put the frighteners on 'im, but whoever it was, he weren't telling. I tried to press 'im but the man stepped in and told me not to be harassing the lad, who had to battle all day to clear the mud and got but a pittance by way of exchange.'

'You don't know who the man was?'

'Refused to give me 'is name. Said he was nobody. And he certainly looked no better – scrawny hair, matted beard, filthy coat. Though I do recollect thinking there was something in 'is manner that suggested 'e'd 'ad a fall in life.'

'Have you seen either of them since?'

'The man, no. But I did see the lad again, only yesterday as it 'appens. It reminded me that I 'adn't heard anything for a good long while about the Cass case, so I went and 'ad a look at the files. Just out of interest, you know 'ow it is. But there was nothing there.'

'The file was missing?'

'No, the file was there all right. It's just that all the details – the doctor's report, all of that – it were all gone. There was nothing to say it wasn't just the usual sort of street robbery the sergeant told you it was. No different from the rest of 'em.'

'And that's not all,' he continues, leaning forward and lowering his voice. Charles realizes suddenly that the lad's not unnerved by what he saw after all, he's positively revelling in it. As a more celebrated novelist than I once said, "We can sometimes recognize the looks of a century ago on a modern face, but never those of a century to come". And this lad – had Charles but known it – is the very model of a modern teenage geek.

'This boy,' he whispers, 'the crossing sweeper – he's mixed up somehow in whatever it is that Inspector Bucket's investigating. I can't tell you what it is, 'cause none of us at Bow Street know anything about it, 'e keeps it so close to his chest. But there's one thing I do know. I saw a messenger come for 'im last night, and I recognized 'is face. His name's Knox, Jeremiah Knox, and he's—'

'Chief clerk to Edward Tulkinghorn.'

'Oh,' says Walsh, evidently disappointed, 'so you already know 'im then?'

'I know him,' says Charles.

His voice is firm, but for the first time in months – and certainly for the first time since he started this case – he's beginning to feel afraid. Afraid enough to be glad he can now fire a gun with reasonable accuracy, and that he has it about him, even now. Afraid enough to go straight back to Buckingham Street and issue Stornaway strict new instructions on bolting the doors front and back, even during the day. But not afraid enough – yet – to think again about the wisdom of what he's doing.

Or change his mind.

An hour later he's been to Newton Street and found the crossing-place occupied not by a lad, but by a thin faded girl. Everything about her from her straw bonnet to her coarse wool cloak to her wan skin seems bleached and colourless. She's sweeping the street rather erratically with a series of odd juddering movements and cannot be persuaded to leave off, though she is – eventually – coaxed into revealing that 'Toughy' did indeed once sweep here, but she has only the vaguest notion of the passing of time and cannot say for sure how long it was since he left or where he might be now. Thankfully Abigail Cass proves a rather easier quarry. The constable has furnished him with an address, and within the hour Charles finds himself at the entrance to a narrow cul-de-sac near the Foundling Hospital. It's so narrow, in fact, that a coster's cart can only just negotiate it and the inhabitants on opposite sides of the road can talk comfortably to each other by looking out of their windows. One house has a heap of mussel shells by the kerb, another a soggy pile of yellowing vegetables. There are strawberry baskets hanging by some doors, and grocers' sieves and barrels of herrings at others. Long poles stretch above his

239

head and lines of old patched sheets hang drying in the damp air. Four old men are sitting on the ground near the junction playing cards, seemingly oblivious to the vehement row taking place a few yards further down, where a woman with slicked black curls is leaning out of her first-floor window and yelling abuse at a chimney sweep in the road below.

'That villain dragged her in 'ere by the hair,' she cries at the crowd gathered round him, 'and then 'e kicked her till she was black an' blue! You should see 'er face! Make 'im show you 'is boots – I'll wager there's blood on 'em still!'

A woman in the crowd shouts at her that she's a 'vicious old cat' and shakes her fist at her, while people in the windows all around the court applaud and whistle.

Charles skirts past the crowd to a house at the far end of the yard, where the door's opened by an old Irishwoman with a black eye and a nightcap tied tight around her head. She looks at Charles with some suspicion at first, but a shilling soon gains him entry. The room she shows him into has a sloping roof, with little black-framed pictures round the walls. Most are too fogged to make a guess at their subjects, but there's one of a sailor smoking a pipe, next to Jesus with a bright red bleeding heart, and a portrait of Daniel O'Connell. There's a flypaper hanging from the ceiling and in one corner of the room a recess with a bed pushed flush against the wall. A stout lad is asleep on top of the bed, still clad in his outdoor clothes. The blue-striped shirt is missing one sleeve and the black trousers look as greasy as tarpaulin.

'What happened to your eye?' says Charles, not much to the point.

The old woman puts a hand to her face. She's wearing grey fingerless mittens and there are pulls and snags in the dirty wool.

'T'at blackgeyard t'ere gave it me, shame on him. It's t'e liquor I blame – he's not such a bad lad when he's sober. And I canna turn him out. I need t'e money.' Her fingers close more tightly round the coin Charles gave her, as if apprehensive he might demand it back.

'I'm here about Abigail Cass,' he says. 'I think she lodged here. About a year ago?'

'Ah, what a nice lady!' says the old woman. 'Such a dridful thing as happened to her. Nice God-fearing widow woman like her. And no-one on hand to pay for a decent burial.' She shakes her head. 'It's not right, it's not right at all.'

'How long had she been living here before she was killed?'

'Oh, not long. A week or two, no more. She said when she came it was just for a short while, until she found a new position. People like her, they get t'eir lodgings t'rown in. Not like t'e rest of us.'

'I'm not sure I understand you.'

'To be sure, I t'ought as you were a friend of hers? She was a nurse, wasn't she – only t'e place she was working at let her go, and she had to find anot'er situation. I told her she might be better off going home, to her own people, but she said t'ere was no work to be had t'ereabouts, and in any case she had not lived t'ere for many years and had no family left to speak of. Apart from her brother, of course.'

Charles has wandered to the window in the course of this, but turns now and stares at the old woman, who's started to fiddle fretfully with the mismatched plates and cups stacked on the tiny chest of drawers.

'Abigail Cass had a *brother*?'

'Oh yes. Very nice man, if a bit rough round t'e edges for my taste. Came here a few mont's a'ter she was killed but I couldn't tell him anyt'ing he didn't already know. Poor man, he'd only just found out she was dead – dead and buried in a pauper's grave and too late for him to do anyt'ing about it. But t'en he was a fearsome long way away when it happened, and t'at's the trut'.'

The lad on the bed turns over heavily on to his back and starts snoring loudly. The old woman comes closer to Charles and looks up at him. 'Seems Mrs Cass had written to him just before she died, only t'e letter was mislaid and he only got it weeks later. Poor man was cursing and crying and taking on so, it weren't easy to follow what he were saying.' She sighs. 'I've seen it take people t'at way before – t'ey lose a loved one unexpected and look for someone else to blame. Most often t'ere's no trut' in it, and I'm sure t'at's what poor Mr Boscawen realized in t'e end.'

Charles sees it coming, but only just, and it's a shock all the same. The final definitive connection he's been searching for.

He puts his hand in his pocket and takes out half a crown. It's bright. New-minted.

'This hospital where she worked – where did you say it was?'

She flutters a mittened hand. 'Oh I couldn't tell you – I don't t'ink she ever mentioned it. Or at least not in my hearing.'

'And she said nothing about why she left?'

'We-ell, not exactly—'

The old woman turns away and starts to tinker with the crockery again. Charles moves a step closer, 'Mrs O'Driscoll?'

She glances up at him and then at the figure prone on the bed, but whatever it is she's so hesitant – or so fearful – to confide, he is surely in no fit state to hear it.

'I'm no listener at keyholes, sir, I can assure you, but t'e rooms here are so small and t'e walls so thin—'

'I quite understand. I'm sure that if anyone raised their voice in here you could hear it the other side of the court.'

'Ah, but t'at was just it. He didn't raise his voice at all. Mrs Cass – she was quite distressed – angry even – but for all t'e noise he made you might'a been forgiven for t'inking she was talking to herself.'

So much, thinks Charles, for not listening at keyholes, but he lets no trace of the thought appear on his face.

'Was it an aristocratic voice? A gentleman's voice?'

'Oh I couldn't tell you. It were too low. Little more t'an a whisper, but it was a strange one, t'at's for sure. Sent cold shivers right down my back. I told Father Conor, it reminded me of what it says in t'e Bible about a voice "going like a serpent". T'at's what it sounded like, and no mistake. A serpent.'

'But you didn't hear what he was actually saying?'

Mrs O'Driscoll shakes her head. 'No more than a word or too. Not'ing as made any sense. Mrs Cass, now, t'at was different. She was defending herself, t'at was clear enough. I remember t'ere was something about a girl having been cruelly used, and cruelly wronged. It had such a ring to it, it stuck in my mind. And t'en she said she knew what was going on, and all t'e noble rank and money in London would not be enough to conceal it, not if she had anything to do with it.'

The expression is more eloquent, but the meaning is just the same: *I naw what yow did. I will make yow pay.*

Charles takes a deep breath; his heart is beating faster now. 'But you have no idea who the man was?'

'I never saw him. But t'ere was one thing that stuck in my mind. T'e door was a little ajar, and t'ere was a smell like baccy, only sweeter somehow.' She shakes her head again almost wistfully, and pulls distractedly at her shawl. 'Lovely it was – I'd never smelt anyt'ing like it before.'

So, thinks Charles, she may not be able to identify a gentleman's voice, but she can identify a gentleman's tobacco all right.

'And when was this, Mrs O'Driscoll?'

'Last September. I remember exactly, because it was less than a week later t'at she was killed. Poor, poor lady.'

'Did you tell the police about the man you heard?'

She looks offended. 'But of course I did. T'ere's some round here as wouldn't hold out a hand to a policeman to save him from drowning, but I'm not one of t'em. I told t'at nice inspector everyt'ing I just told you and he said it was – what was the word, now – not *relevant*.' She folds her hands. 'Not relevant to t'e investigation. T'at was his exact word. Not *relevant*.'

How very interesting, muses Charles – what's an inspector doing coming round here, when there are any number of constables to take on such a menial task? He can make a pretty shrewd guess who it was, too, but he needs to be certain. Absolutely certain.

'Do you remember the man's name? The inspector?'

She beams at him. 'To be sure! It were such an odd one, I could hardly forget. Didn't sound like a real name, if you take my meaning. Bucket. T'at was his name. Inspector Bucket.'

Chapter Eighteen

Attorney and Client

When he emerges from the stairway, Charles is unsurprised to see the crowd has dispersed and the court is empty of all but the four old men sitting on the kerb, still dealing their worn brown cards. Disputes between neighbours flare like summer storms round here – full of sound and fury, but not very enduring. At first he barely remarks the imposing carriage waiting at the junction with the main road, beyond noticing in a rather distracted way that it looks a little rustily old-fashioned in its heavy black accoutrements. That, in itself, could have been warning enough, but Charles' observational skills have deserted him this time – so much so that when he draws level with the carriage and sees the man standing at the door, he is completely unprepared.

'Mr Maddox,' says Jeremiah Knox, touching his hat. 'Good day to you.'

Charles spins round, his eyes scanning the passers-by for someone he recognizes – someone who might have been tracking his steps. A cluster of closed chary faces stares back at him – he knows none of them – has not, to his knowledge, seen a single one of them before, but that in itself proves nothing more than his adversary's formidable powers. The fact remains that Tulkinghorn knew he was here, so how

245

much more does he know? How long now has his every movement been followed? Only since the attack in the City Road – or was it before that? And if that's the case, how in God's name did he let himself be so deplorably careless?

Knox, meanwhile, has opened the carriage door. Charles is seriously considering pushing him to the ground and taking to his heels, when there's a movement out of the corner of his eye and he sees a figure descend from the groom's seat at the back. He seems hardly much more than a boy, but he wears no livery, and his manner is cocky and insolent as he stands staring at Charles with not even the slightest suggestion of deference in his pale yellow eyes. Knox alone he could handle, but two of them will be harder to evade – not, at least, without creating a disturbance and attracting the attention of the constable giving directions to a well-dressed couple on the other side of the road. Charles hesitates, then steps quickly inside.

The journey is scarce worth such a ponderous conveyance – indeed the traffic is so heavy Charles could have walked it quicker, but he's only too aware that the purpose of the carriage is to guarantee his presence, not spare his feet. Barely fifteen minutes later he's mounting the steps to the house in Lincoln's Inn Fields, followed hard by the silent but persistent Knox. Tulkinghorn's room is much as it was, the disconcerting figure on the ceiling still cushioned in his flowers and his overgrown cherubs, and still gesturing, in his strangely unconvincing way, down from the clouds. And if, by some odd trick of perspective, that plump and insistent finger of his seems to be pointing now in Charles' direction, then Charles does not see it. Mr Tulkinghorn, by contrast, has departed not only from his accustomed place, but from his

246

customary demeanour. He has abandoned the station of honour behind the desk, and stands instead against the chimney-piece, where two candles in antique silver candlesticks are struggling to dispel the shadows from the shuttered and stuffy room.

'So, it's you, is it?' he says. 'I have been to a great deal of trouble to find you, sir.'

'So it appears.'

'I recall, rather distinctly, that I instructed you to return Sir Julius' letters to me, the last time we met in this room. Since you have not done so, I have been compelled – at some inconvenience – to dispatch my clerk to fetch the said correspondence. Indeed, he has called at Buckingham Street on, I believe, some four separate occasions, but to no avail. Each time he enquires, he is told you are not at home, you are engaged, you cannot be disturbed.'

'That was quite true. I have been much pre-occupied with a case.'

'You know quite as well as I do,' says the lawyer, tapping his ring of keys irritably against the marble mantel, 'that that statement is a lie. You have been evading me, sir, and I am not accustomed to overlook such impertinence.'

'And I,' counters Charles, moving a step or two further into the room, his blue eyes darkening, 'am not accustomed to being waylaid in the street, and set upon by a vicious ruffian. You might tell Sir Julius that, when next you see him. I am no more a man to cross than you are, Mr Tulkinghorn.'

The lawyer looks at him warily. He has made, Charles notes, no reference at all to his conspicuously bandaged hand. 'You were paid to undertake a particular task—'

'Paid!' retorts Charles with derision. How he wishes, now, that he had kept those sovereigns, so that he could take them

247

from his pocket and hurl them back in the lawyer's face.

'You were *not* paid,' continues Tulkinghorn, ignoring the interjection, 'to meddle in matters that do not concern you. Since you have elected to do precisely that, you must accept the consequences.'

'So you are not denying that I was attacked, and that this' – he holds up his disfigured hand – 'is the result?'

'I am neither denying nor confirming anything of the kind. I am, however, giving you a further warning. I had hoped that you possessed sufficient intelligence to render such a tiresome reiteration unnecessary, but I appear to have been mistaken. I repeat: you are interfering in matters you cannot possibly understand.'

'Oh, but I do,' replies Charles, moving another step towards the lawyer. 'I understand a good deal more than you realize. I know that you only hired me to find Boscawen so that you could have him silenced, just as you had already silenced his sister. I know you had Lizzie Miller killed – because there was something she might have told me, had she lived. And I know that you are prostituting your fine reputation to conceal the sordid secrets of a rich and powerful man.'

Tulkinghorn is celebrated among his associates for his inscrutability, and he has never looked more impenetrable than he does now.

'Let us consider then,' he says eventually, tapping the mantel once again with the key-ring and looking imperturbably at Charles all the while, 'how the matter stands. You are determined, I take it, to continue in this extremely ill-advised course of action.'

'There is nothing you can do to stop me.'

'You intend to pursue your enquiries until you discover

248

what – in *your* opinion – really lay behind William Boscawen's monstrous persecution of my innocent client.'

'It is not a case of my opinion, it is a case of the truth.'

'And if and when you ascertain this "truth" of yours, I imagine you will not let the matter lie idly by.'

'You may collude in a such repugnant concealment if you wish. I have no intention of doing so.'

'And should such circumstances arise, I assume you would, therefore, consider that you had an obligation – a duty, even – to expose Sir Julius. In the newspapers, for instance.'

Charles flushes, realizing, suddenly and too late, that he has been put on the stand and there is no advocate in London who can compete in cross-examination with this lacklustre little man, with his dull black clothes, and his limp white frill.

He lifts his chin, defiant. 'There can be no higher cause than the truth, Mr Tulkinghorn.' Surely he's heard words like that before, and recently? But he cannot for the moment remember where. 'I would hope that you, as a bastion and mainstay of our great and much-admired system of justice, would be the first to concur.'

If a note of sarcasm has crept into his voice, we can perhaps forgive him for that. The lawyer, by contrast, persists in the same monotonous tone.

'Very well. Then I am authorized to inform you that we will – with some reluctance – advance you the same sum as the one you have already received, on the strict condition that you return my client's property to me forthwith, and cease at once and forever from this outrageous pursuit. Consider well, Mr Maddox. I will not offer such leniency again.'

'Keep your money, Tulkinghorn. I despise it almost as much as I despise you.'

'You surprise me, my friend,' the lawyer observes composedly. 'I hardly thought a man in your precarious circumstances could afford to turn money away in such a cavalier fashion.'

'My finances may be precarious, but my integrity is not. You, it seems, suffer from exactly the opposite predicament. I know which of the two I prefer.'

'So you will not desist.'

'I will not.'

Tulkinghorn nods slowly. 'Very well. And if I were to tell you that I have it in my command, by the stroke of my pen, to have you dragged from your bed this very night and hauled naked through the streets to a prison cell, what would you say to that?'

'I think,' Charles replies coolly, 'that you should save your threats for the sort of pitiful wretch likely to be intimidated by them.'

'You may think that if you choose,' returns Mr Tulkinghorn, taking out his handkerchief and blowing his nose. 'But it alters nothing.'

'You are bluffing. You cannot terrify me.'

'Clearly not,' says the lawyer, 'but I can make good on my threat all the same.'

'You have no cause. I have done nothing wrong. Unlike your despicable client.'

'Ah, ' says Tulkinghorn with a smile, 'but it can, regrettably, be the way with our great and justly admired system of justice that one does not have to commit a crime to be hanged for one. As a former member of the constabulary I need hardly, I am sure, tell *you* that. The name Silas Boone, for instance, will not I think be unfamiliar to you.'

He puts away his handkerchief and adjusts his frill, then looks Charles straight in the eye, for very possibly the first time.

'Let us be clear, once and for all. If I hear word that you are continuing with this investigation of yours, I will see to it that you are shut up in jail under hard discipline. There is a treadmill, sir, in Coldbath Fields where the inmates stand and grind for eight hours a day. And an iron crank requiring ten thousand daily turns. A man with an injury such as yours would scarce last a week under such a regimen. I will give you no further warning,' he concludes, a rare spot of colour appearing in both cheeks. 'And be assured of this: cross me again, and I will not flinch. For I make no threat I have not the will and the power to accomplish, and to the utmost extremity.'

Charles nods. 'You have been admirably clear. Now let me be so.' He crosses the three feet that still separate them in one stride and takes Tulkinghorn's flaccid throat hard in his hand. 'This conversation is the last – the very *last* – time you will seek to impede my enquiries. If I am hindered again in any way – whether by violence or otherwise – you will live to regret it. Do you understand?' he whispers, his breath hot on the lawyer's papery flesh. 'However well you bolt your door, however strong you think the key, I will come here, in the night, in the dark, when you least expect it, and you will discover to your cost that I, too, have never yet made an idle threat, and I, too, *will not flinch.*'

He stares in the lawyer's watery eyes for a long moment, then pushes him against the wall, and turns and leaves without looking back. He does not, therefore, see Knox emerge from where he has been standing behind the door and make a few notes in a small leather pocket-book, before going quickly to his master, who has staggered to his heavy mahogany chair and thrown his head back against it, and is now lying there gasping, staring sightlessly at the inscrutable

251

figure of Allegory above him, whose finger points now even more insistently, from the flowers, and the pillars, and the painted clouds.

Chapter Nineteen

Perspective

For all Charles' bravado, the next few days mark a pause. Or perhaps a *recul pour mieux sauter*. I'm not at all sure even Charles knows, fully, what he intends to do, but I do know that he spends the best part of two whole days in the Buckingham Street house, venturing out only to meet briefly with Sam Wheeler over lamb chops to check on progress with the Miller case (none), and to practise (three times) at the shooting range off Leicester Square. It's on one of these occasions that he arrives to find an unaccustomed gathering of people at the far end of the gallery – or rather, if we are being strictly accurate, a standing of unaccustomed people, for the figures he can see gathered with the trooper by one of the little cabins are very far indeed from the establishment's usual clientele. There is a little plump bald man with a shining head and a clump of untidy black hair who seems familiar to Charles from somewhere, though he's clearly never held a gun in his life, and beside him a tall dark young man with sunburnt skin and a calm but troubled face. The gallery is – other than these – quite empty of custom.

The little bald man seems anxious to be gone, and once the trooper has shown him out, he makes purposefully towards him with his usual military tread and – somewhat unusually – extends his hand.

'I am glad to see you, Mr Maddox.'

'Are you in some sort of trouble?' asks Charles, glancing past the sturdy shoulder. He has picked up, here and elsewhere, that the old trooper has money worries – money worries that may be entangling him in an even deeper predicament. But his interlocutor shakes his head.

'No trouble, Mr Maddox. At least not for me, and not for today.'

He takes Charles by the elbow. 'The last time you came, I believe you mentioned that you had been looking for a young crossing-sweep?'

'The lad from Newton Street? What of it?'

'And I believe you said that this lad – if you could find him – might be able to help you discover who had murdered an innocent woman?'

'*Two* innocent women. I think the same man this lad saw has also killed at least one other woman since, and probably set that fire in Bell Yard as well, which killed a dozen more.'

'But if you were to find him, I'm sure you would not wish this lad any harm, or hand him over to those as might wish to harass him or move him on.'

Charles frowns. 'That is not in my nature, as I hope you would know.'

The trooper bows. 'Right enough, sir, so I do. But it is a delicate matter and I'm sure as you'll understand my method of proceeding soon enough. You see, the lad is here.'

'*Here?* How on earth did he come to be here, of all places?'

The trooper gestures briefly towards the back of the room. 'He were brought here by that young gentleman. A surgeon by trade. Seems he found the boy in the rookeries. Seems he knew him – or of him. There be some sort of connection between them, that I do know, though neither has said what it is.

Anyhow, this young doctor took pity on the lad, and brought him, by a rather roundabout route that need not trouble you, to me. He has been here two days now, and Phil and I have been doing our best to care for him. Having been found, when a baby, in the gutter, Phil naturally takes an interest in the poor neglected creature.'

Charles stares at the trooper, then starts eagerly towards the cabin, but the man holds him back. 'The lad is clean now, and fed, and as comfortable as we can make him, but he is quite worn out with all that has befallen him, and not long for this world, I should say. Go gently with him, sir, and keep the doctor by.'

The little cabin at the back is dim and cramped, but it's clean, and the mattress is provided with sheets that have been lately washed, albeit a little worn. There's a small shelf of medicines on one side of the bed, and on the other the figure, hunched now, of the young doctor. He looks up when Charles enters and motions silently to a place by his side.

'He is sleeping. Rest can do more for him now than I can.'

He reaches across and lays a hand gently on his patient's heart. The boy murmurs at the touch and his bony chest heaves and rattles. His eyelids flutter, but there is no ignoring the deep hollows under his eyes, or the thin fingers clutching at the bedclothes.

'How long has he been like this?' asks Charles softly.

'When I found him he was the most abject figure you can possibly imagine – all in rags and cowering against a wall, with a hand over his face as if the only things life has ever dealt him are blows. Which is probably not so very far from the truth. Not so much a human being as a rat, or a stray dog.'

There's a bitter ring to the doctor's voice at this, and the lad stirs and opens his eyes. He sees the doctor's face, and huge tears well up and spill on to his emaciated cheeks. 'You's not angry wiv me agin, are you, Mr Woodcot? I is wery truly hearty sorry that I done it and I never went fur to do it, and I wos a-hoping as you'd be able to forgive me in your mind.'

'No, Jo,' says the doctor, though his tears are falling too, 'I'm not angry with you. You had a reason for what you did, and you could not have known what consequences it was to have. And I know the young lady forgives you too.'

'What's he talking about?' whispers Charles.

'Oh,' says the doctor, passing a hand across his eyes. 'It is – another matter. Unconnected with your own.'

He takes the lad by the hand and bends over him. 'Now, Jo,' he says kindly, 'there is a gentleman to see you. He wishes to ask you some questions.'

'He ain't the police, Mr Woodcot?' cries the boy, his eyes flaring with terror.

'No, Jo,' says the doctor soothingly, 'he is not the police. But if you can tell him what he needs to know, you'd be helping to catch a very bad man, and that would go well with you, would it not?'

'I'll do anythink as you say, sir, for I knows it's good.'

'Very well then.'

The doctor motions Charles closer, and he crouches close to the little feverish face.

'I want to ask you about a woman, Jo. A woman you saw once, in the street.'

'Not the lady in a wale and the bonnet and the gownd as sed she wos a servant?' The boy is suddenly distressed again, and catches at the doctor's hand. 'Not the lady at the berryin-ground! Don't as make me talk about that, Mr Woodcot! I sed – it is her and it an't her and I don't know nothink more about it.'

Charles looks bewildered but the doctor gently interjects, 'No, Jo. Not that lady, another one. Mr Maddox here will explain.'

He nods to Charles. 'Go on.'

'I think this woman was dead when you found her, Jo,' says Charles. 'Do you remember that? It was something over a year ago. Do you recall seeing a woman lying dead in the street around that time?'

The boy nods slowly. 'It were near the berryin-ground. It warn't the lady in the wale but it war nigh the same place. She war lying on her back, wiv her legs up. And there were blood. Lots of blood, Running like water, it wos, like wen it rains bad and my broom ain't enough to kip the mud away.'

'Did you touch her, Jo? Did you take anything from her?'

The boy looks fearfully from one face to the other. 'It warn't me as killed her, Mr Woodcot!'

'We know that, Jo,' says the doctor. 'Mr Maddox is just trying to make sure that the woman he's concerned about is the same woman you saw.'

The boy looks away. 'I knew it war wery bad and I deserve to be punished and serve me right, but I wos wery hungry and poor and ill, I wos, and they warn't no use to her no more.'

'What weren't, Jo?'

'Them pretty rings. Bright gold they wos, and shining,' he mumbles. 'Only not a bit like the sparkling one wot the t'other lady had – her as wos and yit as warn't the t'other lady – her wiv the wale and the bonnet and the gownd. Can't have been, 'cos they only gave me five bob for all three on 'em.'

Charles nods quietly, and edges closer to the boy; already the rank smell of death hangs heavy about him.

'This next question is very important, Jo. Did you see a man nearabouts where the woman was? The man who might have killed her?'

The boy's eyes widen, and he looks back at the doctor imploringly. 'I told you, Mr Woodcot, I dustn't. I would but I dustn't.'

'But that was about – the other matter,' says the doctor, a spasm of pain crossing his face. 'This is something quite different, Jo.'

'No,' whispers the boy, his voice breaking. 'No, it's all the same – all on it. He ses to me, "Hook it! Nobody wants you here. You move on, or you'll repent it." And I am, Mr Woodcot, I am!'

The doctor turns to Charles. 'I am afraid he is still confusing the two occasions. I happen to know that what he is saying is the truth – he was indeed told to move on, but that was in relation to the other matter, and the two things cannot possibly be connected.'

Charles shakes his head. 'I'm not so sure. Is it possible that the real reason the boy was told to move on was because he saw something that night that certain people did not wish to come to light? Because he witnessed a murder?'

'It's an extraordinary theory, Mr Maddox—'

But Charles has already turned to the boy on the bed. 'Who was it, Jo? Who told you to move on?'

'I dustn't name him,' says Jo. 'I dustn't do it, sir.'

'You may trust me, Jo, just as you trust the doctor here.'

'Ah, but *he* may hear,' replies Jo, shaking his head in distress. 'He is everywheres, all at wanst. I dustn't give his name!'

'I know who it is he speaks of,' the doctor tells Charles in a low voice. 'There is no need to alarm him further.'

Charles swallows hard, then reaches out and places his hand on the boy's damp forehead. 'Don't think about that now. Just think about that night. When you saw the woman dead. Do you remember the man you saw? Think carefully, Jo,

258

and tell me the truth. You know, don't you, that it's wicked to tell a lie.'

But that was clearly the wrong thing to say: Jo's eyes are now round with terror. 'I don't know nothink. It war wery dark, sir, that it wos, and I niver saw his face or nothink. I wish as I'd never gone a-nigh her – don't let them took me away agin, Mr Woodcot!'

'Don't worry, Jo. You're quite safe here. I'm not leaving you now.'

Charles reproaches himself silently, and tries another tack.

'If you didn't see what he looked like, did you perhaps see what he was wearing?'

Jo thinks for a moment, then nods warily. 'I remember there wos a hat and a coat. Long and dark it wos.'

'And was he tall? Taller than the doctor, for example?'

Jo shakes his head, but his eyes are losing their focus. 'I've been a-chivvied and a-worried and a-chivvied but now I is moved on as fur as ever I can go and can't move on no furder. It's time fur me to go down to that there berryin-ground, Mr Woodcot,' he falters, 'and put along with him as wos so good to me. Let me lay there quiet wiv him and not be chivvied no more.'

It takes him a long time to say this, and they have to stoop to hear much of it, but he slips, finally, into sleep, and the doctor gestures to Charles that the interview is over. The trooper has been standing silently in the doorway all this while, and the three of them leave the cabin and return to the table, where Phil is cleaning his tools.

'I do not know if that was any use to you, Mr Maddox,' says the doctor with a sigh, 'but I fear you will get little more. His heart has very nearly given up, and will labour but a little further.'

259

It's only now, in the full light streaming from the windows overhead, that he notices Charles' hand.

'May I?' he says, gesturing to the dressing.

Charles nods. It may not be such a bad idea, after all, for a professional to take a look.

'Has a surgeon seen this?' says the doctor with a frown, echoing Charles' thought.

Charles shakes his head, watching the bandage removed by a practised and skilful hand. As the last strip of cloth lifts from the wound, he winces, then shakes his head again as the doctor eyes him with concern. 'It's nothing.'

'On the contrary. This is a serious injury, and must be very painful, even now.'

He lifts the hand so he can examine it more closely, then touches here and there, but gently, so as not to cause unnecessary pain.

'You have had a good nurse,' he concludes eventually. 'I see no sign of infection at present, but you must remain vigilant. You risk losing the hand, if not worse.'

He asks Phil for a basin of water, then cleans the hand again and dries it, and binds it up in a new dressing. And as he does so he asks, with what is perhaps a rather artificial nonchalance, 'I have had occasion recently to treat a number of people wounded in a wreck at sea, but this injury does not resemble any of them. The cut is too clean, too expert. This was no accident, was it? Someone attacked you.'

Charles smiles bitterly. 'I found out to my cost that if one approaches too near the knuckle with the likes of Mr Tulkinghorn, one risks having the metaphor turn to reality in the most unpleasant fashion.'

He sees the trooper start at this, and a look flashes between him and the doctor.

'I see you know the name,' says Charles, his interest aroused.

'As I said to the doctor only yesterday, Mr Maddox, I know the name. Aye, I know the name, but only to my sorrow.'

The trooper rubs his large hand over the back of his neck, sending his thick hair standing on end. 'You have gathered, no doubt, that I am in difficulties just at present. It is this man, this Tulkinghorn, who is at the root of it. He has the power to turn me out of this place neck and crop, if he chooses, but he does *not* choose. He threatens, and then he withdraws. Even when I have money to give him, he passes me from here to there, refusing to see me, keeping me hanging on until it fair maddens my mind to fury.'

The trooper's face is by now as red as the soiled bandage cast aside on the table, and he heaves a heavy sigh, as if fearful of what else he might say.

'And you say this Tulkinghorn is responsible for your injury?' says the doctor to Charles, stopping for a moment in his bandaging.

'Not directly, of course,' replies Charles. 'He would not dirty his hands with such disagreeable matters, even if he had the heart and stomach to undertake them.'

'Aye,' agrees the trooper. 'As I said to the doctor here, I wish I had the chance of setting spurs to my horse and riding at that bloodless old man in a fair field. For if I had that chance, he'd be the one to go down, I can promise you that!'

'And the police?' asks the doctor calmly, still intent on the dressing.

Charles shrugs. 'I have no proof. And even if I had, I suspect Mr Tulkinghorn's word would weigh more heavily with certain officers at Bow Street than even the strongest and most incontrovertible evidence.'

It is the doctor's turn to glance up now and his face is troubled.

'I told you a few minutes ago,' he says slowly, 'that I did not believe there could be any connection between the crime you are investigating and the callous moving on of this poor lad. I am not so sure of that now. Indeed,' he continues, 'I always found it odd that such a man should have taken so much time and trouble to pursue and harry that pitiful creature – a proceeding which has unquestionably brought him directly to the sad state into which he has now descended. To track him as far out of London as the house in which he was found' – and here the shadow passes again across his face – 'and then have him taken away in the dead of night. What was there to be gained from it? Whom could it possibly benefit?'

'I think you know the answer now, sir,' says the trooper, his face grim. 'It is this Tulkinghorn – this man who hoards the private secrets of a hundred noble families, and whose sole concern is to preserve them from prying eyes and common tongues. You have a dangerous enemy, Mr Maddox, and his reach is long.'

Charles looks from the trooper to the doctor, who takes up his thought again. 'Indeed, this would seem to be the only explanation for another otherwise inexplicable aspect of the affair. The fact that the boy remains – as you saw – in a quite irrational terror of the person who ordered him to keep out of the way. He still believes this person to be everywhere, and to know everything.'

'I know to my own cost,' returns the trooper, shaking his head, 'that this person he speaks of is undoubtedly a rum customer – and a deep one. The boy is right about that, in every particular. I never saw a man with such an outward appearance of candour, and yet so secretive a way of going on.

262

Nor did I ever meet a man who seems so clearly to be marching straight ahead, only to veer off, at the last moment, in another course entirely.'

'Of course,' says Charles slowly, as the final recognition dawns. 'Inspector Bucket.'

Chapter Twenty

Hester's Narrative

And now I come to a part of my story touching myself very nearly indeed, and for which I was all unprepared. It was some months after Clara had been ill, and yet I felt still that there was some strange and inexplicable shadow between us, and yet in every other way my life was just as it had always been. Until that day – oh, that terrible day! – when I first felt myself unwell. My dreams the night before had been unusually tangled and hectic, and when I woke the room was still dark and I could not free myself from the impression that something had happened during the night, though I did not know what it was, that had left me with a curious sense of fullness, as if I were becoming too large altogether. I made myself a little tea, and sat down heavily before the dying fire. And as the room grew gradually colder and colder I found I was shivering from head to foot, and yet I was growing all the while not more wakeful but more somnolent, and my thoughts soon became so confused that I began to lose a sense of who I was – now the girl in the room was me, and now she was Clara, and now she was poor confused Miss Flint, distraught and tormented, and crying aloud in fear in the darkness.

I do not know how long it was that I remained there, but my next recollection is of the grey light of morning stealing between the curtains, which I must have left open. I rose, somewhat stiffly, and went to close them. It was still very early, and the sky overcast and drab, but I was sure I could see figures in the garden. I believe – I am sure I caught a glimpse of white – that one of them was Anne, the boarder I think I referred to once before. She was walking on the farther side of the lawn, accompanied by one of the maids and another woman I had never seen. I should have remembered if I had, for though her figure was comely and her manner elegant, I could see even from my window that her face was ugly. I am not being unkind, I assure you – her skin was swarthy, her forehead low, and her features almost masculine. I had no looking-glass to compliment my own looks, but I could not help feeling a most pleasant satisfaction with them – such as they are. Looking back at what I have just written, I realize that I have omitted to mention that Anne had recently returned to our company after an absence of some months. To my mind, she seemed rather changed from when I had last seen her, but my Guardian said she had been very ill and the slight changes to her appearance were no doubt due to the effects of that illness. Did not my own darling pet look rather different now than once she did? And no doubt he was right, in this as in all things.

But to return to my narrative. When Carley came to wake me, I asked her who had been in the garden and she looked at me in some perplexity and replied that I must be mistaken. There had been no visitors at that hour of the morning, she said, and none of the maids would have the leisure for a walk at such a time. And in truth, I was by then feeling so much worse that I was no longer sure of what I had seen. Indeed, Carley soon saw that I was very indisposed, and helped me to return to my bed before going at once for Miss Darby. She must have come, and come quickly, for I remember her placing her cool hand on my forehead, and the taste of something dull and bitter between my lips. That day turned into night, and the night into another day, and I had not left my bed, or seen anyone but Miss Darby. Though I found it difficult to talk, I asked once or twice for Carley, but was told she was indisposed, and unable to come. Soon after that I heard my darling in the corridor outside, but Miss Darby went to the door and said that I was asleep. I heard her whisper softly, 'You must not come in now, Miss Clara – not for all the world!' And then I knew how ill I must be, and turned my face to my pillow and wept.

I lay sick a long time, and my old life became like a distant memory. Everything I knew and loved seemed to have retreated to a far remote place, leaving me alone and abandoned in that shuttered room. There were times when all my recollections seemed to run into one another and melt together, so that there was one moment when I thought I was a little girl again at my mother's knee, but there was my Guardian sitting with us too, caressing my mother's face and running his hand over my hair. This vision was painfully real to me – the colours too bright, the lines too sharp. I doubt that anyone who has not experienced such a thing can quite understand what I mean, or why I shrank from this vision as if it were a thing of terror, though it was, in every respect, a picture of love. There were nights too when I thought myself harnessed to a terrible treadmill, or forced to work forever some unbearable machinery that burned my hands and brought hot tears to my eyes. But there were other times when I talked quite lucidly with Miss Darby, and felt her hand on my head. But I dare not even think of that worst of times, when I felt drowned in a dark place, while my whole body was ripped apart in some never-ending agony, hour after hour, and I heard a voice calling out in pain, and knew it to be my own.

But perhaps the less I think about these terrible things, the quicker I will forget them. I do remember the final utter bliss of sleep, and thinking, even in my frailty, that it was over now, and I could rest. I do not know how long this period of convalescence has lasted now. Days, perhaps weeks. I do know that the year has turned, and the weather with it. I sit at the window, wrapped in my shawl, and look down at the grey garden and watch the slow drops fall – drip, drip, drip – upon the terrace. And I remember Amy telling me of the footstep on the Ghost's Walk, and I wonder if perhaps it might be true, and if it is, what does the sound most resemble? A man's step? A woman's? The tiny feet of a little child, ever getting closer, and never coming near? It affects me, now – that sound – as it never has before, in all the long years I have lived in this house. I cannot explain why. And in all this time of my recovery I have never seen my pet. Miss Darby makes up the fire, and brings me my meals on a tray, and she is as always the soul of kindness, but other than her I see no one.

No one, that is, until this morning. I slept badly last night, disturbed by the dreary and monotonous drumming of the rain on the roof overhead, and I had only just drifted into a troubled and restless slumber when I heard a noise in the passage outside my door, and then the soft careful sound of the key turning in the lock. I sat up stiffly in bed, wondering why Miss Darby should be waking me at such an early hour, but it was not Miss Darby's face I saw. It was Carley's. She closed the door quietly behind her, then came quickly across to me and took me in her arms, and I could feel her body shaking. After a few moments she sat back and held me by the shoulders, and started to speak to me. Her voice low, and her eyes always, always fixed on mine.

And now she is gone.

I have been sitting here, in the bleak dawn light, for a long time, thinking about what she said, and shedding some bitter tears. I know Carley loves me, and I know – or thought I knew – that she would never lie to me. She said so again – over and over – that what she was telling me was the truth, and yet, how can I believe it? How can I accept what she says, without questioning everything I thought I knew – everyone I thought I trusted – every word that has been said to me in this house since the day I came here? I have gone over it in my mind, a hundred times, and still I cannot – *cannot* – believe my Guardian could have done such a thing.

And even if it were true – even if he did – even supposing—

Chapter Twenty-one

Mr Bucket

It is moonlight tonight. A clear, cold night full of sharp shadows, and the restless silence of a city that never fully comes to rest. In the attic at Buckingham Street a large black cat sleeps unchallenged and undisturbed on a tangled expanse of pale sheet, and in a room downstairs an old man stirs before the fire, his brow pressed into frowns, his mind astray in a thicket of memories that mingle and separate and re-combine in strange new patterns that he will not remember when he wakes.

Across town, in that immense but dreary mansion in its dull but elegant street, my Lady Dedlock's soul is troubled, and she is heartsick. The spectre of her pursuer fills her mind, and the prospect of that pursuit, and of never being free of it, casts a shroud before her eyes. And not a mile away from her, in a small room, and a small street, another woman she once employed nurtures the like dark thoughts of the like implacable man, and festers a bitter hatred that she cares not to contain.

And then, suddenly and without warning, the air splits open with a hissing crack that sets the dogs barking for a mile around. Those few people still out of doors stop in their tracks and look up into the sky, but it is clear, and threatens no thunder. A firecracker? But no, Guy Fawkes is long gone, and the street-urchins sleeping. A window opens, then another. A man looks out, and calls down to those on the street. What made that noise – do any of them know? A sprat-seller who's passing claims it came from over yonder near the Fields, but his voice is drowned in the sudden chiming of the hour, and by the time the last bell has faded, the street is silent again, and the moment, or incident, or whatever it was, has passed.

The morning finds Charles, once again, at the shooting gallery. Where he has been all night he does not say, but his lined shirt and shadowed jaw have their own tale to tell. As, perhaps, does the deep line that has now settled between his brows. What it is that has made him so angry – so angry that the air about him seems to crackle with furious energy – will become clear soon enough. For the moment, though, we will content ourselves with watching. And we will not be alone.

He has come, it seems, to the funeral of the crossing-sweep, though that is rather a grand term for such a meagre affair. The half-starved body lies in its open coffin, and though there are cuts on the bare feet and sores about the mouth, the thin face is finally – and perhaps for the first time – at peace. Jo has found his rest at last. The trooper has done what he can to dress the lad in clean clothes, and a heap of half-rotten verminous rags are now being fed into the rusty grate by an unusually grave-faced Phil. Charles stands with the doctor as the stern and ponderous beadle has the lid screwed down, and the coffin lifted on to the cart and wheeled towards the door. Their destination is the cemetery where Jo's dead friend was laid, and though it's scarcely possible to think of a worse horror than an eternity in such a place, the lad seemed to gain comfort at the end from the thought that he would lie close by the only person who had ever showed him a little human kindness.

Leaving Phil to attend to the morning clientele, the others take their places behind the cart as it creaks its way along the long whitewashed passage, followed slowly by its small cortège. There may only be three of them, but that's more than Jo's wildest dreams would ever have pictured, and certain it is that he is more lavishly attended now than he ever was in his short and disregarded life. It's only when the cart swings out into the road that Charles seems to realize, with a start, that the procession now numbers four. They did not see him come, they did not hear his tread, but he walks there beside them all the same. Stout and sombre in his unexceptionable black suit, there seems at first glance nothing noteworthy about him at all. Nothing, perhaps, aside from the rather odd way he has suddenly materialized, and a certain glint in his eye as he contemplates Charles.

Two of the three mourners are clearly well aware of the identity of their new companion, but while the trooper's face merely sets yet grimmer and more silent, the very sight of this apparently inoffensive little man seems to douse hot oil on Charles' dry fury.

'What in God's name are you doing here?' he says, gripping the man by the sleeve and swinging him round to face him. 'Haven't you done enough harm to that miserable little wretch without turning up here now to gloat over your handiwork?'

'Now, Charles, my lad,' says Mr Bucket, taking his hand from his arm, 'that's hardly the way to speak to an old friend, now is it? And all may not be as you currently believe it is, in respect of the boy.'

'He'd done nothing to you. He'd committed no crime.'

'There was nothing charged against him,' replies Bucket, rubbing his face with his forefinger, 'but that is not to say he was innocent neither. No – I tracked the boy down because I wished to keep a certain matter quiet that risked being made public in a very unpleasant manner, and bringing all kinds of trouble on the heads of his betters. He'd been more loose-tongued than he should have been about a service he'd been paid for, and that sort of thing won't do at all.'

'Not, at least, when the man paying for that service is Edward Tulkinghorn,' Charles retorts sardonically.

Bucket looks at him with his habitual attentiveness. 'That's as may be. Rather more to the present purpose, I gather you have had dealings of your own with that gentleman of late. Dealings that you have also, in your turn, been paid for. And handsomely too, or so I hear.'

Charles steps closer, his eyes darkening. 'I'm going to find out the truth of this, Bucket. And then where will you be, you and your loathsome masters? However much Tulkinghorn's paying you on the side, it won't be enough. Not nearly enough – not when I've finished with you.'

'Ah, there's no call for that now, is there,' says Bucket brightly, taking him by the elbow. 'I will come along with you for a moment, if you've no objection.'

'In fact I have a very strong objection indeed to spending a single minute more in your society. You have no business here and none, as far as I know, with me.'

He turns to go, but Bucket still has his hand on his arm. 'Half a minute, Charles. I should wish to speak to you first.'

He stops, looks about him, then claps Charles suddenly against the wall of the alley. The cart is by now at least fifty yards ahead and the doctor turns and hesitates for a moment, not knowing whether to intervene. But it is only for a moment; he must have decided that Charles has some business with the newcomer, and is more than capable of looking after himself.

'Now, Charles,' says Bucket softly, as the coffin and its followers disappear at the end of the street. 'You know, and I know, that your great-uncle was a friend of mine once – friend

272

and mentor – and I don't want this little matter to get in the way of that, not if I can help it. I will endeavour to make things as pleasant as they may be, but you must be under no misapprehension. You are in *my* custody now, my lad, and you know what that means, none better.'

'Custody?' scoffs Charles. 'What the devil for?'

'Now, now,' says Mr Bucket, reinforcing his words with his insistent forefinger. 'As you know very well, I am under an obligation to inform you that anything you might say will be liable to be used against you. Therefore, I advise you to be rather careful what you *do* say. You may drop the pretence now, there's a good lad. We both know I have come about the murder.'

'You can't intimidate me that easily,' says Charles, pushing Bucket's hand away. 'You know as well as I do that I didn't kill Lizzie Miller. I have an alibi. Which I've been through already – and in detail – with Wheeler—'

'Now, now,' interrupts Bucket, tapping his forefinger – perhaps unadvisedly – on Charles' chest. 'Think carefully, mind, before you speak again. There has been a murder. Last night. In Lincoln's Inn Fields. Shot, he was, right through the heart, clean as you like. You know who I mean, and I know you know. And now you understand what I'm doing here, don't you?'

Charles stares at him, then puts both hands on Bucket's shoulders and shoves him, none too gently, away. 'I was nowhere near there last night. I reviled and despised Tulkinghorn, yes, but I didn't kill him. Though I'd like to shake the hand of the man who did. You'll have to try harder than that, Bucket. You can't pin this one on me.'

'Now, Charles,' returns Mr Bucket, seemingly unperturbed, 'you know full well that I can. This murder I speak of was done at around ten o'clock. If what you're telling me is true, a bright lad like you will know where he was at that particular time, and will be able to prove it.'

'No,' says Charles quietly. All his stridency has suddenly evaporated and his face is white. 'I cannot prove it. I was – it doesn't matter where I was – but it wasn't Lincoln's Inn Fields, or anywhere within a mile of that accursed house. You have my word.'

'Well, I'm sure you'll understand that I don't have a mind to accept your word, on this occasion,' says Mr Bucket with a smile. 'After all, as you will recall from your own days in the Detective, when a certain person has been seen more than once at the scene of the crime, when that person has, indeed, been heard arguing with the victim – even, perhaps, threatening him – a threat witnessed by a most unimpeachable source – then it's in the natural way of things that I should seek out that person and bring him in for questioning. So, young Charles, am I to call in assistance, or is the deed done?'

Charles stares at him for a long moment, as if weighing his options. And he must have concluded he has very few, because a moment later he nods slowly. 'There's no need for that. If I have to come, I'll do so quietly.'

'All the same,' says Bucket affably, 'this is a very serious charge, Charles, and I have a preference to do such things by the book.'

He takes a pair of cuffs from his pocket and stands, holding them, waiting. Charles starts back angrily but says nothing, and eventually holds out his hands in silence.

Mr Bucket busies himself in one or two small adjustments, then stands back. 'There, how is that? Will they do? If not, I have another pair about me that are just as serviceable.'

Charles shakes his head. 'For God's sake, get on with it. Let's get this over with.'

*

It is, mercifully for all concerned, a very short way to Bow Street, so it is barely half an hour later that Charles finds himself in an underground cell, the iron-bound door of which he knows only too well, even if this is the first time he has seen it from the inside. But it is long, very long, before Bucket elects to visit his prisoner, and when the door is unbolted, he finds Charles pacing up and down, striking his fists against the rough brick walls, his coat cast on the bench. Although the cell is freezing his shirt is damp and there are unsightly patches of sweat under the arms. If it's true that it's the innocent who rage against wrongful arrest while the guilty go quietly to sleep, then there is surely no more blameless man in London than the man in this cell. And even if the latter is a very modern insight, Inspector Bucket is a very insightful man, and well able to draw his own conclusions. Not that he seems mindful to share them. Now, or at any other time.

'Now, young Charles,' he begins, taking a seat as if he were in his own sitting-room, and the bench as comfortable as his favourite armchair. 'I hope this little interlude has given you some time to think, and consider your position. For it's not a good one, all things taken into account. It's a bad look-out for you at present, and no mistake.'

Charles, who remains standing, looks down at him without any attempt to conceal his distaste.

'Point one,' continues Bucket, telling them off with his fat forefinger. 'You was heard, only a few days ago, by the deceased's clerk, threatening his life – and in rather lurid tones, I may add. Point two, as the whole station-house here knows, you have a gun, and are competent to use it. Point three, you cannot – or will not – furnish an alibi for the time of the crime. So, young Maddox, can you give me one good reason why I

275

should not be a-charging you with this murder right here and now, and having you taken down to Newgate without delay?'

Before Charles can answer, there's a noise in the passage outside, and Sam Wheeler's carroty head appears round the corner.

'Just to say they've brought 'im in. The deceased, sir. 'E's in the back room upstairs.'

Bucket betrays no irritation at the interruption – if indeed he feels any – but merely nods and goes out, calling to the guard to come and lock the door, and leaving Charles and Wheeler alone together. It's only to be expected that Charles should beg a word with his friend, but neither of them have any idea that they are not the only ones to take part in the conversation that follows, even if the third party is more by way of an eavesdropper than a participant in the full sense of the term. But Inspector Bucket is nothing if not patient, and he is quite content to sit quiet and unmoving in the darkened cell next door, listening intently and waiting for his moment in his own comfortable manner. He has built his career on that way he has, and his reputation on ruses such as this, and he is rarely if ever disappointed. When Wheeler leaves a few moments later and he hears the bolts slide to, Bucket glides from his hiding-place without making a sound – he is surprisingly light on his feet for such a solid little man. And having let you into this particular secret, you will guess at the next one easily enough. He has a shorter wait this time, having had the foresight to allow the prison guard an early luncheon, and to have made a certain amount of fuss at the front desk about a carriage he requires for an urgent call he has to make on an eminent member of the baronetage. And so it is that the station-house falls unusually quiet for the time of day, and Bucket has only to wait in stillness in the closet next to the

276

room where they have laid – rather unceremoniously, it must be said – all that now remains of a man who once stood at the shoulder of half the peerage in the land. Once in a while he takes his fat forefinger and pushes the closet door an inch open, then lets it fall softly to. It has been much in evidence of late, that finger. When he is on the trail of a crime, this finger of Bucket's will be seen placed close to his ear, or held in the air, or rubbed along his nose; but as every one of his subordinates knows, it never fails, be it soon or late, to finally point out the guilty man. But here, for the moment, it performs only the function that God – or evolution – intended.

And pat they come. Wheeler flushed, fidgety, transparently a guilty thing surprised; Charles pale, slightly hectic still about the eyes, but from the way he starts to examine the corpse, his presence of mind has not yet abandoned him. Bucket observes him for a few moments and sighs silently to himself. He has few regrets of a professional nature, but this young man is one of them. And there is something preoccupying Charles now – something that seems to be almost literally eating away at him, that Bucket would dearly love to fathom. His forefinger twitches in sympathy, as if itching to prod and probe this little mystery and make all plain. He watches as Charles circles the table and comes to a halt by the old man's head, where the sheet is pulled tight to the drooping chin. Even in life Tulkinghorn was a parched thing, a thing of sallow paper and old desiccated confidences, but in death he seems to have shrunk back inside his own bones. The blotched and withered skin sags from his skull and the old hair clings in scraps to the wrinkled scalp. From dust we come, and to dust we return, but in Tulkinghorn's case the process seems to be starting long before he is committed to the ground. Bucket knows well enough what lies beneath that all-concealing sheet, and

Charles must surely guess, but all the same the young man takes a deep breath before he takes hold of it and pulls it back. It seems the lawyer is a lawyer yet, clad still in his time-honoured suit of black, his lustreless knee-breeches tied with ribbons, and his wilted white stock. But this impeccable palette of monochrome tones glares now with colour – colour almost scandalous in its gaudy flamboyance, its ostentatious indifference to all those qualities of silence and reserve and anonymity the old man once stood for. It's doubtful anyone ever saw Tulkinghorn, night or day, with his coat unbuttoned, but this particular indignity is only the first of many his dead flesh must now bear. The fine lawn shirt is soaked with a deep red taint that spreads from neck to gut, but the red is rawest, and the stain is densest, and the bloody cloth is bloodiest, around a small tight black hole in the centre of his chest, hard by the heart few of those who had dealings with him ever believed he possessed. Charles stands there a moment unmoving, and Bucket nods unseen, as if reading his thoughts. Who, indeed, would have thought the old man to have had so much blood in him? But a minute later he hears Wheeler hiss at his companion from the doorway, 'Come on, Chas – we ain't got all day.' He's so nervous he can barely keep still, and keeps darting his head into the corridor, then back again into the room. ''Ave you got what you came for, because if you 'ave, let's get out of 'ere, and quick.'

'I was right,' says Charles slowly. 'See this bullet wound? It's far too small to have been made with a bullet from my pistol.'

He looks again at the corpse. 'In fact, I think the shot was fired from only a foot or so away. That means Tulkinghorn knew his killer, and trusted him. Or at the very least saw no threat in having him at such close quarters. Which is precisely the opposite of what Bucket is alleging where I'm concerned.

If he's going to rely on my supposed threats to make his case stick, how does he explain the old man allowing me to get so close?'

Wheeler edges nearer, interested despite himself. 'But if it were close range there'd be powder marks and you've got next to no chance findin' 'em. That moth-eaten old rag's too dark to show anythin'.'

Charles turns the coat against the light and is forced to agree. But as Bucket already suspects, he's the last and very possibly the best pupil his great-uncle ever had. A moment later Bucket sees him dip his head against the body and breathe deeply. A gesture, incidentally, that you would have seen Bucket himself performing no more than an hour ago, when the body was first brought in. Which means he knows exactly what conclusion the young man is drawing: overlaid on the dankness of old clothes and the sweet metallic aroma of new blood, there is the faint but unmistakable smell of burnt gunpowder. When Charles straightens up, there is a hard little smile on his face, but the smile dies when he lifts his eyes and sees who else is now in the room.

'Well done, young Maddox,' says Mr Bucket genially. 'You're a quick study, that's what *you* are, and no mistake. And so you think you've found the answer, do you? And I suppose, moreover, that you'll soon be a-persuading me that this *is* the answer, and expecting me to unlock these doors and put away my cuffs, and escort you with all due courtesy to the front door? Of course you do,' he continues conversationally, 'and very odd indeed it would be if you didn't.'

'Don't blame Sam,' says Charles quickly. 'It's my fault. I persuaded him to let me in.'

'Oh I know all about that,' says Bucket, tapping his nose with his busy forefinger. 'And you do right by him, so you do, for taking the blame. Now don't *you* be a-fretting,' he says, throwing a glance in Wheeler's direction. 'I know what's what, and who's who, and loyalty's a quality I prize a good deal even when it's misplaced. As it looks to be in this case. Well then, I'll tell you something, young Wheeler. I think you'd be best, all things taken into account, to take yourself back down to the desk and wait for me there. I'll be wanting a word with you in due course, but I have one or two for Mr Maddox here first.'

Wheeler shoots an agonized look in Charles' direction – which the latter does not see – then stumbles out of the room. Bucket hears his feet in the stone passage, first walking, then quickening to a run.

'Now then,' he resumes, 'I heard what you were a-saying about the deceased, and I am obliged to say that I am minded to agree with you.'

'Then you'll let me go—'

Mr Bucket's finger is raised in the air.

'But if it wasn't my gun—'

'Don't you be jumping to conclusions,' says Mr Bucket, 'and you'll find it goes much better for you. Now,' he says, 'I'm sure you realize, being such a quick study, that it would be as easy as winking for you to have borrowed another gun. That you might a-done so precisely for that reason – to lay me off the trail.'

'Where could I have found one like it? This gun can't have been much larger than a pocket pistol – I don't think I've ever even seen one, much less fired one.'

'Ah, but you would know someone who has, I think?' replies Mr Bucket affably. 'You do, after all, frequent a well-known shooting gallery, where all types of tastes are catered for, and all types of firearms are readily to be had. Indeed I'll bet a pound that if I were to rummage about a bit in the said establishment, I might find any number of the like weapons, and recently discharged to boot.'

'On the contrary—' begins Charles, before faltering. It seems he was about to come to the trooper's stout defence, but something is suddenly holding him back. Something, muses Bucket, like a case of little pearl-handled guns, kept neatly in a drawer. But he says nothing of this, and merely watches Charles with his most watchful eyes and smiles his most knowing smile.

'As it happens,' the inspector resumes presently, as if for all the world there had been no interruption at all, 'I am inclined to believe you on this occasion. Which is lucky for you. Even luckier, I should say, is the fact that certain new information has come into my possession, which diminishes the suspicions I had entertained of you and raises them in regard to another party. That being the case, I am willing to discharge you, for the present, on your own recognizance. But with certain conditions. That does not surprise you, I am sure.'

'And they are?' asks Charles evenly.

'First, that you keep away from that shooting gallery and have no intercourse – written or otherwise – with the trooper who runs it.'

The young man gives little away at this, beyond the slightest of flickers behind the eyes. He's a cool customer, thinks Bucket, and that's a fact.

'And if I refuse?'

'Oh, you won't do that, I'll wager,' replies Bucket complacently. 'You're a clever young man, and a sensible one on the whole, and your business is a business that requires a reputation for trustworthiness and an unsullied record. I'm sure it ain't necessary to say to a man like you that it's the best and wisest way that this little matter of your arrest should not come to your clients' ears.'

Charles' face is set; he knows, and Bucket knows, that he has him there.

'And the other conditions?'

Bucket smiles. 'In a case such as this one, all is not always what it seems. In my experience, and I dare say in yours, things are apt to come to light, and secrets laid bare, that in other circumstances would no doubt have lain long dead and buried. I say it again, and you would do well to heed my words: all is not always what it seems, even to those most closely involved.'

He regards Charles with a thoughtful eye. 'I am asking you, lad, as a present member of the Detective to a former one, to trust me. I am sure you see me, just at present, as your opponent. Your enemy, even. You know a little of my dealings with Mr Tulkinghorn, and you have extrapolated that little into a very great deal indeed. Moreover, you have picked up other bits and pieces here and there, and have fitted them likewise into the same great puzzle. I can see how this has occurred. I might even – in your place – have made the like error. But it *is* an error, Charles. I hope it will not be long before you see that. I can say no more than this for the present, but you have heard me say often enough, to the victims in like unhappy affairs, that I will not turn out of my way, right or left, or take a sleep, or a wash, or a shave,' this with a rather pertinent glance at Charles, 'till I have found what I go in search of. And when that day comes, you may discover that we are, in fact, working the same case – albeit from opposite ends.'

'And you ask me to believe that – to take it on trust? On your word merely?'

'Dear me, no,' says Bucket, 'not on that alone. On your knowledge of me, and my methods, and the fact that I learned those methods from a master of our art. Now you know who I mean, and I know you know, so we need say no more on that.'

They stand, eyes locked, for perhaps a minute, then Charles shakes his head. 'I'm sure you'll understand,' he says drily, mocking the detective's words, 'that I don't have much of a mind to accept your word, on this occasion. I will keep away from the gallery, but that is as much as I am prepared to pledge.'

Bucket nods slowly. 'And you still refuse to tell me where you were last evening?'

Charles shakes his head. The livid anger has returned to his face. 'At ten o'clock last night I was with a woman – though not in the way *you* probably think. She was helping me. But as I'm sure you are only too well aware, anyone who offers to help me these days has a more than passing chance of turning up dead very soon after. I don't want any more needless deaths on my conscience, and I'm certainly not going to be responsible for handing you another victim – you or Sir Julius Cremorne.'

If that name means anything to the inscrutable Bucket, then he makes no sign.

'Very well,' says the inspector eventually. 'I will make arrangements to have you discharged. But I caution you this: you are making a mistake, my friend. A very grave mistake. I hope it does not cost you dear.'

Chapter Twenty-two

A *Turn of the Screw*

A nd now, having concealed for so long where our young
hero has been, and why – more to the point – his mood
has taken such a turn darkwards, it is time to rewind a little. To
that conversation between Charles and the trooper and the
surgeon at the shooting gallery, and the allusion to Bucket by
name that seems almost to have conjured his all-too-solid
appearance in the flesh. That much you know. But what you
do *not* yet know is that barely five minutes after he left the
gallery, Charles was tracked down on his way back to
Buckingham Street by Billy, who, out of breath and red in the
face, handed him an envelope. An envelope that contained a
rather formally worded letter from the chairman of the Royal
Geographical Society, which eventually, after much preamble
and prevarication, revealed itself to be an apology. The society
had, after 'mature reflection', and 'due consideration', and
various other carefully measured pairings of adjective and
noun, finally determined that the ban laid upon him after the
'unfortunate occurrence' (another fine example) on the
evening of the 7th inst., had now been rescinded, and he
would be welcome to join them at their forthcoming meeting,
at which Dr Joseph Dalton Hooker would be discussing his
'Fourth Excursion into the Passes of Thibet by the Donkiah
Lah'. The signature at the bottom was suitably ponderous, but

284

there was a postscript underneath that seemed to have been written by the man, rather than the mouthpiece: 'Though the manner of it was unquestionably inopportune, your intercession was nonetheless a salutary reminder that however similar things might initially appear, they are not always what they seem, and therefore it is of the utmost importance, in every branch of scientific study, to employ the most rigorous criteria in the matter of taxonomy.'

At which point Charles made a face that would have left no one in any doubt of his views on the matter, before screwing the paper into a ball and turning to Billy.

'I can't believe you came hot-foot all this way just to give me this.'

'No, Mister Charles, but seein' as I was comin' with t'other letter, I thought as how I may as well bring that as well.'

'The other letter – what other letter?'

Billy fished in his rather grubby pockets and pulled out another envelope. No elaborate wax closure or fine watermarked stationery this time. A single sheet, folded, and clearly unsealed. Charles flashed a glance at Billy, having formed a rather lower estimation of his trustworthiness lately than the one the boy came with. But then he remembered: Billy could barely read. And when he turned to the note, it was clear to Charles at once that the writer of it was scarcely much more literate, and certainly far less effusive. A single line only: an address.

'He said it was urgent,' said Billy, eyeing Charles with undisguised interest.

'I bet he did,' muttered Charles, wondering for a moment who it could be from, and concluding that Jacky Jackson was probably the likeliest suspect. He stood with the paper in his hand for a few moments more, half-tempted just to screw this letter up too and throw it in the dung at the side of the road. More than half-tempted, in fact, because that was exactly what he did. Only to change his mind a moment later and scrape about in the mud to get it back. Much to the amusement of both Billy and the gang of scavenger boys who were working the same gutter, and were far better at it than he would ever be. So why the sudden change of heart? Simple: it was already dark, it was Friday night, and the Argyll Rooms would be in full swing, and at full staff. So how could Jacky Jackson be demanding to meet with him urgently, and at an address near Waterloo? It didn't add up.

'You said he told you it was urgent, Billy – the man who came with this note.'

Billy's eyes widened in a mock innocence that wasn't fooling anybody. 'Oh, it weren't no man, Mr Charles. It were just a boy. One of the costers, I shouldn't wonder. 'E said she gave 'im threepence—'

'*She?*'

'That's right – 'e said it were a woman as gave 'im the note. All dolled up smart like, but talked no better than a fishwife.'

Lizzie, was his first thought. But no, of course, not Lizzie. Lizzie was dead. But someone like her – someone like her.

'All right, Billy, you can go. Tell Mr Maddox I'll be home directly.'

He stood watching as Billy disappeared into the crowd, his mind working and re-working. He could still see the look on Lizzie's face – the old woman bearing down upon them, and Lizzie opening her mouth to tell him something else. *But meanwhile*, she'd said, he remembered that now, but that was all – he never got to hear the rest. What if she'd been about to suggest someone else he should talk to? Someone else who knew about Sir Julius Cremorne? Someone else besides Lizzie who could tell Charles the real truth – who could supply the missing link between Boscawen and Cremorne, and give Sir Julius his motive for murder?

Someone *like her.*

An hour later he came to a halt under a lamp-post on the corner of a road running parallel with the new Waterloo railway line. A grimy, noisy, unprepossessing neighbourhood, but notable in 1850 for a very different reason: this was one of Victorian London's most infamous red-light districts. All along the road the ground-floor windows were uncurtained and fully lit, the dazzle of gas turning each front-room into a cheap peep-show. From where Charles was standing he could see three women lolling in chairs in one room, their breasts completely exposed despite the cold; two more were hanging out of the next-door window calling raucously to passing men, and in a third room a girl who looked little more than thirteen had her skirt yanked up about her waist and was peeing ostentatiously into a chamber pot, to the whoops and cat-calls of a crowd of young men on the pavement. Another girl – probably her sister, so alike they looked – took a coin from one of them and bent coquettishly towards him over the windowsill, so he could stare down her chemise and have a private panorama of her naked thighs and pubic hair.

The house Charles was looking for was two doors further down, and – unusually for the place and the time – was both shuttered and dark. He tried the front door, then went down the narrow passage to the paved court at the back, where the two-storey houses backed directly on to the station shunting yard. The air was thick with soot and raucous with metal and wheels. But someone was listening, all the same, and his first knock brought a movement to an upstairs window, and the sound of feet on the stairs. Then the door opened, but only a crack.

'Who is it?' A girl's voice.

'Charles Maddox. I had a message to come here.'

''Ave you got it wiv yer? So I knows you're genuine.'

Charles took out the letter and slid it through the gap. A moment later the door edged open and the girl appeared. She, like Lizzie, was tiny – less than five feet – and huddled in a thin woollen shawl. Her face was very pale, and her hair brashly and unnaturally blonde.

'Was you followed?' she whispered,

'I don't think so. I took care.'

'I don't want no one knowing you was 'ere. I don't want to end up cut to pieces like poor Liz.'

She beckoned him down the hall to a tiny back room, which was clearly her place of work as well as rest. There was a brass bed in the corner, draped in cheap embroidered moreen coverings evidently designed to look luxurious. The rest of the room was bare, apart from a table and chair in one corner, and a small armoire hung with a pale-coloured peignoir trimmed with feathers. The curtains were drawn and a lamp on a table in the corner threw shadows across white walls blotched here and there with damp. The only decoration was the mantel-shelf, which carried a choice collection of copper-plate impressions from the Galaxy Gallery of British Beauty, showing society ladies in a sequence of stylish gowns and equally stylish attitudes. It's not a species that has ever excited much interest for Charles (though its subtle variations of plumage, habitat, and courtship ritual are as complex a taxonomic challenge, in their way, as anything presented to the Royal Geographical Society), but even at that distance he could recognize Lady Dedlock, she who occupies so central a place in the fashionable

288

world, posed on a terrace, with her fur-lined shawl draped over a stone urn and a heavy gold bracelet on her arm.

The girl stooped and turned the lamp up a little, and Charles saw for the first time that one cheek was swollen and badly bruised. Seeing his glance, she turned away and put her hand to her face.

'Who did that to you? It wasn't—'

She shook her head. 'No, it were just Arnie. Just a little knock to keep me in my place. He means it kindly, mostly.'

Charles has seen it many times before, but still doesn't understand it – the way these girls cling to their pimps, taking any sort of bad treatment as no more than they deserve and considering it a mark of character to bear pain without protesting. And it's not just the prostitutes either; he once caught one of the coster lads beating his girl almost senseless, merely for talking to another man, but the girl refused to complain, saying she liked it when he larruped her – 'cause it proved he still cared.

'What's your name?' he said.

'You don't need to know that. Best you don't. I know who *you* are. That's what matters. And more to the point, Liz said I could trust yer. I saw 'er that night. It was the last time I ever did.'

'So you know what I was asking her about.'

She nodded. 'She said you was all right, and I could talk to yer. Said it wouldn't come back on me. But that was before someone took a carving knife to 'er. Poor cow.' She folded her arms, 'So what I want to know is, what are you goin' to do to make sure that don't 'appen to me?'

'I can't make you any promises.'

'So why the hell should—'

They had raised their voices, and Charles was suddenly aware of a noise in the adjoining room. A whine at first, rising to a howl. The girl threw him an angry look, then crossed quickly to the far door. He heard her hush the child and the creak of a rocked cradle. A few moments later she appeared again, and closed the door behind her.

'Look,' said Charles, moving towards her, 'I think you may already be in danger – whatever it is you know, it makes you a threat to this man, whether you talk to me or not. But if you do, I will at least have some chance of bringing him to justice.'

He took a step closer. She barely reached his shoulder, and he could smell the fear on her now, sharpening the cheap scent.

'It would be for Lizzie,' he said softly. 'Justice for Lizzie.'

She opened her mouth, but then stopped. Living the life she did, she probably had a pretty good idea of her chances, and they weren't good.

'I could give you some money,' he said, reading what he thought might be crossing her mind. 'You could get out of London for a while. Take the child to the seaside.'

'*Her*. It's a little gel. And anyway, Arnie wouldn't like it.'

Charles nodded slowly, wondering whether that was what she really feared, or whether she was more concerned she might lose the only real protector she'd ever had, even if he did beat her half-senseless on a weekly basis.

The conversation was going nowhere; it was a risk, but he didn't feel he had much to lose. He took the now dog-eared sheet of newsprint from his pocket and held it out to her. 'This is a likeness of Sir Julius Cremorne.'

The girl looked, then turned her face quickly away.

'You recognize him.'

She swallowed. The moment hung in the balance: she could go either way, and he wasn't at all sure which it would be. But then: 'Neither Liz nor me ever knew 'is real name. None of the girls do. All we know is 'e's a bastard. A bloody disgusting vicious *bastard.*'

The loathing in her voice reverberated like a curse in the narrow room, and the child whimpered and stirred beyond the door. Charles looked at her. 'Is he really so much worse than all the rest?'

Her venom shifted suddenly to scorn. 'Oh yeah, *much* worse. Shows you what the likes of you know about it. I've been raped and buggered and belted more times than I can count, but nothing, *nothing* like what he done to me. And what makes it worse is that your Sir Julius bloody Cremorne is only interested in little girls – or those of us as can pass ourselves off as such. Same type every time. Always blondes. And the younger the better. Ten, eleven – one of the pounceys even found him a girl of six once. I can look younger than I am 'cause I'm little, but I still 'ad to dress up like I was straight out of the nursery. Ribbons, ringlets, pink dress, the whole friggin' farrago. He even gave me a bloody doll to hold while he was on top of me. Couldn't seem to get it up otherwise. And never took 'is clothes off the 'ole time, not even 'is gloves. Then afterwards 'e makes me take the 'ole lot off and watches me take a bath. Even then I thought it was bloody weird. Then when I got out and turned round, 'e was 'olding this 'orrible-looking knife – Christ, I thought me last hour 'ad come. But it turned out all 'e wanted was a curl of hair. You know – from down there. For 'is *collection,* 'e says.'

By now the girl had started shivering uncontrollably. 'State I were in by then, I didn't care what 'e took as long as 'e left and didn't come back. I burned everything 'e made me wear soon as I shut the door. Bastard pays well, though, I'll give 'im that. Couple'a sovs if you're lucky – but then again 'e ain't got much choice. I couldn't work for a week after. God knows what state that six-year-old was in when he'd done wiv 'er. Poor little cow.'

She lifted her head, defiant. 'So now you know – who 'e is and what 'e done. So my question is, will it 'elp? 'Elp find whoever it was did them terrible things to Liz?'

Her eyes were huge now in the half-light. Huge with fear and pleading.

'Men as high as him are hard to bring low,' said Charles. 'But if I can make him pay, I will, I promise you that. Lizzie was my friend too. I'm going to miss her.'

There must have been something in his eyes at this, because the girl looked at him for a moment, then nodded and took a step back. Charles turned to go, but she wasn't finished. Not quite.

'One more thing. It ain't just what 'appened to Liz. One of the pimps was found in the street wiv 'is throat cut after a run-in wiv Cremorne, if that really is 'is name. 'E ain't 'ad no trouble since – everyone's too scared. So if it's 'im you're getting tangled up wiv, then watch yer back.'

Charles held up his bandaged hand. 'I know. To my cost. But it's not me you should be concerning yourself about.'

He slid a coin into her hand. It was gold, and he saw her eyes widen.

'Think again about that holiday, will you? And you know where to find me if – well, if you need to.'

Back out on the street Charles took a deep breath and let it out in raw gasps. There was a pain in his chest like a dead weight. He knew – anyone in the police knew – that there were literally thousands of young girls being prostituted in London every night, as often as not by their own families, and in their own homes. And most of what Sir Julius Cremorne was doing was – in the strict sense of the term – perfectly legal, since the age of consent in 1850 was twelve, not sixteen, and as Maddox had already observed, the girls were doing it, most of them, of their own free will. All the same, even to someone as case-hardened as Charles, there was something particularly perverted, something pitilessly brutal, about a man who set his sights on children as young as six. And who did so in a way that could terrify even such a girl as this. Charles couldn't imagine what Cremorne must have done to her, and yet he knew that her word alone was nowhere near enough to bring a viable case against the man, and that none of it – yet – explained Tulkinghorn, or Boscawen, or Abigail Cass. But there *was* a link, somewhere, of that he was quite sure. He had only to find the flaw in the fabric, the treacherous loose thread, and wind it slowly backwards to its grim and hidden source.

So now perhaps you understand why, when we saw him at Jo's funeral, there was a new hardness in his face that we have not seen before. And why, as even Bucket has now perceived, a flint and arid rage has settled on his soul.

And now we watch as he is taken up the stairs and through the Bow Street station-house, Wheeler at his side and a constable at his heels, and it is obvious that this seething anger has not abated one jot. But once at the front desk, the sergeant seems rather more concerned to be ordering Bucket a carriage than finding the key to the cuffs on Charles' wrists.

'You there,' the sergeant calls to Percy Walsh, who is nervously avoiding Charles' eye and making it quite obvious thereby, to anyone who cares to look, that the two of them have met before. 'Get your sorry arse outside and hail a hansom. Inspector Bucket has another appointment in Belgravia, and he won't want to be kept waiting.'

Wheeler grins as Walsh slopes unwillingly out into the

freezing air. The weather has turned cold again, and the evening clouds are heavy and yellowish with unfallen snow.

'Poor old Walsh. He's spent half his shift the last couple of days out in the street looking for cabs. Seems to me Bucket might just as well move in with bloody Sir Leicester Dedlock, *Baronet*, if he's going to spend so much time there—'

The rather premature end to this sentence can be accounted for by the sudden appearance of one of the persons referred to in it; in fact, the aforesaid Bucket rather prides himself on his ability to appear and disappear at will, in an almost supernatural manner. It may, indeed, be at the root of his otherwise unaccountable ability to know facts to which he has no right, and no other conceivable access. Wheeler's face is red to the ears with embarrassment, but Bucket affects not to notice, merely scouts about in his plethora of pockets for the key to the handcuffs. But when Charles turns to the desk sergeant to retrieve his coat and gun, he finds the latter, at least, is not forthcoming. Seeing the look on his face, Bucket takes him quietly aside.

'I've been mulling over what you said earlier, my lad. On the subject of bullets and such like, and whether or not the shot was fired up close. My interest has been piqued, that's the truth of it, and when a man in my line of business finds himself in such a position, it's as well for him to follow his nose, that's *my* view. And seeing as that's the case, I would like, with your agreement, to undertake a few little experiments of my own.'

There is a moment's hesitation on Charles' part, but Bucket reads the thought in his usual unerring and unsettling fashion. 'Don't you be afraid that this might turn back upon you. It's all right as far as you're concerned. It ain't your gun I'm interested in, insofar as it belongs to *you*. Only as a comparison, if you take my meaning. I promise you, as a man and as a Detective, that you shall have the gun back in your hands tomorrow, and no more said about it. Now that seems perfectly fair and reasonable to me, in the interests of justice and the solving of a crime. Don't you see?'

What Charles sees, like so many before him, is that Bucket has inveigled him into an impossible position. He's on the point of saying as much when a movement by the door catches his eye and he looks up to see two other officers bringing in the trooper, just as he himself was brought in only a few short hours before. He's about to start forward when Bucket takes him by the arm and whispers softly in his ear.

'Now, my lad.' he says. 'Just you be remembering your promise, and don't be doing anything rash.'

'But—'

'Like I said, you will have to trust me. I know what I'm doing, whether you believe that or not. So you pretend not to have seen the trooper there and come quietly along with me to the back door, there's a good lad. And remember – as I said to you before, things may not always be as they first appear.'

Left to himself on the back steps, Charles reflects on those last words and on the number of times in the last few days he's heard – or read – something similar. As a proposition, the idea that appearances can be deceptive is hardly radical, so why does it strike him so forcibly now? Why is he so convinced, suddenly, that there's something he's missing? That for all his scientific theory and practical experience there's a connection somewhere that he's overlooked? But as we already know, he thinks better when he's walking, so it's no surprise to see him turn up his collar and head purposefully down towards the Strand. It's such a short step to Buckingham Street that he has little time to collect his thoughts, which are at best rather

295

ragged after so little sleep. So much so that it's only the swift intervention of two passers-by that saves him from being knocked down, as a large carriage careers to a halt outside the grand stucco-fronted townhouse that hosts one of London's most exclusive gambling clubs. Charles is about to thank the two men who stepped forward to help him – one of them with a high forehead and slightly wild dark hair under his tall silk hat, the other plumper, bookish-looking, with small metal-rimmed glasses – when he realizes he's seen the carriage before. It's the one he saw in Lincoln's Inn Fields – the one that bears the arms of the black swan. He watches as a man comes out of the club and stands for a moment, gathering his cloak about him. It's the man with the scarred hand – the same man Jacky Jackson described drinking and gambling with Cremorne at the Argyll Rooms, the same man Charles might have seen that day nearly two weeks ago, going into Tulkinghorn's house, had he been looking – or lucky. But if chance deserted him then, it's on his side this time, for the man is suddenly seized with a dry hacking cough that forces him to stop under the gaslights at the door, and when he puts his hand to his mouth you can see the red scar as clearly as if it were broad day. But in the time it takes Charles to register this – to make the link, and realize what it means – the man has moved quickly down the steps and into his carriage, and the coachman is spurring the horses away. Charles looks back at the building. He knows the place well enough to be sure he will gain neither entry nor assistance there, but there is a source of information this man cannot conceal – one that, on the contrary, he is flaunting even now for all to see. Because even though the carriage has already turned into the Strand, Charles looked at it more closely this time, and has seen something he did not notice before. The arms on the panelled door bear a small but unmistakable badge on the canton of the shield. And while he may not know the name of the man whose equipage this is, he knows exactly what is signified by such a *sinister hand appaumy Gules*. It's the red hand of Ulster. The man is a baronet. A *baronet*.

And while the 'Sir' of a baronet may look the same, and sound the same, as the 'Sir' of a knight, they are as dissimilar, as species, as a mythical unicorn and a Common Eland. Indeed, why else should Bucket keep repeating the *Baronet* in Sir Leicester's name, if not to emphasize the immeasurable distance between that great county family and those who may use the same designation before their name but can lay claim to neither the same ancestral lands nor the same ancient lineage? And what was it Mrs O'Driscoll overheard Abigail Cass say? That a girl had been cruelly used, and cruelly wronged, and 'all the noble rank and money in London would not be enough to conceal it'. Now as Charles is well aware, a mere baronet does not – on the most scrupulous technicality – actually qualify for the ranks of the nobility, but a woman like Abigail Cass is unlikely to have known that. What she *would* most definitely have known, on the other hand, is that despite the enormous fortune amassed by the Cremornes – rumoured to exceed even the Dedlocks' – there is an invisible but adamantine barrier impeding Sir Julius that not even an alliance with an earl will ever entirely do away: unlike Sir Leicester, who owes the title before his name to nothing more than accident of birth, Sir Julius has earned his money in trade, and achieved his knighthood by dint of his own toil.

Charles is furious with himself for not realizing it before, but he sees it all too clearly now: the man Abigail Cass was talking about can't have been Cremorne at all, but *someone else entirely*. Someone, it now seems clear, who not only knows Cremorne, but in all probability has the same tastes as Cremorne, the same secrets as Cremorne, and the same reasons as Cremorne to have those secrets silenced and suppressed. And who better to do so than that dusty old mausoleum of all that is treacherous and compromising, Edward Tulkinghorn? Did Abigail Cass discover what they were so concerned to conceal and threaten to expose them? Was *that* why she had to die? And who are 'they' anyway? Charles remembers – not before time – those four men he glimpsed in Tulkinghorn's ante-chamber, and realizes with a jolt that it is quite possible Cremorne was among them. One of them certainly fitted the description Jacky Jackson gave of the stiff old man with grey hair seen in Sir Julius' company at the Argyll Rooms. So does the same dark conspiracy envelop them all? And if that's the case, who else is involved, and how long has it been going on? A host of questions suddenly, but for a man like Charles, it may not be as difficult as it first appears to start unearthing some answers.

He covers the last few yards to Buckingham Street at a run, leaving his two Good Samaritans looking down the road after him, denouncing his discourtesy and wondering at such an uncommon incident. But both of them being writers of some note, as well as friends, I would not be at all surprised to find one of them making good literary use of it one day or another.

Back at the house, Charles clatters up the stairs three at a time and nearly collides with Molly, who is scrubbing the first-floor landing. Up in the attic he spends half an hour ransacking the crates for his long-lost scrapbook of English heraldry, which he does indeed manage to find, but which turns out not to contain anything even remotely resembling the black swan adorned with the red hand. Which is infuriating, but not, thankfully, the only way of getting at what he needs. He could wait until morning and go to the British Library and pore over learned tomes for hours, or he could take a short cut. The latter will undoubtedly be quicker, and will furnish him besides, with intelligence no library could ever provide, but is he prepared to take such an enormous risk?

On his way back downstairs, Charles stops at Maddox's door, and gently pushes it open. The old man is asleep in his chair by the fire, his mouth slightly open, and the coals burnt low. Charles hesitates, wondering whether to wake him and tell him what he's discovered, and what he plans to do now, but he remembers what Stornaway once said about how fast his uncle's grasp of the world plunges as the day declines, and decides he might be doing more harm than good. There'll be another opportunity, he tells himself. I can talk to him tomorrow.

Chapter Twenty-three

Closing In

T he room is darkened and still. A thin sliver of moonlight slices between the shutters from the street outside, and zigzags crookedly down the *columbarium* of iron boxes marshalled like a silent legion of the dead behind the empty chair where their master once sat enthroned. He is as silent now as they are, encased in his own dark box downstairs, awaiting the moment when he too will be allotted a narrow niche that bears his name. This room was never much given to receiving company, and seems to have lapsed with relief back into its familiar emptiness. There is no sign, now, of the dozens of uninvited feet that have trod these floors these last few days, sifting every locked drawer, and staring, many of them, up at the ominous ceiling, with its prophetic pointing Allegory, who gazes down as blindly now as he did before, at the mahogany desk and the stiff-backed chair. There is still a bottle of wine and a glass upon the table, and still the two silver candlesticks at either end. But there is a stain on the ground before the table now that was not there when last we visited this place. It's not so very large, that stain, nor so very dark, but it's curiously compulsive, and once noticed you cannot seem to escape it, and find it lurking at the corner of your eye, wherever you look about the room. Many a housemaid will try to get that stain out, and many a housekeeper berate them for incompetence, but soap and scouring will neither rid nor blanch it, and in the years to come that fact alone will endow this room with a fearful fascination for all who come here – a fascination that swells into shivering frisson when they raise their eyes to the ceiling and contemplate Allegory, pointing down now with a terrible accuracy at the very spot on the floor where Tulkinghorn lay, all those dark hours alone, face down and bleeding, with a bullet in his heart.

Time passes. The blade of light creeps, inch by inch, across the floor, turning the flecks of floating dust to diamond in its cold brightness.

And then – what's that?

A noise. Too muffled by stone and brick and wooden doors to hear distinctly. Is it merely the breathing of the old house, or has someone penetrated its closed and curtained seclusion and found a way within, despite the heavy bar now nailed across the high front door? Yes, yes – look there, on the stairs – the ghost of candlelight grows and takes shape, and wild shadows shudder up the wall. But as the unknown man emerges on to the landing and stands for a moment before the door, shading his candle against his palm, we can see that the hand that holds it is bound about by bandage. And who, indeed, but Charles Maddox would have the impudence to intrude on a house of mourning – for surely these walls must lament their master's untimely passing, even if no living soul ever will.

If he hesitates as he stands there, it's only because the candle is guttering badly in the draught, and he's concerned not to advertise his presence to anyone watching from outside. He crosses quickly and noiselessly to the window and pulls the shutter close, then moves to the desk and tries the drawer – the drawer he's seen Tulkinghorn open so often, but always, in the past, with a key. But Bucket has been here before him, and this time the drawer slides open and the ring of keys he's seeking lies revealed. And next to it, that small obsidian paperweight that Charles once coveted so much. He should have expected to see it there, but it seems to snare his attention all the same. After a moment he reaches out to touch it, and finds to his astonishment that the stone is warm, even in the chill of that cold room – as if its master's grasping fingers cannot quite relinquish it, and have left what heat they ever had, locked inside this hoarded trophy. A voice in Charles' head tells him to take it – tells him to slip it into his pocket, unnoticed – tells him that no one will ever know, and that whoever it is who will now take possession of Tulkinghorn's many treasures, he could not possibly appreciate this obscure object of desire more than Charles does. Is he tempted? Of course, but it is the ring of keys that his fingers close upon. Then he turns to the racks of boxes behind him, and takes the little set of worn library steps in his free hand. We can already see, just as he soon does, that some of these boxes are no longer quite as dusty as they were when Charles first came here, even if others are slumbering still under years of neglect. The next thing he finds – and it's with a surge of quick elation – is that the boxes are marked not only with the names of Tulkinghorn's clients, but with a small etching of their armorial bearings. A weakness this, perhaps, in the old lawyer's otherwise impregnable facade, a hint of vainglory, of overweaning professional pride that has now met with all too vertiginous a fall. Resisting the urge to go immediate swan-hunting, Charles turns first to the Cremorne coffer and spends ten fruitless minutes flicking through wills and title deeds and dull affidavits. Little of it is recent, and none of it is even remotely personal in nature, but on second thoughts that is not so very odd, given Tulkinghorn's almost preternatural concern for caution and circumspection: Cremorne is the only name Charles has ever been given, so if any one box here has had its compromising contents removed elsewhere, it is surely this one. Though he cannot fail to notice, in passing, that the box on the shelf below dedicated to Dedlocks dead and present has also been emptied of most of what it must once have contained. But that he suspects is the inspector's handiwork, not the lawyer's. He slides the Cremorne box back into its place and begins his search for the black swan. And now even the alphabet proves to be on his side: no Vavasour or Smithson this, but filed neatly under 'G' a mere two shelves further down. The box has the thinnest film of dust, and no recent fingerprints, so it seems Bucket's incursions have not stretched this far, though it appears very possible that Tulkinghorn himself was busy about this box in recent days.

Charles pulls the box out and takes it to the table. Then he sits down at the desk, and opens the lid, holding the candle so close to the sheaves of dry paper that they seem to uncurl and stretch in the heat of the flame.

He's so absorbed in trying to make sense of this correspondence, so intent on discovering the crime – for crime there *must* be – that lies concealed behind the bland legal language, that he is not as alert as he should be to the creak of the boards – not as suspicious as experience should have taught him of the elaborate oriental screen so carefully and so conveniently positioned. But what he does not hear, he soon senses in another way. Faint at first, but unmistakable. Just as it was once before, in this very room. The aroma of the finest Turkish tobacco.

He raises his head and sees at once a figure in the shadows in the far corner. How long he has been there, Charles does not know. Pure instinct tells him it's Cremorne, but he sees almost at once, even in the half-light, that this figure is surely too slight, too short. But if not Cremorne, then—?

The floor creaks again as the silhouetted shape moves closer, but when he emerges at the edge of the circle of light cast by the candle, Charles almost laughs out loud with the absurdity of his own fears. The man in the shadows is barely a man at all – so small, in fact, that his black coat skims its tattered hem along the floor. The assailant his mind manufactured in the darkness is no more fearsome in reality than Tulkinghorn's groom. The strange-looking lad with the queer yellow eyes. The rush of relief is just giving way to mystification about what on earth he's doing here – now, in this room, in the middle of the night – when the boy puts his fingers to his mouth and Charles sees what is in them.

A cigarette.

It's not merely that the boy is smoking in the house that shocks him, though it does, no question. In fact, it's not so much *what* he's doing, but what he's doing it *with*. Charles' upper-class contemporaries may be partial to cigars, but the working man of 1850 smokes only a pipe – indeed it'll be at least another four or five years before English soldiers in the Crimea are introduced to cigarettes by their Turkish comrades. And even if there are fine hand-rolled versions available in London this very November evening, it is only from one very expensive and exclusive shop in Bond Street (though the name above the door would probably be familiar to you). That this lad – this not-much-more-than stable boy paid no more than ten shillings a week – should be smoking one, and smoking it in so casual, so pointedly nonchalant a fashion is utterly unaccountable. Or at least at first. Because the cigarette is not the only thing he's holding. As he moves slowly forward and into the light, Charles sees what was invisible at first, and is even now partly concealed by the folds of the coat. In his left hand, catching in the candle flame, is the glint and glitter of a long ebony-handled blade.

It takes a fraction of a moment for Charles to realize he's been wrong all along – not just wrong but hopelessly, disastrously wrong. The long dark coat Jo saw on the killer of Abigail Cass – the same long dark coat worn by the man Lizzie Miller was with the night she died. The smell of a gentleman's tobacco that made Charles think it was indeed a gentleman Mrs O'Driscoll overheard. The voice that whispered in his own ear as a knife sliced into his flesh.

'So it was you,' he says slowly, getting to his feet. 'You killed them all. Cass, Boscawen, Lizzie Miller. And it was you who attacked me in the City Road.'

The lad smiles, a curious off-centre smile that does not reach his eyes. The more Charles looks at them, the more saurian they appear. Who is this parody of a child, who commits such appalling murders with such frozen proficiency?

'Worked it out, 'ave yer? Took you long enough.'

His voice is of a piece with all the rest – high-pitched, nasal, whining. Easy to mock were it not for the knife in his hand, and the pictures in Charles' head.

'Think you're so clever, with all yer fancy *methods* – you 'aven't got a bloody clue. I'd been following yer for days before that, but someone like me, we're beneath the notice of the likes of you. I could have 'ad you there and then if I chose' – he draws the knife across his own throat in an arc so perfect, a gesture so practised, as to be almost beautiful – 'but that weren't what I was being paid for. Not then.'

'Whereas now?'

'Ah, well now it's different. *Then* you was just making a nuisance of yerself. *Now* you *know*. Or soon will, unless someone puts a stop to you.' He smiles, and turns the knife so it catches the light. 'Guess that'd be me then.'

They stand facing each other, little more than a yard apart now, both knowing that the first move will in all probability be decisive. Charles has the advantage of height and size, but he has no illusions – and, more importantly, no *gun*. It's not the first occasion he's had cause to rail at Bucket, but never before with such a perilously good reason. His fingers tighten imperceptibly around the candlestick. It's the only other weapon at his disposal, but it will give him one chance, and one alone, and like as not he'll destroy the only evidence he's ever likely to get in the process – evidence he hasn't even got to the bottom of yet – evidence that's cost him so much time and pain to find, and for which others have paid an even higher price. But what other choice does he have?

A second later – and without ever taking his eyes from his opponent's gaze – he drops the candle into the box of paper and the parched leaves leap up like bushfire. Before the boy can move or react, Charles flings the blazing box in his direction and dashes for the door, to a howl of burning curses. He's halfway down the stairs before he hears footsteps start after him on the floor above and realizes that even if he makes it back through the kitchens and into the courtyard he'll be tracked down long before he can scale the six-foot fence. But even as that thought takes shape his fingers stub blindly against a crack in the plaster. No – not a crack – Tulkinghorn tolerated no such faults in this flawless house – it's the edge of a door, the hidden entrance to the hidden gallery, the frame so perfectly crafted as to be almost invisible to the naked eye. Charles turns and fumbles up and down the jamb until he hears a soft click and the door swings heavily open. It's as black as death at the top of the stairs, but he knows from experience that it will be lighter lower down. And there is a full moon.

He pulls the door closed behind him and takes the stone steps as fast as he dares, the sound of his own blood beating in his chest and a new ache in his mutilated hand, as if by some sort of sympathetic magic it can sense the presence of its old aggressor. At the bottom of the stairs he stops, listening, hoping that he hasn't shut himself into a trap of his own making. But silence reigns still above. He makes his way – slower now, in all this priceless clutter – to the galleried room, hoping frantically that his memory holds true and he can remember how to find the mirrored alcove. The busts and marbles stare at him from their blind stone eyes as he turns the corner and a dim and distorted version of himself looms momentarily from the glass. He seizes a statuette from the nearest shelf and slides into the narrow space behind the god of panic and irrational terror, aware, in a small and remote part of his brain, of the aptness of that irony, and filing it away to entertain Maddox with over the drawing-room fire. If he ever makes it that far.

A heartbeat, two, three. Charles is still holding his breath, his ears straining against the fizzing silence, and after what seems an age there's the dull distant thud of a door somewhere closing. I'm not sure how long he leaves it after that. Perhaps five minutes, perhaps a lot more, but eventually even Charles decides it must be safe to emerge. But as he moves quickly back around the gallery he catches sight of a light beneath him in the darkness, and pauses, his heart drilling again in his chest, until he realizes that it's only the candle in the niche by the Egyptian sarcophagus, burning still in the room below. Despite himself, despite the danger, he cannot resist the urge to look down again at the unravellable mystery of that majestic piece of stone, knowing that this will no doubt be the last time he will ever see it, and wondering in passing where all these astounding artefacts will end up now.

And that's when it happens. The blade against his neck. The voice in his ear. Someone else's sweat against his skin. It seems this eerie man-boy had a point when he said Charles was far too clever by half, and surely now he is indeed caught in his own cunning snare. His reactions are quick though – maybe just quick enough, because he has his hands round the boy's wrists before the knife makes blood and is pushing backwards against him with all his strength. The right instinct, as it proves, because the boy cannot hope to match him for weight. He can smell the tobacco and the cheap cologne as he forces the boy down on to the floor and tries to get enough purchase on the stone figure to aim a decent blow. They roll over and over, kicking and clawing, and suddenly the statue has slipped from his grasp and the boy is staggering up and trying to get away. Charles catches at the long coat but it pulls away in his hands and the boy is on his feet, stumbling, aiming for what he thinks are the stairs. But now it's Charles who has the advantage – Charles who commands the terrain – Charles who knows that the staircase at the corner of the gallery is mere *trompe l'oeil* – a mural that's hallucinatorily realistic, even in daylight, and fatally deceptive now. As the boy clatters into brick wall, Charles is on his back before he even realises what's happened. They fall backwards and the knife spins away across the floor and over the side of the balustrade, clattering on to the stone floor twenty feet below. Charles straightens and they stand, face to face, just as they did in Tulkinghorn's chamber. The only difference now is the thin streak of blood running down the boy's face.

'Think you've got me, do ya?' he gasps, his pale eyes even stranger in the glimmering dark. 'Think you have the balls to finish me off? 'Cause that's what it'll take, Maddox. If you don't kill me now you'll spend the rest of your life looking over yer shoulder. Never knowing if it's you I'll come after, or someone close – someone you care about. Someone you don't want me takin' me time over. Like that black whore of yours – what's 'er name? *Molly* – that's right.' He leers at Charles and runs his tongue over his cracked lips. 'The best ones – they always take longest. Once you've got 'em gagged you do what you like with 'em – cut 'em, fuck 'em, watch 'em die—'

Charles may know, somewhere in his brain, that the boy is deliberately using Molly to provoke him, but that knowledge is not enough – never has been enough – to prevent him from being seized with such a boiling fury that he hurls himself at the boy and the two of them hammer backwards against a table of terracotta figurines, sending emperors and divinities crashing to smithereens. And now the boy has the advantage not of weight but speed, and is the first to reach out for something – anything – that could strike a final blow. But even he's not fast enough to get the grip he needs, and the two of them writhe on the floor like serpents – much like the model of Laocoön that they are even now crushing into splinters on the ground beneath them. Hard to tell who has the upper hand now, but as the table rocks and begins to fall, it's the boy who is lurching to his feet and Charles who is still on the floor – Charles whose injured hand is crushed without mercy beneath the other's boot, Charles who lets out an animal cry of pain. The blood is pouring from a new cut on the back of his head as the boy half-reels, half-crawls to where the statuette lies on the floor, but as he bends to reach it Charles is on him again and they struggle, first one then the other crushed back against the stone balustrade, until sheer momentum takes over and they plunge, still locked fast together, head-first, down to where the ancient vessel of the dead awaits them.

Chapter Twenty-four

Pursuit

The chophouse on the corner of Lincoln's Inn Fields is unusually busy for such a late hour. There's a card-game under way in the corner, and amid the smell of sawdust and beer and tobacco-smoke, you can hear the clink of browns being laid as bets and a constant patter of gaming slang. So only the most curious customer, or those who have particular reasons of their own – as we do – would cast anything other than the briefest of glances in the direction of the stout black-suited man occupying the window seat, who is, to all appearances, a very commonplace sample of the human species. He's taking his time over his coffee, this ordinary little man, and he drinks it very strong, but he seems on a second glance to be far more interested in what's going on outside than what's contained in his cup. His sharp little eyes have, in fact, scarcely left the windows of the large and darkened residence on the opposite side of the square, which is clearly visible from where he sits. Indeed the shop's proximity to this house might explain his otherwise rather unaccountable choice of late-evening venue, since he must surely have a homely hearth and an equally homely wife, who keeps both his slippers and his supper warm and whose society he surely appreciates more than he does this noisy draughty corner. But then – he is gone. As sudden and unseen

310

as he came. And if you look across the square now you will be too late to see what he saw – too late to observe that in all that tall forbidding facade, there was, just for a moment, a flicker of life.

Less than a minute later the same little man can be observed on the steps of that same house in the company of two young police constables who are – extraordinary though it sounds – in the process of taking a crowbar to the metal bolt nailed across the door. Once inside, the air in the great hall is thick with dark, but the little man is unperturbed – indeed, we can now see that he has a small bull's-eye lantern with him, which he must surely have brought with this very purpose in mind. Leaving the two constables wheezing in his wake he takes the broad marble steps at a sharp pace, and comes to the door of Tulkinghorn's chamber. And now it's clear from the light reflecting up on to his face that he has not found what he expected. He stoops and inspects a pile of half-burned papers on the floor, reading a line here, and a word or two there, and then turns over the iron box to inspect the name emblazoned on the front. Then he lifts the lantern a little higher and looks about the room, throwing a pallid gleam on the blood-red walls. If there are clues that will tell him what has happened here, it will take a deductive genius to read them. But this, after all, is Mr Bucket of the Detective. And yet when he retraces his steps towards the stairs you can see that his expression is grave – graver, in fact, than we have ever yet seen it. In the last few days he has searched every inch of these chambers, and thought there was no secret in all this house of secrets that he had not laid bare. But there, it seems, he was wrong. For now, as he looks back down the way he came, he sees the pale outline of a door against the smooth plaster – the merest shadow of a shadow it is, and easily missed, but it is there.

Perhaps fifteen minutes have now passed since he saw the light in the window, and when he pushes open the hidden door and stands at the top of the stairs leading down to Tulkinghorn's private museum there is no sound or movement below. He beckons to the constables – one of whom, we can now see, is none other than Sam Wheeler – and the three of them descend into the maze, the stout Bucket with his eagle eyes, and the others struck with wild surmise, as the arc of the lantern beam reveals shelf after shelf, and wall after crowded wall, one artefact after another emerging from the dark, sharp-edged in the glare and shimmering like the monstrous spectres in a travelling phantasmagoria. Mr Bucket is not a man easily or needlessly impressed, but he comprehends in a moment what a task it would have been to fashion this place. And likewise, even if he has neither the eye nor the mind for art, deception in all its forms is something of a speciality of his, and he perceives at once that whatever this place is, it is most certainly not what it first appears to be.

'Look sharp now, my lads,' he warns over his shoulder. 'Don't be breaking anything by your clumsiness, and mind you be watching where you put your feet.'

Knowing what we do about what has just happened here, it's yet more agonizingly slow minutes before they reach the inner gallery, and turn the glower of the bull's-eye on the wreck of Tulkinghorn's treasured trove. Pieces of priceless antiquity lie in fragments about the floor and grind into red dust beneath their feet, and as the lantern beam swings round, the younger constable suddenly starts and cries out as a ghostly reflection of himself rears up before his eyes. Bucket stops and turns, but even as he does so Wheeler has reached the balustrade and seen what lies below.

'Mr Bucket, sir – over here! Quick!'

In a moment the inspector is by his side, looking down into the stone sarcophagus, and if his face was grave before, it is lined with apprehension now. Apprehension that only increases when he realizes that in this hall of mirrors and distortions even the staircases are an elaborate hoax. Every corner they turn leads nowhere, and there's a note of panic even in Bucket's normally unruffled manner by the time they discover the hidden steps and penetrate to the lower level. Bucket rushes to the plinth where the sarcophagus lies and lifts the lantern. In the bottom of the trough, face down in a layer of blood, is the body of a young man. There's a deep gash on the back of his head, but he's breathing – he's alive. And when he stirs slightly and raises his head, we can see that it's Charles, and Bucket can see that it's Charles, and there's a look on the older man's face now that seems to spring not just from relief but a deep affection. Something that might also explain the gruffness of his voice when he calls to the constable and tells him to fetch a doctor and be quick about it.

'There's a reputable man lodging at Portugal Street, no more than a step from here,' he calls after him, then turns to Charles. 'Hold up, my lad,' he says kindly. 'Hold up. I will stay with you until the doctor comes. Now you grip tight to me, there now, and we shall see if we can sit you up. Because that's what a strong lad like you will want to do, of that I'm sure.'

His plump arms go round the young man's shoulders with an almost fatherly tenderness, and eventually, slowly, Charles is not only upright, but able, holding hard to Bucket's hand, to climb out of the coffin and sit heavily on the ground. By some miracle there seems to be nothing more wrong with him than bruises and cuts. But his speech is slurring slightly, and Bucket begins to wonder whether the injury to his head isn't rather worse than it appears.

'Did you see him?' demands Charles, his chest heaving as if he's struggling to breathe. 'Did you see that boy? Tulkinghorn's boy. He was here. He must be here. There's no other way out.'

Bucket nods. That much he has guessed already. And indeed it is not so very difficult to deduce that there has been a desperate struggle in this place, and that Charles did not hurl himself over the balustrade on the whim of the moment.

'Take the bull's-eye, Wheeler,' he says, beckoning to him, 'and have a good look hereabouts. We're after a stable-lad. Small and lean and pale-haired he is, but don't you be under-estimating him for all that.'

'There now,' he says amiably to Charles, after Sam has gone. 'There's no need to fret yourself over that lad of Tulkinghorn's. We will find him, and we will discover what is at the bottom of all this.'

'I had it there,' says Charles, his breathing a little easier now. 'In my hand. In the box. The letters. What Tulkinghorn's been doing. What they've all been doing. I was piecing it together. And then— and now—'

He strikes his hand against the floor, angry and impotent, tears starting in his eyes as they have not done since he was a little boy.

Bucket watches him for a moment. 'Two heads are often better than one. That's my experience. How's about you tell me what you found?'

'That's the whole point. I didn't find *anything* – there wasn't enough time. There were some references to an address in Hampstead, and to money being sent there, but I don't know why, or even what sort of place it was. That box I had, the papers related to a baronet – I saw him tonight. His arms are a black swan—'

'I know him,' interrupts Bucket quietly. 'I know him.'

'Whatever Tulkinghorn did for him, he appears to have done exactly the same for Cremorne, some time before. God knows what – those damn lawyers seem to practise to deceive – but I do remember a letter from Tulkinghorn that said something like "based both on my own experience and that of my clients over many years, I can confirm that the establishment in question is ideally suited to dealing with delicate cases such as yours". But as to what that "delicate case" actually was, I am none the wiser. Though I do know that there is something vile at the bottom of all this. Vile, and far-reaching, and of long standing. There is no other explanation.'

'Maybe, maybe not,' says Bucket, in that careful way of his. 'And yet I agree there would be no call for any of this – no need to have Boscawen done away with, or employ a villain like Robbie Mann, if there were not more to it than we have yet discovered.'

'The stable lad – is that his name? You know him?'

'Aye,' replies Bucket, 'I've had my eye on Robbie Mann for a good while. Abandoned in the Whitechapel workhouse he was, by a mother no better than she should be. I first came upon him when he was taken on suspicion of setting fire to a warehouse, down at Essex Wharf.'

'Like at the rag and bottle shop.'

Bucket nods. 'And from what I heard, the exact same method was employed on both occasions. After all, even a lad can lay his hand to a flagon of camphene, and no questions asked.' He sighs. 'No more than ten years old, Mann was, when he first crossed my path.'

'But if he'd committed arson—'

'Oh, I knew it, and he knew it, and he knew I knew it. But I had no *evidence*. I've kept half an eye on him always from that time, knowing I was likely to pick up his trail again, if I looked sharp.'

'And since?'

'Nothing as could be laid to his charge in a court of law. Petty pickpocketing mostly. Even if he do frequent inns like the Sol's Arms that you and I both know to be the haunts of far rougher thieves.' Bucket's face darkens. 'Though bad rumours have come to my ear in the last few months. Seems Mann's natural cruelty has been sharpened of late by a vicious and most *un*natural pleasure in inflicting pain.'

Charles glances at him, then looks quickly away.

'There was an incident with a poor half-starved cat I will not distress you with,' continues the inspector, 'but there was nothing *then* to suggest it would go further – no hint he would turn his malice on his fellow men. Or women.'

'What I don't understand is what could possibly have induced Tulkinghorn to employ such a blackguard?'

Mr Bucket waves his fat forefinger, which has lain quiet for much of the previous exchange. 'Now that, my lad, is the pertinent question, if you don't mind my saying so. For he knew, did Tulkinghorn, all about this lad. I told him so myself. It troubled me at the time, so it did, why he should want such a scoundrel in his service, but I could not work out the why of it. Now, it seems, we may be nearing our answer, and it may be the service Tulkinghorn had in mind had very little to do with the upkeep of his carriage.'

'So you believe me? You actually believe me – even with no proof?'

Bucket sighs. 'There was a time, my lad, when you'd not have needed to ask such a question. But recent events being what they are, you have become mistrustful, and I don't rightly blame you. But you know me, and you should know that I could never condone anything crooked, and as to concealing it—'

Charles nods. There is a drilling ache in the side of his head and his vision is slightly blurred. 'I'm sorry. I assumed that—'

'That because I was assisting Tulkinghorn with one matter of a rather delicate nature, I must, of necessity, be doing the same with another, and worse. Nay, lad, all I have done, I have done for the other.'

He takes a deep breath. 'And since all seems aright between us, I'll tell you a thing I couldn't tell you before. Though a brave lad like you will do me the justice of recalling that I tried to give you a hint on it, at the time. Suspicions I did have and that's a fact, but they were of quite a different order. I knew about Cremorne and his friends, with their titles and their estates and their fine ways, but I believed their crimes to be crimes of greed. Greed and greed alone, mark you. And I had my reasons. There's an old inspector friend of mine in the City New Police division who has been head over ears in a fraud case these three months now, and from what he told me – in confidence, mind – I was ready to lay a hundred pound that these men were mixed up in the very same business. So I bide my time, and I watch 'em. And when Tulkinghorn asks my help in identifying a mysterious woman seen one night by that young crossing-sweep, then naturally I accept, even if I wonder why such a minor matter should concern so mighty a man. But I told myself his motives were not my business, and *my* business was to fathom the fraud. But it seems all the while I was a long way off the mark, and the right direction was another way entirely.'

It's the closest Bucket has ever come to admitting he's wrong, but Charles scarcely notices. 'I heard that there had been irregularities at Sir Julius' bank, but as far as I could discover, his own associates lost larger sums than almost anyone else.'

'Ah!' says Bucket sharply, raising his portentous forefinger and tapping it against the side of his nose. 'That was indeed what you were designed to think. And no doubt all sorts of pieces of paper can be brought for'ard to prove it. But from what I've been a-hearing, they have contrived very nicely to line their own pockets and all the money lost has made its way to their own private purses. And not before time, at least for some of 'em. That baronet you mentioned has so encumbered his estate by debts got by gaming, he inveigled an innocent young woman to marry him, merely to lay his hands on her fortune. A young woman who has now died not long since, and all unexpectedly.'

Charles frowns, as the memory returns to him. *'A girl cruelly used, and cruelly wronged.'*

Bucket turns to him with a question in his eyes, but it's at that very moment that they hear the rush of footsteps and Wheeler returns with the lantern, alarmed and out of breath, to tell them that he has searched both gallery and house and of Robbie Mann there is no sign. Charles is on his feet before Sam has even finished.

'And where do you think you're going, my lad?' says Bucket sharply.

'God knows how that boy has managed to evade us, but if he *has*, there's only one place now where we can hope for any answers – that address in Hampstead. We may be somewhat early for polite visiting hours, but to be frank, courtesy is the very least of my concerns.'

Bucket consults his pocket-watch, suddenly aware that the light seeping through from the hexagonal dome above them is not the sharp silver of moonshine, but the slow grey of a winter dawn.

When he looks up again at Charles, he sees that there is colour now in his cheeks even if the cut to his head is still bleeding. Now where, thinks the inspector impatiently, has that doctor got to?

'Will you come with me?' asks Charles, and there is possibly just the faintest hint of pleading in his voice.

Bucket shakes his head and gets to his feet. 'The man who was once master here is to be buried this afternoon, and I have an official appointment to attend, as well as reasons of my own that require my presence. But I know, and you know, that this may not end well, and that being the case you had better be accompanied. Sam here will go with you. And all things duly considered, you had better have this.' He reaches into his pocket, and we can see now that he has had Charles' gun about his person all this time. Something else he must have brought with him with an exact purpose in mind. They look at each other for a moment, then Charles gives a slight bow of his head and stows the pistol in his coat.

They make their way back to the entrance-hall and find, much to Bucket's relief, that the doctor has finally arrived. It's the same young surgeon who attended the crossing-sweeper, and he seems just as startled as Charles to see who his patient has turned out to be.

'I knew you lodged nearby,' says Bucket matter-of-factly, though in due course Woodcourt will wonder how, and indeed why, the inspector has furnished himself with this information. 'I'm reluctant to let this lad go a-rushing hither and thither without the say-so of a medical man.'

'I'm perfectly recovered now,' says Charles quickly, motioning Sam to go out into the square and look for a cab, 'and I don't have time for this.'

'I'm afraid I agree with this gentleman,' says Woodcourt, eyeing the new blood seeping through the bandage round

Charles' hand. 'That injury alone looks to me to need further attention. If you wish, I will come along with you and the constable, and examine it on the way.'

And so it is that the three of them are in a carriage before sun-up, rolling swiftly north under a heavy sky, where a haunted light glows in the east. The streets are almost empty, save here and there a ragged child huddled in a doorway, and a few coke fires still glowing on street corners, ringed by a shabby crowd of beggars, some smoking, some sleeping on the cold ground, and some already beginning the grim business of survival, picking over the heaps of rubbish for bones, rotting fruit, or oyster shells. Bucket, for his part, and for all his talk of obsequies to attend, and preparations to make, turns back into the house when the carriage has gone, and makes his way back to the hidden door and the gallery below. Alone now, as is his preference, there is no nook, no shelf, no compartment, no drawer he does not examine and inspect, keeping his own mental account of everything he finds, and a memorandum on occasion in a large black pocket-book. And then he leaves everything exactly as he found it, and goes back up the stairs to the clerk's hall, and the desk, and the door to the street.

In the cab, meanwhile, the noise of hooves on the wet stones does not permit much by way of conversation, and even if that were not so, none of them seems particularly inclined to talk. Though it's clear, from the glances he casts in Charles' direction, that Sam, for one, would very much like to know where it is they're going, and what he should be expecting when they get there. Charles, by contrast, is sunk in thoughts of his own, and Woodcourt watches him thoughtfully as he unwinds the stained cloth and re-dresses the wounded hand. The sleet is just starting to fall when the carriage slows to a walk at the entrance to a long tree-lined drive off one of the main roads leading out of London. There is a little lodge house, and there are two iron gates, but they already stand open and the lodge-keeper waves them through. A few moments later they come to a stop in front of a large redbrick porch, and Charles springs down without waiting for the driver, looking a good deal more confident than he actually feels. The bell is answered almost immediately, and by a woman. Thin, middle-aged, and wearing a white apron over a plain grey merino gown. When she sees Charles her face falls, and he realizes she was expecting someone else entirely. Which goes some way to explaining her promptness, and – perhaps – the open gates.

'Oh,' she says, her mouth falling into sour folds, 'I thought you were the doctor.'

Woodcourt steps down from the carriage. 'I'm a doctor, madam. May I be of assistance?'

'We have our own medical attendant. Your presence is not needed here.'

'In that case,' says Charles, 'I would like to see the proprietor. My name is Maddox.'

'I'm afraid that won't be possible. He is very pre-occupied at present, and can see no one. One of our patients is unwell.'

Charles and Woodcourt exchange a glance.

'What sort of establishment is this?' asks Woodcourt, his dark eyes grave.

The woman looks at him narrowly. 'I'm not sure that is any concern of yours.'

Wheeler takes a step forward. 'This is a police matter, madam. I'm sure you wouldn't be wishing to impede our enquiries, now would you?'

She sniffs, clearly unimpressed by either his uniform or his tone. 'It is a private lunatic asylum. And if that is all, I have better things to do than—'

The door is closing, but Charles has his foot against it, and the next minute he's pushed past her into the empty hall. There's a large refectory on one side with a smaller office opposite, and straight ahead of him a heavy carved staircase that branches left and right to the two wings of the house. And then at last the pieces shift, slide together, and form – finally – a pattern. This is the 'service' Tulkinghorn provided for Cremorne and his associates and all those other clients over the years – this is the 'establishment' that is so suitable for handling 'delicate cases'. And if that is so, there must be a link – a connection – not only between this place and Cremorne, but between this place and the baronet of the black swan.

He turns to the woman, only a few paces behind him now. 'Do you know a man named Sir Percival Glyde? Does he pay for the upkeep of a patient here?'

'I am not at liberty to divulge—'

'You'd be advised to answer the gentleman,' says Wheeler quickly. 'It'll go better for you in the end.'

'I'm sure you know exactly who I'm talking about,' says Charles, moving slowly towards her. 'Between forty-five and fifty, I should say, with dark hair starting to thin and an extremely distinctive scar on the back of his hand.'

She flushes; there is a line of bright colour now on her thin cheekbones. 'We did have a patient here whose treatment was paid for by Sir Percival—'

'*Did* have?'

'Anne Catherick—' she hesitates, 'is no longer with us.'

'And what exactly does that mean?' demands Charles. He is by now barely three inches from the woman, and towers over her.

'I do not know who you are, and I am equally unacquainted with whatever it is that gives you the right to behave in such an unmannerly and intimidating manner towards my staff.'

They turn. The man who has just emerged from the office is tall, with a heavy grey beard and a large gold watch, rather showily displayed.

'I am the owner of this institution. As you have already been informed, one of our patients is very ill, and that being the case I must ask you to leave the premises at once.'

'I'll leave,' says Charles, 'when I have some answers, and not before.'

'Very well,' says the man, smiling in a very unpleasant way. 'What is it you wish to know?'

'What happened to this woman Anne Catherick?'

The man spreads his hands. 'Before I answer that, you should know that this establishment is one of the most highly regarded of its kind in London, if not in England.'

Charles glances at Woodcourt, but the doctor is intent only on the proprietor's face.

'No expense is spared on the treatment provided here, which conforms to that recommended by acknowledged experts working in the fields of hysteria, imbecility, epilepsy and other such predominantly female maladies.'

The doctor frowns slightly, but says nothing.

'You must also understand,' the man continues, 'that Anne Catherick was an extremely disturbed young woman. Had been so, indeed, from a very early age. In the course of time the symptoms of her mental affliction became so severe and so alarming that there was no alternative but to place her under

323

full medical supervision. Her mother having rendered faithful service to Sir Percival's family for many years, he was generous enough to defray the expense of her daughter's treatment here, thereby avoiding the necessity of admitting the girl into a public asylum.'

'Not that she was grateful, the conniving little minx,' snaps the woman. Her employer glances at her quickly, then looks away.

'What do you mean, "conniving"?' says Charles, trying to divine what message it is that has just passed between them.

The man shakes his head. 'It was most regrettable, most regrettable. Especially for an establishment as punctilious as this has always been on such matters. Miss Catherick contrived to ingratiate herself with one of the nurses here – a girl, I may say, who had been with us only a few months – and escaped one night from the grounds. It was some time before she could be traced and returned here for further treatment, during which interval Sir Percival was unstinting in his efforts to assist in retrieving the unhappy child. But by the time she was eventually found, her condition had markedly deteriorated. Indeed, you might scarcely have believed her to be the same person.'

Charles sees another look pass between the man and the woman; there is something here, something they are concealing from him, but what can it be?

And just then – as he stands there, looking from one to the other – there is a sound from upstairs. Somewhere a long way away, over their heads, a woman is screaming. Charles looks at Woodcourt, and the two of them race up the stairs with Wheeler at their heels, only to find themselves confronted by a long dark corridor, its line of windows curtained against the light. Door after door stand before them, all closed. Charles nods to Woodcourt and he moves quickly to the rooms at the farther end of the passage, while Charles turns to the door in front of him and reaches for the handle.

He thought he knew what he was going to find. He's seen the worst of London's squalor in his time, the darkest of its many darknesses, but he has seen nothing – nothing – that compares to this.

The room is no more than ten feet square; there is no fire in the tiny hearth and the barest of blankets on the iron bedstead. And in the corner, muttering incoherently, there is an old woman cowering away from him on the filthy floor, her night-dress yellow with old urine and an empty bird-cage gripped in her gaunt and crooked fingers. The next room is an exact copy of the first, only here Charles finds a young man with wild disordered hair and ink-stained hands, surrounded by a great quantity of textbooks, their pages bristling with snippets of paper. He does not even look up when Charles enters – does not even notice he's there – so engrossed is he in turning frenetically from one book to another, and making tiny notes in a minute illegible hand. Charles can hardly bear to look at him – it's like some obscene parody – a terrifying and insane mirror image of himself that touches a deep and buried fear that even now he will never discuss, and which haunts him like a figure seen only in a dream, advancing towards him down a long colonnade; now in shadow, now in light, now invisible, now half-seen, now a stranger, now with the face of one he once loved.

He turns away, sick at soul, and finds Wheeler has gone before him and is already standing staring in the neighbouring doorway. And it's soon clear why. The golden-haired girl who stands looking listlessly out of the window is as beautiful as a Botticelli Madonna, but what stops Charles' breath and freezes his heart is the short rose taffeta dress she wears, and

325

the sight – all innocent as it seems – of an old rag-doll lying on the chair.

> *'Sir Julius bloody Cremorne is only interested in little girls – or those of us as can pass ourselves off as such. Same type every time. Always blondes. And the younger the better. Ribbons, ringlets, pink dress, the whole friggin' farrago. He even gave me a bloody doll to hold while he was on top of me...'*

At that moment the young woman turns and sees him, and shrinks back in terror against the wall. 'Don't touch me! You mustn't touch me!'

'I won't hurt you,' says Charles quickly, retreating backwards. 'I want to help you, if I can. If you'll let me.'

Her eyes widen. 'I don't believe you. Uncle Julius says men are not to be trusted. Especially young men. He says I must always be on my guard because I am so beautiful.' She tilts her head and twists one of her ringlets about her finger. 'Do *you* think I'm beautiful?'

'Very beautiful. But I hope you will realize that you *can* trust me, whatever your uncle says.'

She smiles at him coquettishly, all her fear apparently gone. 'I will have to introduce you next time he comes. I will tell him you are my new beau and we will make him *very* jealous. It is no more than he deserves, for not coming to visit me for a whole *week*.'

'Does he come often, then?'

'Oh yes, very often,' she replies carelessly. 'He says he cannot bear to be without me. Because he loves me dearly and no one will ever treasure me as he does. It is our special secret, and I must never tell anyone. Not even my closest friend.'

'Does she live here too?'

'Oh yes. We used to have rooms next to one another, until I became ill.' Her face clouds and she dandles the doll a moment before flinging it on the bed. 'Such a long time it was, that I was sick. But Uncle Julius says we may be allowed to see each other once again, when she is well. And if I am very good.'

'Is your friend sick too?'

The young woman nods vigorously. 'But they tell me she is getting better and I will see her very soon.'

There is a noise in the passage and the woman in grey appears, labouring a little from the effort of climbing the stairs.

'And just what do you think you're doing?' she begins in an irate tone, dragging Charles out of the room and shutting the door behind him. 'Don't you know that these patients are extremely susceptible to disturbance or commotion of any kind? Storming unannounced into their private rooms in this way may have serious consequences for their course of treatment.'

'Treatment? *Treatment?* Do you call leaving an old woman in her own filth treatment? Do you call what you're letting happen to that girl *treatment?*'

The woman looks at him. 'I haven't the faintest idea what you mean.'

'This girl – who put her here? It was Sir Julius Cremorne, wasn't it?'

'Miss Adams is Sir Julius' niece, certainly, though what business that is—'

'And he visits her. Spends time with her. In this room – behind a locked door.'

The woman gives him a venomous look. 'She is his ward. He is entitled to privacy.'

'And is he entitled to have her dress like a nine-year-old child?'

'Clara Adams came to us when she was around that age. Do not be fooled by her charming appearance – when she first arrived here her language was most unseemly and her conduct decidedly inappropriate in one so young. We have – by dint of patience and the careful application of suitable remedies – brought her to a state of comparative calmness. It comforts her to wear such clothes, and we see no harm in it.'

'And do you see no *harm* in practising a barbaric form of brain surgery that has left its hapless victim little short of cataleptic and scarcely able to walk or talk?'

It's the young doctor; he's coming towards them down the corridor, his handsome face as angry as Charles has ever seen it. He gestures back the way he's come, his hand trembling with suppressed fury. 'There's a young girl along the hall here who still bears the scars of that out-moded procedure, and another chained to her bed and strapped into a strait-jacket.'

'I can assure you,' says the woman, her voice rising, 'that Miss Augusta had been subject for years to debilitating seizures of the most alarming kind. We were assured by the doctor that trepanation was perfectly safe, and had been carried out with great success on many similar cases, and I am pleased to say she has not had a single attack since that time. The operation was, therefore,' this with a pointed look at the doctor, 'a *complete success*. As for Miss Caroline, well, I am afraid it is well-nigh impossible to induce her to demonstrate the self-control fitting to one of her sex without resorting to such restraints. Without them she will refuse her medicines, or conceal them from the staff, and become so unruly as to be a constant disturbance to the other patients, tearing her clothes and laughing immoderately, while at other times descending into fits of sulkiness that last for days on end.'

328

'So you manacle her in a strait-jacket,' says the doctor grimly.

'We use the camisole, yes. In *her own interests.*'

'And was it in Miss Adams' interests,' interrupts Charles, 'to be debauched time and time again by her own uncle?'

Woodcourt turns to him, his face grey. 'Please tell me that is not true.'

'My God, Woodcourt, I wish I could. She's in there. One of I don't know how many other young women incarcerated here by Edward Tulkinghorn over the years, for the sordid convenience of men like Julius Cremorne. How many more are there like Clara Adams?' he says to the woman, seizing her by her thin arm. 'How many other girls here have wealthy so-called *protectors* who are "entitled to their privacy"? *Answer me,* damn you!'

The woman starts to splutter a reply, but a look from Woodcourt silences her and he opens the door and disappears inside.

And then – louder now – closer now – they hear again what first brought them here. The sound of a girl screaming, accompanied now by the drumming of fists. 'Help me – please! If there's someone out there, please help me!'

It's coming from the room at the farthest end of the passage, but the door will not give, not even to Wheeler's sturdy shoulder. But Sam is not defeated yet. He starts back along the corridor to where the woman in grey is still standing,

'Do you 'ave the key to this door?'

Charles has rarely seen his old friend so determined, and something of this must have communicated itself to the woman, because she puts her hand in her apron pocket without another word and hands him a heavy key. A moment later the locked door is open and there's a young woman half-fainting, half-collapsed in Charles' arms.

'You have to help me,' she gasps. 'It's all my fault. She's gone, and it's all my fault.'

Her eyes are wild and her face is stained with tears, and Charles is about to call for Woodcourt when he realizes with a shock that she, too, is wearing a grey merino gown. He frowns, 'Do you *work* here?'

'Yes, yes, I'm not a patient – I'm one of the nurses. My name is Alice. Alice Carley.'

'So what on earth are you doing locked in this room?'

She looks at him, and then away, the tears falling.

'I told Hester what had happened. But they made me do it – Mr Jarvis and that woman Darby. They *made* me do it.'

She's becoming frantic, and Charles is relieved to see Woodcourt emerge into the corridor a few moments later and come quickly towards them. The doctor kneels by the sobbing girl. 'I examined Miss Adams,' he tells Charles in a low voice. 'And your suspicions are, I am sad to say, entirely correct. I would not wish to see a sister of mine so knowing on such intimate subjects. Or any woman I hoped to marry,' and here the shade passes across his face that Charles has seen once before.

'And I'm afraid that is not even the worst of it,' continues the doctor. 'Miss Adams is with child, and it will not be her first.'

He has kept his tone low, but Alice Carley hears him all the same.

'Not Clara! Oh, please, not Clara! You must believe me – I never knew it was Clara!'

'I am a doctor,' says Woodcourt gently. 'There's no need to be afraid. Just tell us what happened.'

He passes a hand over her forehead, and she is immediately calmer and more composed.

She takes a deep breath. 'I swear I never knew Clara had had a baby, sir. But if she did, it won't have been the only brought

330

into the world in this place. There was another child born here not two months ago.'

Charles and Woodcourt exchange a glance. 'I've seen no nursery,' says the doctor, 'heard no cry.'

Alice looks at him pleadingly. 'They *told* me it was born dead. And you could tell, sir – there was no way the poor mite could have lived long – so tiny and twisted – with such an odd unnatural look about it. All the same—'

She stops, and bites her lip.

'Go on,' urges the doctor quietly. 'Tell us from the beginning.'

She drops her eyes and shakes her head sadly. 'One day in October, Mr Jarvis summoned me to his office, and told me that one of the patients had given birth to a stillborn. I didn't know, then, whose baby it was – they'd kept Hester close for weeks, telling us she was ill and letting no one near her. And you've seen the shapeless gowns they make them wear – it was no wonder none of us knew. Mr Jarvis said he had no idea how it could have happened – that she must have "consorted" with young Mr Cawston, but I couldn't see how that could be – none of the patients are allowed alone together without one of the nurses – *never*. And what would he have seen in such a queer misshapen little thing anyway? Mr Jarvis said it was all very regrettable—'

'A favourite word of his, it seems,' interrupts Charles bitterly.

'– but they needed to dispose of the body. Discreetly, he said. Because above all else it was vital that they prevented a public scandal. I said I wanted nothing to do with it and we should summon the police, but Mr Jarvis made it very clear that I either went along with what he demanded, or I would lose my position. What else could I do?' she pleads, looking from one to the other. 'My whole family relies on me, now Pa is gone. Even with my wages, it's barely enough to cover the rent.'

'A fact of which Mr Jarvis is no doubt fully aware,' says Charles. 'So what did he ask you to do?'

'He sat me down by the fire and started to tell me about a graveyard he knew near St Giles Circus. I remember the look on his face as he was talking, and thinking I must be in some horrible nightmare. He said this place was somewhere a child like this might be buried in consecrated ground without anyone even noticing – a place where plenty of young women got rid of babies they didn't want. I was revolted at the very idea of it, but Mr Jarvis looked stern at me then and said I would lose my post – like that other girl who let Anne Catherick escape. So I told myself that if the babe really was dead when it was born, there could be little real harm. Especially if he was right and it was consecrated ground.' She looks at Woodcourt, the tears starting again. 'But that was before they gave me the baby. That woman had wrapped it in a blanket so I couldn't see it, but I couldn't help myself. I knew then that they'd lied to me. I'm a nurse – I know the signs. I saw the bruises, and when I touched its little face I could feel its wee nose was broken. Someone had smothered her – poor lamb – and they hadn't even done it with a gentle hand.'

Her voice catches with a sob. 'I couldn't bear to see her after that, so I put my handkerchief over her little face, and swaddled her properly, like a baby should be swaddled. And held her for a moment against my heart, like a baby should be held.'

Tenderness, thinks Charles, remembering how that word had forced itself on his mind in the burial-ground, as he stood over the tiny body rotting in its shallow grave, the scrap of white cloth still wound about its neck, and wondered how any woman could have shown such gentle care, and yet done such a terrible thing. He couldn't understand it then, but he can understand it now. That child was Hester's child, and the woman who buried it, this woman.

Alice Carley wipes her eyes. 'That night they sent me into town in the carriage. I had to get out somewhere near Oxford Street and walk the rest of the way on foot, but Mr Jarvis said I had nothing to fear – that no one would remark a young woman carrying a child. They'd told me where I had to go, but I lost my way in the dark and had to ask a crossing-sweep. I wouldn't have found the place without him, though I wish to heaven I'd never laid eyes on it.' She shudders. 'I will never forget the horror of that graveyard – never forget trying to open the grave with nothing but a little trowel, in the stench of all those decaying bodies.'

'Corpse gas,' says Woodcourt. 'You were fortunate not to become seriously ill.'

'You must believe me, sir, that I did everything I could to give the child a decent burial, but no one could have borne staying in that terrible place long. I was half out of my mind with fear. The fog had come down, and as soon as I'd closed the gate behind me I was sure that someone was following me – I could hear noises and the sound of footsteps. And a few moments later I felt a hand on my shoulder and my heart froze. And when I turned and saw this huge man looming over me, I nearly lost my senses – I thought I was about to be garrotted – or worse. And what would happen to my brother and sister then?'

She takes a deep breath. 'But then the man said he wasn't going to hurt me – that he just wanted to talk to me. I was so terrified I could scarcely hear what he was saying, but I eventually made out that his sister used to have my position here, and that exactly the same thing had happened to her. Mr Jarvis told her the same things he'd told me, and she'd buried three babies in that unspeakable place before being dismissed without a penny, for allowing Anne Catherick to escape.'

'William Boscawen,' says Charles quickly. 'Was that the man's name?'

Alice nods. 'He said that after she was dismissed, his sister planned to blackmail Mr Jarvis by threatening to tell all she knew, but that was the last he ever heard from her. It was months later that he found out she'd been killed. That's when he came to London to find out the truth. He started to get very angry then – he said he'd discovered what was really going on at the asylum, and he was going to confront the guilty men with the evidence of their sin.'

'What did he mean by that?'

Alice takes out her handkerchief and holds it to her mouth. 'It sickens me even to think of it, sir – how anyone could—'

Woodcourt puts his hand on her shoulder. 'Take your time. We have a policeman here with us. You have nothing to fear now. Just tell us what Mr Boscawen said.'

She looks up at his face and seems to gain courage. 'He told me he'd dug open the grave where the babies were buried and – and – cut the hands away from the corpses. He said he was going to send them one by one to the men who'd fathered them. To punish them for what they'd done.'

Charles stares at her, understanding at last the riddle of the letters, and the terrible menace the last one had contained. Julius Cremorne had opened that package to find the decomposing hand of his own bastard child; a child born of incest and rape, a child he had instructed Jarvis to do away with. Small wonder he went as white as death when he saw it; small wonder he looked as if he'd seen a ghost.

Alice glances up at him fearfully, mistaking his grim expression for disapproval. 'I told that man Boscawen I didn't want to hear any more about it – that I had to go – that the carriage was

334

waiting for me. Then as I ran down the passageway I heard him calling to me that he would write to me and explain, but I never heard from him again.'

The tears well and spill again. 'I don't think poor Hester even knew she was with child – how could she, an innocent like her? Half the time she seems scarcely more than a child herself, playing make-believe that she's the housekeeper here and that I'm her maid, not her nurse. You'd never think this place was a lunatic asylum, to hear the way she talks of it, but we none of us have the heart to disenchant her. And then she was so weak for so long after she had the baby it made my heart bleed, just to look at her, and in the end I felt so wretched about what I'd done I made up my mind to tell her the truth – tell her what had really happened. So I went to her early this morning and told her that she'd had a baby – that that was the real reason why she'd been so sick. I said I'd made sure it was given a Christian burial, and that it was in a Better Place now, but then the poor girl started crying and crying and talking wildly about her mother leaving her behind and how she would never do that to her baby, and then she said she wanted to see it and however much I said that was impossible she would not leave it be. It takes her that way sometimes, poor little thing, but I can usually calm her with a dose of opiates – it always seems kinder to me than that dreadful camisole Miss Darby insists on. But in my haste to fetch the medicine bottle I must have left the door unlocked, and when I got back the room was empty, and Hester had vanished.'

'And that's why Jarvis locked you in here.'

She nods. 'And because I wouldn't tell him where she had gone.'

'But how in God's name could you possibly know?'

'It's not so very difficult to guess, sir. Hester has never left this place once in the ten years she's been here. Where else would she go? She's gone to see her baby,' she says softly. 'She's gone to Tom-All-Alone's.'

Charles gets to his feet, knowing now what he must do next and wondering for the first time what has happened to Wheeler. A question quickly answered when they get to the landing and see Sam coming up the stairs towards them.

'No sign, Mr Maddox,' he reports, reverting, no doubt unconsciously, to the courtesy Charles was entitled to when he still had rank in the Detective.

'What do you mean?' asks Charles, with a jolt of alarm.

'Given what that young woman was saying, I thought we ought to make sure that bastard Jarvis didn't give us the slip, but I've searched all the rooms downstairs and I can't find him anywhere.'

Charles follows him quickly downstairs, where they find the woman in the hall, berating another young woman clad in grey.

'Where's Jarvis?' interrupts Charles, forcing her round to look at him.

'*Mr* Jarvis had to step out a moment.'

'This is a police investigation, madam, and he has serious allegations to answer.'

'*He* may be a constable,' she snaps, pointing at Wheeler as if he were a species of insect, 'but *you*, as far as I can tell, have no official standing whatsoever. If you *had* I am sure we would have heard about it long before now. And Mr Jarvis has been charged with no crime – has, indeed, *committed* no crime. He is perfectly free to come and go as he sees fit and you have no right to detain him.'

At that moment there's the sound of wheels on the sweep, but by the time they emerge on to the front step the carriage is already turning down the drive and gathering speed.

Woodcourt turns to Charles with a look of disgust. 'No doubt he is endeavouring to "retrieve" Hester just as he did Anne Catherick. But this time, thank God, he has no idea where the poor girl has gone. You will be able to reach her long before he does.'

Charles looks round; something about this sudden departure is making him uneasy. And then he catches sight of the woman's frosty face and sees the look that's now upon it.

'She heard it all,' he says to Woodcourt. 'She was listening to every word we said – she knows where Hester went, and now Jarvis has gone after her.'

He calls to Wheeler to have the cab brought round, and fast, and he's already stepping into it when Woodcourt catches his arm and offers to go with him. 'She will be distraught and very possibly in need of medical attention—'

'I've had some training, myself. Not much, but enough. I know what to do. And your presence is more urgently required here until more help arrives.'

It's clear from Woodcourt's face that he cannot argue with that conclusion, but he is not done yet. 'At least,' he says, his hand still on Charles' arm, 'at the very least, take Miss Carley with you. Imagine yourself in this young girl's position – she has just made a terrible discovery, then finds a man pursuing her she has never seen, in a huge and dangerous city she does not know. She is weak already, and I dare not speculate as to the consequences of further distress so soon after her confinement.'

Charles nods and the doctor goes quickly back inside, returning almost at once with the nurse, enveloped in a blanket clearly taken from one of the beds upstairs.

'She is willing to go with you, though Heaven knows she could do with hot tea and a few hours' sleep.'

'I am quite well,' insists Alice. 'The only thing that matters is that we find Hester and take her somewhere safe.'

'I pray to heaven we can,' replies Charles, climbing up to the box beside the driver and telling him to make all speed towards London, with a crown at stake if he can catch the carriage ahead of them.

As they clatter towards town, Charles stops every coach and vehicle coming towards them, picking up the trace of Jarvis each time but finding him ever just too far ahead, ever maintaining his crucial advantage before them, until they reach a crossroads where four roads meet and have to make a choice: the road to Finchley, the road to the West End, and the road to London. The driver draws up – they can reach their destination by two of these ways, but which is best – which did Jarvis choose? Charles sits hesitating a moment, before noticing a young man on a small stool at the side of the road, sketching the sun rising over the city and the steeples and house-tops lifting through the mist in the slanting rays. Charles jumps down and strides towards him, asking if a carriage has passed this way.

'The driver was in a green greatcoat, and the man inside had a thick grey beard.'

'And a rather large watch, I believe,' says the young man. 'Yes, I saw him. He has some fifteen minutes' advantage of you. But I sent him the wrong way.'

'I'm sorry, I don't understand—'

'He asked about the young woman. She passed this way too, something over an hour ago. A strange little creature in a long dark cloak, but I could see she had only a nightgown on underneath. She asked me the way to Tom-All-Alone's. I told her that polluted graveyard was no place for a young girl, but she began to weep in a piteous fashion, saying I had no right to suspect her and it was the fault of others that she was alone here in such strange circumstances, and something more I did not understand about a "guardian". She became so agitated then, all the while shrinking from me as if I might molest her, that I agreed, much against my better judgement, to find her a cab and give her the money to pay for it. Not before time, I think. She seemed ready to drop with fatigue.'

And not just fatigue, thinks Charles, attempting to press several shillings into the young man's hand.

'That is not necessary, sir,' he says, pulling away. 'It was little enough of a service after all, and I can tell you mean her only kindness. That other gentleman *said* the same, but there was something about him that made me doubt it. Not least the fact that he called her a cripple, and a freak, and various other terms I am too humane to repeat. That and the look of the groom he had with him made me uneasy, so I sent them on the other road, telling them she was still on foot.'

Charles' heart turns to iron in his breast. 'This groom – what did he look like?'

'He was little more than a boy, in fact, but the strangest-looking boy I ever saw in such a—'

'Sandy hair – a long dark coat?'

'And a bad bruise to the side of his face. Indeed I am surprised his master allowed him in public in such a state—'

But Charles is already running towards the cab. He climbs back up, urging the driver to a gallop and cursing himself for not realizing that Mann would have made for the asylum just as he did, and imploring a God he does not really believe in that they will find this wretched girl before he does. It's not long before they're descending fast into narrow streets and gloomy overhanging thoroughfares where the morning has not yet penetrated and the street-lamps still cast their sickly yellow.

Perhaps it's the fall he took, perhaps the chill of the exposed seat, but his vision starts to blur again and his mind begins to play tricks with him. The few people they pass in the streets seem hardly alive, and as they raise faces to him that seem now as blank and eyeless as in a long-repressed nightmare, the kaleidoscope pieces of the case start to shift and mingle with his own haunted memories – his mother gagged and bound, her eyes streaming and imploring, her bare feet kicking against the two women struggling to carry her away. The stifled incoherent screams that even now are inextricable from the cool impersonal voice of the doctor ensuring his father that he had made the right decision, that the institution was a model of its kind, and that Mrs Maddox would be treated kindly there and given the time she needed to reconcile herself at last to the loss of her daughter. He never knew how much his father had believed of this; all he did know for sure was that he never saw his mother again. And that all of it – from the beginning – was his fault, and there was nothing he could ever do that that would put it right.

With the clocks striking nine they come to a halt by the grimy side-street where we followed him once before. As Charles swings down to the ground into the steam from the horses, he hears the sound of hooves and turns to see a carriage disappearing towards St Giles, and knows with a hopeless certainty that despite their haste – despite the young man's help – they were still too slow: Jarvis has got here before them. He hastens Alice Carley from the carriage and the two of them begin down the alley towards the covered way. He thought once before how apt this place was for ambush, and as they approach the bend before the tunnel he can just make out a slumped figure lying face down at the side of the path. But it's only when Alice Carley gasps and shrinks back against his side

340

that he recognizes who it is. The cape and the tall silk hat mark him out as a gentleman; the greying beard identifies him as Alexander Jarvis. But the heavy gold watch is long gone. Charles kneels by the man's head and sees at once that all the talk of garrotting in this part of town is not just the hype of an over-heated press. There's a deep weal around Jarvis' neck and he is struggling to draw breath.

'What happened?' says Charles, taking him roughly by the collar. 'Where's Mann?'

'We were set upon,' he gasps. 'Thieves – four of them. I felt the rope around my neck and hands dragging me down. I called to Mann to help me. But he just laughed.' He chokes, coughing spittles of red over his white stock. 'He just laughed in my face and left me here in the filth.'

'So where is he now?'

Jarvis lifts a heavy hand and points. 'He went ahead. After the girl.'

Charles gets to his feet and covers the final yards to the tunnel with his heart hammering at his bones. Up ahead, where the lamp is still burning over the iron gate, one slight figure is bending over another, lying prone on the wet ground. Charles takes out his gun, but his eyes are dim and he cannot make out his target. He starts towards them again, and even as the images lurch and separate before his eyes he thinks he sees the low glint of a blade – thinks he sees an arm raised – and he knows he cannot make it in time – knows there is only one thing he can do—

He lifts the pistol and shoots into the air.

The recoil has his boots slithering on the greasy cobbles and he slips to his knees. Then all at once he senses Alice Carley come up behind him, and though he cries out to stop her she gives a cry of horror and runs forward to the gate. When he gets to his feet and staggers after her he sees, alone, lying on the step, the twisted body of a young girl, one hand clutched around the iron bars, the skirts of her white nightgown stained dark red. And Alice Carley is already weeping as she takes the girl's head in her lap and cradles it there, rocking to and fro, the tears running down her cheeks.

Charles stoops down, and puts his arm about Alice's shoulders. And then, with the gentlest of gentle hands, he puts the long dank hair aside and touches Hester's cold scarred face.

Chapter Twenty-five

The Appointed Time

Noon, Waterloo Bridge.

From where we stand we can look up towards Whitehall and Westminster, and down towards the City, where the lines of barges and lug-boats are advancing slowly up from the Essex marshes, laden with timber and coal and barrels of porter. The river moves sluggishly beneath us as if filmed with oil, but the wind is starting to get up now, scattering the stench of excrement and whirling the gulls upwards in sharp gusts. Down among the gravel and the black sand a group of mud-larks are wading about up to their naked thighs in the freezing water, aprons tied about their waists, looking for iron, copper nails, discarded junk, pieces of rope – anything as might earn a few coins to eat by. The sound of their voices floats up to us in fits and starts – a curse, a cry of success, even, once or twice, laughter. On either side of the bridge we can see crowds of people going about their ordinary business – street-traders and hawkers, patterers and pedlars – but it is a cold day and few are choosing to eat their midday meal in the open air. Fewer still have either the leisure or the inclination to do what we're doing, and merely stand and stare. But there are exceptions. A few hundred yards away, on Salisbury Stairs, there are two men sitting together in what seems to be a companionable silence.

And I can tell you, moreover, that they've already been there for some time. The one tall, young, blue-eyed; the other small, black-suited, thoughtful.

'So she will live,' says Charles eventually.

Bucket glances at him, then nods. 'She was very cold and she had lost a deal of blood, but Woodcourt says that with proper care, she has a chance. Though even if her body heals he is not sure he has the medicines that can mend her mind. But if there's a doctor in London who can do it, I'll wager it is Woodcourt. And who knows, mayhap she will find that there is love in this world that is not cruel and disfigured, and that will help bring her back.'

'And what happens now?'

Bucket rubs his forefinger against the side of his nose. 'I will pursue Mann, if I can. But my guess is the evidence will not be strong enough. What he boasts of to *you*, he will not confess to *me*, and I fear he will simply disappear back into the slums of Whitechapel whence he came. But you have no need to fear – for yourself, or those about you. I will keep my eye on him, as long as I have breath, and as long as I am Mr Bucket of the Detective. He shall not stir, shall do no harm to so much as a street dog, without my a-knowing of it. Let London look to itself thereafter, for I dare not predict what savagery that young villain might be capable of, or what cruelty he is willing to inflict.'

A cloud passes across the sun and the gulls whirl suddenly upwards in a shrieking spiral of wings and claws and razor beaks.

'And the others?'

'We have enough to pursue Alexander Jarvis. Fortunately for us, he was not as cautious in his record-keeping as his paymaster in the Fields. I suspect we will find plenty enough paper-work at the asylum to bring charges against Cremorne and his associates. Though one of them is already being held to account at a far higher court than I could bring him to. I have just got word that Sir Percival Glyde has been killed in a fire in Hampshire. What the circumstances of this fire be – accident or arson – is not yet clear.'

Charles turns to him with a bleak look on his face. 'How many of them were there?'

'The young girls? There is some mystery surrounding Anne Catherick that I have not yet got to the bottom of, and that I fear may not be unconnected with that young wife of Glyde's so lately dead, and that fortune of hers so greatly wanted. There is more to Anne Catherick's confinement in that asylum than an obligation to an old servant, you mark my words. And when I hear tell that the second time she was brought to that abominable place she seemed quite different and strangely changed, I prick up my ears and I ask myself why, and I wonder how it is that she is not there still. But all that,' he sighs, 'will have to wait for another day. What I do know is that Woodcourt found three more young women like her in the other wing of the asylum, and Jarvis' records show there have been many more over the years, some of whom seem to have stayed there only a few short weeks. I fear we will discover that they too had been dishonoured and betrayed by uncles and fathers and men of like kind, and it was Tulkinghorn who arranged for 'em to brought to the asylum, so as to keep the men's secret, and dispose of its consequences. Who knows how much innocent blood he had on his hands, by the end.'

Charles looks away, sick at heart. 'And Miss Adams?'

'I am making arrangements for her to be placed in Lady Cremorne's care, with the strong recommendation that she removes with her to her own family's seat in Derbyshire. The girl went to live at Curzon Street for a time, they tell me, after her parents died. She had hitherto been a mild and peaceable child but grew capricious and unsettled almost at once. Suffered badly with her nerves and became altogether ungovernable. It was about this same time that Lady Cremorne suffered her unfortunate accident. And as you may remember from your time in the Detective, I am no great believer in coincidences.'

'You mean, she *knew*?'

'Did the fall not take place in the middle of the night? When the rest of the household were a-sleeping? And was it not impossible to account afterwards for what she was doing there? My guess, my lad, is that she discovered the two of 'em together – her husband and his niece. Discovered it and either ran away in terror, or took issue with the man and paid the price. But I would lay a hundred pound that she will never tell. It seems that all this time she has believed the girl had been placed in a distant asylum, far from London and beyond her husband's reach. Though it appears she has been making efforts to find the child of late. But why now, after such a stretch of years—'

'The letters,' says Charles quickly. 'The anonymous letters. *She* must have known what they referred to all along, even if she didn't know who was sending them.'

Bucket nods; even he has not made this last connection. 'That would explain it, I grant you. And it would likewise explain why she has been writing so many letters herself in recent weeks – enquiring discreetly of all her acquaintances about establishments where the girl might be found.'

'But how could she have agreed to have a mere child committed to a lunatic asylum in the first place – even if it was meant to protect her?'

Bucket is silent a long time, twisting the great mourning ring on his little finger, but finally he turns to Charles. 'Not all

Jarvis' patients were put there by Edward Tulkinghorn. Some were entrusted to him by their own families – well-meaning people, most of 'em. The young lad Cawston, for instance, was the apple of his family's eye. A fine young fellow he was once, and full of promise, but he became so fixed in his habits, and so prey to monomania, they could no longer manage him. The grandmother who brought him up sincerely believed she was doing the right thing – that Jarvis would effect a cure. In my experience, people are more often committed to such places out of love than wickedness. Love and ignorance. The mind is a singular thing, Charles, a singular thing, and it has depths that even your finest science has not yet fathomed. I have known women,' and his face is drawn now with the memory of an old and unhealed pain, 'who have so longed for a child that they can think of little else, and sink into such a pit of melancholy that there is no recovering them. And what can even the most loving of husbands do at such a pass but follow the advice the doctors give? There is no solving such cases, no knowledge of the heart that can bring back a mind so clouded and astray.'

Charles thinks of his own mother, driven from her reason by the loss of a child, and of the sister he knows he will never find, and it is a long, long moment before he remembers that the present Mrs Bucket was not the first. And that even now, Bucket has no children of his own.

They sit in silence again, and it is Bucket, in the end, who breaks that silence first.

'I must be away soon, to Lincoln's Inn Fields, and to the funeral, but before I do, I should tell you what I found there this morning. It's why I suggested we took a stroll down here. Open air, my lad, is best for evil deeds.'

347

He turns his eyes again to the river. 'There were secrets in Tulkinghorn's house, my friend, that even you did not discover. Like a wall hung with priceless pictures that turned out to be no more than a wooden partition. Like a little brass clasp that unlocked that partition, and allowed it to swing open. Like another set of pictures, hung inside, of an obscenity such as I have never seen in all my years in the Detective. Images of children, mostly, as would wring your heart and incite you to a blistering vengeance had you laid your eyes upon them. And were that not enough, there was a little parlour hidden behind, in the heart of the spider's web, where I found the last and worst of all Tulkinghorn's secrets. There was a box of papers there that chilled the very blood in my veins. Seems that this young Hester was *his* daughter. Secreted away, all these years, where no one would think to look. Seems he styled himself her 'Guardian', and never revealed, even to Jarvis, that he was the father. Not even when he got her with child – that same child that even now lies mouldering away in the foul earth of Tom-All-Alone's. Seems Hester's mother was his own niece, whom he ruined when she was still little more than a girl herself, and then traced to the workhouse when she was turned out of doors, for bringing such disgrace on the family credit.'

Charles turns to him, his face aghast. 'What was the girl's name – the mother?'

Bucket eyes him a moment, then nods. 'So you are there, now, are you? I wondered how long it would take for you to marry it all together. You see, now, why I am in hopes that this bruised and wounded girl may yet find love in the bosom of her own proper family. For your guess is right, my lad, and your case is solved against all expectation. The name of Hester's mother was Honoria. Honoria Chadwick.'

*

Half an hour later Charles is walking the short step back to Buckingham Street. The thin sun is warming his back and despite all he has witnessed, and all he has undergone, for the first time in weeks his mind is at rest. He parted with Bucket at the top of the steps, where the inspector turned to him and took him by the hand. 'If you ever see your way to returning to the Detective, then you have only—'

Charles smiled but shook his head. 'It is a kind offer, but I think not. And now I must get back to the house. My uncle will be missing me.'

'Give him my compliments, my lad. And my best respects. And Charles—' he said, as he made to go, 'a piece of advice. Given in a spirit of kindliness. You may take it, or not, as you think fit. But if I were in your place, I would make peace with my father. And once that is done, go with him to see your mother. I know what you are a-feared of, but not all asylums are as wretched as Jarvis'. You may take my word on that.'

Charles looked at him, then nodded, and started to turn away, before recollecting something and turning back. 'And the trooper? You don't still believe—'

'Ah,' said Bucket with a smile, his fat forefinger again in evidence, 'he's all right. Before this day is done, he'll be discharged with no stain on his character. You may take my word for that. I can tell you now that I no more believed it was George as done the deed as I believed you capable of it, but there was evidence against him, as there was against you, and that being the case I had no choice but to take him in under guard, while I concluded my investigation. But as things stand now I know the truth of it, and I will soon have all the proof I need for an arrest.'

And with that Mr Bucket buttoned himself up and went quietly on his way towards the Strand, looking steadily before him as if he already had the face of his culprit before his eye.

The house is hushed and still when Charles opens the door and pauses for a moment in the empty hall. It is so quiet he can hear the faint ticking of his uncle's clock, and the sound of sheets cracking and whipping like sails in the yard at the back. Laundry, he thinks, abstractedly. Molly must have done the laundry. There is a visiting card on the hall-stand which he picks up without really looking at it, before climbing the stairs slowly one by one, aware, for the first time, how much his body aches and how much he wants a hot bath. But first he must look in on his uncle, and tell him what has passed.

The drawing-room curtains are still half-closed, and Charles waits as his eyes adjust to the dim light, breathing in the scent of a wood fire burning low in the grate and the faint aroma of port from the glass at his uncle's side. Maddox's eyes are closed, his mouth slightly open, and his sombre and motionless face gives no hint of the dreams within. He must have fallen asleep in his chair, for his pillow has been carefully tucked behind his head, and a blanket drawn up over his lap. A lap where, as Charles now sees, the black cat is curled and sleeping, his ears twitching every now and then at the tiny crackles from the subsiding fire. Thunder has never sat with Maddox before, and Charles is smiling as he tiptoes over to the chair and bends to give the cat a quick caress before reaching to his uncle's hand. But while the cat has warmed in the fire's glow, the old man's fingers are chill; and though Thunder stirs now and stretches at his master's touch, Maddox lies rigid still, and does not wake.

And as he sees this – and as his heart lurches to what it means – there's a sudden catch in Charles' throat that has him kneeling quickly by Maddox's side and pushing the hair gently from his uncle's brow – an echo – all unconscious – of what the old man used to do when he was a boy – little enough in itself, but a gauge of deep affection in an age uncomfortable with intimacy, and a family chary of love.

'The doctor came but he says there's little we can do but keep him warm, and trust to hope. And there is hope, Mr Charles, there is hope.'

Stornaway is standing in the doorway, and although his words are brave there is a break in his voice. And as Charles reaches again for his uncle's wrinkled hand, there is a new and different catch in his throat, and he can scarcely see for tears. Everything he'd wanted to say – everything he now so wants to share – Maddox will not hear it now. May never hear it. Charles told himself it could wait till tomorrow, but tomorrow is here, and it is too late.

Stornaway comes slowly forward. 'It came on so sudden – I thought at first it were just another of his turns. He'd been fretting about you, and I was trying to turn his mind to other things. I told him he had no cause to worry on your account – that you'd become a fine detective in your own right, and even the highest in the land were now knocking on your door—'

'I'm sorry, Abel, I don't understand—'

Stornaway looks at him, 'That card in the hall, Mr Charles, did you not see whose it was?'

Charles wipes his hand across his eyes and puts his hand into his pocket. The card itself is over-embellished and a little pretentious, but otherwise hardly very remarkable. But the name – the name!

It's scarcely conceivable that two short words can conjure such a fever of contradictory ideas, but even in his first confusion Charles knows that this man must be – can only be

351

– a son who bears his father's name, for the man now venerated by some almost to idolatry died an outcast and a pariah almost thirty years before, his heart cut out and his body burned on a windswept Italian shore.

Charles turns to Stornaway. 'You showed my uncle this?'

Abel nods. 'I wish to God I hae never done it, but how could I hae known he would take on so? All on a sudden he was shouting wildly about things long ago and then he gripped me by the arm and said a name I have nae heard from his lips for half a lifetime or more. The next thing I knew he had fallen back in his chair with no stir of life about him, just as you see him now.'

'He said a name? What name?'

Stornaway sighs and shakes his head. 'He loved once, Mr Charles. Loved and lost. He never spoke of it, after they parted – not to me, and not to Fraser. But we knew, all the same. They met when we were in Northamptonshire working a case, but in the end she upped and married another. I never knew what became o' her after that, or if he ever saw her again. But it was her name, Mr Charles – the last word he spoke to me was her name. It must hae been her – with the life he's lived I know of nae other.'

Charles looks at Stornaway, and then at the card in his hand, and wonders suddenly if he has another answer to that question, however extraordinary and unlikely it may seem. For he knows – as Stornaway may not – that the woman whose son has left this card was once as infamous as the man she married, the brilliant daughter of brilliant parents – an old woman now, if yet she lives, but celebrated once for her beauty, and her cloud of red-gold hair.

'Mary,' he says softly, half to himself, but as he glances up at Abel's face he sees the old man's eyes widen in sudden amazement, and realizes with an absolute clarity that whatever this card means – whatever demands are made of him, or questions asked – there is an unguessed secret that lies unseen, in the darkness and vacancy of his uncle's cold repose.

Acknowledgements

These acknowledgements include details of the novel's plot, so readers may want to wait to read them until the end.

As any Dickens devotee will know, 'Tom-All-Alone's' is not only the name of the notorious and disease-ridden slum described so vividly in *Bleak House*, but one of the titles Dickens originally considered giving to that book. I've always considered *Bleak House* to be without question Dickens' masterpiece, and it is the first and most important of the three great mid-Victorian texts that inform my own novel.

Bleak House was first published in instalments between March 1852 and September 1853, and is a wonderful, complex, and compelling work. It's a gripping story, a powerful social commentary, and a panoramic portrait of contemporary London life. It also manages – single-handedly and almost in passing – to create a whole new literary genre: the detective mystery. For a writer who aspires to write 'literary murders' herself, it could hardly be richer territory to explore, and I hope that anyone who loves Dickens as much as I do will enjoy seeing how I have interleaved my own mystery with the characters and episodes of his novel, and used his chapter titles for events in my own, though each time with a new twist, and a rather different meaning. In doing this I have, of course, drawn extensively on *Bleak House*, and also on others of Dickens' works, especially his *Overland Tour to Bermondsey*, the *Sketches by Boz*, which includes his account of Seven Dials, and *On Duty with Inspector Field*, a piece he wrote for the *Household Words* magazine about the real-life police inspector who may well have been the model for Mr Bucket.

The second of my three great works is *The Woman in White*, written by Dickens' friend Wilkie Collins, and published in 1860. Even if the relationship between this novel and my own is not made explicit until the closing chapters, the moment when *Tom-All-Alone's* really came to life for me was when I realized that the time-scheme of *Bleak House* could be made to run parallel with Collins' very precise chronology for *The Woman in White*, which culminates in Sir Percival Glyde's death in a fire in late November 1850. This allowed me to create a 'space between' these two great novels, where I could locate a new and independent story of my own, and explore some of the same nineteenth-century themes of secrecy, madness, power, and abuse, though with the benefit of twenty-first-century hindsight.

Last but not least of my three is *London Labour and the London Poor*, by Henry Mayhew. This huge work was originally published in the form of sixty-three pioneering articles in the *Morning Chronicle*, which were then collected together in book form in 1851. *London Labour and the London Poor* is the closest thing we have to an oral history of the crowded, rowdy, filthy streets of the mid-Victorian city: Mayhew conducted hundreds of interviews with real people, and gives many of their words almost verbatim. The result is an account so immediate that it's almost as if we're walking those streets by his side, and eavesdropping on his conversations. In fact this is exactly what I do during some of the episodes of *Tom-All-Alone's*, most notably the rat-killing, where I send young Charles Maddox to the Graham Arms on the very night when – with a little artistic licence – I imagine Mayhew himself might have been there.

I talked just now about looking at the nineteenth century from a twenty-first-century perspective, and there's another obvious reference point for *Tom-All-Alone's* which famously took a similar approach, though set some seventeen years later. John Fowles' *The French Lieutenant's Woman* has long been one of my favourite modern novels, and when a close friend casually observed to me that there was 'room for a *French Lieutenant's Woman* for this generation', I realized at once that this could indeed be one of my ambitions for *Tom*. Much of my novel was already written by then, and it seemed a wonderful coincidence that I had already named my young hero Charles after his great-uncle, and made him an amateur scientist, even if in a different field from that Charles Smithson in Fowles' novel. It's Fowles who is the 'celebrated novelist' I refer to in Chapter 17, and readers who knows his book well will spot a very young Ernestina Freeman walking with her nurse in Hyde Park, and the deliberate echoes of Sarah Woodruff in my own 'Sarah'.

Anyone who has visited Sir John Soane's Museum in London will recognize his extraordinary collection in my depiction of Tulkinghorn's underground gallery, though Tulkinghorn's more infamous items are his, and his alone. I have taken one or two architectural liberties, but the museum is essentially as I describe it, and in 1850 this real collection had already been amassed in Soane's real house in Lincoln's Inn Fields, the same square where Dickens sets his lawyer's fictional chambers. Dickens himself says nothing of Tulkinghorn having such a collection, of course, but nor does anything in *Bleak House*

357

preclude it. In fact one of the great delights, for me, in writing this book was the chance it gave me to add new layers to a character like Tulkinghorn, from the secrets of his private museum to the even more horrifying secrets of his private history.

I would like to thank Timothy Duke, Chester Herald at the College of Arms, for his kind help with some of the finer points of English heraldry, and Jan Turner, Deputy Librarian at the Royal Geographical Society's Foyle Reading Room, for her assistance with the history of the Society, and with Baron von Müller in particular. Most of the speech I give him was indeed his own, and formed part of an address he delivered to the Society in March 1850 (though everything else is my own invention). There seems to be no trace of him thereafter, so it may be that his belief in unicorns was indeed his professional downfall, though not, needless to say, at the hands of one 'Charles Maddox'! James Duncan is another real historical figure, though having him and his drawings in the British Museum is also my invention.

I read a number of books about London in the 1850s as part of the research for this novel, including Jerry White's fascinating *London in the Nineteenth Century*, Catherine Arnold's *Necropolis: London and its Dead*, and *The Victorian Underworld* by Donald Thomas. Books like this also helped point me to useful primary material, as did the excellent website www.victorianlondon.org.

As for Robert Mann, I owe a debt of gratitude to Mei Trow's book *Jack the Ripper: Quest for a Killer* for providing a new suspect in the Ripper killings who was old enough to have started his murderous career as early as 1850, and who might – just possibly – have been prevented from any further atrocities until the 1880s by the vigilance of a man like Inspector Bucket.

Finally I would like to thank my husband Simon, my 'first reader', and my excellent agent, Ben Mason of FoxMason, whose input was absolutely invaluable as the novel took shape. I would also like to thank my two wonderful editors, Krystyna Green of Constable & Robinson, and Kate Miciak of Random House, for everything they did to make this book as good as it could be.